MOB RELATED
GROWING UP AROUND THE OUTFIT

MOB RELATED

GROWING UP AROUND THE OUTFIT

FICTION

By:

Joseph Senese

**Family Saga/Organized Crime/
Nostalgic/Adult Humor/Coming of Age**

*DISCLAIMER

This book is a work of fiction. All of the characters, events, businesses, and organizations depicted are fictionalized or used fictitiously. No representation that any statement made in this story is true or that any incident depicted in this novel actually occurred is intended or should be inferred by the reader.

To my four sons
Michael, Joseph, Dominic, and Anthony

PROLOGUE
* In Retrospect

Having an imaginary character deliver an unorthodox retrospective prologue sounds like literary suicide. However, considering Victor DaBone's unique role in this narrative, especially the later chapters, his perspective works best.

As a pre-teen in the mid-1960s, I was allowed to watch unlimited television and listen to all kinds of rock music and adult comedy records. Thanks to older friends and cousins, I also tagged along to see the most popular 'M' for mature and 'R' for restricted-rated movies. What mother and father weren't concerned about their adolescent children's exposure to those impressionable media outlets during one of the most culturally changing times in our country's history? That would be my mom and dad, Nicky and Grace DaBone.

Sure, we sit back and laugh about it now. But, don't believe for one minute that it stops my incessant teasing about the questionable choices they made in the child-rearing department during my formative years. Of course, my mother always has her famous go-to line at the ready when we discuss this.

"You should hit your fucking knees every night and thank God."

I'm always quick to remind Mom that any reference to 'God' and 'fuck' in the same sentence is considered blasphemy. (My father always gets a kick out of it when I say that.) However, the back and forth banter we share on this subject usually comes to an abrupt end when I bring up the unique, curious, and up-close-and-personal adult interactions I was privy to as a youngster.

I've heard the ability to say something without actually saying it is a gift, so here's my gift to you. Certain men I grew up around were, in some way, shape, or form, associated with a particular Italian subculture. So, what did I decide to do when I got older? I wrote a book and created characters loosely inspired by their uniqueness, nuances, mannerisms, and traits. That was a ballsy move considering who I was related to. Even though my novel was fictional, it was questionable judgment to choose that subject matter. Nevertheless, I decided to run with my idea, literally. But that's getting way too far ahead in the story. For now, it's probably best to stick with only early-on examples. I took the liberty of translating Italian words and phrases into English and deciphered street terms and references, which you may or may not be familiar with. Lastly, I shared a few personal things about myself because I want you to fully understand where I came from, seeing, hearing, and experiencing life as I did at a VERY young age.

Mom, Dad, Zeus (our 125-pound full-blooded German Shepherd) and I, lived on the top level of Grandma and Grandpa DaBone's building on Fillmore Street in Chicago's Little Italy neighborhood. My grandparents lived on the first floor since 1921. My father's sister Teresa and her husband Tommy lived upstairs for a while when they first married, right before moving into their Maple Creek home in the early 1950s. My parents saw how well it worked out for them, so they did the same right after getting hitched in 1955. One of the biggest jokes in our family is how Dad and Aunt Teresa took a giant matrimonial leap relocating a whopping total distance of 15 stair-steps away from where they were born. Grandma and Grandpa were always quick to remind all of us that their first married move was over 5,000 miles!

The first Syndicate-related story I ever pieced together on my own involved Japeto's Restaurant directly across the street from our house. It took years of secretly gathering information before I thoroughly understood how and why everything happened the way it did.

The famous newspaper restaurant critic, Frank Bruno, called Japeto's, **"THE PLACE IN LITTLE ITALY"** to enjoy delicious, timeless recipes cooked to perfection in a friendly, casual atmosphere. That's how it started out. What was added later was an unseen second layer. Japeto's also became a front for one of Chicago's most lucrative, Mob-protected bookie joints. That was thanks to the owner's son, Frankie Pope, who everyone lovingly called "Fat Frankie."

To Frankie, being referred to as "Fat Frankie" wasn't an insult, it was a fact. He was fat, and there was no getting around that, or him, especially in tight quarters. Fat Frankie conquered every conventional bathroom scale he ever stepped on. There was a rumor about him going down to SouthWater Market one afternoon to pick up a few bushels of eggplant for the restaurant. Supposedly, Frankie climbed onto one of the industrial scales used by the workers to weigh loose bundles of fresh produce, and the needle went around four complete spins before it stopped at 444 pounds!

When it was hot, when it was cold, when he handled food, and when he counted money and took bets for the Syndicate, Fat Frankie sweated. That's the direction he took when his father, Japeto Pope, died suddenly from a massive heart attack a few days shy of Frankie's 25th birthday. Frankie's mother, Graziella, only spoke broken English and knew nothing about the restaurant business outside of commandeering the kitchen. Gina, Frankie's little sister, was just finishing her senior year in high school at that time. Japeto Pope was the backbone, heart, and soul of that restaurant, and with him gone, the establishment's future was in jeopardy. Someone had to do something, and that someone was Frankie. He devised a plan, crunched numbers, and ran multiple scenarios in his head. What he concocted was nothing short of brilliant. It was a hand-over-fist, money-making scheme that also involved keeping the doors of his family's restaurant open. Unfortunately, there was one major flaw in his business design. It was unlawful.

Now, if anyone was planning on doing the slightest thing south of legal on the Near West Side, they needed Mob approval. Absolutely nothing went down in the neighborhood unless Emmanuel "Manny" Ingalleretta gave it the green light. Manny personally knew Frankie and his family for a long time and always liked them. Frankie was surprised that Manny suggested their meeting be face-to-face at Mama Sue's Cafe. That was very uncommon for Manny. Since his rapid rise to power, the heat and scrutiny of law enforcement surveillance had plagued him. It was the main reason he shied away from any one-on-ones with anyone about Outfit business, especially in public.

It was different with Frankie. As far as anyone knew, including law enforcement, Frankie Pope was just a local guy whose family owned a restaurant.

Manny's plan was for the two of them to sit right out in the open and share a meal and conversation as friends usually do. However, Manny had an ulterior motive. His well-calculated real intention was to use his open-air meeting with Frankie to send a subliminal message to the organized crime agents sitting out in their cars, standing across the street, walking by his dinner table, and peaking out the windows. Manny wanted them to understand that Little Italy was his neighborhood, and he would not hide from them. As far as he was concerned, the agents had two options – either pinch him or go fuck themselves. One thing about Emmanuel Ingalleretta, he might have been physically diminutive, but he had King Kong-sized testicles.

Before they got down to business, Manny told Frankie a couple of stories. Fascinating was Manny's back-in-the-day account of plain-clothes law enforcement agents disguising themselves to snoop around the neighborhood. Everyone that lived in Chicago and the suburbs knew about Taylor Street. It carried a mystique that had endured the test of time, distinguishing itself as either home or a starting point, for quite a few Chicago Outfit members. Most of those guys did their best not to draw attention to themselves. Instead, they blended in with thousands of other Italians who worked legitimate jobs and wanted nothing to do with the Mob or the black mark it left on their precious heritage.

Local and federal government agents, often referred to as the 'G,' were not clueless about what was happening. They were well-trained, educated, honest, hard-working, and serious as a heart attack. They had one goal, to obliterate organized crime and demolish its infrastructure. Their biggest drawback was, oddly enough, the federal and state laws they pledged to uphold. (Even mobsters have legal rights.) Also impeding their success were dozens of Outfit lawyers manipulating and interpreting the United States Constitution. Last but not least, when their cases did make it to court, they were usually held in front of corrupt judges or paid-off jurors eager to submit 'Not Guilty' verdicts.

The misdemeanor arrests the G made in the neighborhood were primarily braggadocious bust-out gamblers or minor theft offenders boasting that they knew this one and that one. As a result, agents were usually very disappointed when they found out the men they apprehended knew less about the Mob than they did.

Manny laughed when he told Frankie the G was so desperate for inside information that they even recruited the older female secretaries from their Clybourn Street office to dress up in faded yellow pantyhose, wool coats, and babushkas. The women were instructed to go shopping in the neighborhood and write down license plate numbers and tape conversations with bulky, portable recorders they hid in their large purses and bags.

When the social conversation part of their evening ended, Manny listened to Frankie's idea as they sipped several cups of cappuccino. Initially, he liked what he heard, but Manny had a significant concern. Japeto's was in the neighborhood, HIS neighborhood. Manny lived only a couple of blocks away on Castle Street. He was quick to remind Frankie how two dozen other Mob-connected friends of his also resided nearby. Frankie explained that it was for that exact reason that the plan would work perfectly. He asked Manny if he knew anyone who would be foolish enough to fuck around with a place that had that kind of protection. Manny bombarded Frankie with questions. They ranged from his response to a police raid to how he'd handle money exchanges. A half-hour and five cannolis later, Frankie not only correctly answered his questions, but he took it three steps further. He outlined his plan on coordinating wagering slips, betting lines, gambling collections and phone communications.

When Manny ran out of queries, Frankie brought up his additional idea, offering extensions of betting credit for heavy gamblers. Frankie explained how a bettor would use collateral instead of cash by creating partnership documents. That meant legal access to their businesses, real estate holdings, stocks, bonds, and cars. In addition, if a gambler lost and couldn't immediately pay, it offered them another outlet to make good on their debt before seeking the services of a loan shark, which, as Frankie pointed out, were already on the payroll. Manny was thoroughly impressed with both ideas, especially taking over legal businesses, which he'd already been doing for a few years.

Once the word got out about Ingalleretta and Fat Frankie Pope sitting together, there was rampant speculation on why they met. But, there was one thing for sure that everyone agreed on. Frankie was more than just a fat guy from the neighborhood who owned a restaurant. He was one of the few people that had Manny Ingalleretta's ear. Less than one year after that meeting, Fat Frankie Pope's new venture was up and running.

I've known Frankie forever. He's like an uncle to me, and he's been a great friend to our family. I would've never been able to connect the dots on his story without secretly listening to the years of conversations he shared with my dad, my uncle, and their neighborhood cronies.

When his new Outfit endeavor first began, Frankie was under a ton of stress. His coping method was food, which was no surprise to anyone. Because of that, he dealt with his fair share of health issues. Add to that his constant battle with profuse sweating, and you could say Frankie was a walking, talking science project. He didn't perspire as an average person did. Instead, his sweat beads built up like tidal waves on the sides of his forehead, then dripped down to his chubby, always brightly blushed cheeks. The circus tent-sized polyester shirts, the ones he swore up and down to his mother, 'fell off a truck' near Maxwell Street? By midday, every day, they were soaking wet. After a few doctor visits, Frankie found out why his cheeks always looked like he had rouge on them. It was due to off-the-charts sky-high blood pressure. Thank God it wasn't a tomato allergy because the thought of not eating red sauces and gravies would've indeed killed him before any weight-related health issues could've.

I think I was in about third grade, I paid homage to Frankie. I created a game that I played only with myself. The challenge was to see if I could guess how many times the crease in his pants tucked and un-tucked inside his butt-crack. I privately referred to it as "Asshole Hide-N-Seek."

Watching Frankie's ritual as he exited his white Lincoln Continental was classic. First, he always drove his car backwards into the Japeto's parking lot. Then, he'd open the door, grab the top of the driver's side roof backward with his left hand, and swing his massive left leg out first, using the steering wheel with his right hand for support and leverage. Last but not least, my favorite part. He'd huff and puff his big ass to the small back door of the kitchen, open it as wide as it would go, and then have to turn sideways just to make it inside!

Frankie's poor steering wheel needed replacement three times in two years. All of them snapped in half from the pressure of his weight when he pushed on it. Dad, Uncle Tommy, and the older guys in the neighborhood brutally teased the shit out of him about that.

My father made Frankie a special present for one of his birthdays. It was a hand-carved wooden block encased inside of a glass frame. Mounted on the block was the third broken steering wheel. The attached golden plaque above it read:

FAT FRANKIE: 3
STEERING WHEELS: 0

Frankie loved the gift so much that he proudly hung it in a place of prominence, right next to the fully-stocked faded green refrigerator in his private office.

Besides owning a restaurant, Frankie's most significant weight obstacle was his voracious appetite. Every morning like clockwork, once he squeezed through that back door at Japeto's, he yelled for his number one waiter, stuttering Danny "Peanut Butter" Rodrigo to make him something to eat.

"Hey, Peanut Ba-aaaaa-aaaater, make me a couple of braised pork and broccoli rabe sandwiches and grab a bottle of that chocolate fa-aaaa-aaaacking Kayo!"

Danny had a slight speech impediment ever since he was a kid. Since his stutter wasn't communicatively debilitating, that meant only one thing in the neighborhood, his verbal stammering and stumbling were fair game to fuck with. Peanut Butter and his family lived on Troop Street, just off Roosevelt Road. Frankie busted Danny's balls about his verbal faltering just as much as everyone else did, but the truth was, Frankie could be as kind as he was immense. When Danny turned 18 years old, Frankie hired him as a waiter. Danny learned to embrace and somewhat control his stutter, playing it up in a humorous, comfortable way. He always had the staff at Japeto's in stitches with laughter. When restaurant customers joined in on the teasing and light-hearted fun, they always made sure to tip Danny very well. On the rare, slower nights at Japeto's, Danny kept busy bussing tables, washing dishes, and cleaning restaurant equipment instead of his usual server position. He insisted that the older, more senior waiters with families make the gratuities. Frankie was impressed by Danny's selflessness, so he always made sure to casually tuck a small wad of cash in Peanut Butter's top pocket as compensation for his missed tips. Danny would try and refuse, but Frankie would jokingly corner him, knowing full well that the circumference of his belly surrounded Danny, making it humanly impossible to get by him without accepting.

By the time I was eight years old, I knew most of the Japeto regulars by name. If they were from the neighborhood, I knew where they lived. If they had relatives who also lived in Little Italy, I knew who they were and where they lived. It got to the point where I could distinguish restaurant customers from the regulars from my upstairs window. That got a lot tougher for me to do once Frankie was full-fledged up and running, doing his behind-the-scenes Mob bookie thing. There were dozens and dozens of new faces. My dad called those guys "Wannabes." According to him, they were alcoholics, losers, moochers, gambling degenerates, and worse. So, whenever a group of wannabes walked into Japeto's at the same time, my father's favorite thing to say was that they looked like a bunch of bust-out chooches (Dummies/Idiots) bum-rushing the joint. They gambled heavily, borrowed money, and hoped to rub elbows with the guys that had the real ties to the Outfit, which our neighborhood had its fair share. The wannabes ordered tons of food, bought rounds of drinks, paid for bar and dinner tabs, ordered more food, and heavily tipped bartenders, waiters, and busboys if they won their bets. If they lost, they borrowed money, credit bet, drank heavier, and nervously waited for the next game or race results to see where they stood. Any way you looked at it, it was a win/win for Fat Frankie, Ingalleretta, and the Mob. One of the saddest things I learned about the wannabes was that they thought knowing the names of a few connected guys in local crews also made them part of the big Outfit picture. It didn't. Dad told me a thousand times not to grow up and be a wannabe. It was even more confusing when he said I should be who I'm supposed to be, not someone I pretended to be, like them. I guess you could say I learned my very first street lesson without even realizing it. Don't be a wannabe.

    As I mentioned earlier, the whole Japeto's Restaurant/Fat Frankie Pope story took me years to piece together. However, other things I witnessed didn't take nearly as long to figure out. We were only fourteen days into January of 1964, and I had already observed four incredulous interactions. Number five was on deck. As usual, I'm sitting at the desk in the dining room, NOT minding my own business when I hear faint whispering and shuffling coming from the kitchen. My parents thought I was busy reading the new releases of MAD and Cracked magazines they picked up for me at the Zayre Store on First Avenue in Maywood. I was, but I wasn't. My curiosity once again got the best of me. I tip-toed into the kitchen hallway and quietly stood under the picture of the Blessed Virgin Mary, the one with her holding her own pierced and bleeding heart in her hands. (You're not considered a true-blooded Italian-American Catholic without that picture being displayed somewhere in your home.) I peeked around the corner, and there was my father, stacking piles of money on the kitchen table. My mother is sitting at one end with a pencil and paper. I listened and watched them for a good 10 minutes. I remember their conversation like it was yesterday.

    "Okay, Grace. Listen to me very carefully. First, I want you to write down Louie Buonyidall for three hundred. Then, I'll put three hundred dollars next to it."

    "Nicky, I don't know Louie Buonyidall, and I have no clue on how to spell Buonyidall."

    "For Christ's sake Grace, you know too much already. Louie from Miller Street, the fat jagoff with the limp, I think he's Barbara the slut's brother."

    "Wrong! You mean Louie Torcamatta. He's from Polk Street, not Miller Street. He limps because he got shot in the war. Barbara is his cousin, not his sister, and she's not a slut."

    "Okay, good. Now you at least know who I mean."

    "Nicky, I still don't know how to spell Buonyidall."

    "Fine, just write down four hundred for the whore's gimpy cousin. I'll know who it is."

"Is it three or four hundred? First, you said three hundred. Now you're saying four hundred. So what is it, three hundred or four hundred?"

"Make it four hundred. I'll throw Buonyidall an extra C-note for getting shot in the war."

"You are unfucking believable, Nicky! Are we almost done here?"

"No, we are not. This next one is very important. Grace, I want you to write down Tony Shit-Stains for two-fifty."

"I AM NOT WRITING THAT! And who in the name of God is Tony Shit-Stains?"

My timing has always been very decent. So, when I heard that, I felt it was the perfect opportunity to chime in and show my parents what and who I knew and how helpful I could be.

"Mom, Tony Shit-Stains is Anthony Indolini. He lives alone on the second floor of Red Fontanelli's building on Racine and Taylor. Everyone calls him 'Shit-Stains' because when he gets drunk, he shits his pants."

Dead silence from the kitchen.

Since my answer didn't have the effect I hoped for, I turned around and walked back to the living room. But, right before I sat back down, I looked at the big mirror on the opposite end of the connecting wall, and what did I see? I caught the side reflection of my mother and father in the kitchen, hunched over, shaking their heads, their hands covering their mouths, and finger-pointing in the direction of where I was. It took me about a minute to figure out what they were doing. My parents were doubled-over, trying not to laugh. My mom could barely choke out the words, 'Thank you, Victor,' to me. Now, I'm full-blown, intrigued. I figure not only must I have correctly identified Tony as "Shit Stains," but no one yelled at me for swearing. I waited a few more minutes, then took my position back under the Blessed Mother picture. That's when I saw roughly 10 paper bags lined up on the table. They were the very same my mother used to pack my school lunches in. I knew the cash was now inside those bags. There was only a single stack of money remaining. It was colossal. I figured it had to be at least six inches tall because it was almost even with the ceramic heads of the Jesus and Mary figurine salt and pepper shakers, but not quite as tall as the Saint Joseph napkin holder. My father dropped that last mound of cash into a Florsheim shoebox and handed it to my mom.

"Grace, Tommy's in the empty lot. Tell him it's the full order of cabbage for Mr. E."

I ran to the side window, and sure enough, there's Uncle Tommy in his brand new black Lincoln. He leans over the railing, grabs the box, and kisses my mom. She whispers in his ear. He nods, gets in his car, and pulls down the alley towards Loomis Street. I knew everyone called Emmanuel Ingalleretta from Castle Street "Mr. E." I was positive Uncle Tommy was on his way there. Another thing I was sure of was that there was no cabbage in that shoebox.

A couple of days later, I was watching television and happened to stroll into my parent's bedroom. Their entire bed was covered in jewelry. Probably a hundred separate pieces arranged in neat little piles. There were rings, bracelets, watches, broaches, necklaces, and even a bunch of loose-multi-colored stones that looked a lot like the marbles my friends and I used to call 'beauties.' Within four, maybe five hours, after a few visits by Fat Frankie, Uncle Tommy, Aunt Teresa, and a couple of guys I didn't recognize, the only things left on the bed were a couple of rings, a pair of earrings, and a few gold necklaces. My mother wore every piece of remaining jewelry to the dinner table that evening. I remember how surprised I was because there wasn't one bit of conversation about the flurry of gems, gold, and silver that flew out of our house that afternoon. It was almost like it never happened.

    For the next hour, the only thing my father talked about, actually, the only thing he boasted about, was how Uncle Tommy was 'in' and that meant business was going to explode for all of them. I had no clue what they were talking about at the time, but my parents seemed delighted. So, once again, I just listened. I also remembered that Uncle Tommy being 'in' must be a good thing. That same evening we ate steaks for dinner. But, this tasty beef didn't come from Mitzie's Butcher Shop like it usually did. Instead, tonight's T-Bones were hand-delivered in a sealed wooden crate by some guy who looked like he just had the living shit kicked out of him. I wondered what he did to get beaten so badly. His left eye was purple and swollen. He had a fat lip and fresh cuts on his nose and cheek that were still lightly bleeding. He stood by the back alley door, handed my father the crate, and awkwardly passed Dad an envelope. I say 'awkwardly' because I've seen enough smooth envelope exchanges in my time to know how they should look. There's an art form to it. Although I couldn't hear their entire conversation, I did hear my father tell this poor bastard to be back every week until 'it' was paid off. I never found out what 'it' meant, but this guy showed up religiously at our alley door with crates of steaks, every week, week in and week out for about three months. Every time I saw that man (I later found out he was some stroke from Berwyn that everyone called "Creeper,") it looked like he just received a fresh beating. The lesson I learned? Having to pay 'it' off was a bad thing.

    I felt I did a good job putting two and two together, so after dinner, feeling confident and content, I went to my spot on the radiator. That warm ledge was my go-to seat in the house during the cold weather months. Since it was below zero outside, the radiator was working overtime and way too hot to sit on. To me, that meant only one thing, time to morph a Hershey chocolate bar to the perfect consistency, which was warm and gooey enough to scoop off the tin foil wrapping with the back of my front teeth, then roll it around my tongue until it gently melted down my throat. One of the first times I tried that the chocolate was so hot it burned my tongue, lips, and roof of my mouth. So when I shouted out "MOTHER FUCKER" at the top of my lungs, it got everyone's attention, especially Fr. Geno from Our Lady of the Shroud, who just happened to be visiting us that day. I remember how pissed off I was that my family was more concerned about apologizing to him than they were tending to the heat blisters forming inside my mouth.

    Speaking of mouths, I had a bit of a swearing problem back then. It happened even more often than you'd expect from a Taylor Street kid. It's not like I knew what every word meant, and most of the time, I only repeated what I overheard others saying. Mrs. Chinetti, from across the alley, always yelled when she heard me cussing around her kids. I never really understood that because her sons, Marky and Tony, were no angels in that department. I think the first time I heard the word 'cocksucker,' it was compliments of Marky Chinetti, or maybe it was my father. I honestly don't remember. And my dad, besides having his own set of profane words, always had a couple of irons in the fire. When he wasn't busting his ass at his tool and die job or helping Uncle Tommy, he relaxed on the couch watching television, the main form of entertainment in our household.

    Initially, the shows my older relatives watched, I couldn't stand. I referred to those programs as 'their' shows. They were huge fans of "The Red Skelton Show," The "Lawrence Welk Show," The Jimmy Durante Show," "The Danny Thomas Show," "Perry Mason," "Dr. Kildare," "The Milton Berle Show," and those God-awful westerns, "Gunsmoke," "Wagon Train," "Bonanza," and "Rawhide." Watching television with only my parents was way more fun. I loved to see the expressions on their faces. Sometimes, they laughed so hard, they cried. I didn't fully understand the humor, but I laughed right with them. Some of their favorite shows were "Candid Camera," "I Love Lucy," "The Andy Griffith Show," "The Ed Sullivan Show," "The Beverly Hillbillies," reruns of "The Honeymooners," and real late at night, "The Johnny Carson Show." My personal favorites to watch together with them were "The Dick Van Dyke Show" and "Leave it to Beaver." (Dad was crazy about Eddie Haskell!) When "The Alfred Hitchcock Hour," "The Twilight Zone," or "The Outer Limits" were on, my parents would deceptively try and shuffle me away from the television. They knew those programs gave me nightmares. Still, if I put up a big enough fuss and begged them to watch, I was allowed. No big surprise there.

    As much as my early life revolved around television and comic books, it was my introduction to music that really hit a nerve. It's like when I listened, my mind functioned in a completely different way. At first, it was only local AM radio. I couldn't wait to hear the never-ending loops of songs from Elvis Presley, Chubby Checkers, The Beatles, Smokey Robinson, The Supremes, The Carpenters, Herman's Hermits, Simon and Garfunkle, The Cowsills, The Temptations, Sonny and Cher, Stevie Wonder, The Beach Boys, The Jackson Five, and The Osmonds. The older teenagers I emulated were also into the same music. I guess I kept my ears open around them, too, because that's how I first learned about late-night F.M. radio. The whole musical vibe was more intense. The singers, groups, and musicians were on the darker side of rock and roll. You could also add an extra dab of hipness for yourself if you thought the main reason the disc jockeys played the longer songs so late at night was so that they could sneak around corners and smoke marijuana in their radio station closets and bathrooms. It didn't matter. As long as they played The Animals to Led Zeppelin and everything in between, the thought of them getting stoned only added to the whole rock and roll mystique. There were hundreds of nights I laid in bed wearing my cheap, thin-wired, white earplugs, tossing and turning, thinking about some of the confusing events of the day. Then, I'd finally fall fast asleep while listening to Steppenwolf, Deep Purple, Jimi Hendrix, The Yardbirds, The Kinks, Vanilla Fudge, Cream, Iron Butterfly, Grand Funk Railroad, The Who, and The Rolling Stones songs not aired because of content during daytime hours.

Between television, the comic books, the MAD and Cracked Magazines, records, radio, and going to the movies once or twice a week, you would think that was enough to keep any kid busy, but not me. Instead, I always found the time to blend inconspicuously, wandering amongst the adults, eavesdropping and memorizing their conversations, watching their actions, and learning about things no school would ever teach.

Getting back to me waiting impatiently for my Hershey bar to melt on the radiator, I passed the time flipping through magazines and comics while mixing a few potions with the chemistry set I won for selling the most boxes of Christmas cards in my class. My dad's lying on the couch watching one of his favorite shows at the time, "The Man from U.N.C.L.E." He's thrilled because the network did away with its black and white format and broadcast the new season in Technicolor. What perfect timing for a brand new Zenith Color Combination Console with 240 watts of peak music stereo power and basket weaved sliding doors to have been delivered to us just a mere two days earlier. Mom told me that my father won it in a raffle. A RAFFLE! That was a good one! What an amusing coincidence Uncle Tommy and Aunt Teresa, Fat Frankie, my grandparents, and three other relatives also got new television sets, right about the same time we did. And, wouldn't you know it? Low and behold, theirs were the very same make and model as ours was, right down to the light scratches where the manufacturer's identification tag and shipping label used to be.

So, while Dad's playing around with the new wireless remote control, I decided to check out what was happening at Japeto's. He sees me do this, and out of the blue, he casually tells me how the wannabes pissed in their pants every time Uncle Tommy showed up there. I asked if the wannabes pissed their pants when he walked in. Dad laughed, I laughed. I felt we bonded. As far as I thought, that was the end of the conversation, but it wasn't.

Now, I realize I've sidetracked at least twice already, but I must once again take a detour. I've only briefly mentioned my Uncle Tommy. That's doing both you and him and injustice. So, let me scratch the surface and give you a small glimpse of Tominucci LaCosta.

For starters, many people called him by a shitload of other names. There was "Tommy," "Tominucci," "Alleged Gangster," "Tee," "Tommy Bari," "Underworld Figure," "Tommy Market," "Big Banana," "Reputed Mobster," "Manny's Guy," "Taylor Street Tommy," and "Friend to the Outfit," just to name a few. The inside information on Tommy has been ongoing. It's a never-ending process that's piled high since I was old enough to know he was much more than just my uncle. He's that type of person, constantly evolving, slightly mysterious, multifaceted, and yet helpful, loving, kind, and caring. Tommy is my father's sister, Teresa's husband. He's also my baptismal and conformational Godfather. Having Tommy as an uncle is great, it's like having a second father. And, it was because of him that our family had its ground-floor introduction to the Chicago Outfit.

Tommy was barely in his mid-twenties when he really came into his own with a handful of other trustworthy, well-versed street-smart operators. They generated tons of cash for the Syndicate. In my opinion, Uncle Tommy's most immense Outfit contribution was helping them broaden their ethnic spectrum. He forged solid relationships with a few key people of color, enlisting their help with his brokered capers and jobs. Those groups reciprocated and included him and the Mob boys in a few of their dealings. The amounts of cold, hard cash those rainbow collaborations brought in for all involved parties were, at times, staggering. White, black, brown, or beige, your skin color didn't matter, it was all about the green. Later on, you'll find out how an innocent single act of kindness started Tommy off in the Outfit and made him an unassuming Taylor Street legend with a vast array of contacts and connections that extended up and down the wazoo of the Syndicate.

At first, the whole Outfit thing was like one giant puzzle to me. Looking at it that way helped me make sense of what it was. I pegged Uncle Tommy early on as one of those small, essential, inner pieces that connected multiple, more significant-sized pieces. I wasn't sure where he or the other men I knew precisely fit in the big picture, but thanks to all the inside information I was accumulating, my Mob puzzle borders were coming together nicely.

As I was saying, my father and I were bonding, sharing a laugh, compliments of my masterful use of the word, 'piss.' All of a sudden, here comes my mother. She's charging in from the kitchen with a full head of steam, screaming her ass off to Dad. The next thing I know, she's telling him about how Sister Antonini pulled her aside after school because I called Johnny Sanflippo an asshole. Johnny Sanflippo was an asshole. Mom didn't stop there. Next, she tells Dad how she had to biff me on the head because Mitzie, the butcher, didn't like it when I told him the sausages hanging inside his window looked like a bunch of swinging dicks. They did. Then, Mom drops the giant bomb, beefing to my father about me calling old man Charlie Landa a fucking jagoff right to his face. Indeed, I did. Charlie Landa was a fucking jagoff. And, he looked like Adolph Hitler, mustache and all!

Dad appeared disappointed but not furiously mad. He would've been really irritated if he knew that I overheard how Charlie Landa owed Fat Frankie and Salvatore "Sally Boy" Domenico, a union boss from the neighborhood, lots of money. Landa was so far over his head from gambling, bad investments, and failed business ventures, that the only thing left for him to do was sign over the title to his four-story, middle-block Taylor Street building. I also overheard Frankie tell Uncle Tommy that Landa's structure was solid, and all that was needed was some wall patchwork, fresh coats of paint, and upgraded fixtures. Charlie must've buried himself in debt because once he signed over the title of his building to Anna Marie Domenico, Sally Boy's wife, no one ever saw him again. After that, the rumors about Landa's sudden disappearance were off the charts. My personal favorite was that Fat Frankie ate him!

Speaking of Frankie, he and Sally Boy worked out a sweet arrangement. Instead of taking what Charlie Landa owed him, Frankie retained a rent-free top-floor corner unit in the building. It was the only apartment with a balcony that faced southwest and the sole flat with unobstructed views of the Fillmore and Loomis Street intersection, Japeto's parking lot, and the back of our house.

Let's get back to my mother and her one-woman crusade to clean up my vocabulary. For the record, she swore almost as much as my father. Earlier that day, I heard her call Goldie Fantozzi a miserable cunt. Mom was right. Goldie Fantozzi was a miserable cunt. But, I didn't feel the timing was right to bring up our mutual agreement on Goldie's cuntiness.

My mother, Grace Rose Benidetto DaBone, the dark-haired Sicilian beauty with quite a mouth of her own on her, was in her late 20s back then. At five-foot, four inches, barely 120-pounds, she looked and acted like a fiery, European version of actress Natalie Wood. Biting her tongue and not speaking her mind was something Mom rarely did. I wasn't yet aware of the famous idiom about the apple not falling far from the tree. I definitely would have used that to defend my swearing. But, the bottom line on that night was that I was going to lose. Mom was the mother, and I was the kid. What and who I knew didn't matter. The only thing left for me to see was whether I was on the right side of wrong or the wrong side of right for trying to talk, act, and share as an adult.

I should thank my lucky stars that my parents weren't hitters or spankers because if they were, I probably would've looked as beaten up as Creeper did when he delivered the crates of steaks to our house. Instead, Mom tells Dad that she's had it with my swearing and that enough was enough. So here's the three of us, blankly staring at each other in uncomfortable silence. Those 15-20 seconds felt like an hour. Mom saw I was getting upset, so she walked back into the kitchen without saying another word.

Dad knelt next to me and said I should've known better. He was right, I should've. The only thing I knew for sure was that I just got reprimanded by my mother in front of my father, one of the most humbling and humiliating experiences for a young boy to endure. My bottom lip quivered, my jaw shook uncontrollably, and small tears welled up. I was way too embarrassed to make eye contact, so I sniffed, wiped my nose with my left sleeve, and nodded in agreement.

My father got up to comb his hair in the bathroom. He knew I was on the verge of crying but didn't make a big deal out of it. I ran into my bedroom, grabbed a brush, and bolted back to the bathroom to join him. So, while I bobbed and weaved behind Dad trying to catch a glimpse of my reflection as we combed, he looked in the lower corner of the mirror and saw what I was doing. He turned around all serious. I knew he was getting ready to bless me with yet another pearl of fatherly street-wisdom.

"Victor?"

"Yea, Dad."

"Charlie Landa is a fucking jagoff."

I remember I felt vindicated, but it didn't last long. Not two seconds later, my mom stuck her head in the bathroom.

"Nicky! You asshole! I heard that! You're not helping me with him. Goddamn it!"

Dad didn't answer. Instead, he smiled and blew Mom a kiss.

"Nicky, you can shove that kiss straight up your ass. You wanna make nice? Why don't you and the Taylor Street Swearing Machine go to Snafuro's Bakery before they close. Grab us some eclairs, a few cannolis, and see if they have any cheesecake left."

Mom smiled even after her red-faced whining and complaining about my foul language. Talk about mixed messages! What about the way she and Dad swore with their creative cursing? Why was it was okay for them to talk like that, but not me? Next, I considered asking about the cash on the kitchen table, where it came from, and how they decided who got what amount. And after that, the jewelry on the bed, the unknown whereabouts of Charlie Landa, the new televisions, Creeper's steak delivery and what he was paying off, and why shit was going to explode because Uncle Tommy was in something. Then finally, what I wondered about ever since I was old enough to know what a memory was. Why did almost everyone that stepped foot in our house either drop something off or pick something up?

Looking back on it now, those inquiries still hold up. But, I never got to ask my questions that day, and it was because of the Dean Martin song, "Welcome to My World." It played on the kitchen radio before I had a chance to open my mouth. So, instead of getting myself into further trouble, I decided to do what I did best, I listened. It was as if the opening words of Dino's ballad were written explicitly for me.

(Dean) "Welcome to my world."

(Chorus) "Welcome to my world."

(Dean) "Won't you come on in?"

(Chorus) "Won't you come on in?"

Then and there I realized it. An ordinary life in this family wasn't in the cards for me. Not by a fucking long shot.

CHAPTER ONE
FROM THE BEGINNING

GIUSEPPE AND MARIETTA

Giuseppe (Joe) DaBone and Marietta (Mari) Spaccia were married in 1921. Their relatives and friends cooked for three days straight in preparation for the festive occasion. Wedding attendees dined on multiple handmade pasta dishes, assorted fresh fish, and delectable pastries. In addition, gallons of full-bodied, homemade red wine were poured and consumed. Local musicians played romantic Italian songs while Joe and Mari danced and kissed passionately in their hometown of Bari, Italy, surrounded by those who loved them. The young, brave, and slightly naïve newlywed Italians were the first in both of their families to come to America three months later.

The money Joe and Mari earned while in Bari, sometimes working two jobs each, was all spent on an affordable two-flat home in Chicago's Little Italy neighborhood. The early years in their adopted country weren't easy for the newly immigrated couple. Mari had to ride along with Joe in the streetcars every morning. He didn't know the language yet, and she wanted to make sure he correctly got to where he was going during his employment search. Mari taught herself to communicate in English thanks to the Italian/American translation books she began reading a full year before arriving in the United States.

During a worker will-call at Polina Construction Company, Joe was fortunate enough to be hired as a laborer. The company owner, Bruno Polina, was a flashy guy with Mob connections. So when Bruno needed the kind of assistance only the Outfit could provide, they helped him. In return, Bruno supplied materials and labor for his Syndicate-connected friends' private homes, cottages, and side projects. Unfortunately, Bruno got stuck paying out of his pocket for their work and material costs on more than a few occasions. That's how the Mob is, they'll toss you in the awkward position of paying for them or their stuff, and when you do, they don't even thank you. Instead, they get insulted because you didn't thank them for the honor of picking up their tab!

The secret reason Bruno never refused to do a favor for his Outfit buddies was that unbeknownst to them, he was amassing quite a fortune extorting kickback money from his immigrant laborers. The mounds of cash he was piling up were more than sufficient to finance the room additions, home remodels, new driveways, and construction requests made of him. So, Bruno never complained. He felt granting favors for his gangster buddies gave him a leg up with the Outfit. The Syndicate bosses figured as long as they had their arm around him and got their materials, supplies, and construction labor for little to sometimes nothing, they were right as rain. So the trade-offs between Polina and the Mob went on for a very, very long time.

Bruno's right-hand man was Dan Doogan. It was Doogan's job as company foreman to intimidate the laborers into paying those kickbacks. Doogan made sure to have Italian, Polish, and Irish translators on hand to avoid miscommunications. Polina knew his coveted laborer jobs not only paid very well but were hard to come by. Joe DaBone and his fellow immigrant co-workers knew that as well. So the laborers had only one move, to turn over a portion of their hard-earned wages in cash, week in and week out. The few workers that complained about the kickbacks were terminated and banned from Polina's future construction projects.

A new cement worker, Bowser O' Sullivan, was hired about six months after Joe. O'Sullivan was more than well aware of the kickback arrangement. When it came time to make his payment, he loudly refused to pay. To top things off, he was intoxicated. O'Sullivan staggered and swayed his way up to Doogan, filled with a snoot full of liquid confidence that the few extra pints gave him. He stood nose-to-nose with the foreman, screaming, slurring, and spitting in drunken Irish.

"Hey, Doogan, you're a Wop-owned, crooked, potato eating Mic. You got green runnin' through your veins, laddie, all the way up to that big fookin' head of yours!"

Even though O'Sullivan was blind drunk, he was right on the money about Doogan's head. He was an above-average-sized man, but what everyone saw first was his abnormally large skull, similar to an African Forest Hog. Doogan couldn't find a safety helmet that properly fit him. Even the largest sizes available dangled precariously on top of his dome.

Doogan turned away from his intoxicated countryman, reached down, and lifted a 50-pound bag of powdered cement like it was a sugar packet. He swung it and hit O'Sullivan square across the chest. Bowser dropped to the ground and spewed bloody puke on himself. He choked and gasped for air. All eyes were on Doogan, who was no stranger to violence, having resorted to similar enforcement tactics in the past.

"Any of you other Mics, Greaseballs, or Polacks got something to say? Speak up, mother fuckers!"

Everyone remained silent.

As O'Sullivan continued coughing up a phlegm and blood mixture, he was able to make it to his knees. Doogan grabbed him by the rear of his jacket collar and dragged him off-site. That was the last time Joe DaBone and his co-workers ever saw Bowser O'Sullivan. From that day forward, whenever a worker caught a beating at the hands of Dan Doogan, they referred to it as a 'Bowser.'

Bruno Polina's kickback scheme lasted for over two decades, but that all changed once the Mob-entrenched labor unions became heavily involved in the construction industry. The Outfit and their partners in the labor movement combined their strengths. They focused on organizing non-union construction companies with the common goal of pressuring them to become unionized. The newly formed Mob/Union alliance became so powerful that when their demands weren't met, they placed strangleholds on material delivery and enforced work stoppages. Even the most massive construction sites were sometimes at a standstill. The general contractors in the Chicago land area were forced to double and triple their already inflated job bids. That was the only way to compensate for the staggering amount of payoffs and no-show jobs they had to come up with if they wanted to work the larger, more profitable projects.

The construction trade laborers realized it was the dawn of a new day for them. Now, they had union representation, backed up by Mob-muscle. The newly-organized workers were no longer intimidated by management threats and wage shake-downs. Polina's guys were among the first to confide in their union representatives about the weekly payoffs. Those business agents wasted no time relaying the story to their Mob partners.

Bruno knew he was in deep shit. He ran to his so-called Outfit friends, hat in hand, a bend at the knee, and tail between his legs. His explanations and excuses of ignorance fell on deaf ears. Polina's third and fourth-tier Syndicate cronies received word from their bosses about Bruno's greediness, so they did the smart thing; they all took two giant steps back from Polina and what they referred to as 'his' problem. Bruno's Mob buddies, the ones he openly boasted having, ran away from him like he had leprosy. All those dinner checks he picked up, the unrestricted use of his elaborate Lake Geneva, Wisconsin summer home, and the gratis construction work – none of that was taken into consideration. Bruno's predicament was so severe that he got called on the carpet to meet with Outfit Underboss Sergio "Ouzo" Calluzo. This meeting made Bruno extremely nervous. He privately rehearsed in front of his office mirror, believing a heartfelt performance would grant him Syndicate absolution.

Sitting in the hot seat facing Calluzo, the first words out of Polina's mouth were pleas for forgiveness. He apologized profusely and offered all types of financial reparations. But, Bruno didn't receive the immediate mercy he expected, so he broke down and wept big, salty, crocodile tears.

Calluzo took Polina's offer back to the Bosses. They decided to heavily tax Bruno for his indiscretions and insist on a substantial one-time payment. Once he agreed to that, Polina figured he would be out of the woods and back in the Outfit's good graces. It took the Mob only five months to figure out Bruno hoarded substantial money. The Bosses were pissed. They saw it as being fucked out of their fair share. Bruno needed to learn a very crucial lesson. When you decide to do business with the Chicago Outfit, you better make goddamn sure that every penny is accounted for.

An example needed to be made of Bruno Polina, so the Mob took almost everything he owned. In the end, it cost him his company, along with a couple of fingers and a thumb, which he explained away as an unfortunate accident with a faulty circular saw. It was no accident. Polina's digits were hacked off by a guy he trusted and depended upon for years. That man was officially the new legal owner (on paper with the Mob's blessing) of Polina Construction. He was company foreman Dan "Doogs" Doogan.

With his knowledge of the construction business, willingness to follow Outfit directions, and eagerness to get his hands dirty with more than just cement dust, Doogan was a perfect choice to step in and operate things on behalf of the Mob. As a result, he was one of the first full-blooded Paddies in Chicago to break crime-circle nationality barriers, choosing to work for the Italian Syndicate instead of an Irish Gang.

The Polina/Outfit situation was Joe DaBone's first time experiencing organized crime in action. In Europe, as widely spread as The Mafia was, Joe never had any direct knowledge or associations with them. But he wasn't in Italy anymore. Joe was in America, the land of opportunity. Thanks to the gossip of his Italian Taylor Street neighbors, he quickly learned that someone he knew from the old country was seizing every illegal opportunity he could. That man was Joe's slightly older childhood acquaintance, Emmanuel "Manny" Ingalleretta.

Joe was only seven years old when he first met Manny. They ran and played all day on the grassy hills of the Bari countryside. Manny was a watchful and thoughtful companion to young Giuseppe. Even though their time together was short, Joe always kept him in high regard. Manny arrived in Chicago's Little Italy about six years before Joe and Mari. Manny and Joe finally reacquainted at a neighborhood Columbus Day celebration held on Loomis Street. They shook hands, hugged, and remarked how quickly the years had passed. Manny was cordial. Joe was hoping for a more heartfelt reunion with his old friend. Instead, everybody in the neighborhood told Joe it was best to keep a respectful distance from Mr. Ingalleretta.

As he sat on his front stairs that night with Mari, Joe realized Manny wasn't the teenage boy he remembered, but instead, a man that chose a life dedicated to organized crime. Manny made all the right moves and rose quickly. The Mob ultimately granted him control over Little Italy, which was just the beginning. Joe's childhood friend was well on his way to becoming one of the most powerful and influential men in Chicago Outfit history.

BENJAMIN AND GRETTALICIA

Benjamin Benidetto was born in Palermo, Sicily. He was intelligent and handsome, with thick hair, a lantern jaw that housed a cleft chin, a tall, slender physique, and a quiet demeanor. Benjamin's first job in Sicily was as a police officer in the Carabinieri. The only reason he took that position was to pay for school tuition. His passion was chemistry, and he was amongst the top in his class. When he graduated, Benjamin immediately left the police force and took a job as an Assistant Chemist at a laboratory in Trapani.

Early in 1920, after two years of logging in countless hours of lab time, Benjamin was officially certified. Equipped with his newly acquired professional title and hopes for a better life, he followed in the footsteps of his friends and decided to do what they had done, relocate to America. His arrival placed him in Chicago's Grand Avenue neighborhood.

With his education and credentials, Benjamin landed a job at a local chemical plant on Erie Street in no time. While attending a church function six months later, he met Grettalicia "Gretta" Turconi. Gretta arrived from Sicily with her family about three months after Benjamin did. Their attraction to each other was strong and immediate. Their friends continually teased the lovebirds, telling them that it looked like they were hit by a thunderbolt. Benjamin and Gretta married less than a year later, surrounded by family and friends of Carpenter Street and Grand Avenue. The Benidettos quickly became parents. Gretta was pregnant almost non-stop for the first twelve years of their marriage! She never had the time to have a real job, so Benjamin was the sole bread earner. He spent the majority of his time focusing on a pet project, a freeze-dried formula that targeted specific food groups.

Max Rochelle, Rochelle Laboratory owner, saw some future potential with Benjamin's endeavor. So he approved extra hours of pay for his young Sicilian chemist. After months of research and testing, Benidetto developed a chemical equation to freeze-dry doughnuts. Instead of opting for co-ownership of the soon-to-be-approved patent, Benjamin accepted a one-time payment of $2,500 from Max Rochelle in exchange for full ownership. Rochelle was unscrupulous and cunning. So was his attorney, Abe Angel. Angel confused Benjamin with a cunning barrage of statutory jargon combined with inaccurate legal advice. Nevertheless, Benjamin trusted both men, accepted the bonus, and signed the ownership papers. Rochelle had Benidetto over a barrel. He knew his employee discovered a valuable, marketable formula. Rochelle also knew Benjamin had many children to feed and clothe and that his valuable employee would jump at the chance to pay for his family's mounting living and medical expenses. One week later, Benidetto handed over all documents and research transcripts to Abe Angel, crooked attorney at law. Angel attached the Rochelle Laboratory name to the patent.

*See Rochelle Laboratory at the end of this chapter.

Less than two years later, Max Rochelle opened a subsidiary company near his summer home in Michigan for the sole purpose of testing Benjamin's formula. The highly successful testing results were in. Max Rochelle's freeze-dry formula was on its way to becoming a staple in the frozen food industry.

Benjamin Benidetto died of a heart attack at only 45-years old, almost two years after his twelfth child, Grace, was born. Max Rochelle did not attend Benjamin's wake or funeral. Instead, he sent Abe Angel with a bouquet of roses. Angel hugged Gretta as the Benidetto children watched. The younger kids cried, struggling to understand the sad mystery of death. They thought Benjamin was asleep and unable to awaken.

Abe used his extensive vocabulary when he spoke to Gretta. He expounded on Benjamin's wonderful character traits. Rochelle instructed his attorney to intentionally vocalize his words loudly and clearly so all the Benidetto friends and relatives could hear him. The shifty lawyer handed Gretta a sympathy card. He explained it was from Mr. Rochelle, who could not attend due to urgent company business. (The truth was that Rochelle was in a Michigan hospital suffering from a severe case of the clap.) His unprotected indiscretions with a Portuguese hooker finally caught up to him. The final act in Abe's performance was handing Gretta a card from Mr. Rochelle. He asked her to stand in front of Benjamin's casket and read it aloud. Inside were five $100 bills. She read the short, standardized offer of sympathy on the pre-printed card. The money and generic words did not comfort her. Gretta was left facing an immense task. She was a young widow raising nine small children and a few teenagers on her own during the country's most devastating economic time, The Great Depression. The three oldest Benidetto children never made it past the 10th grade. Instead, they got jobs to help support their younger brothers and sisters.

To keep young Grace occupied, her older siblings put her in charge of the family's pictures. She took that responsibility very seriously. No matter how old she got, every time Grace looked at the old, peeled, yellowing black and white photographs, she cried. It got easier for her to deal with it as more time passed, and her sadness and tears eventually faded, just like the tattered, colorless pictures of her father.

*The Rochelle Laboratory

The Rochelle Laboratory is currently a publically-traded company. Patents, real estate holdings, equipment, stock, and net worth are over $2,375,000,000. Benjamin Benidetto's freeze-dry formula was the reason a small Erie Street basement chemical testing business evolved into a multi-billion dollar company.

CHAPTER 2
THE DABONE FAMILY OF LITTLE ITALY

Joe DaBone retired when he was 68 years old. The wear and tear his body he endured from years of hard, physical construction labor had taken their toll. Joe was a quiet, proud man, always simply dressed in clean but faded overalls. He enjoyed yard work, gardening, and the challenge of a home repair.

But, when it was time to relax, he loved nothing more than being surrounded by family. His three younger brothers from Bari also came to America thanks to him. They all lived within a few blocks from each other, which meant almost next door in neighborhood terms.

Dominic DaBone, affectionately called "Minore" (Youngest), was the last brother to settle in America, but oddly enough, the first to move to the suburbs. In the warmer months, Minore visited his brothers often to enjoy their favorite pastime, drinking Joe's neighborhood-famous homemade wine and playing "Briscola" and "Scopa," addictive, shrewd, and popular Italian card games.

Victor DaBone, Joe and Mari's only grandchild, was Nicky and Grace's son. Early on, Victor was a real handful. He had the bilingual swearing repertoire of an Americanized Italian soldier on shore leave, compliments of the over-zealous conversations he mimicked to perfection during his grandfather's back porch card games in the 1960s. Victor attentively sat, watched, and listened to the broken English and slang-Italian used by his grandfather, great uncles, and older neighborhood men. He couldn't wait to hear and see the mock fury over an incorrect discard, the swearing about a poorly dealt hand, or the misinterpretation of the many facial signs commonly used to signal a drawn trump or high-point card to a partner. Sometimes, Joe would really scream his ass off at his brother Jimmy.

"You stupid some-ana-beech, I said go lesce!" (Pronounced Leesh. Means less.)

"Va fancculo! (Fuck you!) You don't know how to play. I gotta get a new goddamn partner!" Jimmy would fire back.

They would all laugh between small sips of the best red in all of Little Italy, Joe's vino. He made it using plump grattiola grapes purchased on SouthWater Market and then squeezed them using the wine press he bought from Chiarugi Hardware on Taylor Street. Pa DaBone's wine was the nectar of the gods.

Jimmy was the second oldest DaBone brother and the most fun to watch. Between his singing, swearing, dancing, and chewing his crooked DiNobili brand cigars until the only thing remaining was wet tobacco leaves dangling from the corners of his mouth, he was priceless.

The drunken meter on just how intoxicated everyone was, came when Mari opened the back porch door. If the brothers erupted into song, it was a done deal. The more they drank the louder and the more off-key they sang, especially Uncle Jimmy. Everyone called Vincenzo DaBone, "Uncle Jimmy" and Joe DaBone "Pa," including their family and neighbors.

Mari always worried about the men being too loud. The last thing she wanted was gossip about her family after Sunday church, or far worse, whispers and pointed fingers as she waited in line at Mitzie's Butcher Shop, Snafuro's Bakery, LaJoy Foods, Romeo's Groceries, or Falbo's Cheese Store.

"Siete tutti urbriachi di nuovo?" (Are you all drunk again?) Mari often asked, even though she knew the answer.

What sealed the deal was when someone tossed a Louis Prima record on the Victrola. Louis Prima's music always set off some genetic alarm in the older Italians. Comedian Pat Cooper, whose real name is Pasquale Caputo, said it best in his stand-up act.

"And when that Louis Prima music comes on, forget about it! Every Greaseball west of Rome, even the crippled ones in wheelchairs, get up and start dancing like they're having a fucking epileptic seizure!"

There were no strings attached to the DaBone family's commitment to one another. There were no jealousies. They all took a chance when they came to America and raised their children as best they could. If one brother needed help, they all contributed. If one came into good fortune, they all shared. You'd be hard-pressed finding a clan tighter than them.

The DaBone brothers sat on Joe and Mari's back porch with family and friends for decades, while the world revolved around them amidst the sights, sounds, and smells of Chicago's Little Italy.

CHAPTER 3
THE BARI ORPHAN AND SOUTHWATER MARKET

Tommy LaCosta was only nine when he came to America in the early 1930s. His mother died a few years earlier, and his father, a sickly alcoholic, also died young at only 26 years of age. Tommy had no living relatives and no reason to remain in Italy. When he heard what others were doing, he decided to do the same, be a stowaway on a boat bound for the United States. Tommy made it halfway before a couple of drunken friends of his father saw him huddled in a dark corner of the ship's bow. They cared for him until the boat docked at Ellis Island in New York. Then, they left him. Tommy was alone in a foreign country, with nothing more than the clothes on his back and his shadow.

Young LaCosta spent his first year in New York with a few different families thanks to an Italian-American senator's immigration program. It was designed to compensate families of the orphaned Italian children offering a few extra dollars every month. The money was barely enough to feed the children enrolled, but it was something. Mari's cousins, Concetta and Marco, were the last family to sponsor Tommy. But, unfortunately, their tiny apartment was filled with their own children and other relatives. Concetta was devastated Tommy couldn't remain with them due to the government's sponsorship time limit. If a child did not have a legal guardian within that time frame, they were sent back to Italy. Tommy's two-year probationary period as a sponsored orphan was almost up. Vivian wrote letters and sent pictures of this young, handsome boy to Mari. It was Mari's idea for Tommy to come and live with her and Joe in Chicago. She couldn't bear the thought of him being denied a family. Mari also noticed her daughter Teresa was became attached to Vivian's photographs of Tommy. After weeks of filling out legal paperwork and supplying needed documentation, Tommy traveled to Chicago and settled with what he hoped would be his forever family, the DaBones.

When Tommy and Teresa met, there was an immediate, undeniable bond between them. Tommy was amazed by Joe and continuously followed him around the house and backyard. Tommy loved Mari, hugged her tightly, and kissed her at every possible opportunity. Joe and Mari knew they made the right decision when they signed young Tommy's legal guardian papers.

Because of Tommy and Teresa's closeness in age, their unique bond was always under constant scrutiny by those who lived on their block, especially Vincenza and her daughter, Roberta. On many occasions, Joe voiced his frustration to Mari about the mother/daughter tandem and the obnoxious questions. He would point out that the two women had the most giant mouths and oversized asses in the entire neighborhood. Besides huge asses, mom and daughter also had overbites in common. Roberta's oral protrusion was so bad she could've opened a quart of motor oil with her mouth.

Vincenza and Roberta Snafuro were permanent fixtures at 10:00 a.m. mass every Sunday at Our Lady of the Shroud Church. Joe said the pair's interest was not

not the church but the free pastry table supplied by parishioners. Like vultures swooping down over fresh roadkill, Vincenza, Roberta, and the other female neighborhood gossipers hovered over that dessert table. They filled their plump faces with todalles, cannolis, eclairs, and sfogitelles. Vincenza and Roberta never missed a Sunday mass or a sweet table. Then, with their stomachs filled, they questioned Mari about Tommy and Teresa's relationship.

"Are they cousins?"
"Is Tommy an adopted brother?"
"They don't sleep in the same room, do they?"

Joe referred to Vincenza and Roberta as "Face Brutes." (Pronounced Fa-Che Brutes. Means Ugly Faces.) He and Mari dreaded the never-ending barrage of questions asked by Vincenza, which usually came in a rapid-fire form while white powdered sugar from the free desserts sprinkled across one of her chins. Roberta would sit silently, gaze at Tommy, then cry when she got home. She had a massive crush on him, and he didn't reciprocate those feelings. Instead, Tommy made fun of Roberta behind her back. He puffed his cheeks out like a blowfish and then looked at Teresa to make her laugh.

"Vincenza should stoppa eating alla the goddamna time and worry about her daughter's bigga ass," Joe complained in his broken English.

Vincenza knew she could say what she wanted to. After all, her father was Jacco Snafuro, retired Sicilian Mafia Boss and owner of Snafuro's Bakery. At almost 70 years old, he was dubbed the "Unofficial Godfather" of Taylor Street. Even the real Bosses recognized Jacco's previous Cosa Nostra status overseas. Because of that, everyone in the neighborhood paid him respect, and in turn, tolerated his daughter and granddaughter.

The DaBones didn't officially adopt Tommy. Instead, they were his legal guardians. They also thought it was best for him to keep his LaCosta birth name as a reminder of who he was, and where he came from. Living in the basement would be another reminder for young Tommy. The sweet fragrance of grapes from Joe's homemade wine reminded him of his father's breath, the weak man who chose to drink himself to death because he couldn't survive without his wife. Tommy took it very hard that the father that brought him into this world decided to drown himself in a pool of wine and sorrow.

Tommy barely graduated from eighth grade. High school was not in his future. Instead, he was hired as a hustler on SouthWater Market five months after his 14th birthday. SouthWater was the primary fruit and vegetable hub in Chicago, and "Hustler" was the position name given to guys who loaded and unloaded trucks and railroad cars. Everyone called SouthWater "The University" because those fortunate enough to work there received the street-smart education of a lifetime. It's been facetiously said that if a person wanted to know, or aspire to know about any topic on planet earth, that they could learn everything necessary with just a single visit to Chicago's SouthWater Market. Everyone who worked there had information and opinions about every subject under the sun.

One of the biggest employee perks was access to the freshest produce in the city. Tommy brought home small boxes packed with assorted fruits and vegetables every week. He didn't pay for them. Instead, the tasty provisions were finagled off trucks and railcars. That box of unpaid fruits and vegetables was universally known as a "Peter Rubi."

There were two myths about how the term Peter Rubi originated in the produce business. The first myth points to an Italian husband and wife named Peter and Rubi. In the early 1900s, the married couple peddled fresh fruits and vegetables door-to-door with their horse and buggy. Their reputation spread rapidly as their produce was like none other. Expectant residents would excitedly shout out, **"PETER RUBI'S COMING!"** as the bell of their horse jingled down the street. The second myth was that Peter Rubi was a notorious thief who stole fruits and vegetables off trains before delivering the products to merchants. As that story was told, Peter Rubi was never caught because he was never just one person. What evolved from both of those myths was that Peter Rubi was the official name given to a box of successfully purged fruits and vegetables from previously filled boxes without disrupting the appearance that those boxes were still full. Creating a Peter Rubi was an art form, but most importantly, it was NEVER paid for.

There was one way to get in and out of the Market. It was an old, narrow road initially meant for horses and buggies, not trucks and tractor-trailers. Buyers and shop owners arrived while it was still dark outside. They bartered over the freshest produce starting as early as 1:00 a.m. every morning, except Sundays. SouthWater was a one-of-a-kind place where millionaire businessmen and company owners often dressed worse than homeless people. Many drank their morning coffee as they yelled at bums pissing off the dock, almost dousing their pallets of fresh produce. Besides fruits and vegetables being bought and sold, there was always something else happening. Other common occurrences included loan sharking, drunkenness, racketeering, gambling, and union business agents puncturing the tires and radiators of the trucks owned by merchants delinquent with dues or bribe envelopes. Those illegal activities remained behind the scenes and were invisible to those not savvy with the Market's underbelly. In addition, crooked cops turned a blind eye to loads of hijacked goods making their way to storage areas, big-money card games at multiple locations, and anything and everything illegal in between. SouthWater was a world within itself filled with tough talk, rough people, and impatient customers who would much rather fight first and ask questions later.

Tommy stayed away from the Market counter-culture and minded his own business. He concentrated on loading and unloading trucks because if those trucks weren't loaded properly, God wouldn't even be able to help him. Early on, Tommy's workday began at roughly 4:00 a.m. He always took the same route to his job, about three miles one way. It was Fillmore to Troop, Troop to Roosevelt, and Roosevelt to Racine, and then he continued walking about four more blocks from there. A few times during those vicious Chicago winters, the young Bari orphan physically got stuck in a couple of snowdrifts and almost didn't make it out. Luckily, some truck drivers helped him and gave him a ride.

Eventually, Tommy's hard work, a steady diet of produce, and Ma DaBone's pasta had molded his once frail frame into a six-foot-one inch, two hundred ten pound strapping man that was able to unload boxes and crates as heavy as 80-pounds each, and he did it all day long. At 23 years old, Tommy already had nine years under his belt as a solid worker. His dedication and effort were rewarded, and he received the coveted forklift driver position at Lanzatorri Produce. Tommy was the youngest worker on SouthWater to have that privilege. So naturally, he was ecstatic, especially when Lanzatorri explained there would be a little extra in his paycheck. The elite forklift operators were mainly company owners, their older sons, and the Market Kings. The Kings were a pretty storied group of about twenty-five. Half of them were mobsters that needed to show legitimate income on their tax returns. The other half were well-connected firemen and policemen working part-time and only for cash because they didn't want to violate their individual contracts with the city regarding municipal employees not working side jobs.

Benny Barone was the oldest and most respected Market King. So when he heard about Tommy's good fortune, he wheeled a pallet of Michigan carrots to the end of the dock where Tommy was unloading.

"Let the machine do the work for ya, kid!" Benny congratulated.

Tommy also received a shitload of teasing about the promotion, especially from Lanzatorri truck driver Micky Silvio, who didn't waste a precious second busting his balls.

"Hey, Tommy, did you have to fuck Fat Roberta to get that forklift job? You're such a suck-hole," he joked.

Micky was one of Tommy's best friends. He was also a Chicago Park District Boxing Champion three years running. Silvio was brutal when he stepped into the ring. When he wasn't boxing or working at SouthWater, he moonlighted making collections for the Outfit. If you owed the Mob money, you more than likely received a visit from Micky. You probably also received a couple of broken ribs.

Ernie, the union steward, was the next guy to break Tommy's chops.

"Hey, La Costa, how did Old Man Lanzatori's dick taste, like garlic, piss, and Aqua Velva?"

Tommy quickly responded.

"I don't know, Ernie, you should ask your baby sister. I heard dick tasting is her specialty."

Two minutes later, Joey from Mannina's Tomatoes added his two cents.

"Hey, Tommy, how about a nice hot cup of coffee, you know, to get the taste of cock out of your mouth?"

Tommy cracked a smile. He knew it was the "Market-Way" of congratulating him.

A few months later, while driving the forklift on the back dock, Tommy intervened during a robbery attempt. His good deed wound up opening the door to a whole new world. The little old man about to get jumped wasn't just some poor guy in the wrong place at the wrong time. He was one of the top Bosses of the Chicago Outfit.

CHAPTER 4
I WAS ONLY TRYING TO HELP

Manny Ingalleretta lived on Castle Street, just a couple blocks away from the DaBones. Of course, Tommy knew Manny and his reputation. He also knew the notorious mobster was a childhood friend of Pa.

Ingalleretta temporarily relocated to Oakbay, one of the Mob-infested suburbs, shortly after taking control of Chicago's Near West Side when James "Gentleman Jimmy" Massino went to jail. Ingalleretta wisely kept both residences, choosing to oversee Little Italy by remaining close. When Massino died in a freak prison accident, Ingalleretta rose to the rank of Boss. That was no surprise. Manny was a seasoned veteran in the Chicago Outfit, earning respect since the late days of Al Capone.

Most of the guys who worked at SouthWater had connections to Ingalleretta in some roundabout way. They were usually friends of business associates or relatives of someone from the neighborhood. Manny had a fondness for SouthWater. He also had a vested interest in three of the businesses there as a silent partner. He visited at least two or three times a month, but never on the same day and ALWAYS unannounced.

It was 5:00 a.m. on a stormy April morning. The sound of thunder crashing and flashes of lightning illuminated the early morning Chicago skyline. Tommy finished his bowl of escarole and bean soup, which Teresa made to his specifications - easy on the beans, heavy on the escarole. Their relationship became closer and stronger as they got older. Living under the same roof for the last ten years was awkward. They couldn't express their true romantic feelings and only kissed each other on their cheeks for birthdays and holidays. Their lips burned to touch but never did passionately out of respect for Joe and Mari. There would be no sneaking around, no hiding, and of course, NO SEX. The holy vow of matrimony couldn't come soon enough for either of them.

Before Tommy climbed back onto his forklift, he finished his soup, slurping it down to the last tasty drop. Earlier, he noticed a couple of unfamiliar men in the alley. At first, Tommy couldn't tell if they were bums. He figured they were just the regular guys who floated on and off the Market earning a few extra dollars helping local purveyors and buyers load their trucks. Realistically, they were non-union scabs looking to make a few bucks 'CASH' for maybe a few hours worked. Tommy knew most them. There was, "High-Ass" Charlie, Big Amos, Juanito Stegerando, "Buckwheat," and "Sweet Pea" Jackson. When there were no trucks to load, those guys rummaged through discarded produce, purged what they could, and congregated near the railroad trucks to drink. They usually spent the money they made on cheap liquor and blow-jobs performed by skanky, over-the-hill, wig-wearing, teeth missing hookers.

The rain started to come down harder. The powerful lightning strikes were even lighting up the usually pitch-black alley. Tommy headed to the dock behind

Lanzatorri Produce. He needed to unload fifteen pallets of Michigan cabbage that arrived a couple of hours earlier on one of the trucks owned by Damon "One Eye" Harding from Benton Harbor. After years of working at the Market, Tommy knew to be alert near that alley. Sometimes, bad shit went down there. Just as the forks of his lift slid under a pallet of cabbage, he saw a car slowly pulling up alongside the dock. As he raised the skid in the air, the driver's side door of the vehicle opened. Out walked Emmanuel Ingalleretta. Tommy had no idea it was him. As best as he could make out, it was just a small, older man driving a big car. A large crack of thunder boomed and echoed off the brick buildings lining both alley sides.

    Ingalleretta side-stepped some water puddles and covered his head with a newspaper. As he made his way to the dock ramp, Tommy saw the two bums from earlier rapidly approaching. Another sharp crack of thunder was followed by a bright flash of lightning. At that split second, Tommy saw one of the bums had a knife. He was able to see that because the brightness of the lightning bolt illuminated the shank. The bum raised the blade from the side of his soiled, tattered coat and was only a mere handful of steps away from Manny. Tommy pushed the accelerator pedal of the forklift to the floor. The thousand-pound forklift lunged forward as ten boxes of cabbage, weighing 50 pounds each, bounced and shifted on the pallet. Tommy raised the forks high in the air. Ingalleretta, making his way up the ramp, was unaware of what was happening, more concerned about hustling out of the downpour. As Manny glanced up, he saw a wall of cabbage boxes coming towards him. Just as the forklift wheels hit the curb of the dock ramp, Tommy slammed on the brakes. The two bums never saw it coming. The one yielding the knife got hit first, just as he was preparing to leap at Ingalleretta.

    The top two layers of cabbage boxes tumbled down on both men. One of the crate corners hit the knife-wielding bum square in his face and knocked him off his feet. The second bum got drilled with about three crates that smacked him in the chest, temporarily disabling him. Only five boxes of cabbage out of the original 20 remained on the pallet. All of the others were scattered on the dock and in the alley. Ingalleretta was knocked off-balance by a crate but managed to stay on his feet. Tommy jumped off the forklift and assisted Manny. Ingalleretta, in turn, screamed at him.

    "What the fuck is the matter with you? Do you even know how the fuck to drive that lift?"

    Tommy didn't answer. Instead, he pointed at the bums and the scattered crates. Ingalleretta looked at them, realizing what had just happened. The knife wielding bum attempted to stand as the noticeably dazed second bum was already on his feet. Tommy kicked the tramp with the knife in the balls. The man dropped to his knees.

    Ingalleretta was stunned at what was going on around him. He shuffled in place, eventually regaining his composure.

    "Watch out!" someone yelled from the loading area sidewalk.

    It was Micky Silvio. The second bum was up and racing towards both of them. Silvio flew off of the dock, poised and ready to fight. Instead, the second bum stopped in his tracks and turned his attention to Silvio. That was a big mistake. This vagrant was unaware that he was about to be pummeled by a flurry of well-timed punches thrown by one of the best hand-to-hand combat guys in the neighborhood.

Before the bum knew what hit him, Silvio landed an overhand right, backed away, and sized up his adversary. The drifter, still upright, threw two half-hearted haymakers at him. Micky dodged one punch, blocked the other, and countered with a barrage of fierce body shots, eventually finishing with a solid left hook. It was a punch he perfected during his reign as a champion boxer. The crushing blow took the bum off his feet and dislodged his jaw. After that, it was a done deal. That poor bastard got hit by Silvio so many times he must have felt like three guys surrounded him. Finally, Micky ran up to Tommy and Ingalleretta.

"What the fuck is going on?"

In that instant, Silvio realized who the older man was.

"Holy shit, Mr. E., it' me, Micky Silvio, Gina and Tony's son from Castle Street. Are you ok?

Tommy's heart was beating through his chest. He wiped the raindrops from his eyes and reduced his breathing to short pants.

"Ingalleretta! Holy fuck!" he thought.

Tommy knew Micky's family lived on Castle Street, just three houses away from Manny. Silvio's father and his cousin, Greaser, all got their jobs on the Market because of Ingalleretta.

"Yes, I know who you are, Micky, but I need to know who your friend is," Manny responded, focusing on Tommy.

"I'm, I'm Tommy LaCosta, Mr. Ingalleretta. I live with Joe and Mari Da, Da, DaBone on Fillmore Street," Tommy answered, slightly stuttering like Danny Peanut Butter from Japeto's.

Tommy extended his hand. Manny pushed it away, instead choosing to hug Tommy tightly.

"I know Joe and Mari. You're the orphan boy from Bari, right?" Ingalleretta asked.

"Not anymore," Tommy firmly but respectfully answered.

In the meantime, more than a dozen guys converged onto the back dock area. The two bums struggled to stand up, trying to get to their feet. Sergeant Roger O'Neil, the cop in charge of SouthWater security, also ran up with his gun drawn pointed in the direction of the bums.

"WHAT THE FUCK HAPPENED HERE?" he screamed.

Ingalleretta grabbed his arm, pulled O'Neil in close, and spoke into his ear so no one else could hear.

"Stop drawing attention and put that fucking gun away, you stupid prick!"

O'Neil complied immediately and holstered his piece. Then, he focused on Tommy and Silvio.

"All right, what's going on here?"

Silvio attempted to explain. Ingalleretta motioned to him with his index and shook his head negatively. Micky got the message and immediately stopped speaking. Instead, it was Ingalleretta who answered.

"These two bums tried to jump me. One of them flashed a knife. Then, this guy came to help me," Ingalleretta explained. "That's all you need to know."

Ingalleretta glared at O'Neil and pointed to Tommy.

"THIS KID SAVED ME!!"

Everyone standing on the dock heard what Ingalleretta said. All eyes focused on Tommy. He looked back at everyone, unable to speak. O'Neil appeared perplexed. He turned to Ingalleretta and spoke in a voice only Tommy and Silvio heard.

"Do you want me to pinch these bums?"

The most apparent thing crossed Tommy's mind first.

"What? The cop is asking the mobster what to do?"

Ingalleretta thought for a few seconds and whispered into O'Neil's ear. Then, he leaned into Silvio and did the same. Silvio, in turn, walked over to Benny Barone, grabbed him by the arm, and whispered something to him.

"That's way too much fucking whispering," Tommy thought.

Benny took off and ran down the alley like a bat out of hell. Micky rolled the two scofflaws over the dock's ledge. Big Amos helped him.

"I'm gonna say this one time. I never saw these two mudda fuckers before in my life," Big Amos said loud enough for everyone on the back dock to hear.

Then, Amos turned his attention to the beaten bums.

"Y'all picked the wrong man to fuck with. You guys' fucked now!"

Benny pulled up a truck with a large garbage bin attached to its front. A few of the guys jumped down to the alley and helped throw the bums into the container. Then, Benny drove towards the abandoned railway yard. Everyone standing on that back dock knew the chances of anyone seeing those tramps again was highly doubtful.

O'Neil bent down, picked up the knife, and tucked it inside his police vest. There was a large leaf of cabbage on Ingalleretta's overcoat sleeve. Tommy brushed it off of him. Manny watched the leaf flutter to the dock.

"First, you save my life, now you're cleaning me off!" he joked. "Listen, Tominucci, I want to speak with you privately, maybe this weekend."

"Sure. That would be fine, Mr. Ingalleretta," Tommy nervously answered.

O'Neil whisked Manny away as they hurried to the back stairs of Strube Celery and Vegetable Company. They climbed a few more short steps to the gated staircase that led into the back offices of LaMancha Produce. Ingalleretta never walked into LaMancha through the main entrance due to the many prying eyes on the Market.

While Tommy brushed cabbage leaves off of his own jacket and pants, the workers that had gathered offered congratulations for what he had just done. Old man Lanzatorri threw his arms around Tommy.

"Maddon' a mi, Tommy, you help fight for Mr. E. You save him! Jesus Christ, you gonna have a bigga favor come your way!"

As Lanzatorri went back into his store, the crowd thinned. Tommy noticed many private conversations amongst the group as they walked away. A couple of the guys looked back at him and nodded. Tommy was numb and smelled like wet cabbage. Everything that just happened slowly began to register. Then, it hit him like a brick thrown from a second-story window. He just saved the life of a top Chicago Syndicate Boss!

He climbed back onto his forklift and wondered what would happen to those bums. In his head, he kept repeating that all he was doing was helping some old guy from being jumped, beaten, and robbed. For the rest of the day, he was treated like royalty and congratulated by everyone. A couple of the Market Kings bought him breakfast. A few others bought him lunch.

When he arrived home that afternoon, Tommy excitedly explained what had happened. He saw the worried look on everyone's faces and thought it best to make light of everything, summarizing the events of the day as if it were nothing.

"I was only trying to help.

Pa realized little Tominucci was no longer the orphan boy he took in and watched grow. Instead, his future son-in-law was well on his way to becoming a legend for stepping in and saving the life of an important man like Ingalleretta. Unfortunately, Joe also knew it would only be a matter of time before Tommy became hypnotized by the allure of Outfit life.

CHAPTER 5
CI STO (I'M ALL IN)

  Tommy reluctantly accepted Manny's envelope. Ingalleretta handed it to him directly, without a go-between. That alone spoke volumes. The exchange happened at Snafuro's Bakery while Manny enjoyed coffee with Jacco Snafuro. Tommy was instructed to be there at 9 a.m. sharp. He walked in at 8:59 and was immediately greeted by Snafuro.
  "Come stai, Tominucci? (How are you, Tommy?) Caffe espresso?"
  "No, thanks, Mr. Snafuro."
  "Tommy, call me Jacco. No more, Mr.Snafuro. Ok, figlio?" (Son)
  "Grazie (Thank you) Jacco."
  "Tommy, Manny is outside in the back waiting for you."
  As Tommy walked behind the bakery counter, he parted the red, white, and green beads that divided the customer end of the bakery from the staging area. It was then he remembered.
  "Those Italian flag-colored orbs have been since I was 13 years old!"
  He maneuvered his way through the prep area and the stoves. The smell of freshly baked bread was unbelievable! Next to ovens were long, wooden tables filled with an assortment of homemade pastries, cookies, cakes, and pies. Before he sat down with Ingalleretta on the back porch, Tommy extended his hand and kissed Manny on the cheek. His mind was racing a million miles a minute.
  "I can't believe that I'm sitting down with a Chicago Syndicate Boss."
  Manny lit a Lucky Strike, took a huge drag, and watched Tommy nervously fidget in the chair.
  "Rilassati, Tominucci." (Relax, Tommy) Ingalleretta calmly suggested.
  Tommy nodded and took a breath. As he exhaled, he noticed someone standing in the backyard corner. The shadowy figure was half-hidden by the large, red umbrella sticking out from the middle of the picnic table. Tommy, slightly puzzled, looked at Ingalleretta.
  "Don't worry, Tommy. That's just Vinnie. Have you two met?"
  "No, we have not."
  "Vinnie? It's gotta be Vinnie fucking Champagne!" Tommy thought.
  "Vincenzo, vieni qui, per favore. (Vinnie, please come here.) I want you to meet Tommy LaCosta."
  Out from the corner emerged Mr. Vinnie Champagne. Tommy had seen him a couple of times, but only from far away. Vinnie was Ingalleretta's sometimes driver and bodyguard, and in serious matters, his assassin. If Ingalleretta gave him the word, Vinnie was the guy that ended your life. Tommy heard many stories about him, but the most intimidating thing of all, besides his enormity, was his nickname, "Il Gigante Silenzioso." (The Silent Giant) Tommy extended his hand.
  "This is Vinnie Champagne, Tommy," Ingalleretta introduced.
  "Christ Almighty, this is the largest human being I've ever fucking seen,"

Tommy thought. *"I barely come up to this giant's shoulders!"*

"Hello, Vinnie. How are you?"

"That was a nice thing you did for Mr. E.," Vinnie replied in his deep, baritone voice.

"I was glad I could help," Tommy modestly answered.

Vinnie carried not one but two guns. The first tucked inside his pants, the other in a shoulder holster. The first thing Tommy thought was not that far-fetched.

"I wonder if he's got a third rod (Gun) *hidden somewhere."*

As Vinnie lumbered back to the corner of the yard, Ingalleretta reached inside his coat pocket. He pulled out a large envelope and placed it on the black and white polka-dotted tablecloth.

"This is for you. Before you say anything, you need to listen carefully to what I'm about to say. Then, you're going to take this, put it in your pocket, and not open it until you get home. Capisci, Tommy?" Ingalleretta instructed.

"Si, capicse," Tommy acknowledged.

"Inside this envelope is my gift to you. I'm forever grateful for what you did, and I'm offering you an opportunity. Everyone I've spoken to about you says the same thing. You're smart, respectful, and you conduct yourself as a man's man. You're loyal to your family, you're honest, and you're a hard worker. Tommy, I feel you're someone who can be trusted. So, if you want, I will teach you things and groom you. If you follow my instructions, you'll live a life that you've only dreamt about. I'm certain we can do great things together."

"Thank you," Tommy nervously responded.

"The man who took you into his home, Giuseppe DaBone, he and I have been friends since we were bambinos in Bari. In all the years I've known him, Joe has never asked me for help with anything. But you already know that, right?"

"Pa told me you knew each other as kids in Italy. As far as him ever asking you for anything, I don't know anything about that."

Tommy continued shifting in his chair, crossing and uncrossing his legs. His right hand sat on top of the envelope Ingalleretta gave to him. He slid his thumb over the side.

"That's gotta be over three fucking inches thick!"

"I respect Pa. He's a son of Bari like you are, and like I am. There's no pressure here, Tommy. So, I want you to accept this envelope. Non ci sono stringhe allegate. (There are no strings attached.) Think about what I just said. Read between the lines. Let me know if being with me, being with us, is a place you would like to be"

"Ok, Mr. Ingalleretta. I understand. I'll let you know, and thank you very much for the envelope and your generous offer."

"From this point forward, I want you to call me Manny," Ingalleretta insisted.

Tommy walked around the table, leaned over, and kissed him on the cheek. Ingalleretta grasped Tommy's hand and tightly squeezed.

"Whatever decision you make will be the right one, Tommy."

Snafuro smiled the entire time Manny was speaking, nodding approval.

Finally, Jacco stood, snapped his black suspenders, and appeared ready to talk. Just then, the back screen door to the bakery opened. It was Fat Roberta.

"Grandpa, it's getting busy in here, and people are asking for you."

She spoke to Jacco, but her eyes were focused elsewhere.

"Hey Roberta, how are you?" Tommy greeted.

She took advantage of the opportunity. Roberta reached out with both of her flour-covered hands, grabbed Tommy's head so he couldn't move it, and planted a smooch smack dab center on his lips. It lasted for a good five seconds before she let go.

"I heard you and Teresa are getting married. I guess that's been coming for a long time. I'm happy for you, Tommy. Congratulations."

Roberta's well-wishes were less than enthusiastic, her facial expression forlorn.

"Look at my lovely granddaughter! Isn't she beautiful, Tommy?"

Roberta gazed at Tommy like a starving hippopotamus sizing up its prey.

"She sure is, Jacco. I wish there were two of me, one for Teresa and one for her."

Roberta smiled, and her famous puffy cheeks swelled. Ingalleretta, barely able to contain himself, put his hand over his face to hide the smirk. Tommy followed Jacco and Roberta inside and then continued to the front of the store, where he waited his turn at the end of the customer line. He couldn't resist picking up a tray of pizza and a couple of loaves of fresh bread just being removed from the oven. Ingalleretta stuck his head inside the back door as Tommy's order was processed.

"Tommy, Vinnie is going to help you carry your packages."

"No, it's ok. I got it," Tommy politely refused.

"No, no, no. Let Vinnie walk back with you," Ingalleretta insisted.

Manny put his hand on his shirt pocket and patted it a couple of times, reminding Tommy about the large sum of money inside his jacket.

"Meglio prevenire che curare, Tominucci." (Better safe than sorry, Tommy.)

Nicky and Fat Frankie were sitting on the DaBone's porch. Frankie knew Vinnie, but Nicky had never seen him before. When they got to the backyard, Tommy handed the bread bag to Nicky then took the pizza tray from Vinnie.

"This is my soon-to-be brother-in-law, Nicky. I'm sure you know Fat Frankie from Japeto's."

"Nicky, this is Mr. Champagne."

"Hello, Nicky. How are ya, Frankie?" Vinnie greeted.

Nicky took a few seconds to size Vinnie up from top to bottom.

"Are you two guys or one guy?" Nicky asked him.

Vinnie smiled and turned to Tommy.

"There's not a fucking guy in Chicago who wouldn't give their left nut to be in your shoes right now. That's all I'm gonna say about that."

Tommy nodded. Frankie and Nicky looked at each other. Neither of them knew what to make of Vinnie's statement.

"Give this to Teresa, right?" Nicky asked, motioning to the loaves of bread.

"Yea, pal. Then come and get the abeets. (Pizza) I'll leave it here on the bench."

Tommy set the pizza down and walked towards the back basement door. Fat Frankie leaned over the crooked, metal fence that connected the empty lot to the DaBone's sunken backyard.

"Vinnie Champagne is carrying your groceries? Are you fucking kidding me? So your talk with the Old Man went well, I take it?" questioned Frankie.

"I gotta take care of something. I'll talk to you about it after dinner."

Tommy didn't wait for Frankie's reply. Instead, made haste to the basement's back corner room. That's where Pa stacked the old, empty wine barrels. Since there was no electricity in that area, Tommy lit one of the kerosene lamps on the window ledge. As he closed the door, he reached into his jacket and took out the bulging envelope. Tommy brought it close to the flickering lamp, opened it, and saw it was filled with $50 bills. There was a knot in his stomach. He got about halfway through, stopping at the $5,000 count. He placed half of the money into his pocket and the rest inside a plastic bag. He shoved the bag into the barrel and turned the cover to face the wall. He stood silently for a few minutes and let his life flash before him.

"Ci sto," (I'm all in.) he whispered.

Tommy noticed subtle changes when interacting with people in the months that followed. Socially, there were increased nods, more handshakes, and even a few hugs and kisses. The days of acknowledging his presence with just a quick hello, a wave, or a half-smile, were long gone. Even the Market Kings treated him like he was one of their own. There wasn't a day that passed that the business owners, the union reps and Mob guys, or the patrol cops on the Market didn't stop and shoot the shit with him, asking how he and his family were doing or if he needed anything.

"Hey, Tommy, how the fuck ya doin'?

"How's the family, Tommy?"

"You look like a million bucks! Is everything good? Anything I could help you with?"

"I just got a skid of cherries in. Why don't you take the top show box home?"

Tommy played things as he always did, on the low, confident, and everything in stride. He intended to ride his Mob tidal wave to the shoreline. Old man Lanzatorri loved Tommy long before the whole Ingalleretta intervention. Now, it was like he was Lanzatorri's business partner instead of an employee.

"Tommy, you work too hard. Take a break. If you need to, take a-two-a break. You wanna day off, you take a day off," Lanzatorri began suggesting in his heavy Italian accent. "I stilla pay you."

It got to the point that when Tommy dined at a restaurant, someone always tried to pick up his tab. At the very least, they'd send him a bottle or buy him a drink. But, most of the time, they just stopped by his table to introduce themselves, say hello, or ask him if he knew this guy or that guy. Teresa worried about his newly found Mob-celebrity status.

"Just be careful, Tommy. Please."

"I will, Bella," he always answered. "Ti voglio bene." (I love you.)

The local store owners also jumped on the Tommy LaCosta bandwagon. Ma received extra groceries in her bag, and although Pa was apprehensive and nervous about the whole thing, he was absolutely ecstatic that no one parked in the empty lot next to his house anymore. Mitzie took things to a whole new level when he started hand-delivering salami, capicola, pork neck bones, and fresh, thinly-sliced pink veal to the DaBone's house every weekend before closing his shop. Word traveled quickly throughout Mob circles. Manny had his arm around Tommy LaCosta.

Nicky also cashed in on Tommy's good fortune. The older guys began including him in the neighborhood card games and even occasionally folded a hand or two so he could win. He was also picked early when the softball teams were chosen. Even though he was only in his mid-teens, Nicky was allowed to work at the Market with the union's blessing on Saturday mornings. He wasn't physically big like Tommy but held his own when it came time to unload heavy cargo, never shying away from hard work. Nicky's claim to fame came when Lanzatorri gave him permission to make mechanical adjustments to broken machinery, pallet jacks, forklifts, and refrigeration units. Lanzatorri's distribution equipment became the lightest, strongest, and easiest to maneuver on the entire Market. Then, one afternoon, while rewiring the intercom and phone systems, Nicky met his future boss's brother, Fred. When Fred saw Nicky's improvements, he suggested an apprentice job at his brother Seymour's tool and die company. After discussing things with his family, Nicky jumped at the opportunity.

Tommy also had an apprenticeship. His early Mob endeavors began innocently with envelope exchanges, package shuttling, and whispered messages. Other times, Market store owners, produce purveyors, grocery buyers, connected guys, or union business agents tucked a roll of cash inside his coat pocket with specific delivery instructions. The most tedious of Tommy's responsibilities were when boxes inconspicuously hidden in the middle of fruit and vegetable pallets were required to be dropped off. Those exchanges were usually done while it was still dark outside. Tommy didn't know what was inside of them and never asked.

At least twice a month, Tommy took walks around the neighborhood. He chatted with friends and store owners just like he had been doing since he was in his early teens. His routine basically stayed the same over the years, with one exception. Now, his last stop before going home was Manny's Castle Street front porch. That stoop was Manny's sanctuary. Anyone who joined him was there by invitation only. Tommy and Manny's conversations almost always ended on a personal level, where Ingalleretta talked about not having children, being a widower by the time he was 52 years old, and about Lillian, his deceased wife. Tommy listened attentively. He could tell how much Ingalleretta trusted him, especially when sharing confidential information. Manny gave Tommy advice on conducting business, especially those he was personally involved in. During their hour-long porch conversations, Ingalleretta always held a glass of wine. His reading spectacles hung from the tip of his nose, and his brown suspenders covered his

his white short-sleeved shirt. Tommy would leave the folded newspaper he carried with him on the bench at the end of his visit. Manny would continue sitting, always finishing his glass of vino. Then, he'd pick up the newspaper and walk inside his home to his first stop, the basement bar area. It's there that he unfolded the paper to retrieve a hidden envelope filled with cash.

Tommy became one of Manny's few trusted protégés, earning anywhere from $500 to $1,500 weekly for his services. His end was always delivered to him by Vinnie Champagne or Lenny "The Cocksmith" Gardino. The denominations were $20 and $50 bills, never $100's. The empty wine barrels in the DaBone's basement didn't remain that way for very long. As Nicky got a little older, he also made deposits from his profits buying and selling stolen merchandise. Pa was none too happy when he caught wind of what he was doing.

"I'm keepin' an eye out for him, Pa," Tommy reassured. "Don't worry."

When Nicky was in on a score, he always kicked up cash to Manny and had Tommy include it in the porch-drop envelope. Manny was more than impressed with young Nicky's honesty, respect, and tribute. After all, Nicky was a quick learner, implicitly following Tommy's instructions regarding the pay-to-play Mob mentality.

These two very savvy boys knew how to make money for themselves, their family, and The Outfit.

CHAPTER 6
BIG BANANA, A FEW OF THE BOYS, MOB 101

The next few years passed almost as quickly as the envelopes of cash. Even though Ingalleretta's health was declining, he still firmly controlled his domain, Chicago's Near West Side. Nothing moved without his approval. Manny had a stranglehold on practically all the worthwhile illegal activities, as well as an ever-growing list of legitimate businesses. Mob coffers were overflowing thanks to him.

Tommy became Ingalleretta's guy on the Market, eventually leaving his forklift at Lanzatorri for a LaMancha Produce supervisory position. That job gave him the flexibility to appear and disappear as he pleased. Most of his time was spent overseeing the day-to-day operations of that very lucrative business while tending to his growing list of Mob responsibilities. But somehow, there was always time to coordinate the side deals that just happened to come his way. Besides all that, there was something else on Tommy's already full plate. It was bananas.

Most SouthWater businesses handled at least one specialty item. Besides being known for that, they also carried various assortments of other fresh produce. The thought process was if you couldn't bring a customer in with your showcase piece, you get them in the store by offering other merchandise. But, not a single SouthWater company handled bananas as their main attraction. Merchants usually split half loads from shippers, sighting small profits margins and storage issues due to the various green, on the turn, and ripe stages the fruit went through. Tommy's business strategy was to be the sole wholesale distributor of bananas on SouthWater. To do that, he needed to strike a deal with the two leading growers in the country, Dole and Chiquita. The only other facility with specialty banana chambers for the proper storage and ripening process was grocery giant Gino's Warehouse in suburban Northlake.

The perfect location for Tommy's vision was an affordable, vacant warehouse just across the main Market row on Racine Avenue. Tommy was more than willing to part with a substantial portion of the Mob cash he had already earned to make his dream a reality. With a nod from Ingalleretta and a signed union contract with Sally Boy Domenico's local, Tommy LaCosta was on his way to becoming a legitimate business owner.

The months that followed came and went like a whirlwind. Tommy negotiated a successful deal with both banana companies, and they awarded him exclusive distribution rights on SouthWater. Because of Nicky's mechanical ingenuity, he renovated that old warehouse with state-of-the-art coolers and equipment. The name Tommy chose for his company was "Big Banana."

As if starting his own business wasn't enough, Tommy married Teresa and built a new home in Maple Creek. He was incredibly proud that his house was only a few miles east of Oakbay, the exclusive area where Mob heavies like Ingalleretta, and Primo Montalbano lived. Ma and Pa DaBone stayed overnight many weekends. Pa felt like he was back in Bari with all of the undeveloped land and open fields that surrounded Tommy's sparsely populated subdivision.

A short few years later, Nicky and his steady girlfriend, Grace Benidetto, from Grand Avenue, got engaged. They planned on living upstairs of the DaBone's two-flat just as Tommy and Teresa did. Nicky was also doing quite well. Seymour, the tool company owner, was on the verge of retirement, and Nicky was in a prime position to purchase his business. Moreover, Tommy and Nicky were making money, and their illegal activities were also doing well thanks to their impressive array of firmly-placed street contacts, which were growing by leaps and bounds.

The Mob was also flourishing. They had a new batch of up-and-comers making their mark. Besides Tommy, some of the students at the top of their Outfit class were Frank "Saint Francis" Cirillo, Ronaldo "Ronnie" Bonnaro, Aniello Fontaine, "Choo-Choo" Chuckie Churchirillo, Dominic "Black Dommy" Terranova, Christopher "Christy Frosh" Shannino, Ulysses Fortunato, Bruno Charimonte, Willie "The Kid" Felice, and the Bolino Brothers, Michael, and Johnny.

Boss Joey "Good Times" Balducci boasted that his Crew was the largest and most feared. Primo Montalbano countered by saying his guys were the Outfit's future. Manny never got into their back and forth dick-measuring contest. He didn't have to. His small core group was almost always the most profitable. Manny ran a tight ship, but at the same time, he learned it was best to let his boys do their thing. As long as they respected Mob territories and followed the chain of command, Ingalleretta was more than satisfied with the generous contributions made by his loyal legion.

Manny's Crew, by design, was small. What was massive were the dozens of contacts and connections he accrued due to his Syndicate longevity. Besides his length of Outfit service, Ingalleretta also had a winning leadership style. He always preached to his guys that they were responsible for their involvement.

"Always take care of business first. Go above and beyond for each other in everything you do. If one of us scores, in essence, we all score. Don't ever point any fingers. If there's a problem, fucking handle it. The only buck I ever want to hear about being passed is the one that goes into our wallet."

When Manny spoke to his men, he used lots of 'we,' 'us'" and 'our.' Whatever your role was in the scheme of things, he always made sure you felt like you were playing a significant part in it all. It was just another of the many reasons Ingalleretta's Outfit reign was so successful for so long.

Tommy was one of Ingalleretta's trusted behind-the-scenes guys. An early example was when he helped get Japeto's numbers game up and running. Tommy sent Frankie dozens of heavy gamblers from SouthWater. Of course, Frankie and Tommy had been friends and neighbors for years, which made their collaboration easy. But that type of Outfit camaraderie was prevalent with everyone Manny controlled, and there was one main reason for it. Most of Ingalleretta's close guys and their families had deep Taylor Street roots. Besides Tommy and Frankie, Lenny Gardino, Vinnie Champagne, Salvatore Domenico, Micky Silvio, the four Pirelli Brothers, Anthony Carosha, and Manny's semi-secret ace-in-the-hole, Special Detective Michael Tunzi, all brought something important to the table. The group right behind them was in a category all by themselves. Like Nicky, the Fontanelli Brothers, Rocky Tedesco, and Richie "Big Money" Mazzulla. Their ties were based on the Outfit relatives they had. Every Chicago Crew had some semblance of that second group.

Out of the most recent Syndicate hopefuls, Johnny and Michael Bolino were garnishing more than their fair share of attention in of all places, the unpopular 'dirty deeds' arena. Only in their late teens, the brothers' blood-thirstiness and penchant for violence and brutality were more Mob-hitter veteran-like than their rookie ages indicated. Joey Balducci realized he had diamonds in the rough with these two and was more than anxious to test his intuition about them.

Michael and Johnny grew up on Grand Avenue. Their father Louis was known as "The Black Hand." When the decision was made to kill him, the brothers were only in their early high school years. Louis was a well-liked soldier in Primo Montalbano's Crew. His demise, in part, was due to the constant flagrant disrespect he showed Primo. Louis would have lived longer if not for his problem with Montalbano. Bolino always wanted to be a part of Ingalleretta's Crew, but you don't get to pick and choose whose team you're on in the Outfit. As his unflattering and disrespectful remarks to Primo continued, Louis often found himself in trouble, asking Ingalleretta for help to straighten out several infractions. Manny had a soft spot in his heart for Bolino because his family was also originally from Bari.

Louis's well-known quick and violent temper was similar to a candle. Once lit, it burned red-hot, as it did in the case of Sal "The Barber" Mirando, who was a real-life barber. Besides that, Sal was also a loudmouth, alcoholic, womanizing wannabe that dated Louis's sister Tootsie a couple of times. It didn't take long for her to see through Sal's problems and his many lines of bullshit. She abruptly ended their brief relationship, which broke Sal's heart. Whenever Tootsie went out for dinner or drinks, Sal would show up. For weeks, Tootsie would look out of her apartment window and see Sal's car parked in the street just a few doors away. The Barber's action towards the break-up would be considered stalker-like by current standards. Finally, she confided in her brother, asking for help. Louis was furious when Toots confessed she had gone on two dates with Sal.

"I told you a long time ago about this cocksucker! He's a no-good, rotten, bust-out drunken mudda fucker with a big mouth!"

Sal knew Louis was aware of the unconventional methods he chose in his hot pursuit of Tootsie, but he didn't care. On the contrary, Sal was so enamored with her that he was willing to do whatever it took to win Toots's affections, even if it meant pissing off her ruthless Mob-enforcer brother.

One evening, Louis got word that Sal was at the Lemon Tree Restaurant in Maywood. When he arrived, he was in such a hurry to grab Sal that Louis pulled his car onto the restaurant's front sidewalk and left the vehicle running with the driver's side door wide open. He stormed inside and found Sal sitting comfortably in a booth having drinks with a couple of other gamblers. Louis grabbed Sal by his beautifully coiffed hair and dragged him outside. The other men knew who Louis was so they didn't budge to help Sal. However, they did stare out the restaurant window while Louis issued Sal a severe beating. Everyone in the Lemon Tree

Restaurant also saw and heard him pleading and moaning.

"Louis, please stop! I swear I'll leave her alone. I can't help it! I love her."

Sal begged, trying in vain to stop the punches to his face and kicks to his body. But, by the time Louis was done, so was the damage. Sal was a bloody mess. Louis the Black Hand stood over him and wagged his finger.

"If I find out you go near my sister again, I'll bury you where I find you, you mudda fucker, you," he threatened, spitting on Sal.

It was common knowledge on the street that if you were spat upon, it meant you were not a man but a weak, worthless piece of shit unable to defend yourself. It was as embarrassing as it was demeaning. Louis climbed back into Lincoln Town Car and pulled away. Sal's buddies went outside, scooped up his battered body, and took him down the street to Loyola Hospital. They told the emergency room doctor that he was a robbery victim. It took over 30 stitches to close the wounds. Besides that, Sal's nose was broken and he had two cracked ribs and detached left retina.

Now, Mirando wasn't a connected guy by any stretch of the means. He wasn't considered an Associate, or even a friend of a friend. He was just a fucking barber pretending to be something more. News spread quickly about what happened. Louis thought the beating he gave Sal was justified and that he wouldn't be disciplined by Primo or the Mob considering Sal wasn't close with anyone. The Barber's thrashing was an evident lack of discretion on Louis's part. The Outfit didn't condone that type of violence on non–Mob related matters. Unfortunately for Louis, the beating he gave Sal was akin to hammering a nail in his own coffin. When Primo's New Jersey relatives visited, that was the last shovel-full of dirt Louis threw on himself. When Montalbano asked him to pick up food items from various restaurants, Louis told him to pick them up himself, that he was no errand boy. Que grande culliones! (What big balls!) Although Primo was an arrogant, authoritative prick, he was a Boss. It was a huge no-no to speak like that to someone like him as often as Louis did. After a meeting between top-level guys, they decided enough was enough. Louis had to go. Ingalleretta was the most vocal against this. He reminded the others at the table about all the money Louis made for them, the scores he participated in, and the hits he performed. None of that mattered. Bolino had reached the point of no return. Manny got voted down, and they put a disposal plan into motion.

Montalbano contacted Sal directly and asked him to meet.

"You're gonna do something for me," Primo ordered.

Sal had no choice in the matter. When he heard what Primo asked of him, Sal was happier than a pig in shit. The wheels were in motion. The guise used to lure Louis to his ending worked perfectly. As sharp and savvy as he was, Bolino never saw his hit coming. One of Montalbano's leading hitters was Jimmy Porcella. Louis often worked side by side with Jimmy and trusted him. Porcella called Louis late one weeknight and told him Sal was bragging about fucking Toots. Louis went ballistic. Porcella happily confirmed that he had Sal tied up in the basement of a Canal Street vacant property. Since none of the Bosses ever mentioned anything about the earlier beating, Louis figured it was okay to make this type of judgment call himself, considering the previous inappropriate behavior against his sister. He was wrong, dead wrong. When Louis arrived at the slum cellar, Porcella yelled to come downstairs, where he had Sal tied to a chair under a dingy, flickering light bulb.

"Tonight is your last night on the planet, mudda fucker," Louis threatened, walking towards Sal, reaching for his gun.

When he got about two feet away, Jimmy pulled out his piece and shot Louis once in the back of his head. Bolino's body folded, dropping face-first onto the cement floor. Porcella knelt, untied Sal, and gave him instructions.

"Get the fuck out of here, Sal. Forget about what you saw here tonight, or you'll be next."

Once untied, Sal got up from the chair, stood over Louis's body, and spit on him. Then, as he made his way to the basement steps, the top door opened. Sal looked up and saw Tommy.

"Tommy, that piece of shit Louis is over...."

That's as far as he got. Tommy raised the gun he held at his side and shot Sal in the face. He watched as chunks of The Barber's head spattered against the dirty, gray basement wall.

"I'll take it from here," Porcella instructed.

That was the night Tommy LaCosta made his bones. Ingalleretta explained to him earlier in the week that this was what needed to happen. Tommy knew sooner or later he was going to be asked to perform a hit, to take someone's life, to kill. He had to pay the price to be considered a legitimate Outfit member. He was thankful it was Sal and not Louis. As bad as it was that he murdered, at least it wasn't a friend. Porcella took the gun out of Tommy's hand.

"You can go now. I'll make sure to tell Primo and Manny you did a good job."

Tommy stared at Louis's body. Even though he lay crumpled, bleeding out on the floor, Tommy focused on how impeccably dressed he was. Months earlier, at a retirement party, Louis bragged to Tommy that he could cut tomatoes with the crease in his pants and that his Italian shoes shined like fuckin' mirrors. They toasted each other and laughed. Jimmy put his hand on Tommy's shoulder.

"Louis and I were friends too, Tommy. We took care of a lot of business together. But tonight, his number was up, and I punched the ticket."

"I'll stay here and help you with the bodies, okay, Jimmy?"

"No, you did what they asked. Manny told me he doesn't want you involved with what happens next. You gotta leave now."

Tommy didn't question Porcella. Instead, he went down to the Market and started his day earlier than usual. Later that evening, while dividing the proceeds of their most recent score, Tommy confided in his brother-in-law. He made Nicky swear up and down to keep his mouth shut about what happened.

"Holy fuck! I mean, I understand about Sal, he's been dodging getting popped for years with his bullshit. But, Louis? That's bad. Jesus Christ, I thought Manny liked him," Nicky wondered.

Tommy's answer was right on the money.

"It was more about who DIDN'T like him."

Nicky saw how bothered Tommy was about the shooting. After all, it's not every day that you kill someone. So, he attempted to console him as best he could by justifying the hit.

"Tommy, it's a fucking shame about Louis, but Sal was a perennial jagoff and a piece of shit. Even the handful of pricks that liked him didn't really like him. On the plus side, he's got no family, so you won't be looking into the eyes of any relatives, which is good. Here's the way I see it. Hopefully, it's just a one-and done deal. You're an earner, not a hitter. Manny knows that. You did what you did because you had to. There were no snags, no hesitation, and no problems. Done, done, and done."

"You're probably right, Nick. Thanks," Tommy said appreciatively.

As mentally exhausting as this weighed on Tommy, Nicky couldn't resist the opportunity to throw in a zinger. He felt it was just what Tommy needed to hear.

"Hey, look at it this way, you're the first guy in Outfit history to turn the tables and CLIP a barber!"

Tommy chuckled. As low as he felt, he appreciated the irony of Nicky's analysis.

Three days later, the police received a report of an abandoned car parked in an empty lot across the street from Navy Pier. Upon their arrival, officers immediately noticed a putrid smell emanating from the vehicle's trunk. When they pried it open, Louis "The Black Hand" Bolino was lying in a pool of his blood, piss, and shit. The only thing he was wearing was his pantaloni elegant. (Dress pants) The crease was still intact. Louis's mouth was sliced open from ear to ear. The coroner initially wrote that the deceased's tongue was missing on the autopsy report. The medical examiner eventually found it, jammed 8-inches deep into Bolino's anal cavity. The murder investigation went absolutely nowhere. Nobody was talking. Even the stool pigeons weren't stooling. Ten days later, one of Sal's buddies filed a missing person report when he didn't show up for work. No one ever looked real hard to find him.

Michael and Johnny Bolino were devastated over the death of their father. They made a secret vow in his memory to find out what truly happened with their dad. Then, when the time was right, they planned to exact revenge. Since the brothers had Mob blood running through their veins, they strived to prove their Syndicate worthiness and follow in their father's footsteps.

Montalbano initially complained when Balducci gave the Bolino brothers approval to perform a job for him. Joey didn't want to hear it and took little time setting Montalbano straight.

"The father was your problem. You asked for that problem to go away, and it did. The sons will be my problem, Primo."

Manny also spoke up.

"We heard you, Primo. Now, you hear us. We're putting Louis's sons to work."

A week later, the Bolinos got their first official Mob assignment. Balducci asked them to get rid of an independent drug dealer named Carlos Vega. The bold Mexican made the grave mistake of peddling his wares around Grand Avenue. It didn't matter that those streets had no homes and were lined with only commercial businesses and industrial sections. It was still considered neighborhood real estate. Sources told Balducci that Vega was on the verge of stepping up his cocaine, heroin, and speed distribution thanks to contraband supplied by his Laredo, Texas relatives. Therefore, the Outfit needed to send a message. Grand Avenue was off-limits for drugs and drug dealers of ALL ethnicities.

***See NARCOTICS at the end of this chapter.**

Alejandro Perez, Vega's second cousin, made a colossal mistake the night he chose to brag to some workers at a Grand Avenue steel factory. After he sold a few grams of coke to some guys in the parking lot of Hoto's Taqueria, he bought them a few beers. Alejandro boasted how the Mexican Mafia was taking over. He boldly gabbed that NOBODY was stupid enough to fuck with him and his cousin, especially the Wops. Alejandro was not a bright boy. The bartender just happened to be a friend of Michael Bolino. When he overheard Perez's conversation, a phone call was made.

After two nights of surveillance, the Bolino brothers grabbed Vega and Perez behind their apartment. Johnny hit them both with a tire iron rendering them unconscious. The Mexican cousins were blindfolded and shuttled to a vacant apartment in the Cabrini Green neighborhood. Before the Bolinos even questioned them, they were beaten and tortured. Perez was the weaker link. He cracked first and told Michael and Johnny everything, including the garage's address and secret hiding spot where they stashed their newest shipments of drugs and cash. The brothers drove to the location and found the concealed wooden panel behind some old auto parts. And just like Perez confessed, there were six cans stuffed with roughly $22,000 in small bills and a box filled with cocaine and heroin packets. When they got back to the apartment where Vega and Perez were bound and gagged, Michael removed their heads with ax and Johnny hacked off their arms and legs with a dull saw. The dismembered body parts were disposed of in various garbage cans throughout the Pilsen neighborhood that same evening, except for the heads. The severed noggins were covered in lye, bagged and sealed, and dumped in the filthiest part of the Calumet River, a few hundred feet from the shoreline of a chemical plant owned by Rochelle Laboratory.

The Bolinos turned over all the drug packets they found, but they weren't as honest about the money. The brothers only handed in $10,000, splitting the remaining $12,000 between themselves. As far as they were concerned, the only loose ends not tied in this score were each other. Balducci was happy with the job's resolve and gave the boys $1,500 each. He kept $2,000 and dispersed the remainder as part of the weekly take.

After many successful Outfit ventures, Michael and Johnny Bolino received a combination nickname. The two were known as "Fratelli Della Morte." (The Death Brothers.) They thought their father would've been proud of them. Michael and Johnny were inducted into the Mob as "Made" members less than five years after hitting the Vega cousins.

The decision to induct someone as a "Made" member is because of their willingness to perform valuable services. Some examples are a consistent generator of cash, an essential connection or go-between to an important contact, a supplier of illegal contraband, or a hitter/murderer. If you combined a few of those services, there was a good chance one of the Bosses would eventually sponsor you.

A handful of men in the Chicago Outfit were not Italian, but they were still members. They were not officially Made but admitted to the Organization due to their substantial contributions. Your membership to the Outfit was life-long. Once in, your expectations were undying loyalty, honor, respect, silence, and obedience. The only ways to get out were death or removal by the Bosses. Earning a more prominent position was based on a member's contribution and length of service. It was similar to ancient Rome's army, which the Mob closely emulated. But, there were positions in organized crime families that you would never find on any army chart. A few were "Consigliere," "Underboss," "Street Boss," and "Caporegime." The guys in those positions acted as multi-level buffers between the top tier and soldiers. If you considered the "Lieutenant" and "Captain" positions, which some crime families used instead, it became quite confusing as to which ranks had the most power. The bottom line for a member was to know who they immediately reported to and who the Bosses were. As good as getting a bump up in Mob ranks was, some bad news also accompanied it. Elevated status in the Outfit usually generated additional legal heat. The higher you rose, the bigger target you were for law enforcement. And if that wasn't enough to contend with, there were added responsibilities and pressures. Finally, if you were clever and lucky enough to maneuver through all that, there were the personality conflicts and petty jealousies between members and Crews. It came down to this - just about everyone in the Syndicate gets judged on the thickness of their last envelope.

*NARCOTICS.

The Chicago Outfit's participation in the narcotics trade consisted primarily of large deliveries with quick cash turn-arounds. Significant shipments and purchases went down at desolate locations in the far southern and western suburbs. Most contraband usually went to street gangs, biker clubs, and a small handful of select, big-time dealers. Thanks to the country's rural, wide-open spaces, the Mob conveniently placed "Spotters" (Men armed with high-tech binoculars and walkie-talkies) in various road positions. As a result, they could see any type of law enforcement approach from miles away.

When it came to drugs, the Chicago Outfit did have one crucial obligation – to maintain their deep saturation on Rush Street and the North Shore. The demand was constant, and profits were gigantic. Those were Mob territories, and they were just as off-limits to unauthorized peddlers as the old neighborhoods were. The family responsible for supplying the chemical taste treats to the wealthy that lived and worked in those affluent areas were the Steins, Sherman, Gloria, Marvin, and the youngest son, Benny

The heavily Syndicate-protected Stein Family oversaw dozens of dealers servicing bars, nightclubs, exclusive restaurants, and million-dollar private residences in and near those plush areas. Their responsibility was quenching the insatiable appetite of their customers by selling the highest quality nose,

mouth, and vein candy available.

As a result, the Steins constantly fed the heads of their well-to-do clients. The Jewish Pharmacy was a gold mine that never closed, which meant one thing. The parties never ended.

CHAPTER 7
THE RACKETEERING HEARINGS, NICKYISMS, MANNY MENTIONS A FAMILIAR NAME ON LIVE TELEVISION

National Law enforcement hierarchy decided to take advantage of a failed drug exchange between two mid-level Mafiosi at a New Jersey port to bolster their public appeal. They were tired of being perceived as stiff-neck, hemorrhoid sufferers who wore cheap suits and trench coats. The G's collective ego was crushed when a quote from Paulo "Greasy" Greco, one of the apprehended mobsters, appeared in east coast newspapers. Although not too intelligently, Greasy also spoke to television reporters as he got in and out of squad cars. He was a typical, street-level tough guy, through and through.

"These cops flooded the pier, flashing them cheap cartoon badges, waving illegal search and seizure warrants. They probably graduated at the bottom of their class from some Mickey Mouse police college. I'll be out of jail and enjoying breakfast in my kitchen by tomorrow morning. They got nothing."

The directors of the National Organized Crime Division in Washington were pissed. They responded by putting together a crack team comprised of their sharpest legal minds, best agents, and most knowledgeable advisors. The time had come to put known, high-level gangsters on the stand and ask them about the Mafia in a courtroom setting and broadcast it all, live on national television. Initially, the G felt pressuring these old-timers with public scrutiny would make them crumble. The government's interrogators were also banking on the advanced-age Bosses folding at the thought of losing their wealth and power for hard jail time. The G's plan was to show the American public the faces of the underworld. So, they subpoenaed more than a dozen reclusive New York and New Jersey big boys, with criminal records and histories dating back decades. The legal team was successful early, hitting a sensitive organized crime sore spot. The Bosses loathed publicity.

The first of the two scheduled television-authorized Racketeering Hearings was held at the Metropolis Court House in May of 1963. The G was confident. They felt one or more of the mobsters would lose their cool and say something that could be construed as incriminating. At the very least, they figured to get an informant or two out of it. So, the government rolled the Mob dice. They crapped out and lost.

Although the television viewership for the Racketeering Hearings was a ratings extravaganza, none of the alleged criminals were detained past initial questioning. Not one snitch, stoolie, or beefer amongst them. Mobster after mobster took the stand. They all plead the Fifth Amendment. The only thing the G proved beyond the shadow of a doubt was that they could not indict or arrest any of the subpoenaed Bosses.

Attorneys and their investigative team scrambled for control. They needed to cut their losses and erase the negative media attention they created. It was too late. The public consensus was that the notorious gangsters were invincible. In general, people around the country were rooting for them, enamored with how they were portrayed. The government agents looked like a bunch of goofy Keystone Cops. All of the newspaper headlines appeared in bold print. Eager writers and columnists with an abundance of swollen adverbs and adjectives wrote articles favoring the mobsters.

About two hours after the Metropolis debacle aired, federal agents stormed into the office of head-honcho network executive Jerry Blomberg. They squeezed Blomberg tightly until he agreed to televise the upcoming Chicago hearings ONLY in the Midwest and NOT nationally. Blomberg's willingness to agree with their request was mainly due to the damaging financial documents federal agents presented him with. Those forged investment papers would have sent Blomberg, his junior-executive amphetamine-addicted son, Allen, and their snake-in-the-grass accountant, Norm Stonefield, to prison for at least ten years. (The cunning agents planted incriminating evidence and backed it all up with false testimonies from what they said were 'protected' confidential sources. The G proved once again that they could be just as unscrupulous and unlawful as their Mob counterparts when necessary.)

Since the Big Apple Bosses didn't crack and rat on each other, you knew the Midwest Chieftains sure as shit would be every bit as uncooperative. The following week, tens of thousands of families in Illinois and the surrounding states gathered around their television sets. It was their turn to watch the local Syndicate guys they had read so much about thumb their bent noses at the government. Most Midwesterners only heard of or read their names in the newspapers. At the most, they saw old, black and white mug shots or unclear pictures of the alleged gangsters from years earlier. But now, they had the opportunity to connect a Mob character with how they currently looked.

Avid followers of Outfit-related news couldn't wait for the circus to arrive in Chicago. You have to give the G credit for the guys they corralled. If it was heavy hitters you were hoping to see, they scored a knock-out. From Wisconsin: Anthony "Bella" Santo, George "Georgie Cheese" Arrito, and Johnny "Lake Geneva" Generrosa. From Indiana: Anthony "Tony the Bomb" Valentino, and Morgan "Hungry Mo-Mo" Hackett. From Kansas: Antonio "The Turk" Toucarelli, and Frankie "Irish Guns" Riley. From Missouri: Gaetano "Capone" Lavato, and Robert "Roman" Romenelli. From Chicago, there was: Joseph "Joey Good Times" Balducci, Emanuel "Manny" Ingalleretta, Primo "The Hitter" Montalbano, and James "Jimmy Crap Game" Rio.

Ingalleretta, Balducci, and Montalbano were the most expensive items on the government's Midwest menu. The G had many questions regarding the Outfit's growing interest in Las Vegas casinos, and in their pursuit to save face, they decided to step it up a notch choosing U.S. District Attorney Oliver Calhagan to lead them. He knew about organized crime and its players. He was also intelligent, experienced, and cunning in court. Calhagan treated the hearing as if it were his screen test for senator, a position he dreamt about since his career began some 20 years earlier. When the trial started, Calhagan grilled one mobster after another, playing to the camera with full, fist-slamming authority. In his heart, he knew the Bosses were going to plead the Fifth Amendment as was their right to do so. Still, he intended on milking the media for every ounce of sensationalism it was worth. He got louder with every top gangster that took the stand.

"I am asking you, Mr. Irish Guns Riley, are you an associate or member of a nationwide criminal society known as La Cosa Nostra?"

"I plead the Fifth Amendment as is my right to do so on the legal grounds that my response may or may not incriminate me," Guns replied.

Riley was hungover from the night before. He and Jimmy Rio had been out playing the high-stakes card game "Between the Sheets" until almost 4:00 a.m. As usual, Guns won big, over $60,000! The government suspected but could never prove that Guns was the Syndicate's leading weapons supplier. He was. Riley also designed bombs and unique military-grade firearms. If the Mob needed a gun to shoot or a bomb to explode, Guns was the man they went to.

One after another, the Midwest Bosses took the stand and pleaded the Fifth Amendment, just like the New York leaders. There they sat, wearing expensive suits, flaunting Mob confidence and an air of invulnerability for all to see. When the barrage of questions stopped, they were excused from further interrogation. They were in, and then they were out. It appeared this hearing would also be wrapped up in a neat little 2-hour package, legally accomplishing what the east coast hearing did, nothing.

The DaBones gathered around the television at Joe and Mari's home watching, and listening to every word. Nicky made the same exact comment every time Calhagan opened his mouth.

"What an asshole!"

Victor's ears immediately perked up when he heard someone swear, especially his father. It was like he had to join in. For now, he remained silent but he was paying very close attention.

When the back door swung open, Tommy walked in carrying a massive Peter Rubi filled with assorted produce, meats, and cheeses. Zeus lovingly yapped, jumped up, and playfully chomped on Tommy's forearm like he always did.

"Did I miss anything?" he asked.

"Lots of Fifth," Nicky answered.

Victor piped up.

"Uncle Tommy, Dad says the guy talking on TV is a real asshole."

"Oooooohhhhhh!" everyone voiced collectively.

Tommy laughed. Grace knelt down next to Victor, explaining why 'asshole' was inappropriate to say. (It was the third or fourth time that month.)

"My friend hasn't been on yet," Pa said, referring to Manny.

Forget that Ingalleretta was old school. Forget he was a Chicago Boss, and forget that he was one of the most powerful mobsters in the Midwest. The only thing that mattered to Joe was that Ingalleretta was his friend.

"They saved Manny for last," Nicky added.

Pa sat up in his old, red leather recliner. It was worn and had indentations of his body. Many nights he drifted asleep on that chair after working long, hard days at Polina Construction. Today, he was as awake as he'd ever been.

When the doorbell rang, Zeus barked like crazy, just as he had done since he was a pup. Victor sprinted right behind him to see who it was. As he parted the window curtain, standing there filling the entire doorway, stood Fat Frankie. He was balancing two loaves of freshly-baked Italian bread from Snafuro's and a banquet tray filled with cavatellis, meatballs, sausages, and bracciolis. When Zeus jumped up and saw Frankie, his tail wagged, and his bark turned into a playful yelp. Zeus was no dummy. Fat Frankie had been feeding him under the table for years. Victor turned and yelled back into the room as he opened the door.

"It's Fat Frankie. Hi Fat Frankie, is that for us?"

Victor leaned in close to Frankie, so no one else would hear.

"I'm fucking starving."

Frankie cracked a smile, putting his index finger up to his mouth to shush Victor.

"No swearing, Vic. Yes, this is for all of us."

Mari shuffled to greet Frankie. She was starting to hunch over a bit. Her silvery-white hair was tightly pulled back by an old ribbon that had definitely seen a much darker mane. She was also slowing down physically as well as becoming noticeably more forgetful.

"Why do you always feel that you have to bring food when you come here?" she asked, hugging and kissing Frankie.

"That's because I love you! Plus, I know you and Pa love the cavatellis," he answered, grinning from ear to ear and chin to chin.

Frankie bellied his way into the dining room like nobody's business while planting a smooch on everyone's cheek. When he got to Nicky, they shared a bear-hug. Age-wise, Frankie was right in between Tommy and Nicky. Growing up, he spent almost as much time with Nicky as Tommy. Frankie and Nicky also had each other's back at an early age. A case in point is when Frankie broke Vincenza's second-story bedroom window. It was an accident, but Vincenza carried on like it was murder. Frankie committed the crime when he showed Nicky how to hit a 16-inch softball properly. Frankie whacked a solid line shot, for the record, his first ever, and BAM! Nicky and Frankie laugh about it now, but Frankie was shitting himself at the time. Every kid in the neighborhood was questioned. Nicky never gave him up.

After they hugged, Nicky soaked Frankie in from head to toe. (It took roughly a minute, a minute and a half.)

"Hey, did you lose weight?"

Frankie knew Nicky all too well. He smiled, wagging his sausage-sized finger at him.

"Nicky, don't start. You say that to me every time I see you."

Nicky raised his left hand and put his right hand over his heart as if he were taking an oath.

"Frank, I swear to Christ, you look like you've lost weight."

Pa was unable to hide his smile. Jimmy Durante, Red Skelton, Milton Berle, Sid Caesar, and Nicky were the only ones to get a real laugh out of him. The worst thing about Nicky was that he always kept a straight face through his deceivingly devious sarcasm. Fat Frankie looked down at his stomach and reached for the waistline of his pants. He tugged at them, hoping to achieve the appearance of lost weight. Sadly, it didn't. Grace slapped Nicky on the arm, knowing full well where her husband was going with his off-handed compliment. Nicky looked at her.

"Honest to God, Grace. He looks like he lost weight."

Then, Nicky leaned over and whispered into her ear.

"He probably just took a healthy shit."

Grace couldn't control herself. She high-tailed it into the kitchen overcome by another awkwardly induced fit of laughter from her husband, just like a thousand times before. Grace called them "Nickyisms."

Nicky rarely showed mercy with his comments. It's like there was nothing and nowhere sacred to him. Whether it was during a mass, a wedding, a funeral, it didn't matter. Everyone and every place was fair game. He was always prepared with humorous, inappropriate remarks at the most inopportune times. Not only did his family know that about him, but so did everyone else who knew him. A few months earlier, Nicky uttered one of his most famous Nickyisms. It was at the wake of Barney "Penny Pincher" Bartenzo from Schiller Park.

Different Outfit and neighborhood people showed up at Greemo and Son Funeral Home. The press and undercover police were all stationed across the street, following their routine - taking pictures, and jotting down vehicle license plate numbers. It was pretty common knowledge that Bartenzo's Mob claim to fame was juice-loans. 'Juice' is the term used for the high interest charged on a street loan usually made by an individual referred to as a "Loan Shark." In most cases, the Loan Sharks are backed by organized crime due to the unscrupulous and treacherous methods they sometimes use to get their money back.

Bartenzo brought his idea to the Outfit years earlier and the Bosses liked what they saw, especially the profit Barney was amassing. So, they spread over a million dollars on the street. That number soon tripled. Degenerate gamblers, hustlers, and schmucks lined up for the cash they needed. The juice alone on those loans flowed like blood on the river of ancient Babylon. Sometimes, it equaled or surpassed the original amount lent. Even worse was when original loans were rolled over at even higher interest rates. When borrowers couldn't repay even the vig (Vigorish/Interest), they found their options were few and far between. They needed to pay what they owed, or else, and or else was never a good thing. Loan sharks and their street collectors were literally burying the delinquent customers in debt, and sometimes, in holes.

For almost a year and a half, Bartenzo gave the Outfit their cut. It was a generous portion, but he made the lion's share. Some speculated it was well over a million dollars, and likely, much more. When the Bosses got heavily involved and got a handle on just how much money was coming in, they took over the whole shebang from Penny Pincher. It didn't matter. Even though he had all that money, Bartenzo was a stingy fuck that always ate alone, fearing he'd have to pick up a meal tab. Fittingly, that's precisely how he died, withering away by all by himself on a used, second-hand hospital bed set up on the fly in his dining room.

Some of the local Mob guys and associates who attended his wake were from Grand Avenue, Melrose Park, Cicero, Taylor Street, Berwyn, and the far southern suburbs. They were all dressed to the nines, solemnly shuffling around the casket. Bartenzo's only living relative was his grandson, Philip, more famously known as "Philly the Waste."

"I can't believe he's gone. I was just talking to him. But he didn't answer me because he was already dead. He was always there for me."

Philly incoherently babbled during the entire wake, blowing his nose and sniffing profusely. He was a useless, unstable, druggie with an insatiable appetite for cocaine, heroin, and acid.

Bartenzo confessed to Philly on his makeshift deathbed that his stacks of old, crusty $10, $20, and $50 bills were hidden in the outdated cast-iron water heater in his basement. Philly couldn't wait to dive headfirst into his grandfather's stashed cash.

As Nicky stood poised and polite at Penny Pincher's coffin, he nodded and shook hands with others who came to pay their respects. Philly continued carrying on.

"Oh my God, he's gone, he's gone. I can't believe it. I just can't!"

Just that quickly, during a moment of complete silence between Philly's rants, Nicky loudly commented.

"Hey Phil, for Christ's sake, give it a fucking rest already. If you really wanna make sure he's dead, drop a buck next to the casket and see if he reaches for it."

Of course, Nicky was referring to Bartenzo's well-known cheapness trait. The entire place went up for grabs and let out an inappropriate whoop of laughter. Then, they all scattered like a hand grenade was about to go off. You never saw so many Italian guys in silk suits hustling towards the lobby, the washroom, and the exits. They needed to be anywhere, except where they were, in front of the coffin. Every eye in the place was now on Nicky. Philly remained at the foot of the casket. He also looked at Nicky, first with a little bit of shock and then embarrassment. That lasted briefly. Then, Philly got the joke. He began laughing out of control hysterically. It was a repetitious, billowing howl, a true "Fuck you, grandfather, I'm finally laughing AT you and not WITH you." Philly knew all that money was his, and all he could think about were the drugs, hookers, and booze he would buy with it.

As Nicky walked to the rear of the parlor, people shuffled in from the lobby to see what the loud ruckus was. Philly couldn't contain himself and was bum-rushed out the back door by Johnny "Shovel" Greemo, embalmer and co-owner of the funeral home. When Tommy caught wind of what happened, he yelled at Nicky.

"You can't do shit like that, pal. Do you know how much money that old cheapskate jagoff made for the Outfit? If somebody beefs, you're gonna have some explaining and apologizing to do. And, you'd better be real fucking sincere about it."

Nicky half-heartedly agreed with Tommy at first. But, the more he thought about it, the more worried he became, so for the next week, he asked Tommy three times a day if there were any rumblings. Ten days later and there were still no complaints about his comment. That meant no apologies to be made, and most importantly, no repercussions. Nicky was fortunate.

As the Racketeering courtroom saga continued, Frankie walked into the DaBone's kitchen. He neatly arranged the braccioles and poured gravy over the cavatellis. Just then, Ingalleretta took the witness stand. Manny appeared gaunt, even smaller in stature than he was in person. The bright lights and television cameras were not at all kind to him. He was pale and sweating like Richard Nixon did when he debated John F. Kennedy. There was rampant speculation about his health, not just within the neighborhood but also within the Outfit and government. Tommy voiced his concern to Joe.

"Jesus Christ, Pa. He really doesn't look good."

Joe sat up in his recliner to get a better view. In the past, Pa skirted conversations with Tommy about his obvious closeness to Ingalleretta. Joe knew their relationship, but he and Tommy never really spoke to each other about it.

Although he was still pretty sharp, Manny's grasp of the day-to-day operations was slipping a bit. The G hoped Ingalleretta would rattle and not remember to plead the Fifth. Or, maybe, say something he shouldn't. The cards were shuffled. It was time for the deal. Calhagan began quickly, wasting no time to verbally intimidate Ingalleretta.

"Mr. Ingalleretta, are you a Boss in any organization known as "The Outfit," "The Syndicate," "The Mob," or "The Mafia?"

Calhagan didn't wait for Manny's answer.

"Mr. Ingalleretta, is it true you and your underworld associates are responsible for multiple crimes and illegal activities? Is it true that those crimes include, but are not limited to, murder, corruption, intimidation, gambling, hijacking, theft, extortion, arson, narcotics trafficking, armed robbery, prostitution, blackmail, fraud, and loan-sharking?"

Everyone at the DaBone house was silent, except for Nicky.

"Well, that about sums it up!"

"Stai zitto!" (Be quiet!) Pa demanded.

Nicky looked at Fat Frankie and shrugged his shoulders. Frankie suppressed a laugh, but just barely. The camera focused tightly on Ingalleretta as he glared at Calhagan. Manny cleared his throat.

"Here we go," Tommy said, bracing for Ingalleretta's reply.

It was the Fifth Amendment. Manny recited it perfectly, and he did so time and time again after every vicious question Calhagan threw at him. Ingalleretta drew immediate applause from some of the Mob-planted court spectators in the room. A collective sigh of relief came over the DaBone household. An irate Calhagan was pissed. He began to sweat and lose his temper. The louder he got, the quieter Ingalleretta's responses became. Manny knew precisely what he was supposed to do and answered like the stand-up champion he was.

Pa sat back in his chair and cracked a faint smile. Teresa ran to Tommy and hugged him. Mari put her hand on Joe's shoulder. Nicky looked at Frankie, furrowed his eyebrows, curled his mouth, and opened his arms as if to say, "Was there ever a doubt?" Absolutely no one was prepared for what was happened next.

"Mr. Ingalleretta, isn't it true that you've spent most of your life as a member of the Chicago branch of La Cosa Nostra? In fact, don't you owe your comfortable lifestyle, wealth, and power all to the Mob? Is it true that you are willing to die rather than break your silence about this so-called brotherhood?"

"I owe my life to one man and one man only," Ingalleretta replied.

"And what is that man's name, sir?" shouted Calhagan.

Ingalleretta sat silent. The DaBones looked around the room at each other. Other than pleading the fifth, Manny wasn't supposed to speak. Tommy's stomach turned. Suddenly, he felt nauseous.

"Please, for the love of God, don't say it!" he thought.

Ingalleretta leaned into the microphone and boldly stated as clear as day.

"That man's name is Tommy LaCosta. He saved my life!"

Victor took advantage of the opportunity.

"NO FUCKING WAY! That asshole just said Uncle Tommy's name!"

Victor caught a pass. Not a word from anyone about his swearing. Everyone at the DaBone house looked at Tommy, even Zeus. The camera zoomed in on Calhagan. He was noticeably rattled, caught off guard by Ingalleretta's response. As he nervously fidgeted through papers on his desk, Calhagan finally focused on his team of advisors. They were perplexed. Calhagan went as ballistic as he could on live television.

"TOMMY LACOSTA? ANYONE? WHO IS TOMMY LACOSTA? DOES ANYONE HAVE ANYTHING ON A TOMMY LACOSTA?"

Ingalleretta's lawyers tugged at his jacket, leaned into him, and whispered.

"Manny, PLEASE don't say anything else."

Calhagan's team was busy shuffling through notes and documents. Then, finally, one of the law clerks spoke softly into the ear of the visibly shaken head attorney. Calhagan pulled away after heating only a few words.

"So what you're saying is that there's nothing on LaCosta?" Calhagan asked, attempting to cover the microphone with his hand.

It didn't work. Everyone in the courtroom and those watching television heard Tommy's name mentioned for the umpteenth time in less than three minutes. One of Calhagan's assistants walked around the table.

"We were instructed to focus on today's witnesses only," he apologetically said. "LaCosta's name was penciled in on the chart just a day or two ago. According to Agent Carpino from the Chicago Task Force, LaCosta is barely a person of interest, and he's not even listed. There's over a hundred known Chicago associates and probably twice as many unknown ones. The only thing we had time to do was see if he had an arrest record. He didn't. Not even a parking ticket or speeding citation. His name never came up at any of our meetings. He's probably just some Little Italy friend or something."

Calhagan got in the assistant's face.

"Probably? Is that the best you can do? LaCosta must be somebody! Do you realize that Emmanuel Ingalleretta just gave us a name, or are you a stone-cold fucking idiot?"

Pa's face saddened. He looked at Tommy and shook his head. Calhagan got up from his chair and walked to Ingalleretta. The sounds of cameras clicking, bulbs flashing, and multiple conversation mumbles filled the courtroom. Ingalleretta remained calm and emotionless as he sat at the oak table. Calhagan stopped and stood directly in front of Manny.

"Mr. Ingalleretta. Why do you feel that you owe your life to this Tommy LaCosta?"

Ingalleretta looked up and smiled.

"Because I said I do."

The room erupted in laughter. The moderator immediately banged his gavel, asking for quiet. Calhagan had one last question to ask.

"Is there anything that you would like to add to that last statement, Mr. Ingalleretta?"

"No, thank you, Mr. Calhoun," he replied, mispronouncing Calhagan's last name for all to hear.

Again, the courtroom erupted in laughter. Calhagan knew he had nothing. The befuddled legal team went down in the flames of embarrassment. A disgusted Calhagan walked back to his table and picked up the desk microphone, stand and all.

"I have no further questions for Mr. Ingalleretta. We're done with this hearing."

There was an advertisement for Sinclair Gas Station during the commercial break. The company used a giant, green dinosaur to promote its many services. Victor owned the promotional five-foot plastic blow-up dinosaur, given to valued customers of their independently-owned franchises. (There was no doubt Nicky had something to do with making sure his son owned one of these treasured toys.) Victor often practiced riding, flipping, and throwing it around his living room and the backyard.

Pa had heard enough and headed for the basement. Teresa remained silent throughout the televised proceedings, but not for long. She was unsuccessful in hiding the 'worried' in her voice.

"My God, Tommy!"

"Everything's gonna be fine, Tree," he calmly responded.

Tommy followed Pa downstairs and found him bent down in front of the most recent barrelful of his homemade wine. Pa opened the spigot, filled two Mason jars to the top, and handed one to Tommy. There was no toast. Joe just gulped his right down. The first words out of Tommy's mouth were apologetic.

"I'm sorry if I embarrassed our family."

"Tommy, now the whole world is gonna know what the neighborhood knows, that you're with them."

"Pa, you knew I helped Manny what, fifteen or so years ago? The lawyers were worried about what he might say because of his brain disease. But, you know how Manny is. He told me last week that if Calhagan irritated him, he was going to tell him to go fuck himself all the way back to Washington."

42

The basement walls closed in on Tommy every time he went down there. It was always damp, and the surroundings remained primarily unchanged since he had slept there years earlier. When he and Teresa visited, Tommy only went down there to tuck cash into a wine barrel or two. In his mind, the peeling paint on the brick walls, the wooden beams, and the smell of wine that permeated the air reminded him of the fears and nightmares of his early youth when he first came to live there.

"Tommy, I hear the stories about you and the others. I know they're not all true, but now, this thing on TV? Maybe, it brings problems, or worse, maybe some people get jealous of you. Today, I was only worried about Manny, now look what happened? They said your name ten fucking times!"

"The government isn't interested in someone like me, Pa. If they were, they would've known my name. I mean less than nothing to them. I work, and I pay my taxes. My business operates legally. Whatever bullshit the government wants to say or think, let them try and prove I'm doing something wrong. Manny slipped up. That's all it was. He got confused, just words and ramblings from a sick old man. So, he mentioned my name, big deal."

Pa didn't buy into Tommy's response for one split second.

"Tommy, don't blow smoke uppa my ass. I watch the news, I told you already I hear the talk in the neighborhood, and Ma reads me all the merda (Shit) in the newspaper."

Pa pointed to the wine barrel in the back corner of the side room. It was placed in an uncharacteristically upright position.

"I found the money you and Nicky put in that barrel. I can't even count that high! And what about your friend, you know, the boy who always dressed so sharply? His parents were from Bari, I think. What was his name, Bolino, right? Wasn't he the paisan that Manny and everyone liked so much and thought highly of? I guess they didn't like him enough, did they? Dead and bloody in the trunk of his car is how he was found. Is that how you want to wind up?"

Tommy realized Pa knew more about what was going on than he had initially thought.

"I don't wanna see you, or Nicky or Fat Frankie get hurt, understand?"

Pa opened his arms and hugged Tommy tightly. Tommy pulled away slightly and looked intently at the man he admired more than anyone in the world.

"Everything's gonna be fine. I promise."

Nicky stuck his head in the basement.

"If you guys want to eat, you'd better hurry up. Fat Frankie's on his second helping already!"

Joe reached inside his overalls and took out one his family famous red and white polka-dotted handkerchiefs. He wiped his moist eyes and blew his nose.

"Forse Mari ed io saremmo dovuti rimanere a Bari," he thought. (Maybe Mari and I should have stayed in Bari.)

CHAPTER 8
WHO YOU WITH?

It was an extremely cold and wintery morning on Christmas Eve in 1966. Victor was pissed because he was missing Saturday morning cartoons. Every kid in the 60s lived for Saturday mornings. Chicago's television line-up began at about 7 a.m. with The Bugs Bunny Cartoon Hour, Scooby-Doo, Gigantor, Shazam, and Underdog. Weekday choices were few and far between, so time was filled watching Ray Rayner, Chelveston the Duck, Frazier Thomas, Garfield Goose, Captain Kangaroo, Mr. Green Jeans, Bozo the Clown, Ringmaster Ned, and Oliver Old Oliver. It was lots of slightly light-in-the-lap middle-aged men dressed in costumes, wearing makeup, and interacting with puppets and stuffed animals while talking to inanimate objects pretending they were real. It didn't matter. They were fantastic!

On this particular Saturday, Victor had to help his dad pass out Christmas gifts to the Shop employees. Nicky talked non-stop for the entire seven-minute ride from Fillmore Street about the big Christmas party later that night at Uncle Tommy and Aunt Teresa's house in Maple Creek. Sometimes, Victor thought his father acted like a kid disguised as an adult.

"Victor, there's gonna be huge, decorated trees, games, home movies, great food, and presents for everyone," he excitedly explained.

Nicky was exceptionally proud of Tommy and Teresa. Along with Oakbay, Maple Creek was rapidly becoming the suburb of choice for Syndicate guys and their families when they left their Chicago neighborhoods. It was nothing less than ingenious foresight and a slight pinch of coincidence that Tommy chose to build his home there.

Victor's concern was the cartoons he was missing. The only Christmas wish he had for the moment was for his father to stop with the 'Uncle Tommy this' and the 'Uncle Tommy that.'

When they were a couple of blocks away, Victor frantically pointed and shouted.

"Dad, the Shop is on fire!"

The Shop wasn't on fire. When it got that cold, the workers collected scrap wood and burned it in a garbage can to keep warm while waiting for Nicky to open the doors.

"Vic, it ain't on fire. That's just the shines trying to keep warm."

"The who?" Victor innocently asked.

"That's Willie, James, and Robert...you know, the guys," Nicky answered.

Instead of explaining to his overly-impressionable son why he called the three black drill press operators 'shines,' Nicky decided to cool it.

Willie, James, and Robert always took the same mode of transportation to work, the EL (Elevated Train) to Canal and Lake Streets. Besides stopping just a short block away from the Shop, the train came to a halt right in front of Mr. Lucky's Bar. The workers were known to stop in for a quick early a.m. whiskey or two.

Nicky took a long, smooth drag on his DiNobili cigar, compliments of Mike Cee, a retired pitching coach for the Chicago White Sox. Coach Cee was a high school friend of Fat Frankie's that coordinated stolen loads. He also partnered up with Nicky, Tommy, and Silvio on many occasions. The Coach's most recent procurement was a 12-wheeler filled with cigarettes, cigars, and lighters bound for a storage facility in Strongs Prairie, Wisconsin. The truck never made it there. That type of contraband basically sold itself and the entire hijacked shipment was broken down, turned over, and converted into cash in less than one afternoon. The deals on boxes, cartons, and cases were so sweet, you couldn't pass them up. Nicky alone bought two full crates of his beloved cigars. (He gave five boxes to a delighted Uncle Jimmy.) Almost everyone in the neighborhood was inhaling stolen tobacco and lighting it up with purloined lighters. Even the people who didn't smoke were smoking!

Willie waved Nicky down about a hundred feet shy of the Shop. Willie Earl Williams was a great worker. He was also as strong as a small herd of oxen, but unfortunately, smelled just as bad. On a few occasions, Nicky hooked him up with longtime friend, Tank Floyd. Nicky and Tank knew each other since their teenage boxing days at the Sheridan Park Gym. Tank, a staunch, smart, and highly vocal African-American was now the secretary-treasurer of the International Brotherhood of Minority Workers. (IBMW)

*See IBMW at the end of this chapter.

Floyd used Willie to work undercover for the union as a job seeker. As a prospective new employee, Willie gained access to the businesses Floyd was trying to organize. It was Willie's job during that fake interview process to gather as much information as possible about the company, the office layout, the number of employees, and any other pertinent details. As a last resort, Floyd instructed Willie to start trouble in any way, shape, or form he could and to do it as disruptively as possible. That's how the union found out about company security measures. Labor organizers, especially the ones that worked for the IBMW, often used those harsh tactics when facing tough business owners who fought their organizing efforts. Willie worked like a charm. His African Zulu, ultra-dark to the point that it was almost purple complexion alone, scared the living shit out of the primarily white bosses.

As Nicky got closer, he saw why Willie was frantically flagging him down. There was a black Buick parked right in front of the Shop. Nicky remembered the conversation he had with Seymour about two guys in a black Buick that tried to muscle him for street tax. (Street tax is what the Syndicate charges companies to be under their umbrella of protection.) Seymour had many life experiences. He was a Marine veteran, a devout Jew, a family man, and a very shrewd and wealthy businessman. Seymour knew how the Mob worked hand-in-hand with crooked police and politicians.

A few years earlier, with Tommy's help, Alderman Danny Buderick postponed the city's quick deed claim on the empty lot across the street from the Shop. Seymour was eyeballing that property for another business venture. At first,

Buderick gave Seymour a mouthful of standard politician jargon in the form of a high-handed response. Seymour had dealt with some local politicos in the past and was fully aware that nothing spoke louder to them than cold, hard cash.

After a few phone calls and a couple of after-hours meetings with Tommy and Nicky, Seymour paid $10,000, and the problem with the lot across the street from the Shop disappeared. What Seymour wasn't privy to was how his bribe cash was dispersed. Alderman Buderick gladly accepted $3,000 once he knew the involved parties were connected. Ingalleretta's cut was $2,500, Tommy snatched $1,000, and Nicky pocketed $500 for brokering the deal. The balance of $3,000 was kicked up the Outfit tree. Everyone involved got a slice. That's how shit got done in Chicago.

Seymour badly wanted that chunk of land across the street. For years, those prime properties immediately west of the Loop were mainly old buildings, small companies, various mechanical shops, and manufacturing businesses. However, that area was rapidly changing. Seymour knew it, and so did the Outfit. The Mob wanted in on the ground floor before those aged structures were torn down or rehabbed and converted into multi-million dollar establishments, condominiums, and shopping venues.

When the two thugs previously visited Seymour, there was no mistake they were there on the Outfit's behalf. Seymour wasn't about to run to the police, knowing he would be an easy mark for monthly shake-downs from both sides of the law. But, on the other hand, he was definitely not going to pay a couple of strokes just because they were supposedly with somebody, somebody. So he asked Nicky to get Tommy involved again.

"Nicky, if I have to pay these guys, I'll pay them, but can you please check with Tommy and make sure they're with his people?"

Seymour died shortly after that. Nicky was too involved with purchasing the Shop and had put that conversation out of his head. However, his memory quickly refreshed when he saw the Buick parked in his spot. He rolled down the window, not taking his eyes off the car or its two occupants.

"What's up here, Willie?"

Willie bent over and stuck his head inside the car. The pungent smell of whiskey, poor dental hygiene, and repulsive body odor passed through even before the surge of crisp, winter air. He was shivering and had half-frozen snot covering his untrimmed mustache.

"Mr. Nick, those two guys are back again."

Nicky turned to Victor, smiled, and then turned back to Willie. James and Robert also walked up.

"Merry Christmas you guys! James, do me a favor, take Victor over by the fire and let him throw some shit in there," he directed. "Let's see what these two fuckin' balloon heads want now."

"You gonna be alright? I'll come with ya if ya want me to?" offered Willie.

Nicky didn't want to worry Victor, who just happened to be hanging on every spoken word.

"You're fucking aye I'm gonna be alright. Right, Victor?"

Victor felt uneasy. James walked around the car to the passenger's side and opened the door.

"C'mon, Victor, let's throw some boards in the fire," James suggested.

As Victor exited, he looked through the back passenger's door window. He saw his dad reach into the glove box and pull out a gun. As much as that worried him, he did what he was told and silently walked with James to the blazing trash can. Sparks and ashes flew up, quickly disseminating in the cold air. The two front doors on the Buick opened simultaneously. Nicky took a drag on his cigar. James leaned over to Victor.

"Victor, your daddy's gonna be fine, you'll see."

"That's right, Baby Sweet," Willie added. "I'll make sure of that."

Two serious-looking men lumbered toward Nicky.

"Hey pal, how ya doin'?" one of them asked.

As they got a little closer, it was pretty obvious. They both towered over Nicky. The man who hadn't spoken yet was broad, even more so in his huge winter overcoat. It didn't matter how big they were, that never stopped Nicky from speaking his mind. It wasn't going to stop him now, either. So he begrudgingly answered with a tinge of cockiness.

"How am I? Not good. Two big jagoffs have their piece-a-shit Buick parked in my fuckin' spot."

Victor heard how his father answered. It made his stomach turn upside down. The more massive man got pissed.

"You little fucking prick, what are you, some kinda punk?" he growled back.

Nicky didn't flinch or even bat an eye. He also didn't take his finger off the trigger of the .38 caliber piece he concealed inside his left coat pocket.

The angered man took an intimidating step toward him. The other guy smiled like the cat that ate the canary. He put his hand on his partner's chest to stop him, then pointed to James, Willie, and Robert with his other hand.

"They told me your name is Nicky, right?" he asked.

"Okay, let's see where this goes," Nicky thought.

"That's right, I'm Nicky."

The smiling man took his hand away from his partner's chest and continued to talk.

"We spoke to the old Jew, I don't know, maybe five, six months ago. He seemed like a really nice man, but I heard he's dead. That's too bad. I also heard that this joint is yours now. So, now we're here to talk to you about the way things are changing out here."

"And what change is that?" Nicky asked.

"People, Nicky, the people in charge of what happens on the streets, that's what the fuck is changing!"

The wind howled and snapped around Lake and Jefferson streets like a frozen whip. An empty, rusted garbage can tumbled down the alley and smashed into a snowbank. For a brief few seconds, everyone's attention focused on. Nicky remained silent and motionless, which was not normal for him. He figured he would let these guys talk and see if they came up with a name. Nicky assumed they didn't know he was Tommy LaCosta's brother-in-law. He also thought that maybe they didn't know Tommy, or worse, perhaps they did know him and didn't give a shit. There were so many new guys on the street with Mob-ties that it was difficult to keep track of them.

"If they're with somebody, they should've started out with that," he thought.

Nicky also knew it was best to wait until the very last minute before mentioning someone's name, and only as a last resort. Tommy taught Nicky that it was always better to do business and be safe instead of acting like a stiff prick

"Look, Nicky, my name is Carmine, and it's way too cold out here to be playing back and forth kid games. You're gonna need to come up with some scratch if you wanna stay in business. That's the bottom line. We're lookin' for a nice round number, ya understand? We'll be back next week to iron out the details."

As both men turned and walked away, Nicky spoke up, deciding to use a street-smart phrase.

"Who you with?"

The two men stopped dead in their tracks. They looked at each other for a few seconds. It was Carmine who continued doing all the talking.

"You already know my name. This enormous gentleman to my left is Big Charlie. If you feel you gotta run to somebody, then run to somebody. But, you better run really fast because the next time we come and see you, Big Charlie here ain't gonna be so friendly."

Nicky figured that at least he had gotten both of their names. It was a start. He continued trying to get a little more information out of them.

"Let me guess, Big Charlie's your Goodwill Ambassador, right?"

Charlie didn't like Nicky's wise-assed comment and let him know it.

"Maybe I'll come back here just to pay YOU a fucking visit."

Nicky stared into Charlie's empty, piercing eyes with a quick response.

"And that might be the last fucking visit you ever pay anyone."

Nicky knew in the back of his head that he had Tommy and company to fall back on if things really got out of control.

"Next time, things'll be outta my hands," Carmine warned, pointing to one of the parking meters.

Charlie wrapped his massive arms and hands around the metal post and was actually bending it back and forth! Then, about 15 seconds later, he ripped it out of the cement, steel bolts, and all. He threw it to the ground, and it smashed open while quarters, dimes, and nickels sputtered out, dropping underneath the fresh snow. Charlie glared at Nicky and walked away. Carmine concluded with a strong statement.

"Nicky, you seem like a sharp guy. Think about that nice round number, and do the right fuckin' thing here."

When he caught up to Big Charlie, Carmine whispered into his ear. Charlie nodded, and turned back to Nicky flashing a devilish, evil smile. Nicky knew what that intimidating grin was all about.

At first, their car struggled to start. But, once it eventually turned over, the growling engine noise blended with the sound of their tires crunching over fresh snow. Then, the roar of the EL racing overhead across its frozen tracks drowned out all sounds. As the locomotive passed, sparkling snowflakes fluttered down and fell as they turned left on Lake Street. Nicky didn't move until they were out of sight.

"C'mon guys, let's go inside and warm up. Who could use a couple of shots of whiskey, Willie, James, Robert?" he asked.

Victor reached for his father's hand.

"Is everything all right, Dad?"

Nicky pulled the collar of Victor's coat up as the wind picked up.

"Everything is fine, Vic. Just do me a favor. Before we go back to the house, remind me to call Uncle Tommy at the Market."

"Okay, Dad. I memorized their license plate number. It's MS3334."

Nicky smiled.

"You're a smart boy, Victor. Before we pass out the Christmas gifts to the guys, go put the television on in my office. Maybe you can still catch some of your cartoons."

"All right, yippee, and right on!" Victor exclaimed.

Nicky unlocked the door and stood to the side as Willie, James and Robert rushed their way in, anticipating the whiskey. Victor waited and watched his father get back in their Chevy and pull it up to his parking spot. When he got out, Nicky flicked his cigar into the flaming garbage can.

"Dad, don't forget to put your gun back in the glove compartment!"

"Oh, shit," Nicky thought. *"This kid sees every goddamn thing!"*

Nicky knelt down next to Victor.

"Hey, buddy. Listen to me. Never, ever touch that gun. Do you understand? Also, let's not say anything to Mom about this today. You know how she worries about us. So let's see if I can trust my little man to keep a big father and son secret, okay?"

"Sure, Dad, I don't want her to be worried, and I don't want you to get in trouble, so we have a deal

As Victor ran to hold the Shop door open, he reminded his father.

"Dad, don't forget to call Uncle Tommy at the Market to see who those two jagoffs in the Buick are with."

Nicky knew Victor didn't really understand what that meant, but was impressed with his son's accuracy. He playfully grabbed Victor's arm and pretended to shove him down the stairs.

"Go put on the television before I kick you in your ass, Mr. Smarty Pants."

*The IBMW

The International Brotherhood of Minority Workers was an Illinois labor local specializing in negotiating inferior, one-sided, employer-friendly labor agreements, referred to as Sweetheart Contracts. The IBMW president was Stuart "Slim Stu" Vincent. The owners of the companies the IBMW had contracts with were interested in not be buried by set wage requirements and employer benefit contributions. Slim Stu's local also provided these companies

with the labor organization affiliation they needed when biding on jobs that subcontracted only union companies. The IBMW's contracts almost always had lower pay scales and offered no benefits to the members. That meant the companies Slim Stu represented could submit lower job bids than their competitors because they didn't have to shell out money for exorbitant hourly wages or hefty fees for health, welfare, and pension contributions like the other unions did. Slim Stu Vincent was the king of Sweetheart Deals. That's what made his inferior, sub-par union organization so popular with shady business owners.

Unlike Tank Floyd, the other officers, organizers, and BA's (Business Agents) were a mixed bag of cluster-fuck puppets. Some were down on their luck. Others were riddled with problems brought on by their own poor life choices. They couldn't get hired as janitors in more reputable labor organizations if their lives depended on it. So they blindly followed and did everything Slim Stu told them to do, regardless of how illegal, far-fetched, or stupid it was.

The BA's were at their finest when they flounced into companies to pick up kick-backs and pay-off money. They glided right by the mostly minimum-wage workers they represented and into the owner's office to get those envelopes. Then, once the cash was in their greedy little hands, they briskly exited, waving and smiling, leaving their members with nothing more than a half-assed handshake or an 'I'll get back to you on that later' answer when asked about pay-raises, health benefits, or grievance statuses. The organizers that worked for the IBMW were the worst of the unsavory worst. They were often referred to by other labor organizations as 'Vultures' because they swooped in and scooped up workers in secondary industries like material fabrication, food processing, canning, and furniture assembly like buzzards picking at animal carcasses.

If you owned a company with a large non-English speaking workforce, the language barrier was never a problem. Slim Stu always had a few bi-lingual organizers on his payroll who were ready to entice those minority workers in their vernacular to join the IBMW.

While larger labor unions focused their organizing efforts on English-speaking workers involved in trades with established, universally-recognized job classifications well within industry standards, the IBMW concentrated on the unskilled third and fourth-tier laborers. Those workers were the easiest to organize because they barely made minimum wage.

As far as the common courtesies that unions extended to each other regarding 'these trades go to this local' or 'those industries go to that local,' Slim Stu's people couldn't care less. They worked for the IBMW, a catch-all union that didn't give two shits about where you worked, who you worked for, or what it was you did to earn a living. They went after everyone. To them, a dues-paying member was a dues-paying member, regardless of whether they were landscapers, office workers, cement finishers, or stuntmen.

Slim Stu's agents and organizers were also champion bullshit artists.

They charmed hundreds and hundreds of workers into joining their local by promising them everything under the sun on a silver platter. Once organizers had those precious union authorization cards signed, they submitted them to The National Labor Board. When the IBMW was challenged by another labor organization for representation rights at a company, they implemented every dirty election trick in the book and even invented a few new ones. If the IBMW lost a certification challenge or election, Slim Stu's organizers kept in constant touch with a base core of supportive workers at that company. They instructed them to get copies of their newly-negotiated contracts so their attorneys could go through them with a fine-tooth comb picking out anti-employee and pro-employer language. (Some articles were identical to Slim Stu's contracts!) Union reps documented unresolved work issues and broken promises made during the previous election to sour employees against the current labor local. BA's made sure to accentuate any current company/union problems, making them appear ten times worse than they really were. Stu's guys came out of the woodwork and shadows, buying lunches and dinners for the prospective members they were currently balls-deep in bullshitting. The goal was to over whelm the workers with lies and disinformation. When the IBMW won an election, they negotiated 'loose' agreements per Slim Stu. That meant erroneous employer-friendly contract language, bottom-barrel guaranteed wages and bare-minimum yearly increases, and positively no health coverage options. After all, the less a company paid for their union employee's benefits, the more money they had to personally duke Slim Stu under the table. Union reps even went the extra mile and schooled the owners and foremen on targeting trouble makers within the bargaining unit, encouraging them to create paper trails. These negative write-ups usually consisted of employee warnings, notices of misconduct, and unexcused tardiness or no-call/no-show absences. That paperwork was necessary to get rid of uncooperative and union dissident employees. BA's also suggested to the company that they shove a few extra bucks into the pockets of their key 'pro-union' employees to ensure all things labor-related went smoothly.

  It was easy to see why companies that couldn't care less about their expendable employees but still needed union affiliation to be business competitive, eagerly jumped on board to take advantage of that kind of one-sided working relationship with that type of labor organization. If you added up the payoff money and what the IBMW legally collected in monthly dues fees, you had a hefty stream of cash. Not too shabby for a union that was barely recognized as legitimate!

  Everyone in that organization, even the office personnel, had bullshit and chaos down to a science. They knew the ins and outs, shortcuts, detours, evasive answers, and rhetoric necessary to be the leaders of the dark side of the labor movement. Anyone who worked for Stu Vincent that didn't go along with his outrageous strategies and corrupt business plans was usually fired on the spot amidst an array of trumped-up charges or false allegations of union disloyalty.

51

And how did the IBMW get away with those types of devious maneuvers and unscrupulous business practices without suffering National Labor Board complications or the wrath of the Mob-controlled unions they were in direct competition with? Because Stuart "Slim Stu" Vincent was Primo Montalbano's son-in-law. That's how.

CHAPTER 9
LOVE WHAT YOU DO

Tommy loved going to the Market and Nicky loved going to the Shop. The boys thought both of their locations were very business-friendly. The Shop blended in beautifully on the corner of Lake and Jefferson Streets, just outside the Loop's heart. If you hit all the traffic lights, it was a seven-minute drive from Taylor Street, a 10-minute drive from Maxwell Street, and a 12-minute drive from the Market. (Always plan to hit the stoplights.) Most importantly, the Shop was one minute from three major expressways, and you can bet your ass all those times were accurate because for shit to go down as planned, exact timing was everything.

The Shop's official business name was Worldwide Tool & Die Company. Grace teased the shit out of Nicky about the Shop. She said it was his mistress because he spent so much time there, but she knew better. Like Tommy and Teresa, she and Nicky were two peas in a pod. The girls almost always knew what was going on with their boys. Almost. Grace and Teresa were always more than willing to help, especially when a women's inconspicuous assistance was necessary to complete a transaction. Nicky knew that if he didn't have Tommy's connections, his action and profit would ultimately be less significant, so he took every advantage possible of his "protected guy" status to receive and sell everything under the sun. Besides that, he fielded various questions from an eclectic circle of people on any given day. They were not in the tool and die business.

"Hey Nick, I need a favor?"

"Nicky, can you or Tommy talk to (***Insert name here**) for me?"

"Nicky, I got a lead on a truckload of (***Insert merchandise here**) I wanna unload."

"Nick, do you think Tommy could get my (***Insert relationship status here**) a job at SouthWater, Gino's Warehouse, or Streets and Sanitation?""Nicky, I need to make some cash. Do you have anything I could get in on? An affirmative nod usually accompanied Nicky's quick-to-flash warm smile. A one-time payoff was the usual reward for many of the "asks." The bigger the favor was, the thicker the envelope. Just as good as cash was the promise of something sweet and substantial owed in return, a trade, or a piece of the score at a generous discount, like free! Of course, Tommy and Manny would get their ends because Tommy was Tommy, and Manny was Manny.

"You can't keep everybody happy, but if anyone's gonna be happy, make sure you pick the right fuckin' people," Tommy always preached to Nicky.

There was no shortage of Syndicate Associates, political figures, cops, thieves, neighborhood guys, relatives, wannabes, business owners, and even some wayward souls who found themselves at the Shop at one time or another. You never know who would be there on any given day. Half came to visit, while the other half had a mixed bag filled with their own agendas - like borrowing money, inclusion on a score, or a heist proposal. Everyone who showed up had one thing in common bragging rights. After all, they were at the Shop with Nicky, Tommy, and whoever showed up that day. If you needed something, the chances were solid that somebody with ties to the Shop knew someone they could reach out to. Everybody wanted in.

The Shop was almost half a city block long and five stories tall. The EL tracks that ran Lake Street's length were less than 200 feet away. The basement was humongous. It extended underneath Lake Street, then east to Canal Street. During the summer's intense heat, the stagnant, stale smell of machine oil and rotting lumber permeated the air deep in the back section of that basement. The larger punch presses occupied most of the space on the oil-stained cement floors. There were also five dead-end outlets and a couple of insane tunnels that twisted and turned in every direction. Nicky admitted he got lost more than a few times.

"It's like a fuckin' maze down there. Ya gotta drop bread crumbs to find your way back. I could barely find my ass with both my hands and a flashlight!"

Smaller drill presses and various material storage areas filled the other three levels, where dozens of men and women lined up daily at their machines. That's what made the Shop tick, and that's how Nicky made his legal money. He had loyal laborers and a steady workload. Combine that with the illegal activities, and at the end of the week, there was a sweet tall stack of coins. Tommy was proud of how Nicky conducted business and maneuvered.

"Hey, pal, I'm very happy for you. You got a good thing going on here," Tommy would say.

Nicky had his standard response ready.

"I couldn't have done it without you, Tee."

Tommy always smiled when Nicky said that. A long drag on his Marlboro Red usually ensued.

Ever since Victor could remember, he was intrigued by the Shop. Incredibly fascinating were the conversations, hand gestures, and facial expressions used by just about everybody who stepped foot in there. For example, at the Shop, he learned that a nod and a wink were just as good as saying yes. Some of the best scores involved Ned Devane, a sergeant in the incredibly corrupt 120th Precinct. Maxwell Street and SouthWater were a primary part of Ned's jurisdiction. Devane reached out to Nicky when miscellaneous high-end shipments were delivered to those businesses.

In the 50s and 60s, any man or woman that wanted to wear the best and most stylish rags in Chicago shopped on Maxwell Street at Smokey Joe's, Green's Clothing, Lowstein's For Men, or Blue Steve's. Those businesses sold wholesale and retail and were very competitive because of the three short-block radii of their locations. The stores all sold assorted clothing featuring multiple apparel styles, from conservative/designer suits and casual/formal dresses to outlandish Nehru jackets and wide-collared shirts, bell-bottom pants, platform shoes, knee-high boots, and fringed purses. There were bunches of other retail stores and shops on Maxwell Street, but the clothing stores occupied the prime locations and serviced the most customers. Dozens and dozens of trucks and boxcars containing fresh produce, meats, cheeses, groceries, and clothing, were delivered to multiple locations daily in the 120th, and Ned Devane knew about every delivery, route, shipper, and load destination.

No matter what authority police Captain Enrique Martinez thought he had in the 120th, it was Ned Devane who controlled and wielded the behind-the-scenes power, especially the illegal activities of that area. Martinez was appointed as a Captain because of the pressure put on the city by its sizable Mexican contingency. It was nothing more than a bone-throw to shut the neighborhood activists up. Devane had the police support and Mob-juice to get shit done when push came to shove. He controlled the patrol officers, the detectives, the office staff, the store owners, and everyone else who chose to become involved. Martinez was only a figurehead. Devane was the man in the 120th.

Ned's uncle was the late Joseph "Mic" McMahon, a longtime old-school Irish Boss. McMahon worked hand-in-hand with the biggest names in organized crime in his day. He groomed Devane to take over. Time and time again, Devane proved to the top cops and Outfit Bosses alike that he was a stand-up guy, so they started him off by giving him an important task. They put him in charge of all the patrol routes and officer assignments. It was in the best interest of all involved parties to have the right cops on the job in the right places when scores went down. Deliveries to and from came and went at all times of the day and night. And more times than not, those loads either arrived or left a bit lighter than expected. Devane's reward from the Syndicate for his help came from pieces of score profit or chunks of payoff cash. Ned did very well.

As much as Tommy loved the jewelry, electronics, and clothing heists, he really enjoyed hijacked food shipments. To his credit, he was the first one to admit that the only exception to his personal preference of food over all the other scores was when designer clothing and accessories were involved. Tommy knew people wanted to look sharp and wear the best of the best. He always said that there wasn't anyone he knew who wouldn't spend a couple of hundred bucks on brand-name apparel to make everyone else think they spent a thousand.

Tommy always got personally involved when hijacked perishable food items were in play. He suggested to his Mob associates that they target restaurants, mom-and-pop grocery stores, butchers, bakers, and delicatessen owners that were already closely connected. Tommy knew those proprietors would all eagerly jump at the opportunity to save money and stock up on fresh, discounted inventory with many days of expiration time still unused. Once again, LaCosta hit it out of the park. The Outfit's connections in the food industry took full advantage and gobbled up those scores, especially the famous local food chain "Fresh To You!" stores owned by George "The Greek" Korinthos.

The majority of Maxwell Street and SouthWater merchandise arrived at pre-designated times. Store owners discouraged companies from sending loads between 3:00 a.m. to 1:00 p.m., which was the busiest buying time, especially for Market customers. The large semis and tractor-trailers shippers used to deliver their produce caused traffic congestion nightmares for that already cramped area. Store owners needed the limited space available during that peak time for their own delivery vehicles and their customers' large panel vans and trucks. The exception to that Market delivery rule was if a particular product was out-of-stock or if it was an exceptionally scorching commodity on that day. For example, if all of the lettuce suppliers on the Market were out of stock, and there were three truckloads of lettuce sitting in the lot waiting their turn to unload, you could bet your ass those trailers moved to the front of the line and got unloaded quickly. That fortunate store owner now controlled the price of lettuce for that specific day, and sometimes, for the entire week with a profit margin that often quadrupled! Supply and demand is a beautiful thing when you're the only game in town.

    Ned Devane stopped at the Shop at least once a week, and Nicky made sure to always have a bottle of expensive Irish whiskey, fresh coffee, and bagel from Mr. Lucky's waiting for him. And, of course, he would break balls.

    "Hey Ned, how are the stake-outs at those taverns going?"

    Like a true Irishman's Irishman cop, Ned loved his whisky 24/7, and he wasn't ashamed or embarrassed to admit it.

    "Nicky, I watched those fucking bartenders pour my breakfast all morning, and not one of them made a false move! I'm going back there later just to make sure."

    Once the jokes, laughter, and teasing died down, it was time for business. First, Devane laid out all the delivery information. The paperwork included truck and boxcar bills of lading, due dates, points of origin, and cargo destinations. The truckloads were always better than railcars because they could be unloaded at other locations, away from the regular business traffic. Full loads were rarely hijacked, but almost everyone was in on it when they were. The disappearances of partial loads worked best. There was always some hissy-fit thrown, but never a full-fledged investigation over a missing pallet or two here and there.

    Sometimes, the scores were put together at the last minute, thanks to opportune timing and pieces falling precisely into place. Other times, a plan was put into motion even before the goods were loaded at the point of origin! The bottom line was that everyone was an adult. They all knew what they had to do if they wanted to stay in business. If someone was short a few boxes every so often, too bad. Once that load got to Chicago, if anyone locally complained or threatened any legal shit, they could expect some problems with the Mob, the union, crooked cops, or sometimes, all three of them. There were a few formal investigations held over missing merchandise. The truck drivers were always the primary suspects. After all, they were the guys driving the loads. They reported any losses or miscounts to the cartage company, and then the cartage company called the shipper. The shipper quickly reached out to the manufacturers, or in the case of missing food items, the growers, slaughterhouses, or fresh/frozen distribution centers. Sometimes, companies reported losses to their insurance writers for compensation. There was always somebody involved in the delivery chain that caught a screwing. Whoever it was usually kept their mouths shut. (Their silence was always rewarded.) If an account was dropped from receiving further deliveries because of thefts and hijackings, fuck them. There were 20 other companies patiently waiting in line for the business. More times than not, losses were split amongst the players. They looked at it as a write-off, the price of doing business in Chicago. As bitter as the taste was of taking an out-of-pocket hit on a load here and there, everyone took it on the chin. Sometimes, they were forced to swallow.

Nicky's strong suit was coordinating the involved players. One of his particular magical talents was the clandestine instructions he relayed in person and on the phone. If an outsider overheard one of his conversations, they would have no fucking clue about what he was saying. His choice of nicknames for those involved, the abbreviated location names he used, and the sub-par mix of Italian, English, and street-slang he spoke, was a stroke of pure confusing genius. He was a handsome man with a slight, muscular build and naturally funny demeanor. He always contained heaps of positive energy, telling you exactly what you wanted to hear, even if it was the biggest lie in the world. Nicky also excelled at turning pots of shit into bags of money. Some people thought Tommy set him up with everything he had. That was not the case. Nicky was an excellent earner on his own and street-supported by many of the right people. Nicky and Tommy had something in common. If they liked you and you had a problem, they helped. If you needed something, it was yours. If you attempted to screw them or someone they were close to over, they immediately put you on the 'pay-no-mind-to' list. That meant no inclusion on future opportunities and definitely, no favors.

Most mornings, Tommy arrived at Big Banana about 3:00 a.m. Once he checked his inventory and gas coolers, he made calls to his shippers. Then, he walked across the street to The Market Café, where he bought a large cup of black coffee and wheat toast. When his hand-picked employees arrived shortly after, they set up display racks, filled orders, and delivered bananas up and down the entire Market. Tommy was a great employer. He paid union wages and made benefit contributions. He also dropped a little extra cash in every employee's weekly pay envelope. He remembered when Old Man Lanzatorri did that and how much the money and gesture meant. Tommy's guys broke their humps for him, proudly wearing their "Big Banana Brigade" jackets, shirts, and hats every day. Tommy especially liked dealing with the old-time buyers for the smaller stores. He had a soft spot in his heart for them. Especially dear were those of Greek, Italian, and Polish descent. Tommy gave them his best deals and tried to help as much as possible when they needed reduced pricing or discounted delivery. They were all competing with Diamond Foods, Gino's Warehouse, Jewel, and other large chain stores. It really wasn't much of a contest. Those grocery giants would all but ensure the extinction of small, family-owned, and operated neighborhood establishments in the years that followed.

Nicky arrived at the Shop at about 4:30 a.m. Freshly-squeezed orange juice and a toasted English muffin waited on his desk, thanks to the early arrival of Elizabeth Kimbrough, his 68-year-old black secretary. The first thing Nicky did was start the compressors and check material supplies. Once that was done, it was onward to sharpening drill bits, aligning punch-press dies, and setting the piece counts for the day's quota. Nicky was fortunate to have a couple of Seymour's long-term business contracts 'grandfathered in' when he took over. Two of his top accounts were muffler flange stamping for General Motors, and the other was, of all things, a contract with the United States Defense Department for hand-drilling the outer casings of hand grenades and handguns used by the United States military. He also picked up some smaller jobs with local steel and bushing companies for tooling, part cutting, groove setting, and metal and aluminum stamping used for construction projects. The Shop also supplied materials for the field demonstrations die casters and trade instructors often performed.

The G and local Task Force Agents could never wrap their heads around the more savvy Mob-affiliated guys. They were great at alleging and suspecting, but that's usually as far as they got, and that's because the brighter connected boys were extra careful and covered their activities with legitimate jobs or documented incomes. If they were fortunate enough to own businesses or have friends who let them buy in as silent partners, they implemented clever ghost employee payroll techniques and used tax loopholes when laundering and funneling their illegal funds. Most financially secure mobsters could probably be successful accountants.

Nicky, Tommy, and their up before the crack of dawn buddies regularly met for breakfast at Sam Hatchell's Restaurant on Jackson Boulevard. The patrons always talked so loudly that overhearing an outrageous gossipy story being told was easy. So many types of people from all walks of Chicago life began their day there, literally rubbing elbows due to the tight seating. They drank rich, bold coffee and inhaled double-yolk eggs any style with side-orders of thick, flavorful maple bacon, hash browns, and tasty silver-dollar-sized buttermilk pancakes. People dined there for the food, but a close second was the eavesdropping. The guys were constantly entertained by the shit that would run out of people's mouths like diarrhea as they stuffed their faces, talked loudly, and pretended to be necessary.

One early morning, Tommy was seated along the back wall next to a couple of wealthy Greek loan officers from First Community Bank. He picked out bits and pieces of their conversation. What he overheard kept him smiling through the entire breakfast.

It was terrible news for Irving "Irv the Jew" Lowstein.

CHAPTER 10
THE "IRV THE JEW" SCORE

Nicky's Shop played a crucial role in the Irv the Jew score. Tommy, Nicky, Ned Devane, and Ingalleretta's old friend from Maxwell Street, Buddy Green, devised a unique and well-coordinated plan. The total time for the win/win deal to come to fruition? A mere eight weeks.

Irving Lowstein's financial troubles were due to whimsical business decisions, a champagne taste/beer pocketbook lifestyle, drug abuse, gambling losses, and bad stock investments. His once lucrative clothing business was barely making payroll and he was delinquent on all utilities, taxes, and short-term bank balloon loans

Buddy Green was Irv's main competitor on Maxwell Street. There was rarely any fucking around with Buddy or Irv's trucks and clothing shipments. If they were tampered with, it was usually an isolated incident conducted by small-time gangs that pinched a few hangers of shirts and pants. It was never anything substantial. Buddy knew how to take care of the people who took care of him. Whether gifts, clothes, or cash, he always showed appreciation, especially to his go-to guy, Ingalleretta. Irv had a different Mob arrangement. That agreement was running its course.

Tommy told Manny about the bankers' conversation regarding Irv's financial predicament. He immediately told Tommy to reach out for Buddy Green.

"Go talk to Buddy, in person, no phone call. See if he knows anything about it. The fuckin' Jews always know each other's business."

Tommy sprung a significant hard-on when Buddy confirmed the news. He couldn't wait to tell Manny.

"We got him by the balls now. Let's jump on this prick before he busts out. You gave him every pass possible, Manny. This fucking guy is the most ungrateful piece of shit on the planet."

For a few years, Ingalleretta let Irv slide on paying monthly street tax. It wasn't a popular decision, but it was Manny's to make. The only thing asked in return was silence from Irv about the accommodation. So, of course, Irv blabbed, especially to a couple of new collection guys who weren't privy to his arrangement. Irv arrogantly and boldly boasted to the rookie Outfit bagmen.

"Go and check it out. I don't have to pay you grease-balls a fucking thing,"

That sweet deal with Ingalleretta was arranged by Irv's cousin, Hymie Kline. Kline was the Mob's top criminal attorney for years. He told Manny and Joey Balducci that Irv was his cousin. Both bosses doubted that and figured Hymie playing the 'cousin card' as most Italians do when they introduce a close, cherished family friend as a cousin when in reality, they're not. Whatever the tie was, Irv got a pass, thanks to Hymie. The way the Mob looked at it, Hymie was worth his weight in gold for his legal services. The understanding between the Outfit and Kline was that they would let Irv slide - as a favor to him. Tommy often asked

Ingalleretta if Irv had sent anything to show gratitude, especially around the holidays.

"Manny, did this prick drop off anything for you?"

Manny knew his close guys were pissed about that undeserving twat catching a pass and not paying street tax.

"Let it go, Tommy. Vinnie, Sally Boy, Frankie, Lenny, you pains in the ass are always asking me the same fucking thing. Are you all ganging up on me?" Ingalleretta would laugh.

Then, he'd end the conversation with two words.

"Fuck Irv."

As Irving's problems worsened, he chose alcohol to be his special friend, regularly throwing down more than a few Dom Perignon bottles at his north shore country club. Then, he would boast to all who would listen about his ties and connections to the Outfit. When word of his outlandish, braggadocious behavior got back to Hymie, Irv got a call. Hymie reminded him repeatedly to be discreet about anything having to do with his Syndicate connections. But, Irv couldn't help showing off for his big-money friends. It was just about all he had left to brag about after years of squandering his cash. He couldn't squeeze another dime out of any bank and mortgaged his lavish Glencoe home up to the top with absolutely no wiggle room left. He was desperate and had no solution for his financial predicament. The only move was to ask Hymie for help. Hymie knew it was only a matter of time for that call to come his way. When it did, he reached out to Ingalleretta. Joey and Primo agreed with Manny when he laid everything out. They decided the time was now. So on Tuesday night, Manny called Hymie and asked him to meet at Gino and Georgie's Steak House late afternoon on Wednesday. It was the day before Thanksgiving.

When they sat together at the table, Hymie knew Ingalleretta meant business just by observing his body posture and initial hand gestures. Kline was a skilled attorney who enjoyed a long, lucrative career by successfully evaluating the 'tells' of judges, clients, witnesses, and formidable legal opposition in and out of the courtroom. He knew Ingalleretta was about to quote the gospel according to the Outfit.

"Your fucking cousin Irv, or whatever he is to you, has been an embarrassment from the very start," Ingalleretta began.

Hymie opened his mouth to speak, but Manny stopped him dead in his tracks. Kline didn't utter another syllable.

"Never once did Irv show appreciation. Not a gift basket, a nice suit, or even a few bucks in a thank you card. I've never even seen a pair of fancy silk socks. You know, Hymie, the ones he sells for $10 a pair at that shit-hole place of his, the one I'm giving serious consideration into blowing the fuck up."

That comment got Hymie's attention, as did the steak knife being pointed at him. It bounced with every word Manny spoke. Gianfranco, the waiter, attempted to bring some freshly made Italian bread to the table. He took one look at Ingalleretta, did an about-face, and headed back to the kitchen. Manny was funny about having Gianfranco waiting on him because he was the only server that spoke with the with the almost non-existent Bari dialect. There weren't many people that used that form of European region-specific communication anymore.

Ingalleretta's sunken, sleepy, brown eyes glared at Hymie while the knife continued to bob as he spoke. Hymie thought Manny was handling the blade, not so much like a utensil, but more like an inmate wielding a prison shiv.

"Our people backed off of Irv because I told them to. The coppers, the hijackers, the street guys, everyone involved left him alone. We did this because you asked us for a favor."

The following words couldn't have sliced through Hymie any deeper if the Old Man carved them into his chest with the steak knife.

"Well, Hymie, your favor is up. And so is Irv's joint. Now, you can go," Ingalleretta ruled.

Hymie stood, shook Manny's hand, and wished him an early Happy Thanksgiving. When Manny didn't cordially reciprocate with turkey day wishes, Hymie knew that was it. There would be no further discussions to help his fuck-up of a pretend cousin, Irv. Kline played the game long enough to know there was no way around an Ingalleretta final ruling.

Right after Thanksgiving, Nicky ran into Fat Frankie at Snafuro's Bakery. Frankie pulled him on the side and told him that Irv had bad paper all over town. It included IOUs to bookies (not Frankie), drug dealers, and loan sharks. And that was just his street debt. When you added the bills his business owed, Irv was in the shitter for a hair over $200,000!

Early Monday, Tommy got a call at Big Banana from Lenny to set a meeting at the Shop for Tuesday afternoon. Tommy was sure it was about Irv.

"Len, I'll have Nicky order some dogs from Shingle Inn and a few combos from Ba-Ba's," Tommy promised.

Lenny arrived at the Shop at about 2:15. Nicky greeted him with open arms and a desk full of food.

"What's the matter, Len?"
"Nothing's the matter, why?"
Nicky feigned concern.
"You look sad, Lenny."
"I'm not sad. I'm just tired."
Nicky sarcastically feigned relief.
"Whew! That's good to hear, Len. Remember, a guy with a submarine-sized cock like yours should never be sad!"

Lenny was hysterical.
"Nicky, you're the fucking best, pal."

As they exchanged small talk about their families, Tommy arrived through the dock area back door, walking in with James and Robert. They were carrying in two huge Peter Rubis.

"I'll have the guys throw the 'Petes' in your car. The bigger one's yours, the other one is Manny's. Tell him I got the anise for him," Tommy explained.

Lenny handed the keys to Tommy. He took them and shoved them into James's pocket, along with two $20 bills.

"Thanks, guys. I appreciate it. James, one of those $20s is for Robert. Don't fuck him out of it!" Tommy sarcastically advised.

"Hey, Tee, right before you came in, I was in the middle of congratulating Lenny," Nicky interrupted.

Tommy looked surprised, and Lenny? He knew Nicky was up to something.

"No shit, for what?" Tommy asked.

"He was finally able to register his cock with the state as a lethal weapon!"

"It's about fucking time!" Tommy laughed.

Lenny was beside himself.

"Nicky, you are absolutely ridiculous!"

"Tee, I got you two dogs loaded, one tamale, and a dipped combo with sweet and hot," Nicky smiled and winked

Tommy's eyes lit up as he tore open the grease-laden bags. For a few brief minutes, the front Shop office smelled like a tiny slice of heaven. The Chicago-style dog is a work of art. A freshly steamed poppy seed bun housed an all-beef Vienna brand wiener. It overflowed with evenly spread white onions, tomatoes, yellow mustard, bright green relish, and sport peppers. The added specialty was the salted, greasy french fries.

As the boys enjoyed their feast, Lenny talked. He always spoke softly and was hard to hear, especially when the basement punch presses were running. This time, Tommy and Nicky already knew most of what he had to say, so they didn't interrupt, playing it beautifully, acting as if they were hearing it for the very first time.

"The bottom line is that Manny wants the sides retired on all of Irv's debts. You guys are the starting line-up No floating loan papers, no sideline markers, no fumbled passes. Tomorrow, I'll have the final score of what's owed. Tommy, Manny wants you to touch base with Buddy Greene and let him know we'll need his help to retire the sides on this one. Tell him Manny would appreciate the teamwork. Nicky, Mr. E. also wants to use the Shop as home plate," explained Lenny.

The Cocksmith sure loved his sports, often using basic athletic terminology when discussing street business.

The select group picked for this score met at the Shop in the few weeks that followed. They cautiously chose pre-designated times during the day and even got together twice in the middle of the night. The boys were cautious. The Outfit gave Irv $50,000 of their cash to hand-pay a couple of the shippers he was in the red with. This move was nothing more than a thinly-veiled attempt to prove he was liquid with funds. It was also the exact amount needed to free up his purchase restrictions.

Hymie had no choice in also playing a part. He was the go-between who instructed Irv. The first thing Kline did was make sure Irv ordered three times more than he usually did. He also told his fake cousin to explicitly focus on the newest and most expensive men's designer suits and sport coats. Hymie also told Irv to go on record with his suppliers that he was promoting a huge Hanukah/Christmas with television and newspaper advertising.

Irv called Hymie more than a few times to complain.

"Hymie, I'm not some schmuck. This whole thing stinks of a Wop set-up. I'm not taking a fall for those crooks. Let them try and kill me, then those fucking gangsters won't get a dime!" Irv asserted.

Hymie found it necessary to explain the facts of life.

"Irving, my Bubala, (Jewish term of endearment) killing? Killing is what they do! And who knows, maybe they kill me, too. After all, I was the one who vouched for you. And please, don't sit there and tell me that you don't understand what vouching for someone means to them. Look, you received lots of favors. I know, I was the one asking for them. But, instead of using that to your advantage, what genius moves did you make? You shit all over everything! Irving, you've been very selfish and out-of-control. You're standing alone in a corner that you've backed yourself into."

Next on Kline's plate was ensuring Irv was current on his insurance policy and the City of Chicago certificate from the most recent fire inspection. Next, he confirmed Irv the heavy order of high-line suits, sport coats, and leather jackets.

Nicky pulled James, Willie, and Robert into his office the weekend before the caper. He handed them each an envelope with $800 cash. Nicky instructed them to take $100 out and put it in their pockets, which they did. He explained that the remaining $700 was for clothing purchases at Maxwell Street that weekend.

"I want you guys to buy the cheapest men's clothes you can find. I don't give a shit about the sizes, Used, resale, bootleg knock-offs, buy them."

The guys looked at each other. Then, before they could ask questions, Nicky continued.

"Bring everything you buy back here and stack it up to the fucking ceiling inside the spare office."

"If that's what you want, Mr. Nick, we'll do it," James confirmed.

"Good. Also, go separately. I don't want you guys together. Not a word to anyone. No wives, no kids, no buddies, not a fuckin' word," Nicky finished.

At about the same time Nicky was instructing his workers, Tommy met with Silvio to go over which driver and truck they would use. Micky said he would personally drive his 12-wheel rig. Tommy was more than pleased to hear that, knowing Silvio's first rodeo was many moons ago.

When Nicky arrived at the Shop early Monday, he could barely open the door to the back office due to the mountain of clothing stacked to the top of the 10-foot office peak.

"Holy fucking shit!" he whispered.

James diligently worked at his drill press when Nicky tapped him on the shoulder.

"Everything went okay, right, James?"

James smiled. He had about eight remaining teeth.

"We made three trips each, Mr. Nick, got it all done before noon."

Nicky made a quick call to Tommy, informing him that everything on his end was going swimmingly

"Sounds good, Nick. Hopefully, that fuck placed his order.

Ned Devane stopped by the Shop a couple of hours later and confirmed Irv's large order had been placed. Then, after a couple of shots of whiskey and a short rib sandwich from Mr. Lucky's, Devane laid his end out for Nicky.

"One of my guys stopped by Irv's. His order's coming out of New York and should arrive on Wednesday morning, between 5-6 a.m. The bill of lading is a little bit north of $500K."

Nicky's eyes lit up like sparklers.

"Tommy talked to Silvio. His truck will be parked here at about midnight. Are your guys squared away?"

Ned threw down his final shot of whiskey.
"Yes. GiGi from East Coast Delivery is driving."

When East Coast Delivery was involved, things always went smoothly. GiGi was the brother-in-law of Jasper Anunzio, the owner. Anunzio was also one of the largest Mob-connected cartage owners in the New York area. His delivery trucks were used by numerous crime families. Jasper's company and fleet of trucks played a part in hundreds of illegal shipments to and from the five boroughs for over 20 years.

"GiGi's going to call me when he fills up his rig at the Skyway. Then, I'll reach for Timmy O' Toole, one of my patrol guys. Detective Perry Cantone from Grand Avenue will be undercover tomorrow. I've got him driving the unmarked Chevy Impala. O'Toole will lead GiGi through the back, and Cantone will stay in the front. They'll have both ends of the alley blocked so you can do your thing," confirmed Devane.

"It should take about an hour to unload and reload. Your guys okay to be there that long?" inquired Nicky.

"They'll be there for as long as you need them," Devane reassured.

With all the pieces in place, the time had come. Escorted by Cantone and O'Toole, GiGi's truck pulled in the back alley of the Shop at 4:00 a.m. Silvio's truck was parked where it was supposed to be, inside the loading area, facing the narrower alley.

GiGi wheeled 15 full racks of the pricy suits and other clothing down the ramp and into the Shop's basement. Nicky set up a staging platform to switch the suits with the Maxwell Street rags. He tossed that entire load himself in less than 70 minutes! Two ensembles from each clothing rack, one in the front and one in the rear, were left alone so Irv could unzip the covers in front of people, giving the impression every rack was stuffed with imported finery. Once his truck was refilled, GiGi made his way to Irv's. Nicky loaded the mostly Italian suits into Silvio's rig, minus, of course, about a dozen for him and the boys. Silvio's next move was to drive his loaded truck down the street to an old Washington Boulevard warehouse which just happened to be owned by Buddy Greene's recently deceased brother. When Micky got back to the Shop to pick up his truck, he didn't even step foot inside. He was anxious to get to his next stop, Washington Boulevard, where it was Buddy Greene's time to shine.

Buddy made a prior arrangement with a dozen retail clothing shops, mostly owned by his Jewish cohorts. They agreed to take those suits off his hands and include them in their inventory at a slightly-reduced, non-negotiable cash-only price. However, once they saw the high quality of the expensive apparel, some of the store owners got into a bidding war, even paying up to full retail for a few of the choicest colors and cuts!

Tommy drove to Irv's store and waited for the show to begin. He sat inconspicuously in his car, sipping coffee while listening to Wally Phillips on WGN radio. Ten minutes later, GiGi backed into the loading area which was directly in front of Irv's store. Tommy saw Irv himself wheel the racks off one by one while a crowd stood and watched. For the only time in his life, Irv needed to do what he was instructed NOT to do, draw attention to himself.

First, he removed each rack's front and rear suits as planned. Then, he loudly and proudly opened the plastic suit covers displaying the new merchandise to the customers and employees that gathered in front of him. Next, he unveiled each piece of clothing like it was an Israeli artifact from The Holy Land. When done, the racks were quickly zipped up and rolled inside, all by Irv. Tommy was more than impressed.

"This is what it had to come to for this cocksucker to finally listen," he thought.

When Tommy pulled away from Maxwell Street to head back to Big Banana, he saw Silvio. He nodded to Micky through the driver's side window as their vehicles passed each other. Micky returned the nod. That was their sign to each other that everything was going as planned.

Next up to bat was Sammy "The Torch" Rizzo, a retired fireman with over 30-years on the job. His last ten years as a lead investigator with the Fire Department's Arson Division. Rizzo was respected and extremely well-versed with foul play signs when conducting arson examinations. When the Outfit needed something set ablaze, that's who they called.

Sammy's services were often used by members of the Greek underworld, especially the ones who owned restaurants, snack joints, and grocery stores as their covers. Some were degenerate gamblers that pissed away their profits. Others made abysmal business decisions. Whatever the case was, when the time came that they needed money, they'd call Sammy to get their establishments torched. Within two months, they collected insurance money. Sometimes the Greeks opened up somewhere else under a new company name. Other times they just rebuilt what they had. Either way, they started over with a clean financial slate.

Sammy arrived at Irv's a little after midnight. He was given a key for the rear-loading dockside door earlier in the day by one of Ned's Maxwell Street patrolmen. Since Sammy already knew the store's layout, he went directly to the furnace room, conveniently located next to the storage area, where Irv placed the bogus racks. It took him less than half an hour to chip the main cables with the rusted electrical clipper he carried in his arsenal of tools. The Torch planned to make the fire's point of origin appear as rodent damage. He had seen actual cases of it during his career and knew exactly how to duplicate it. Moreover, he and his peers in the Arson Squad agreed that rat-gnawing on wires was a more common than not cause for fires to ignite in older buildings. Irv made sure he unlocked the wire-caged box that surrounded the building thermostat before leaving work for the evening. Also, he wheeled a few pallets of old, dry cardboard boxes and purposely stacked them around the furnace.

As Sammy finished wiring chipping, he heard noise coming from outside. Devane coordinated two tow trucks to drop off a couple of unclaimed vehicles from the city impound just as planned. The stripped cars had to be delivered by a flatbed because they were also without axles. The tow drivers, strategically placed the stranded bundles of metal right in front of the two closest fire hydrants adjacent to Irv's store.

The temperature outside was rapidly dropping into the single digits. Sammy left around 2:00 a.m. Once he arrived home, he turned on his ham radio to the police/fire department frequencies. He made a pot of coffee and waited. Two short hours later and right on schedule, the first of many calls came over about a three-alarm fire at Halsted and Marketplace. Sammy could hear the faint sound of sirens from his Polk Street balcony. The first units that arrived at Irv's encountered a full-blown blaze in process. The wiring Rizzo chipped led to the sparking thermostat that started it all. The fire commander had to call for two industrial-sized ladder trucks. He needed them to move the junk heaps that blocked the hydrants. By the time that was coordinated and done, a partial portion of Irv's roof had already collapsed. And to make matters worse, or better, depending on how you looked at it, only one of the two fire hydrants worked due to the frigid cold. After an hour, fire officials declared 'Containment Only' status. That meant they would let it naturally burn out, prioritizing the surrounding structures only. So, in Jewish layman's terms, Irv's joint was officially a toasted bagel, minus the schmear and lox.

When Irv arrived on the scene at 6:00 a.m., he granted news crew interviews, making himself totally accessible to the media. He appeared genuinely distraught and noticeably devastated when talking about his store and the years he spent selling clothes on Maxwell Street. His picture was even on the front page of the Chicago Sun-Times that evening. If readers looked closely, they could see his tears. Nicky tacked a copy of the newspaper picture of Irv's big puss on his office wall and drew a bullseye. He borrowed a set of old darts from Victor and challenged everyone who came to the Shop.

"Land a dart inside the Jew's big fuckin' mouth, and win a C-Note!"

Irv's picture looked like Yucca Flat after the blast from all the attempts. It took less than three days of dart-throwing to reduce the photo to smithereens.

The Fire and Arson Squad turned in their official findings one week later. Investigators concluded that the cause was electrical wiring possibly damaged by a major rodent infestation. Then, less than 60-days after that, Irv received a colossal insurance check. He begrudgingly turned it over to Hymie, who dispersed it accordingly. Everyone, except for Irv, was more than pleased. When Manny received his cut, it was Tommy who delivered it. The envelope was extremely thick.

"Manny, I hope this is worth all the aggravation you had to put up with for so long."

Five minutes later, after stacking his cash, he answered Tommy.

"Fuck Irv."

Even though all his debts were paid in full, Irv was miserable. Even worse, he needed to search for a job. Buddy Greene hired him as a salesman at his place. Why not? Irv had a decent following of customers. He just didn't have a store. At first, Irv did well at Buddy's. He was even less obnoxious and belligerent. However, his bad habits caught up with him. Irv used third parties to mask his gambling, drug, and alcohol purchases. But, his debts piled high again, surpassing the small portion of insurance proceeds he was allowed to keep. In less than a year, broke, bitter, and beaten, a flea-bag motel maid found him dangling in the closet at the end of a rope.

Nicky and Tommy were at the Shop when Devane walked in for his morning whiskey. Ned shared the breaking news of Irv's suicide, along with a dozen close-up color police photos of the recently deceased. He was wearing an expensive, full-length, hand-woven royal blue lounging robe made from 100 % genuine Mulberry silk. Nicky looked visibly upset. He examined the pictures for a good five minutes, shaking his head in disbelief and making a comment with every flip of the ghastly close-up death photos.

"What a shame this is. It's a terrible tragedy. What, in God's name, is the world coming to?"

Tommy and Ned were dumbfounded. The very last thing either of them thought they'd hear were sympathetic words about Irv. But, whenever Nicky was involved, all you needed to do was wait for his impeccably delivered punch line.

"It's a sin to see a beautiful robe like that just hanging in the closet!"

CHAPTER 11
THE TIMES, THEY ARE A-CHANGIN'

In the late 1960s, business at Big Banana and the Shop were booming, legally and otherwise. But, as great as that was, undeniable change was in the air. Sadly, it was the neighborhood. On the whole, it was slipping and wasn't like it once was. Those that settled years earlier were much older. Their sons, daughters, and adult grandchildren felt living in the suburbs had more to offer. After all, they were now the decision-makers. Some took it a step further and moved to states with warmer climates. They wanted to live their lives according to their ideals, not those held by their aging parents or grandparents. It was a new dawn for the 'today' generation, and the neighborhood's part was becoming more of a walk-on role than the leading star headliner it had been in the past. Some of the beautifully maintained six-flats in Little Italy were also aging, becoming weathered, and desperately in need of work. A handful of the building landlords went all-out and did complete rehabs. Other owners performed only cosmetic updates. A few did nothing, choosing to sell them in 'as-is' condition, leaving the headaches and repair costs up to the new owner. Finally, the oldest of the buildings were structurally unsafe. They were condemned, sitting in that uninhabitable vacant condition until they were slammed to the ground by the city's Urban Renewal wrecking ball.

Near West Side residents who already moved, or were planning on moving, said they didn't feel as safe and secure as they once did. Others that pulled up stakes cited they wanted their own home, a backyard, and a fresh start for themselves and their families. There was a commonality with their relocation reasons - the overcrowded housing projects. Those army barracks-style units were either in the middle or just on the outskirts of Little Italy. The ethnicity of the majority of tenants that lived there was African-American. For them, the mid-1960s was a period of racial awakening. They organized and banded together in a nationwide 'Black Power' revolution demanding equality and fundamental human rights. More times than not, their gatherings, protests, and community activism programs were not met with open arms by the white masses. The tension on both sides of the spectrum usually escalated, resulting in violence. The police, along with older white politically motivated racists, weren't very receptive to the causes of The Black Panthers, The Gangster Disciples, and The Black P. Stone Nation (Black Rangers). When those groups initially formed, they were full-fledged, legitimate organizations dedicated to political and social reform. But, by the time 1968 rolled around, these and other black groups were slowly evolving into gangs. Their focus changed to criminal activity for profit, especially after the Martin Luther King and Bobby Kennedy assassinations. No one was oblivious to the violent movement and rebellion. It wasn't just sweeping through the Little Italy neighborhood but throughout the United States and other countries. These historic occurrences played out on television screens, bringing them home in a way never seen before.

Even through the diversification, some celebrated neighborhood events were still held, like the 16-inch rivalry softball game. The prior year's competition was played at Sheridan Park. The team east of Racine Avenue won 13-10. That after-game meal was compliments of neighborhood favorite Fontanelli Brothers Italian Deli, owned by Donato and Rocco Fontanelli. The brothers went way overboard and provided almost 200 Italian lunch-meat and meatball sandwiches, pop, and snacks. Donato was incredibly happy with the outcome of last year's game. He won a $2,500 bet he had with Fat Frankie. The two agreed to bump up this year's wager to $3,000. To Frankie, the Saturday, July 6th, 1968 match held on the Fillmore Street lot was a good omen. He figured the edge was his since the home team won for the last five years in a row. Plus, Japeto's Restaurant was sponsoring. But, playing at home AND sponsoring? That inspired Frankie to develop a nickname for this year's bet with Donato. He called it a "Fat Frankie Lock." Frankie didn't waste any time letting Donato hear about it either.

"This game is a bonafide Fat Frankie Lock, you fucking Culo Grasso!" (Fat Ass)

Frankie having the audacity to call anyone a fat ass, went miles beyond the pot calling the kettle black.

"We'll see, Frank, we'll see. Just do me one favor? Make sure to use the good sausage from Mitzie's Butcher and not your ground-up rat meat with red pepper and fennel seed," Donato fired back. "I'd rather take my chances and eat something Babe and Shay cooked!"

Babe and Shay were elderly, semi-reclusive, widowed sisters from the neighborhood. They had the reputation of being the two worst cooks on the planet. The ingredients they used were expired, and the meat, fruit, and vegetables in their recipes, on the verge of spoilage. Their prepared dishes were almost considered poisonous. The saddest part about it all was they could've afforded the most expensive meal components available. They were wealthier than the Catholic Church! Nevertheless, when they cooked for you, it was like they hated you. At one of their New Year's Eve parties, the sisters made their mark in Little Italy culinary history. Minutes after choking down Babe and Shay's holiday meal, their family and friends contracted diarrhea so viciously and so quickly that they all wound up on the front lawn with their pants pulled down, shitting uncontrollably during the middle of a brutal snowstorm! Ever since Nicky heard that story, whether it was at DaBone or Benidetto family functions, he would stand up before everyone started eating. He'd raise his glass and say something obnoxious about Babe and Shay cooking the meal they were about to eat. Both families knew the story and roared with laughter every time Nicky made his pre-meal stand-up toast. The exactness of his routines varied, but the bottom line remained the same. His most recent rendition was at Tommy and Teresa's July 4th party.

"I'd like to take this opportunity to thank Babe and Shay for cooking today. Also, I'd like to thank my sister Teresa for her patriotism. The American flag toilet paper design on the front lawn is beautiful, and I'm sure we'll all put it to good use. Everyone enjoy your meal!"

Donato and Frankie had broken each other's balls since Christ shined sandals in Nazareth. They played against each other in the neighborhood softball game was in its infant stages. Both men were a lot younger and about 150 to 200 pounds lighter…EACH! Although the competition was always friendly, it was a hard-fought battle for bragging rights about which side had the better athletes AND the better food. The shit-talking before, during, and after was the funniest, most brutal imaginable. This year, quite a few older teenage guys were on the roster. They were waiting for deployment overseas, and this game was their last hurrah before they shipped out. In fact, "The Last Hurrah" was the nickname given to this year's competition.

Frankie wheeled out the sizeable 10-foot grill Nicky welded together for him at about 9:00 a.m. At the same time, Japeto Restaurant waiters and waitresses set up a dozen chairs and a couple of picnic tables for the neighborhood elders. The lunch menu consisted of cheeseburgers, hotdogs, sausage and pepper sandwiches, snacks, and two huge tubs filled with ice, pop, and beer. By 10:30 a.m., the lot and sidewalk were already filling up with players and spectators. As usual, Pa and Uncle Jimmy sat on the back porch sipping morning wine while Zeus barked at all the unfamiliar faces that walked by. Tommy pulled his car up next to Japeto's and beeped the horn a couple of times. Frankie waddled over and leaned into the open window on the passenger's side.

"What's up, Tominucci! How's the banana king doin'?"

Tommy tossed Frankie the car keys.

"I picked up three boxes of Michigan Melrose Peppers. They're in the trunk."

"Beautiful, Tee, thanks! I'll have my mom start frying them up. What do I owe you?"

"Nothing, just make sure the red flake giardiniera is spicy and oily."

Frankie just finished preparing an extra hot batch.

"Flames are gonna be shootin' outta Big Banana's ass later," he promised.

Tommy wheeled his Cadillac across the street and parked in front of the DaBone's house. Mari was sitting on the front porch with Teresa, who arrived earlier. Tommy got out, walked over, and kissed them both.

"Where's Pa?" Tommy asked.

"He's in the back with Uncle Jimmy. They're hitting the wine already," Teresa laughed. "Grace said Nicky just called. He's running late. One of the machines at the Shop broke down."

"Okay. I'll be on the back porch with Pa and Uncle Jimmy. I'll see if I can calm Zeus down. It sounds like he's going nuts back there."

Grace stuck her head out of the upstairs window.

"Hi, Tommy, how are you?"

"Hey, how's Grand Avenue Grace doin'?"

Grace almost tumbled out the window laughing.

"Tommy, you haven't called me that, in like, forever!"

"How long did Nicky say it'll be before he gets here?"

Grace thought for a second.

"He said maybe an hour, maybe longer. He was pretty pissed about missing the first few innings."

Tommy nodded and walked down the gangway stairs to the backyard. Zeus was jumping on the gate, excited to greet him.

"There's my good boy!" Tommy said, petting the beautiful Shepherd.

"Hey, I thought I was your good boy," Victor interrupted, walking down the back stairs two at a time.

Tommy corrected himself.

"You are my good boy, Vic, especially if you get a couple of hits out there today. Are you ready for the big game?"

"Oh, I'm more than ready. We're gonna beat the living shit out of those fucking chooches from the other side."

Uncle Jimmy burst out laughing, Tommy just shook his head, and Pa looked at Uncle Jimmy for a second before he chimed in.

"That kid? He's a-lost-a-cause."

"Maybe he shouldn't have listened to us while we were playing cards, Giuseppe," Uncle Jimmy laughed.

"He gotta worse-a-mouth on him than Nicky," Pa replied. "Tale padre, tale figlio." (Like father, like son.)

Victor just celebrated his 12th birthday a month earlier. Although his swearing wasn't 100% under control, it was much better than it had been. He was learning when it was acceptable and when it wasn't. Nevertheless, he still belted out a few beauties when the opportunity presented itself.

It was a perfect day for softball. The temperature was 80 degrees with a slight breeze. It was tied at two apiece in the bottom of the second inning. Victor took a couple of practice cuts while he was on deck. Tommy turned to Pa and Uncle Jimmy to let them know Victor was next to bat.

"Victor e il prossimo a battere." (Victor is batting next.)

"Good. I hope he breaks Vincenza's window," Pa joked.

Tommy laughed, remembering the Fat Frankie/Vincenza story from many years earlier. As Victor walked up to the plate, he turned and looked at the back porch. His family was standing by the railing. Victor swung at the first pitch and hit a line drive almost to the alley. He was halfway to first base before anyone even knew it was foul.

"Jesus Christ is that kidda fast," Joe remarked.

"He's probably the fastest guy out there, Pa. Even the older boys can't touch him," Tommy confirmed.

Victor jogged back to home plate and took a couple of more practice swings. He batted lefty, just like Nicky taught him. He slightly adjusted his stance, and on the next pitch, he drilled a rocket down the first base line. Carmie Gamello got a hand on it, knocking the ball down in fair territory. Victor was already rounding first before Carmie even picked it up. Victor knew Carmie had a weak arm. Also, the second baseman, Jimmy Parino, had just dropped a looped infield fly ball last inning. Victor decided to take a chance, so he hit full-stride, racing his way to second base. Parino was in the perfect position to put the tag on him. As Victor prepared to slide into second, he heard his teammates yelling.

"SLIDE! SLIDE! SLIDE!

Victor glided safely into second base with a double, just ahead of Parino's tag.

"When did you get so fucking fast, asshole? Parino asked.

"I had a lot of practice running away from your mother," Victor answered.

Seventeen-year-old Parino just got schooled by a kid that wasn't even a teenager yet.

"That's real funny, Victor. You may be fast, but you're still a little jagoff."

Victor motioned for a time out as he stood and brushed the dirt and dust off his pants. He glanced at the back porch and saw his Uncle Tommy clapping. Grandpa Joe and Uncle Jimmy were smiling and cha-chinging their wine glasses. Victor waved at them.

The next 15 minutes stretched out for an eternity. It started when Luke Capezio, the heir apparent to shatter Micky Silvio's long-standing boxing record, swiftly flew by Victor at second base.

"Get to the alley, get to the alley. MOVE, MOVE, MOVE!" Capezio shouted as the other outfielders ran in.

Victor turned and saw why everyone was running. Blacks of all ages, male and female, were filling the empty lot across the street from the makeshift baseball field. They flooded in from both sides adjacent to Grenshaw Street, carrying clubs, sticks, bricks, and chains. Those sitting comfortably scrambled quickly, tipping over their lawn chairs to make their way to Fillmore/Taylor alley.

"VIC! VICTOR! GET OVER HERE!" Tommy shouted, waving his arms.

Victor was the last one out of the lot. He ran to the back fence, hopped it, and landed squarely on both feet. Zeus was out of control, ferociously barking and jumping on the railing.

Teresa, Grace, and Mari piled onto the back porch.

Grace had a good view from the upstairs window before joining them and let Tommy know what she saw.

"Tommy, there's gotta be at least a hundred blacks. It looks like they're all coming down Loomis from Roosevelt Road."

Pa was pissed. He got up and began walking into the house.

"Goddamn niggers, I'm gonna getta my shotgun."

"No, Joe, please," Mari begged him.

"No, Pa, don't," Tommy said, putting his hand on Joe's shoulder.

"Should I call my dad?" Victor asked.

After some quick thinking, Tommy came up with an impromptu game plan, starting with Teresa.

"Tree, call Silvio and tell him to grab a bunch of guys and get over here, like right now! Victor, I need you to go get Zeus's police dog leash, the thick one from Ned Devane."

The baseball lot was empty. Everyone playing and watching were now lined up three-deep in the alley from Chinetti's back gangway all the way to Little Louie Villicello's Troop and Taylor Street corner house. Fat Frankie sprinted as if he was running the anchor leg of a 90-foot obese relay race. Watching him move that swiftly to the DaBone's porch railing was, in a way, similar to the "Wild Kingdom" television show, specifically the episode where host Marlin Perkins filmed a pregnant water buffalo running from a pack of hungry lions. Frankie was drenched in sweat.

"Where in the fuck are you going, Tommy?' he nervously asked, huffing and puffing.

"I'm going across the street before someone does something that gets people hurt," Tommy answered.

"Tommy, please stay here," Teresa begged.

"It'll be alright, Tree. And if it's not, well, then it's not."

Mari started crying. Teresa attempted to console her.

"Ma, you heard Tommy. He said everything will be fine."

"E se non lo fosse?" (And what if it isn't) Mari asked.

"Ecco quandro prendo il mio cazzo di fucile!" (That's when I get my fucking shotgun!) Pa added.

"PA, STOP WITH THE SHOTGUN! You're upsetting Ma!" Teresa yelled.

Tommy needed to calm them.

"All right, let's all take it easy. Frankie, go to the club and get everyone. Tell them to line up in the alley and stay put. Have the little kids and women go inside somewhere. Silvio's on his way with some Market guys."

"I'm calling my dad, Uncle Tommy," Victor shouted from the top of the back stairs.

Tommy looked at Victor but didn't say anything. Frankie took a couple of deep breaths, made his way to the alley, and headed to the Sons of Taylor Street Social Club on the corner of Taylor and Loomis. As he walked down the gangway with Zeus, Tommy turned to Pa.

"Leave the shotgun in the house, Pa. Please."

Teresa wanted to make sure her father heard that.

"Pa, did you hear what Tommy said? LEAVE THE SHOTGUN ALONE!"

Joe was irritated but reluctantly agreed.

"Goddamn it, Teresa! I'm a-standing right here! I heard him!"

Before Tommy took another step, he inhaled deeply.

"*I must be fucking nuts,*" he thought.

When he got to the front of the house, Tommy couldn't believe what he saw. The vacant lot across the street was wall-to-wall blacks. Nunziata Bonaventi, the oldest guy in the neighborhood, who people guessed was at least 100, the guy that Victor said even smelled old, sat on a chair in front of his building as he did for forever and a day. As Tommy walked by him, Nunziata partially lifted the blanket he always kept on his lap, regardless of how hot it was outside. He showed Tommy the gun he held in his hand. Tommy nodded affirmatively.

"Non ho paura di loro," (I'm not afraid of them.) Nunziata told him.

"Siediti e guarda. Tutto andra bene." (Just sit, and watch. Everything will be okay.)

Nunziata rose slowly, stood, and adjusted his chair to face the lot. Roughly

150 blacks had gathered. Zeus was barking and lunging forward. Tommy stopped for a minute, double wrapped the leesh around his left hand, and gave the agitated Shepherd a command.

"Stop, Zeus!"

Zeus stopped barking within a few seconds, but the hair on his back was standing straight up. Then, as Tommy prepared himself to be the lone white man, facing a sea of angry black faces, a hush fell over the crowd as it parted. Tommy wondered what was going on.

"Keep cool. Don't back down. Be respectful. No one needs to get hurt today."

A tall, slender man emerged. He was accompanied by a snarling Doberman Pinscher. Tommy recognized him.

"That's Lucius Jefferson."

Born and raised in Chicago, Jefferson was the locally famous, well-spoken leader of the city's African-American movement. He appeared on TV numerous times over the last few years, always wearing his signature white silk bandana, which held his full-blown afro-hairstyle in place. As Jefferson approached Tommy, his Doberman began lunging and spewing foam from his mouth. Zeus followed suit and savagely barked. The two men stood a few feet from each other, their dogs, almost nose to nose. Jefferson was the first to break the ice.

"That's a beautiful Shepherd you got there."

"So is your Pinscher, Mr. Jefferson."

"Good, this white man knows me." Jefferson thought. *"Now, let's find out who he is."*

"So, here I am, already at an early disadvantage. You know my name, but I don't know yours."

"My name is Tommy, Tommy LaCosta."

"What's your dog's name, Tommy LaCosta?"

"His name is Zeus. And your dog's name?"

Jefferson smiled before he answered.

"His name is Killer."

Tommy raised his eyebrows. Both dogs were standing on their hind legs, feverishly snarling, drooling, and growling.

"Should we quiet our beasts?" Jefferson asked.

"We should," Tommy answered.

"Sitzen, sei still." (Sit, be still.) Jefferson commanded Killer in German.

Killer sat quietly at attention while Zeus still barked uncontrollably.

"That's some very impressive shit right there, Mr. Jefferson. Is that German?"

"It is. Please, call me Lucius. And, it's okay that I call you Tommy?"

"You absolutely can, Lucius."

"Tommy, I didn't know if Killer was going to listen to me today. Some poor black brother broke into my garage last night. Whoever that stupid nigger was, it cost him. I found a piece of ass cheek and a couple of finger bones on the floor this morning. I mean, you know how these animals are, especially when they acquire a taste of human flesh. Shit, there's no telling what they'll do. It's like they can't wait for their next piece."

Tommy gave two firm tugs of Zeus's leash.

"Stendersi. Nessuna corteccia," (Lay down. No bark.)

Zeus immediately laid down and stopped barking. His paws pointed straight forward, ears perked at full attention.

Lucius was impressed.

"Well, I'll be damned! Y'all got a German Shepherd with a Greek name that understands EYE-TALIAN! I'm sure if Adolph Hitler, Aristotle, and Benito Mussolini were alive, they'd sure be damn proud.

Tommy wasn't interested in getting a history lesson.

"So Lucius, we're on a first-name basis, and we've calmed our bilingual dogs. What's next?"

"Well, until you walked up in here all nice and polite, my people and I were getting ready to make our presence known in Little Italy."

Tommy chose his next words wisely.

"Well, I'm pretty sure you already accomplished that."

The last thing Tommy wanted to do was incite a riot by coming across as belligerent or cocky. Neither side would benefit from that. As their conversation paused, out of the corner of his eye, Tommy noticed one of the black men in the front line throw a rock. Tommy followed the rock's trajectory. It was a perfect toss, shattering the rear window of his Cadillac. Jefferson was irate. He spun around, faced his supporters, and screamed.

"WHO THREW THAT FUCKIN' ROCK?"

The broken window and who threw the rock didn't concern Tommy. What DID worry him was the response from the Taylor Street alley group. About 30 to 50 neighborhood guys walked onto the softball field carrying bats and clubs within seconds of the window break. Right away, Tommy noticed Frankie, and the Pirelli and Fontanelli brothers, and about a dozen familiar faces from the Social Club. Also, Luke Capezio rounded up the older teenage guys and armed them with softball bats and hockey sticks borrowed from Chinetti's garage.

Jefferson angrily yelled out again.

"I WANNA KNOW WHO THREW THAT MUTHA FUCKING ROCK!"

Tommy took a few cautious steps toward the neighborhood crowd. Then, as calmly and non-threatening as possible, he put his hand up.

"No, no, no. Everyone, please stay there!"

Just then, two large trucks rumbled down Fillmore from Troop Street. The vehicles jumped the curb, pulled onto the baseball field, and stopped. Micky and Benny were driving. Their cargo was not fruits and vegetables, but about 30 Market guys.

"*Market Kings, hustlers, and union guys,*" Tommy thought. *"Now, we'll see what we see."*

Tommy wanted to make sure Silvio heard what he had just said.

"Everyone'll listen to Micky," he thought."

"MICKY, KEEP EVERYONE THERE!" Tommy shouted.

Silvio put his hand up then yelled back.

"OKAY, ALRIGHT!"

Lucius corralled the guy that threw the rock and forced him to the ground. The man's nose was bleeding profusely. There was also a small, brown bag sitting on his lap. It was filled with airplane glue.

"Cyrus Flint! That's no surprise at all! You were an embarrassment and a burden to your beautiful parents since you were 10-years old. I'm glad they're not alive to see this day. So, Tommy, what should I do with this rock-throwing, glue-sniffing, nigga mutha fucka?"

The blood dripping from Flint's nose began to soak the front of his shirt. Even though he was bleeding, he still reached for his glue. Jefferson would have none of that.

"Touch that bag of death, and Killer will rip you apart. You are a disgrace to our race!"

There were a few cheers from the all-black crowd. The neighborhood contingency waited, looking for a signal from Tommy. They knew things were being said but couldn't hear from their positions across the street.

"You should get that man some help, Lucius," Tommy suggested.

Jefferson saw an opportunity to preach. It was his specialty.

"I should get him some help? Tommy, this man is beyond help! He is a weak, black brother. We have no room for weak black brothers OR sisters!"

Jefferson's group agreed. They responded by raising their clenched fists, universally recognized as a black power symbol. They all shouted in unison.

"RIGHT ON! RIGHT ON!"

Lucius put his hand up. They immediately stopped chanting.

"JuJu, drag this pathetic mutha fucka away from me!" he ordered.

JuJu Desmond was Lucius's right-hand man, and then some. He dressed in full African tribal regalia. Physically, he was the black version of Fat Frankie, and almost as massive. Almost. JuJu grabbed glue-sniffing, rock thrower Cyrus Flint by his bloodied shirt and dragged him away like he was a bag of dirty laundry. Jefferson reached inside his pocket, pulled out a wad of cash, and peeled off five $100 bills. He extended them to Tommy.

"This should cover your rear window. I see it's a Caddy."

Tommy put the palm of his hand up.

"No, Lucius, I'll take care of it."

"You gonna use some of that 'Mafia Boy' money, Tommy?"

"At least he knows who I'm with," Tommy thought.

"I'm just a regular working guy from the neighborhood, Lucius."

"Uh-huh, I'm sure you are, Tommy. Maybe I just have you confused with one of your EYE-TALIAN brothers lined up across the street. Y'all look the same to me."

Tommy thought Lucius might be testing his patience with that comment, or at the very least, his sense of humor under pressure. So, instead of responding with something witty, he thought for a few seconds.

"This guy must think I'm a fucking idiot, baiting me with the same stereotyping bullshit we say about them. I'm going to let it slide and just smile."

"So Tommy, my black brothers and sisters, we're all lined up too, just like your paisans."

The faint sound of police car sirens blared in the distant background. Lucius sarcastically put his hand to his ear.

"What, pray tell, is that? Correct me if I'm wrong, Tommy, but ain't it the sound of the ALL-WHITE cavalry?"

"And the very first thing they're gonna do is put a nice dent in your afro with their billy clubs," Tommy thought.

"We have about three to five minutes, Lucius. Things are going to take a turn once the heat gets here. Shit'll be out of both our hands."

"And there's no doubt what side they'll choose, right, Tommy?"

This needed to end quickly, so Tommy offered a proposal.

"Stop by my store. We could talk about the future of our neighborhoods."

The sirens were getting louder as they got closer. Squad cars would be rolling up shortly.

"My place is just off of Blue Island by SouthWater Market. It's called Big Banana."

"I know that place. A friend of mine says he stops in there once in a while to have coffee. He used to live right over there," Jefferson said, pointing to a boarded up house down the street.

"Lucius, your friend is my friend, too. Cooches, right? He used to play in this softball game before he moved out."

At only 28 years old, Santiago "Cooches" Cabalarro was the top shot-caller of the largest Hispanic gang in the city, La Familia Mexicana. Tommy helped Cooches's brother, uncle, and cousin get decent jobs on the Market and the Streets and Sanitation Department. Cooches chose a different profession.

Once Cooches was solidly in place as a gang boss, Tommy went to him with a few money-making opportunities. As always, with Ingalleretta's approval, Tommy introduced Cooches to Billy Muir and Wesley White. Those two guys operated a bunch of chop-shops in and around the city. Everyone made a lot of money, whether it was stolen cars, hot parts, or the illegal resale of vehicles. Thanks to Tommy's introduction, Cooches took that criminal enterprise to the next level. La Familia Mexicana became a major city-wide player in the chop-shop business. Both groups have financially flourished, working exceptionally well together.

"So, Lucius, how about we have a conversation and a cup of coffee on Monday?"

Jefferson called JuJu.

"JUJU! JUJU! Get your fat, black, Zimbabwe ass back over here!"

Everyone on the softball field inched closer to the sidewalk. They were posturing and getting antsy while Jefferson and JuJu huddled together. After Jefferson nodded, Lucius turned his full attention back to Tommy.

"Well, Tommy LaCosta. As you said, there's no reason for anyone to get hurt here today, right?"

Tommy extended his hand. Lucius grabbed it, gripped it tightly, shook it, and pulled Tommy in closely.

"I can be back here at any given time with twice as many angry brothers and sisters. Make sure you let them old-ass goombahs know that."

Tommy thought it was best to give Jefferson the play, mainly because JuJu and their group were dispersing and heading back to Roosevelt Road.

"I'll see you at nine o'clock on Monday, Lucius. Let me guess, you like your coffee black, right?"

Lucius smiled. It appeared he appreciated Tommy's humor under the tense circumstances.

"I like EVERYTHING black, Tommy."

Before he walked away, Lucius pointed to Nunziata.

"That old man's been sitting in that same fucking chair since I was a teenager. Does he still hide that gun under his blanket?"

Tommy wasn't shocked Lucius knew that, so he made light of it.

"Nunziata might be the most dangerous guy here."

As he and Killer walked away, Lucius replied confidently.

"I highly doubt that."

Nunziata stood, readjusted his chair, and congratulated Tommy.

"Molto bene." (Very good.)

Nicky's Chevy turned the corner off Loomis Street and slid sideways onto Fillmore, right in front of the DaBone's house. He flew out of the car and ran to Tommy.

"Roosevelt Road's like a fucking Tarzan movie with all them shines. What the fuck happened?"

Tommy turned Zeus over to Nicky.

"We're good here, Nick."

"I see that, but why were they here? Did someone get jumped or something? Victor called me at the Shop and said it was a riot."

"It coulda been," Tommy admitted.

Five squads, two paddy-wagons, and a couple of unmarked police units filled the corner, stopping traffic in less than a minute. Johnny, Luca, Ralphie, and Vito all pulled out their badges. They were the four Pirelli brothers, all cops. Vito was the oldest. Everyone called him "Fazool." Tommy and he had been friends since they were 1940's teenagers. Fazool and his brothers were all connected to Manny. No surprise there. He walked to Tommy.

"Was that the shit-starter moulinyan?" (Pronounced moo-lin-yan. Used as an Italian-dialect derogatory slang for blacks that means eggplant.)

Tommy put his arm around him.

"Faz, could you talk to your guys? Maybe tell 'em there's no problem. Have them all grab a sandwich, a pop, and watch the game."

Tommy inconspicuously passed a wad of bills into Fazool's hand. It was a proper handoff. Fazool took the cash indiscreetly, as he had done hundreds of times before.

"Good idea, Tee. Oh, and just so you know, my brothers and I were heavily dressed, just in case."

Fazool lifted the front of his jacket to reveal the two .38 caliber pistols he had tucked inside his pants. Then, he reached inside his coat, and pulled out two more guns. When the Watch Commander emerged from his squad car, Fazool knew him. Per police protocol, Fazool held his badge high, formally announcing he was a police officer. Then, he whispered into the Commander's ear. You could tell they were friendly with each other. Within minutes, the entire police presence disbanded, except for the Commander and his driver

"Let's play ball!" Tommy shouted.

Everyone yelled and cheered. A few friends hugged Tommy and shook his hand. Some of the guys from the Social Club gathered around the Cadillac surveying the damage. Especially interested in the shattered back window was Cuccinota. He was the only guy in the neighborhood with a single word name. One night, the toughest guy from Peanut Park, Kurtzander West, a rugged German, got in Cuccinota's face, pressuring him to reveal if that was his first or last name. Cuccinota karate-chopped West in the throat, then flipped him through the plate glass window of Judge Mahaney's Bar on Polk Street. After that, no one ever asked Cuccinota, a fifth-degree black belt karate instructor for Army Special Forces and part-time tattoo artist, about his name again, except close friends busting his stones.

"Hey Tee, my cousin Redlin could take care of that for you in a fucking heartbeat. You remember him, right? He has that body and glass joint in Medinah called Anonymous. He does a lot of 'chop shop' shit there, too," Cuccinota offered.

Tommy nodded in agreement

"Can you give him a call for me? In the meantime, I'll park it in Nicky's garage. Oh, before I forget, is Cuccinota your first or last name?"

Cuccinota laughed his ass off. Then, he crouched in a proper karate stance and raised his hands in a chopping-ready position.

"Tommy, the cost of your window repair just went up an extra C-Note!"

Most of the SouthWater workers piled back into the trucks while the Market Kings and the union guys decided to stay, eat, and watch the game. No big surprise there. Tommy gave them all a shout.

"THANKS GUYS! THANK YOU!"

When he finally made his way back to the porch, Tommy asked Uncle Jimmy to pour him a glass of wine.

"Dagli l'intera bottiglia!" (Give him the whole bottle!), Pa joked.

"Just one glass, for now, Pa," Tommy smiled.

"Dad, I got a double!" Victor said to Nicky as he walked up.

"Good job, pal," Nicky answered while petting Zeus.

Victor climbed back over the fence and took his place on second base. Nicky was still curious about what had happened.

"So what the fuck was this all this about, Tee, just the natives getting restless?"

Tommy put his arm around Nicky and then whispered into his ear.

"It's a lot more than that. The sooner you guys move the fuck away from here, the better. The times, they are a-changin'."

"Who are you, Bob fucking Dylan?" Nicky asked.

Tommy got serious.

"Listen, things could've gotten really ugly here today. We gotta ramp up the home search for you guys."

Nicky nodded and walked into the alley with Zeus. Tommy took a large sip of Pa's wine and handed the empty glass over the railing to Uncle Jimmy. Teresa slyly got in the exchange with a buttered piece of toast.

"Is this Ma's black pepper bread?" he asked.

Teresa winked back at him and answered.

"It is. You're gonna need something to soak up Pa's wine!"

Luke Capezio jogged back out to his centerfield position but stopped briefly at second base to say a few words to Victor. Lukie was like a God to all the younger guys.

"Your Uncle Tommy's a fucking legend. First, he saves Manny, and now, this."

Everyone in the neighborhood knew the whole Manny/Tommy/SouthWater Market story.

"He's just Uncle Tommy," Victor answered.

Luke continued out to center, but he wasn't finished talking.

"We'll be telling our grandkids what happened here today, Victor. This is one for the books!"

Unfortunately, that was the last time Victor and Luke ever spoke. Capezio never had the opportunity to break Mickey Silvio's undefeated boxing record. Nineteen-year-old Lukie was shot down six months later as his helicopter flew over a Viet Nam province. He was the first neighborhood war casualty. Little Italy was devastated. When an army ground battalion finally secured the crash site, investigators didn't even find charred skeletons wearing dog tags. A total of four brave soldiers went down in that fiery helicopter, but there wasn't a single trace of human remains. It was like Lukie and his three brothers-in-arms magically disintegrated.

Tommy noticed Fat Frankie and Vinnie Champagne talking. When they were done, Vinnie headed towards Snafuro's Bakery, Frankie walked to Tommy while eating a sausage sandwich.

"Tommy, the old man wants to talk to you."

"Where's he at, Snafuro's backyard?"

Frankie nodded yes.

"Vinnie said he's been watching the entire time."

"Tell Manny hello from Uncle Jimmy and me," Pa insisted.

When Tommy got to Snafuro's, he opened the back gate. Manny was sitting there with Detective Michael Tunzi.

"Tommy, look who came to sit with me. It's Elliot Ness!" Ingalleretta joked.

Tunzi stood and hugged Tommy.

"Michael, how are you?"

"What's up, Tommy? It seems like just yesterday we were playing out there," he reminisced.

"Michael, to this day, you hit the furthest softball I've ever seen!"

Tunzi laughed, remembering how just how far that ball traveled.

"Tee, that fucking rock is STILL rolling past Troop Street!"

As Tommy sat down, Michael asked the question he just had to ask, because after all, he was a detective.

Anything I should know about? I got here about half-an-hour ago. I was gonna join you out there with Jefferson, but Manny said I should wait, so I did. It looks like you handled things nicely."

"Jefferson wanted to remind us how many people he had and how close they were to the neighborhood," Tommy explained.

"Well, I'm glad it ended peacefully. When the Jungle King's involved, it usually doesn't," Tunzi added.

Manny put his hand on Tunzi's.

"Michael, I gotta talk to Tommy for a few minutes, you understand, right?"

Tunzi more than understood.

"Okay, Manny. I'll get back to you on that thing."

Tunzi shook Manny's hand, kissed his cheek, and turned to Tommy.

"As always, it's great to see you. Please give my best to Teresa and the rest of your family, especially that ball-breaker, Nicky."

Tommy chuckled.

"He is a fuckin' ball breaker! Thanks, Michael. I'll send your regards."

Vinnie Champagne stood silently in his usual spot, the corner of the yard.

"Hey, Vinnie, it was nice talking to you!" Tunzi sarcastically said.

The two hadn't spoken a word to each other since they said hello over an hour earlier.

Tunzi looked at Tommy.

"Is it possible Vinnie's getting bigger?"

Tommy smiled, slightly laughing. Vinnie didn't respond or move.

"Behave, Michael. Don't you have some shines to arrest?" Ingalleretta asked.

"No, Manny, I don't. But, before I leave, I think I'll take a few cannolis into custody."

Manny looked tired. His brain cancer treatments were taking their toll. He motioned for Tommy to take a seat.

"Sit down, Tommy. Now tell me, what's with all that nonsense out there today."

"Long story short, it was a show. Manny, I know you don't want to hear this, but the blacks are getting stronger and more organized. They all listen to Jefferson. The key is to keep him happy, so shit like that doesn't happen in the neighborhood."

"Tommy, he's a fucking animale." (Pronounced, On-i-ma-lay. Means animal.)

Manny was many things, but forward-thinking was not one of them. He had no use for the blacks.

"Jefferson's coming to see me at Big Banana on Monday. I invited him for coffee.

Manny, let me feel him out, then I'll get back to you or Lenny. I have a couple of ideas, but first, I want to see what's on his mind. I don't wasn't to start off by dictating our policy to him."

"All right, Tommy, but don't promise anything upfront. This was a slap in the face today. Him, with all those fucking tutsoons (Slang for blacks.) coming here like they were gonna cause problems. By the way, before I forget, very nice out there today, diffusing that shit."

"Yea, thanks. I got lucky. And all it cost me was the rear window on my Caddy," Tommy joked.

Manny wasn't entirely done conveying his feelings about Lucius Jefferson, or for that matter, all blacks.

"If this was 20 years ago, we would've shot that nigger in his burrhead, chopped him up into little pieces, and dumped him in HIS neighborhood. You understand where I'm going with this, right, Tommy? We had no problems with them people because that's how we took care of things."

"I understand," Tommy answered, feeling the need to quickly change the subject.

"By the way, Pa and Uncle Jimmy said to say hello."

"Are they drinking Giuseppe's wine?" Manny asked.

"They are, out of the mason jars. So, it won't be long now before Uncle Jimmy starts singing to the crowd."

Manny got up slowly from his chair. Tommy thought he looked sickly but figured it was just fatigue. Manny looked up and smiled at the clear, light blue sky.

"That Harry Volkman was right on the money again. Not a cloud in the sky. That fuckin' guy really knows his weather."

Volkman was a famous meteorologist who worked at just about every television station in Chicago at one time or another.

"Tommy, did you know that Volkman was the first weatherman to ever issue a tornado warning on television?"

"No, I didn't, Manny."

That comment got Tommy concerned.

"Jesus Christ, Manny's all over the board. First, he's talking about shooting blacks, now he's talking about WGN's weatherman and fucking tornado warnings!"

"I wish I could sit with Pa and Jimmy. What a shame! Too many people watching every fucking thing I do every mother fucking day! All right, I gotta stop. I'm starting to get myself aggravated. Vinnie, let's go. Tommy, you keep me informed, okay?"

Tommy hugged Manny and kissed him on the cheek. Manny was slightly out of breath.

"This is the first time we've talked and he wasn't smoking a cigarette," Tommy thought.

Vinnie took a minute to talk privately to Tommy while Manny ambled slowly through the back door.

"Tommy, he's really slowing down. Sometimes, I have to shake him awake when we're driving because he forgets to tell me where we're going. So I'm taking him back to the doctor next week for more blood tests."

"I've noticed some stuff too, even before that whole television courtroom bullshit. Manny won't let me go with him to any of his appointments. I asked a few times. Vinnie, do you stay in the waiting room or go inside with him?"

"I stay in the waiting room. When I ask if I should go in, Manny tells me to stay put. So, I stay put. You know how he is, Tommy."

Manny stuck his head back outside.

"Vinnie, andiamo!" (Let's go.)

"I'll let you know what I can," Vinnie promised.

As Tommy walked down the alley shaking hands and exchanging a few pleasantries with old neighbors, he stopped in front of Sam and Dolly Amato's garage for a minute to watch the game, which had just resumed. Victor tagged up at second base on a deeply hit fly ball. He barely beat the throw to get him out. But that attempt wasn't made at third base. Instead, it was at home plate! Victor was a blur flying around the bases. The home team fans clapped and cheered. Especially celebratory were the rooters in the DaBone backyard. Grace screamed the loudest, and she wasn't even drinking. Not yet, anyway. But, you could bet your ass there were at least three ice-cold Miller beers in her very near future.

Tommy was pretty amazed by Victor's speed.

"Jesus Christ, am I the only one that sees how fast he is? Maybe it's just because he's my nephew, but what the fuck? It's almost unnatural. I can't remember anyone around here ever being that quick at ANY age!"

The home team won by a score of 15-10. Victor scored twice. And, while playing defense in right field, he also chased down a long fly ball that retired the side when the bases were loaded. (He collided with Rosinski, the kid with the thickest glasses in the western hemisphere to do it, but bottom line, Victor held on and made the catch.) Nicky and Tommy slipped $50 bills in his pocket for playing such a great game. Finally, Grace, Teresa, and Grandma Mari couldn't contain themselves anymore. They showered their favorite player with kisses.

"C'mon, stop it! Everyone's looking over here," Victor pleaded.

"Is Maria DiNapoli watching? I want her to get all gelosa (Jealous) of us!" Grace teased.

"Okay, Mom, that's gonna cost you!" Victor jokingly threatened.

Donato Fontanelli walked sideways (just like Fat Frankie always did) to make it through the narrow back alley door. After saying hello to everyone, he congratulated Victor, then made his way to Frankie. Donato reached inside his pocket and pulled out a wad of $100 bills. He handed Frankie three grand, but not before taking the opportunity to slam his nuts even further, teasing him in front of a captive audience.

"Frankie, when's the last time you cleaned your barbeque grill when Nunziata and Columbus discovered America?"

Pa and Uncle Jimmy almost choked from laughing so hard. Frankie laughed his big ass off too, but it didn't stop him from grabbing that cash like it was the last beef sandwich on earth. He examined the money, smelled it, and then shot right back to Donato.

"Did you and those criminals from the other side of Racine just print this?"

"Only $500 of it, the other $2,500 is the money you paid me when you lost last year," Donato laughed.

"Frankie, all kidding aside, I saw you had Melrose peppers. Where'd you get them from, Tommy?"

Tommy's ears perked up when he heard his name. He was already on his second glass of wine.

"I got them from Joe Ori at Strube Celery. George the Greek and Al at Big Apple bought almost the whole truckload between them, so Joe only had a few pallets left."

Donato wanted in on the Melrose peppers.

"Frankie, your mom gave me one to sample. It was delicious! What did she do, just cut the stems, crosscut the top, and fry 'em in olive oil, salt, and garlic?"

"That's it," Frankie answered.

"I gotta have Rocco grab us five or six boxes. We'll stuff them with sausage and bread crumbs. I think I'll put them on the menu tomorrow. Of course, we'll use OUR meat and not that contaminated salsiccia (Pronounced Sa- Zeech. Means sausage) you make in your basement. I bet if you feed Zeus a piece, he throws it back to you," Donato laughed.

"I got $3000 that says he doesn't!" Frankie boasted.

The rest of the afternoon was the most perfect and memorable ever. Even Ned Devane stopped by to have a sandwich and a couple of shots of whiskey. Detective Tunzi came back too, after official police hours, with Frankie's sister, Gina, on his arm.

The older neighborhood guys chose two-player teams and had a $500 winners-take-all Briscala card tournament in Chinetti's garage. The youngest kids played a softball game at dusk with the help of car and truck headlights. The older teens drank beer and wine and played Morra, an ancient Roman/Greek hand game. The 18-19-year-old rebels amongst them secretly puffed on a few joints in "The Den of Iniquity," their code name for E.D. Seberti's basement.

Every weekend, the oldest neighborhood teens flocked to Eugene Donaldo Seberti's cellar. They drank, gambled, watched sports, ordered take-out, smoked weed, and listened and danced to the music of Led Zeppelin, The Who, The Beatles, The Dave Clark Five, Paul Revere and the Raiders, The Grass Roots, The Supremes, The Rolling Stones, Elvis Presley, Smokey Robinson & The Miracles, Marvin Gaye, Steppenwolf, The Animals, Three Dog Night, The Jackson Five, The Four Tops, and Jefferson Airplane.

Donato came back later in the afternoon with Rocco. They brought one hundred 6-inch Fontanelli submarine sandwiches and four trays of their mother, Gilda's homemade ravioli. When it started getting darker, Vinnie Bonsanto busted out a barrel filled with fireworks, and his brother CoCo, opened up the pump for those wishing to have a late-night splash under the fire hydrant. (Some unsuspecting were unwillingly dragged in!) This was a day that no one wanted to see come to an end.

When that following Monday came around, Tommy and Lucius met as planned. They talked about every topic under the sun. Lucius was particularly interested in the increasing popularity of marijuana and the perspective profit margins that came with it. That's the business move Tommy focused on. Once Ingalleretta approved, Tommy introduced Lucius to one of the Outfit's weed suppliers, Ignatius Archibald. Besides being the owner/operator of a neighborhood gas station, Archibald's family farm in Tennessee was always loaded with their mature mid-grade quality pot plants. It was their main cash crop. Thanks to Tommy and Lucius, the Mob moved more bundles of Ignatius's weed than they ever had before on their own. Six months later, that amount quadrupled. Every dope smoker in the projects and beyond bought tens of thousands of $1, $2, and $3 baggies. Lucius also talked to the black restaurant and grocery store owners in his neighborhoods. He encouraged them to buy their fruits and vegetables in bulk at SouthWater instead of retailing their purchases. As a result, there were at least a dozen or more examples of cooperation between these two very different, very diverse groups. When Manny saw the money pouring in, his hard stance on blacks loosened. He still wasn't a fan, but there was no talk about 'nigger this' and 'moulinyan that.' He also never referred to them as animals again, not even in Italian.

Tommy introduced Lucius to gnocchi, braciole, and red-lead gravy. Lucius reciprocated with St. Louis barbeque rib-tips, collard greens, cornbread, sweet potato pie, and aged Tennessee whiskey. Nicky and Frankie eventually joined in on the visits. They all made each other laugh with racial jokes, ethnic slurs, and stereotyping. They ate pretty well, too. Nicky was pleasantly surprised when he found out James from the Shop was Lucius's second cousin on his mother's side. Lucius expressed rarely-seen heartfelt thanks to Nicky for being his cousin's fair, generous, and decent employer.

Besides a few minor conflicts, the African/Italian American neighborhood skirmishes and confrontations all but vanished. Lucius took some of his earned money and opened up a 24-hour gymnasium on Roosevelt Road. He named it "Black Power." That field house attracted some of the most talented black athletes in the city. Lucius visited Tommy at Big Banana at least twice a month for the next eleven months. They genuinely enjoyed each other's company and even taught one another an important lesson – skin color was just that, a color. They shared many similar views, especially regarding family and business. During those get-togethers at Big Banana, a white immigrant Italian and a black African American exchanged tan manila envelopes containing green. Sometimes Lucius was the recipient, and sometimes it was Tommy.

One Sunday night, as Tommy and Teresa sat in bed watching the Channel 7 news, Fahey Flynn, the avuncular bow-tie-wearing Irish newscaster, opened his broadcast with a picture of Lucius Jefferson. Flynn reported that the local black activist died earlier that evening after being shot in the head at close range. Flynn went on to say that also found very close to the scene of the crime was Jefferson's Doberman Pinscher. The dog reportedly had four bullet holes in his back, chest, and throat. Flynn concluded the Jefferson news piece by saying there were no other details and that no one was in custody. Teresa knew her husband liked Lucius.

"Jesus, Tommy, how terrible is this? You don't' think they'll be riots, do you? We have to get Ma and Pa to stay here, right?"

Tommy thought that was a good move.

"That's very good thinking, Tree. Call them now and set it up, then call Nicky and Grace to let them know."

The following day, at 9:00 a.m., JuJu walked into Big Banana, minus his familiar African dashiki and kufi cap. Lucius always insisted those clothing items be part of his wardrobe, especially when trouble was brewing or the cameras were rolling. Lucius said it made him look intimidating. So, JuJu wore it. Tommy sympathetically extended his hand when the big man walked in.

"I'm very sorry to hear about Lucius."

JuJu tightly gripped Tommy's hand with both of his.

"Thanks, Tommy."

When JuJu sat, it was on the couch's left cushion, the same spot where Lucius used to sit. Tommy found that interesting seeing this was the first time JuJu was ever at Big Banana. Tommy went behind his desk, opened his top drawer, and retrieved an envelope. He walked to the couch and handed it to JuJu.

"This is a sympathy card from Nicky and me. Can you please give it to Lucius's family from us?"

JuJu noticed how thick the envelope was when he couldn't tuck it in his pocket.

"That's awfully kind of you both, Tommy. I'll make sure Lucius's brother gets it. He's driving in tomorrow morning from down south. That's pretty big for just a sympathy card."

"There's two G's in there, JuJu. I'm not telling you that because I want a pat on the back, I'm telling you, so you know how heavy it is."

"Man, that's overly generous. Lucius's brother is a sharecropper, so I'm sure it will help with burial expenses and shit. I stopped by today to let you know that as fucked up as all of this is, it's business as usual. No changes, except now, you'll be dealin' with me. Is that gonna be a problem?"

Tommy was happier than hell to hear that.

"If that's the only change, I don't think that'll be a concern."

"I'm sure the coppers are looking into his shooting. Do they have any leads on who killed him?" Tommy asked.

"Fuck that television lip service they're givin'! I guarantee you that every white-cop bar in the city is filled with blue uniforms celebrating Lucius's dead black ass. They ain't gonna find anyone to pin it on. Remember something, Tommy, you and your EYE-TALIAN boys ain't the only ones who can say 'Abracadabra' and make a mutha fucker disappear."

Tommy more than understood. But he was still curious and couldn't help inquiring.

"So, I gotta ask, did you know the guy?"

"Yea, I knew him, and so did you," JuJu answered.

Tommy looked puzzled.

"I knew him? He was a white guy?"

"Wasn't a white guy, and as far as I'm concerned, even though he was black he was no brother," JuJu mysteriously answered.

Tommy was still baffled, so he shrugged his shoulders. JuJu leaned up, adjusting himself from the couch. The cushion made the same scrunch noise when Fat Frankie sat on it.

"Tommy, I'm gonna tell you something. Lucius always said you were solid. He called you a trustworthy, fair man."

JuJu paused, thought about what he just said, and laughed before continuing.

"He said Big Italian Banana Tommy was one of the 'GOOD' white boys."

"That sounds like something he would've said," Tommy agreed.

"So, in the spirit of forming a bond of trust between us, just like you had with Lucius, I'm gonna tell ya who it was."

Tommy was on the edge of his seat.

"It was that glue-sniffin' waste-of-a-life nigger who broke your Caddy window that day. Cyrus Flint was his name. You remember him, right?"

"You have GOT to be fucking kidding me! JuJu, are you sure?"

"I'm positive. Some Roosevelt Road brothers found Cyrus's sorry ass in an alley about 15 minutes after he shot Lucius. His arm was all torn up, and his jacket had blood on it. I'm thinking Killer must've gotten a few bites in. Flint's empty gun was lying next to him, and the barrel was still hot. They dragged his ass to a spot we have. We beat ole Cyrus for about two hours. The pathetic bitch begged for his life. He swore up and down that he wasn't workin' for man. He was all hopped up on the shit. Cyrus was a jealous nigger who hated Lucius and what he stood for," JuJu confided.

"What a waste of a good man for no goddamn reason," Tommy said, shaking his head.

"The only ones who made out were the dogs. We got a stable of a dozen or so, maybe more. They ripped that piece of shit Cyrus apart and swallowed him up, clothes, bones, and all. So, there ain't nothin' left, except dead nigger stink," JuJu admitted.

As he hoisted himself off the couch, he handed Tommy a piece of paper.

"Here's my phone number. I'll make sure Lucius's brother gets your gift, and I'll be back next week to go over some shit. Maybe you could talk Fat Frankie into making some of that delicious EYE-TALIAN food for me, the same way he did for Lucius? Tell him I'll bring barbeque chicken, oxtail stew, fried shrimp, and red velvet cake."

It wasn't long before JuJu Desmond established himself as much more than the interim guy in charge. He wasn't an activist like Lucius had been. Instead, he was a silent partner and the prime money source behind many black-owned and operated establishments. Tommy and JuJu happily turned over their drug involvement to the major players within their respective organizations. They both agreed it brought way too much heat and hurt their other money-making activities. Neither one wanted a future in that very perilous end of the business. So JuJu's tribe and the Mob goombahs worked out deliveries, shipments, and payment schedules. At first, the transitions were a little dicey. But, all in all, once the glitches and snitches were taken care of, the money both sides made from weed sales alone was boomshakalaka tremendous. And what made it all possible was white Tommy and black Lucius's face to face, dog to dog meeting.

It was an eerie premonition that the neighborhood celebration on that storied Saturday morning was called "The Last Hurrah." Tommy's analysis of the changing times was also fitting. Between Lukie dying in Viet Nam, the mass move to the suburbs by longtime residents, the relocation pressure from the Urban Renewal Department, and the uncertainty of violence erupting from race-riots, the Little Italy rivalry softball game was never played again.

CHAPTER 12
THE UNPINCHABLE FAT FRANKIE, SPECIAL DETECTIVE MICHAEL TUNZI'S BUST, IGNATIUS GETS AN ETERNAL NICKNAME

Within fifteen years of getting his venture off the ground, Fat Frankie Pope sat alone as the top bookie for the Chicago Outfit. He coordinated a dozen large bookies who took bets from about twenty to thirty smaller bookies. All together, Frankie was responsible for monthly betting that, on average, totaled close to $800,000!

There was always action somewhere, and more times than not, those wagers eventually wound up passing through Frankie's extremely thick fingers. Frankie Pope was a larger-than-life target that law enforcement finally saw on their radar. Agents were always lurking in the shadows attempting to pinch him. The police were very interested in where he went, who he talked to, and how he operated. But Frankie secretly carried something in his back pocket. It was invisible, but there nonetheless. It was an 'I Don't Get Pinched' card.

The Chicago Vice Squad had their hands full, investigating illegal gambling and prostitution. Detectives often disrupted the regulars at Japeto's, barging in with search warrants, carrying their big balls on their shoulders. The cops lined up all the wannabes against the bar and squeezed them for any information they could, usually by slinging bogus accusations at them. When the police examined Japeto's kitchen, their investigative methods were disruptive. They tossed around pots, pans and opened sealed bags of food. Graziella Pope, Fat Frankie's mom, often threw her spatula and kitchen rags at agents. Her performances were always Academy Award-worthy.

"You should all be ashamed of yourselves! You're destroying my kitchen! Leave Frankie alone! He's a good boy!" she'd complain.

It was all a show.

Mrs. Pope was one of the few who knew the real story. The truth was that her rotund baby boy Frankie got a pass. Fat Frankie always, always, always, got the heads up before a Japeto's Restaurant raid. That was the deal Tunzi made with the State of Illinois Chief of Police on behalf of Ingalleretta to let Fat Frankie Pope do his thing. It took months to develop a shared dollar amount and agree on the legal scenarios both sides would face if everything turned to shit. But, for as large as the monthly payoff was to State Police Chief Mugnoli, it was worth tenfold to Outfit. Manny let Balducci and Montalbano know it all happened because of Tunzi's negotiating tactics with the police chief. Primo, of course, didn't buy into that. Balducci, on the other hand, did. He let Primo know it by congratulating Manny and complementing Tunzi.

"Give credit where credit is due, Primo. You know how important Tunzi is to us. And we have Manny to thank for that."

Michael Tunzi's official rank was Special Detective. That prestigious position allowed him unlimited, state-wide jurisdiction. Tunzi officially reported to only one person, Chief Mugnoli. Unofficially, it was Ingalleretta. As far as law enforcement was concerned, Tunzi had carte blanche to go after anyone, anywhere, at any time, for any reason. Only two other officers in the entire state had that kind of legal juice, and both of them were hugging desks as their retirement loomed. The special platinum badge Tunzi wore was the most sought-after coveted piece of police jewelry in all of Illinois.

The first time the Vice Squad raided Japeto's, Tunzi came along for the show. He had to. After all, it was his neighborhood, and he was dating the owner's sister. He would've appeared shadier than shit to his police peers if he passed, plus there were also the early whispers in the Internal Affairs Department. How would it look if he didn't participate? So he did. Later, he privately laughed with Mrs. Pope about which of them gave the better performance.

"Okay, Mama Pope, you get the best actress, and I get the best actor!"

Tunzi played his role well, huffing, puffing, and even throwing a head of lettuce at one of the wannabes. But, before leaving, after turning up no incriminating evidence of illegal gambling on the premises, the decorated detective had a message for the bust-outs. He delivered it while they all stood with their hands on the bar, and their faces forward.

"It's just a matter of fucking time, you cocksuckers! I can't wait to see you jagoffs stampede into my office and start beefin' on each other. Then we'll see how standup youse pricks are when it comes time to have a seat inside County, you bunch of fuckin' bend-over, wannabe cunts!"

Tunzi's allegiance to Manny began many years earlier when Ingalleretta intervened with a mysterious problem involving Tunzi's father. Whatever it was, Manny made it disappear, and the very young Michael Tunzi never forgot that. The Mob hierarchy agreed to let Ingalleretta handle Tunzi. As usual, Primo had to gripe about it.

"I don't care how long Manny's known him, and I don't give two shits about him being from Taylor Street. Tunzi's still a fucking copper, just like them four Pirelli brothers!"

There was no doubt Michael Tunzi was a force to be reckoned with. He was a battering ram with a platinum badge and Mob muscle. Tunzi's illustrious career as a detective started with a couple of significant arrests. One was the recovery of a hijacked load of government bonds mistakenly sent out by a new employee from the Federal Reserve. The shipment was confiscated by some Russian gangsters thanks to inside information they had from a security guard. The stolen bonds, worth millions in the open market, were stashed in a southside warehouse and ready to be cashed.

Tunzi, acting on what he officially referred to as a reliable tip, chose a select group of state troopers to seize control of the warehouse. The successful bust received national media coverage. In addition, Tunzi received a medal and a certificate of appreciation from the White House. The accommodation from the Federal Government branded Special Detective Michael Tunzi as a rising star in the eyes of local law enforcement.

Manny wasn't too thrilled about the most recent order of Mob business requiring Tunzi's special touch, mainly because Little Italy was involved. But Manny was overruled. And to make matters worse, Primo Montalbano was overseeing the whole thing because it involved drugs.

"Why not run this deal on the north side, Primo? It'll be easier for you to coordinate. Why is this shit being done in the middle of my neighborhood?" Manny asked at one of the Bosses meetings.

Joey Balducci quickly intervened before things blew way out of proportion

"Manny, this is what works best. We're in for the long play on this one. We show the public we don't condone drug use or sales, especially in that neighborhood. Sure, we have to shoot ourselves in the foot, but that wound will heal. We make the necessary adjustments and inform our guys, the shines, and the spics. The only supply that doesn't get interrupted is to Sherman Stein's family. They must stay fully stocked at all times. Your boy Tunzi gets his bust, we get rid of a problem child, and we move on to bigger and better things."

Joey Balducci was firmly in control, calling all final shots. There was nothing written in stone, but his Crew was the biggest, wielding power and authority over most of the Syndicate's rackets. Manny knew it, everyone in and around the Outfit knew it, and the Organized Crime Task Force knew it.

The problem child Balducci referred to was the whole reason behind that particular meeting. It was Ignatius Archibald Sr., the Outfit's marijuana grower. The overall plan was to put his son, Iggy Jr., in charge as their new weed go-to guy. Sure, Iggy Jr. would need a good talking to, and he'd also have to step up and whip the asses of his backward Tennessee clan of growers. The Bosses knew Junior had a county-mile hard-on for his father. The two fought constantly, and most of the time, it ended with a physical altercation. Junior always wound up getting the worst of it. The Bosses were confident Iggy Jr. would jump at an opportunity to spearhead the operation without his old man hoarding the majority of the profits.

Ignatius Sr. was not a Rhodes Scholar. The Mob found out about his conniving scheme to make money under their table. There was a plethora of flaws in his plan from the get-go. Instead of taking his container of contraband to a neutral, undisclosed location for unloading, packaging and distribution, he instructs his half-wit country cousin driver to go directly to his Sinclair gas station at the corner of May & Taylor Streets. Tunzi was tipped off about the delivery a couple of days before. The heads-up allowed him time to coral his usual hand-picked troopers. Also contacted was the Mob's media guy, Channel 7 news reporter, Chuck Drover. His instructions were to have his television crew ready to roll on a specific date and time for an exclusive. On the day it all went done, Drover and his mobile television van arrived on the scene just minutes after the official call went over the police scanner. Once troopers secured the crime scene, Drover's camera crew set themselves up in perfect position.

Tunzi broke open the airline container just as planned. As the cameras zoomed in tightly, he popped open one of the two hundred tightly stacked canisters. They were all labeled 'COCONUTS.' Besides misty green and magenta colored buds with long red haired pistils, there was a pre-rolled joint, and a pack of Zigzag

1.5 wide rolling papers, the brand with Zouave, the 19th century French solder on the cover. Drover asked Tunzi on live television how much he thought each canister weighed. The Special Detective smartly answered, happily deferring any and all further question to the agents en route. As far as he was concerned, his visibly active part in the setup was done.

"Drug Enforcement agents will be on the scene shortly. Please save your questions for them."

Spectators gathered, applauding Tunzi as he handcuffed and strong-armed Archibald Sr. and his driver, aggressively placing them in separate unmarked squad cars. To his credit, the only thing Ignatius said to police and news crews was, "'Lawyer." Nobody liked the idea of drugs in the neighborhood, but there was big money to be made. The Mob, especially the old-timers, needed to let loose on the reigns of their previous hard-line stances about narcotics sales and instead, start taking advantage of it. The money they generated from their recent concentration on weed was substantial, and they were barely putting any time or effort into it. The action and profits were expanding daily, and truth be told, they weren't sure what to make of the windfall.

Ignatius's punishment for his decision to cheat the Outfit was as a sacrificial lamb. He was served up and portrayed in the news as a rogue druggie from down south trying to tarnish the reputation of the beautiful Little Italy neighborhood. As a result, Detective Tunzi got his arrest and an extraordinary citation from the DEA. In addition, the Mob got some much-needed positive media coverage, thanks to the pre-paid biased reporting of Channel 7's Drover.

Archibald faced a 20-year federal pinch for drug trafficking with intent to sell. A media frenzy ensued. Television reporters from every station filled the neighborhood. The headlines the next day were all about the bust. Although every newsstand in Little Italy was out of copies by 10:00 a.m., there was no shortage of neighborhood gossip on every street corner and establishment.

Reporters went all-out to see whose byline would be the catchiest and capture the most readers. So, naturally, some were better than others.

'RECORD DRUG BUST IN MOB-CONTROLLED LITTLE ITALY!'

'MARIJUANA PUSHER GETS CAUGHT RED-BUD-HANDED!'

'HIGH-GRADE REEFER STASHED IN CANS OF COCONUTS!'

'TODAY'S MENU SPECIAL: HAWAIIAN WEED MARINERA!'

Iggy Jr.'s volatile personal and one-sided business relationships with his father were finally over. He was the Mob's new marijuana frontman. The hillbilly driver that picked up and delivered the airline container received a 6-month jail sentence for transportation of an illegal substance. He didn't know anything about anything. All he did was drive the truck. The Outfit knew he wasn't in on it, but they made him think they thought he was. Good move. Once released from Cook

County Jail, you never saw a farm boy high-tail his ass back to Tennessee so fast!

Archibald Sr. waited for his trial date, a guest of Joliet State Prison. During that time, he refused to cooperate with Narcotics Bureau agents. They interrogated him on three separate occasions. Ignatius didn't speak, per legal advice from his attorney, Hymie Kline.

After a solid, stand-up three weeks of continued silence, four days before his trial, Ignatius Archibald Sr. was found dead in his cubicle swinging from the end of a hangman's noose. JuJu Desmond received a sizeable envelope for his help. He coordinated a couple of his incarcerated black soul-brothers to pay an unscheduled visit to Ignatius's cell. JuJu implicitly trusted the three men who helped stage the fake suicide. The two inmates who assisted were childhood friends doing 3-year stints for robbery. The third man, a corrections guard, was his former brother-in-law, Jeremiah Titus.

When JuJu met Titus to pay him, the crooked guard ex-relative voiced a major concern.

"That ole country boy put up a real fuss before we lynched him! He kept saying he was a Mafia Boss. We're not gonna be in trouble with the EYE-TALIANS, are we?"

After reassuring Titus there would be no problems, JuJu relayed the story to the Outfit guys. They were hysterical! No one ever called Ignatius Archibald Sr. by his real name again. Instead, he was posthumously referred to as "The Hillbilly Godfather."

CHAPTER 13
BAD NEWS FOR THE MOB AND THEIR UNIONS

The 1970s weren't kind to organized crime. Significantly affected were the east coast families. The main reason for that was due to a couple of newly enacted laws. The first was The RICO ACT. (Racketeer Influenced and Corrupt Organizations) Passed in 1970, RICO provided extended criminal penalties and a civil cause of action for acts performed as part of an ongoing criminal organization. That allowed for prosecution and civil penalties for racketeering activity. The most challenging part for federal agents and lawyers was implementing this law, and establishing it as it pertained to a criminal organization.

There are roughly 35 predicate offenses that constitute racketeering. Examples of these are murder, kidnapping, arson, drug dealing, intimidation, and bribery. Included later were mail and wire fraud. With RICO implementation, Syndicate leaders were at risk of being charged for crimes they ordered others to do or assist in doing. It closed a perceived loophole that previously allowed a Boss instructing an underling to be exempt from the trial because they did not commit the crime personally. RICO gave government the power necessary to go after the Bosses, regardless of how many buffers (low-level members) they used to insulate themselves. The G's legal muscles were only as large and robust as their credible evidence in the past. But now, they had the legal authority to indict an entity.

The second law was called The Labor Judgment. It was a written agreement between the government and The National Union of Laborers and Truck Drivers. This document gave the G power to indict a vast majority of wise guys, who up until that point, were only 'alleged' to be connected. The truth was that many of them had burrowed into cushy jobs within labor unions all over the country. The Labor Department was after everyone, even the low-level organizers and union paycheck ghosts. Their telescopic sights were primarily zeroed-in on union agents and officers of Italian descent, especially those rumored to have alleged ties and close associations with well-known, documented members of organized crime. If you had a position in a union, and your last name ended in a vowel, the Labor Department investigated you.

The Syndicate and the unions had a mutually beneficial working relationship for years. But, when the Outfit's hand-picked guys began winning elections, it drew attention from more than just local law enforcement agencies. The government saw this happening more and more throughout some of the country's biggest labor markets, which, as it happened, were also Mob-controlled cities like New York, New Jersey, Boston, Chicago, Cleveland, Philadelphia, Kansas City, Milwaukee, and Detroit.

The Labor Judgment all came about because the national president, Mitchell Preston, got caught with his hand in the union's federally protected pension fund cookie jar. Labor Department and Department of Justice officials jumped all over this opportunity. When agents presented Preston with the damaging embezzlement proof they uncovered, they offered him a one-time deal. He could come clean on organized crime infiltration within all the affiliated locals under his nationwide control and sign a letter asking for government intervention, or go to prison until his last breath. The government badly needed that signed intervention request letter. If Preston refused, the Labor Department was looking at least two years through the court system to present a substantial case - one that had a distinct possibility of being thrown out for lack of credible evidence. Preston faced spending his sunset bachelor years doing a hard-time stint in a federal detention facility's general population locked up inside the walls of a gang-controlled penitentiary. So, not only did he sign, but he also agreed to officially go on the record about what he knew regarding Mob-connections on a state-by-state basis, all against the advice of his legal counsel. As a result, his government cooperation affected almost one hundred union-affiliated representatives at dozens of labor locals nationwide, with supposed ties to organized crime. The government wasted no time hurrying The Labor Judgment through the usually slow-moving legal system.

  Locally, Salvatore "Sally Boy" Domenico was a prime example of the Labor Judgment's one-sidedness when he got barred from holding union office solely based on Preston's testimony. The soon-to-be former president held nothing back when investigators asked about Domenico, a Top Captain and 'Made' member of the Chicago Outfit. The Labor Department already had their suspicions, thanks partly to information supplied to them by Chicago's Organized Crime Task Force. Those agents had watched Sally Boy on and off for years. Although Preston's verbal testimony was officially on the record, he offered no physical proof of his allegations against Domenico, which coincidently, was the same the Chicago Task Force had on Salvatore, nothing. Preston's testimony regarding his version of Sally Boy's Mob highlights included statements about his ties to numerous other labor officials, various high-ranking police officers, and heavy political players in and around Chicago Preston told investigators that Domenico had a very wide reach for almost a decade. (Preston was wrong. It was more like 18 years.)

  The Labor Department knew they had their work cut out for them with Domenico and his union. Unlike other Mob-affiliated labor guys across the country with previous arrest records, Salvatore was clean. What made matters worse for the G's witch hunt, was Sally Boy was never formally charged with labor racketeering, fund money misappropriation, or neglect of his fiduciary responsibilities required of him under his elected position. Strong-armed tactics, bribery, and extortion? Not a claim anywhere to be found. Domenico ran a tight-knit labor local with a loyal and grateful membership. That loyalty was because Sally Boy utilized his union as a personal employment placement business. The shrewd maneuver ensured that the growing majority of his union's membership was in some way tied to him, whether through family, friends, neighborhood people, Outfit connections, or business associates. Before anyone knew it, hundreds of gainfully employed union members at various companies were working because they, or someone they knew, had a connection to Salvatore Domenico, and of course, Ingalleretta. That hiring practice was going on for quite some time.

Chicago crime agencies assisted in the labor investigation against Domenico. They turned over a file which contained a bunch of surveillance photos, some notes, and an audiotape worn by an unidentified, confidential informer. But, all they had on Sally Boy was lots of 'alleged this' and 'reputed that.' The pictures were nothing, just Domenico shaking hands with some Outfit guys at different restaurants. (They did have a nice photo of Sally Boy and Fat Frankie Pope grilling sausage outside at Japeto's during a neighborhood bocce-ball tournament.) Also, there was an old black and white snapshot of Domenico with his arm around Manny Ingalleretta taken in front of Our Lady of the Shroud Church. Sally Boy had a copy of that picture with Manny, too. It proudly sat in a solid 24K gold frame on his bedroom nightstand, right next to his wedding picture.

    The union members in Domenico's local earned top-level wages and enjoyed unbelievable benefit packages. That was one reason why Sally Boy, his board of officers, business agents, and organizers, ran unchallenged in the four previous elections. The other reason was Domenico and his local were Outfit-run. That didn't matter, the G was in. The Labor Judgment went balls-out and successfully removed Mob-connected union leaders, especially Italians, all over the country. Domenico and 14 other Illinois union officials and business agents with alleged ties to the Syndicate were ousted, losing their elected titles and positions.

    Salvatore Domenico's legal team, including a prominent Midwest criminal lawyer and an ex-labor board attorney with 25 years of experience in government intervention cases, never had a chance to admit the boxes of financial statements, affidavits, or hundreds of notarized testimonials from union members into evidence. Their documents even included signed petitions from Mob-friendly company owners asking that Domenico be cleared of the bogus racketeering and criminal conspiracy charges he faced. The judge ruled Preston's taped statements against Domenico were admissible as 'reliable here-say.' Even though the ensuing legal arguments prepared by Salvatore's legal team were valid, he and his lawyers walked out of court with mouthfuls of shit and potatoes. They never stood a chance, just like all the other accused union officials in the Chicago area, as well as across the United States. Those locals were immediately put under court-supervised trusteeship and operated by government-appointed overseers. After that, it was the government and more of the government.

    Loyal rank and file members saw the Labor Judgment as a sweetheart deal between the government and big business to weaken their union by unjustly removing elected officials from office, regardless of the apparent lack of substantial incriminating evidence. What Mitchell Preston saw was a way to stay out of jail for secretly siphoning over 3.7 million dollars from the national pension fund. (He didn't act alone.) Preston, an unhealthy, overweight, insulin-dependent diabetic, died from a massive heart attack only a few days after the government officially filed charges in local labor courts all across the country. As a result, there would be no cross-examination of Mitchell Preston, which the government perceived as a sizable win for them.

    After the rulings went public, they were released to the general public. Over eighty percent of those charged by the Labor Department were of Italian decent.

That news prompted a response from the Italian-American Defamation Society. They held a press conference and had their spokesman, Mario Ronesti, read a prepared statement to the national media. The Society basically condemned the government for their prejudiced disbarment selections. The last sentence of Ronesti's spoke volumes, especially to the honest, hard-working Italian-Americans.

"Our wonderful heritage has been plagued for years by unfair and unjust smear campaigns."

The consensus amongst most Italian-Americans is that their beloved culture and people has been scorned and criticized with automatic assumptions of gangster and hoodlum connections just because they were Italians. But, in the case of ethnicity stereotyping, most Italians are realists. They know deep down inside that they could have fared a helluva lot worse than the general public's perception of them, which were mainly Hollywood glamorized movie renditions.

The government was right about Domenico's union. It was unfamiliar territory to them. Even though he was formally ousted, Sally Boy continued to call the shots, albeit behind closed doors. Labor agents knew it, but they had no physical proof. Domenico's undercover operation to maintain control of his union was nothing less than stupendous. Sally Boy received information and gave instructions thanks to a network of close friends and associates who were more than happy to help the guy who helped them and their families. Domenico loyalists were leaping at an opportunity to be a part of it all. They had no problem delivering or receiving a secret message or two on behalf of Salvatore.

Labor officials patted themselves on the back for successfully removing a heavy Outfit player like Domenico from holding union office. They realized they made it more challenging for the Mob to operate its daily labor affairs without Sally Boy as that local's president. They also knew their efforts were just a mere bump in the road until election time, so their genius plan was to make a bunch of grandiose promises to a small group of dissident union members they felt they could control and convince to run for office. Those poor bastards were hypnotized by government trustees into thinking they would be the knights in shining armor that came to the union's rescue by cleaning up the Mob-blemish of organized crime in their local.

Since most of the union's membership was comprised of guys that worked at SouthWater Market and Gino's Warehouse thanks to Sally Boy, you didn't need to be a rocket scientist to figure out how they were going to vote. The government loaded its campaign with lies, gossip, and propaganda. There was also a mystery mass-mailing to all eligible union voters with a copy of the Organized Crime Task Force's Chicago Outfit Chart enclosed. Salvatore "Sally Boy" Domenico's name was clearly listed. The anonymous mailing, which was obviously orchestrated by G trustees, didn't affect the members as they had hoped.

The "Simon Slate" emerged victorious. It was headed by newly elected president, Tim Simon, a 20-year union steward from Gino's Warehouse. Simon, as well as the entire group of elected officers, were Salvatore's guys. The Labor Department was officially served a bitch-slap in the face. Shortly after the new leadership was sworn in, the government-appointed trustees had enough and quietly walked away. They promised the few supportive union members they had that they'd keep a close eye on all union and fund activities. The appointed trustees and labor investigators knew it was no mere coincidence that the election they just personally oversaw and supervised was won fair and square by a group of longtime Salvatore Domenico supporters.

Members of other locals did not fare as well as those in Salvatore's union did. Once the key players within those Mob-influenced labor organizations were removed, they lost the Outfit juice and leverage previously held over employers. Also, the number of official written complaints filed by members soared. Stacks of grievances were placed on back-burners to be sorted out at an undetermined date. The yearly increases in wages and benefits agreed to in their current labor agreements were all ordered frozen. Company owners were no longer intimidated once the government became involved. They took advantage of the unions' confusing times by manipulating their existing collective bargaining agreements during contract time. The hidden truth was that some had long, personal ties to organized crime members and union representatives with Syndicate connections. For years, almost everything the union asked for during contract negotiations was agreed to. Longtime business owners knew it was in their best interest to agree with what the Mob-affiliated labor locals asked them to do, and they were right, it was.

Now, with government involvement, those old-school winks, handshakes, and envelope-exchanging ways of doing business in the past were disappearing. Also becoming invisible were the side deals between union hierarchy, the Mob, and company representatives, especially when special concessions, favors, and accommodations were needed under the radar.

Some advanced-aged business owners decided it was time to retire. They sold to larger companies while others turned the reins over to their sons, daughters, or relatives. The new owners took every advantage they could of the weaker, troubled locals they had contracts with. The relatives involved in those family-operated businesses couldn't wait to take over. For years they watched family elders easily succumb to union demands. This new breed of owners wanted the bargaining table tilted in their favor for once. At the very top of their list was freezing, reducing, or totally doing away with the costly employer contributions previously agreed to in prior contracts. Every bargaining agreement was scrutinized, article by article, line by line, word, by word. The previous pro-worker language used in past contracts to strengthen union positions was changed and sometimes even omitted in new labor agreements. It was no surprise that those changes mostly favored the employer. Gone were the healthy pay raises and annual increases that members enjoyed in the past. To pour salt on union member wounds, the government placed incompetent, inexperienced 'yes-men' into temporary leadership positions until court-supervised elections could be held. By that time, it was too late for the weaker locals. The damage was already done. Rank and file guys, who just weeks before were loading boxes and driving trucks, all of a sudden found themselves thrust into union leadership roles operating under the strict guidelines of labor trusteeship The newly installed officers couldn't care less. As long as they sat comfortably in cushy positions, they didn't think twice about selling out their union brothers under the government's direction.

The trusteeships were brutally tough on smaller, cash-strapped independent locals due to the cost of substantial mounting outside legal fees. Money-hungry, unethical attorneys specializing in labor law were lined up around the block pitching their firms. They offered help with contract negotiations, labor board grievances, and side addendum drafting. Their incentive was billable hours charged to the union, and if they were lucky enough, to the health, welfare, and pension funds, which contained large amounts of money. Of course, the government turned a blind eye to all of that, secretly hoping those locals would eventually dissolve.

Honest hard-working union members across the country were in jeopardy of facing future wage and benefit reductions, or worse. They were just regular guys like Tony, the dock worker, Ronnie, the truck driver, and Jimmy, the warehouseman. Dozens of labor branches with smaller memberships eventually succumbed to the pressure of remaining unionized. The results were workers voting the unions out, which meant bankruptcy and disbandment of those locals.

A total of seventy-six Italians with questionable Mob-ties working for labor organizations throughout the country were removed thanks to the government. Also, thanks to the government, more than 6,700 longtime union members lost their collective bargaining strength; and, in some cases, their livelihoods.

CHAPTER 14
THE DECADE OF DEATH

The 1960s were a whirlwind of wealth, happiness, and new opportunities for Tommy, Nicky, and their families. But, just like it was for the Mob and the unions, the first half of the 1970s was an entirely different story. Their family was personally spending way too much time at hospitals, funeral parlors, cemeteries, mausoleums, and crematoriums. By 1978, death hit them hard, and it wasn't all due to human loss.

Zeus Von Liebrecht
Aka "Zeus"
1960-1970

Zeus was Victor's present on his 4th birthday. Nicky purchased him from a breeder of German Shepherd police dogs thanks to newly appointed Chicago Police Captain Ned Devane. Zeus's lineage traced back almost 20 years, and he did not come cheap. He cost Nicky $1500 and another $1000 to properly train. Tommy got a kick out of Zeus's full name and the four pages of pedigree documentation that came with him.

"That dog has more legal papers than I did when Ma and Pa sponsored me," he often joked.

Zeus was intelligent, loyal, and explicitly trained by award-winner Clifford Claudia at his exclusive kennel, German Shepherds Only. Pa DaBone was ecstatic when he heard Zeus would also be taught simple commands in Italian. From the first day that little bundle of fur arrived in the DaBone home almost a decade earlier, Zeus Von Liebrecht established himself as more than just a pet and home protector. He was family.

A couple of hours before the vet put him out of his misery using a lethal injection of pentobarbital, the euthanasia medication, the usually robust Shepherd was found by Pa, whimpering in the corner of the backyard, urinating blood, eventually collapsing from weakness. Those beautiful ears that stood at attention since he was just a pup were floppy and limp. First, Pa called Nicky at the Shop and told him what was happening. Then, because it was cold outside, he got a blanket from the garage to cover Zeus. Nicky arrived within 10 minutes. He opened the alley door just as Victor walked down the back steps.

"Hey, Dad, what are you doing home already?" Victor asked.

Their eyes simultaneously met, and then they turned to Grandpa Joe as he knelt next to Zeus. Nicky slowly walked over to Joe and Zeus. He knelt beside them. Victor was mortified.

"Dad, what's wrong with Zeus? Grandpa, what happened?"

Zeus struggled to lift his head. The tail that always wagged with the ferocity of an airplane propeller did not move. Nicky petted Zeus's head while Victor stared at the blood and urine-soaked blanket. Nicky knew right away that whatever was wrong with Zeus was life-threatening.

"Vic, open the alley door. Pa, help me lift him. We'll carry him over to the car."

"Dad is Zeus dying?" asked Victor as he opened the alley door.

Zeus's body was limp, his eyes lightly fluttered but did not open, and he moaned and whimpered from discomfort and pain.

"Victor, sit in the back with him. Pa, tell Grace and Ma what's going on. Call Tommy and Teresa too, please," Nicky asked.

Tears streamed from Victor's face. He held Zeus in arms and moaned right along with him as they sat in the back of Nicky's car, racing to the veterinarian.

Nicky was gulping and staring at them through his rearview mirror. He could barely get the words out.

"Talk to him, Victor. Tell him what a good boy he is."

Nicky thought about the hundreds of pictures taken of them over the years. So incredibly wonderful was the photo of Victor holding Zeus for the very first time as the 4-week old pup lovingly licking his face. That enlarged picture hung proudly on Victor's bedroom wall for the last ten years.

When they arrived at the vet, Nicky carried Zeus inside Dr. Wolf's office alone, fearing the worst. He instructed Victor to wait in the car. Victor kissed Zeus's head, told him he loved him and prayed harder than he had ever done before.

"God, please save Zeus. I won't swear anymore. Honest, I won't."

According to Dr. Alvin Wolf, Zeus was suffering from internal bleeding caused by the swelling of his internal organs, which were deteriorating and failing rapidly. Dr. Wolf told Nicky that it appeared Zeus had ingested poison, more than likely the quick-acting concentrated mixture used by professional exterminators to kill rats specifically. He also explained that Zeus had the same symptoms as other dogs that ate the mini-bags of poison.

"The Streets and Sanitation workers throw those bags in alleys, gangways, and garages to help with the rodent infestation. But, unfortunately, the mixture is lethal."

Nicky walked out of the vet's office about thirty minutes later. Victor saw him through the passenger's side-view mirror carrying Zeus's collar and leash. Nicky paused for a few seconds, leaning against the building, his hands cupped over his head. When he got to the car, he opened the door, large tears streaming down his face. Victor cried as Nicky consoled him. They were both devastated.

"The only thing we could do for Zeus is to put him out of his pain. I'm sorry," Nicky explained to his grieving young son."

The car ride back to Fillmore Street was quiet. Victor clutched Zeus's collar, leash, and dog tags tightly in his hands for the whole ride back home. When they arrived, the entire family was there. Mari, Teresa, and Grace were in the kitchen, crying as they cooked. Joe sat in his red leather chair and blew his nose into his red and white polka-dotted handkerchief. Tommy nervously paced back and forth, his face showing concern. Pa was already three glasses deep into his wine. When Nicky explained what Dr. Wolf said about the rat poison, Victor didn't waste any time speaking his mind.

"NO FUCKING WAY! I never saw any poison bags in the alley or by the garbage cans. The city should pay my friends and me for all the rats we shoot."

For the last few years, he and his buddies made sport of the rodents with their high-velocity .22 caliber CO2 pellet rifles, dropping at least a dozen a week. The family agreed. None of them had ever seen mini poison bags either. That night, Victor took the framed picture of him and his pet down from the bedroom wall and fell asleep with it in his arms. He dreamt of Zeus.

Two weeks later, the Sepe family dog, Major, a stout and sturdy bulldog, suddenly died. Their vet also told them it appeared to be from poisoning. Nicky and Tommy questioned the Streets and Sanitation guys about it. They confirmed they did not use the poison on that specific route, probably partly thanks to Victor and his crew of sharp-shooters.

Nicky was unhappy when Victor told him what happened a few days after Major died.

"Dad, I saw those two black guys with the matching nylon caps in the lot today. They walked a lot closer to our back fence than they used to. It's almost like they knew they didn't have to worry about Zeus anymore. I watched them and heard what they said through the screen door. They were laughing and barking like dogs. Then they grabbed their throats as if they were choking. That really pissed me off."

Nicky had seen those same guys cut through the empty lot before. They always kept their distance from the backyard, especially when Zeus was on patrol. He also remembered seeing them at The Patio hot dog stand on more than a few occasions. That's when Nicky remembered the torn and shredded Patio bags he found in the yard. At first, he didn't give it a second thought, figuring they were blown in by the wind. But, two plus two was adding up. So Nicky asked Frank and Mary Lou Sepe if they also found bags from the Patio in their yard. They did, as recently as the very day their dog Major died. Nicky's first call was to Tommy

"Tee, I bet those two no good, mudda fuckers sprinkled rat poison on Patio food, then tossed them in our yard, AND in Sepe's."

Since the two guys were black, more than likely lived in one of the Roosevelt Road neighborhoods and often went to the Patio, Tommy knew who to ask.

"Nick, JuJu is stopping here tomorrow. Let me run this by him. We'll see if he could find anything out on his end about these guys."

When JuJu and Tommy met, Tommy explained what had happened. JuJu felt horrible, expressing his sympathy and shaking his head.

"That's a fucking shame. Lucius and I talked about that dog and those commands in EYE-TALIAN all the time. Let me see what I could find out."

A few short hours after their meeting, JuJu called Tommy. Nicky's assessment of what he thought happened was correct. JuJu explained to Tommy that the two black guys were identical brothers, Levon and Donald Hayes. Everyone in the projects knew them as "The Heroin Twins." JuJu also told Tommy the Hayes brothers rode the horse real hard and that they had both been hooked on 'H' since they were 15 years old.

"Tommy, they're full-blown junkies. So was their old man. He left home when they were just babies. And their momma? She's a dick-suckin', pussy sellin' whore," JuJu explained. "My people tell me that lately they've been bragging about killing Greaseball dogs."

The next shot of smack the brothers shared was their last. They were way too strung out to notice the balloon of heroin they had purchased was slightly different in color than usual. (When junkies have an itch for a fix, it's all about how quickly they can 'cook up' and mainline than it is about how it looks.)

Levon and Donald Hayes were found side-by-side in the basement of an abandoned building off of Roosevelt Road and Laramie Avenue. The photographs taken at the crime scene captured the brothers in a less than flattering setting. Although they died wearing their signature nylon caps, their close-ups were not worthy of a Cecil B. DeMille film. Dried blood had caked around their noses, mouths, eyes, and ears. A little bit of powder was found on Levon's lap, and a syringe was still sticking out of Donald's right arm. Their blood toxicology reports were identical to the chemical analysis in the heroin balloon. The Cook County Coroner's Office documented the official cause of their deaths as injections of heroin tainted with rat poison.

JuJu refused a stack of cash from Nicky and Tommy for his help. His explanation was simple.

"They got what they got!"

Nicky and Tommy also sent their former neighbor, Cooches, a thick envelope and a large Peter Rubi for his help. It was Cooches that coordinated the sale of the contaminated heroin to the Hughes brothers. He was angered as hell when he heard what they did to the puppies he fondly remembered from Fillmore Street. Cooches also returned the cash, but he kept the Peter Rubi.

Giuseppe Victorio Maximo DaBone
Aka "Pa," "Joe," "Grandpa DaBone"
1900-1970

When Joe DaBone was admitted into the hospital for severe stomach pain, he didn't cooperate with doctors, nurses, and medical staff. Instead, he fought them tooth and nail every step of the way, whether it was answering questions, getting his temperature taken, drawing blood, sitting still for x-rays, or supplying urine and stool samples.

Thanks to Doc Brown, the head of St. Luke's Hospital, the doctors assigned to care for Joe were the finest the city had to offer. But, unfortunately, the diagnosis they came up with was a bleeding ulcer and cancerous, inoperative tumors in Joe's colon and stomach. When Doc. Brown sat down with the family in the conference room, he was sympathetic but did not pull any punches.

"There are no medicines or surgeries to save Joe. I'm so very sorry. The only thing I can offer is an intravenous drip of morphine to help make him comfortable. I'm certain those tumors are painful, but Joe told me he was fine. The x-rays and blood work say differently."

Mari was shocked, barely able to choke out her words.

"Last month, we're dancing at our 50th wedding anniversary party, and now he's dying?"

Mari questioned Tommy and Teresa in Italian, hoping she misunderstood the news. Sadly, the Italian answers they gave her were the same in English. The evening before he passed away, Tommy called the entire DaBone family and asked them to come to Joe and Mari's house. Ma sat in Pa's red leather chair for the first time ever. She was visibly shaken and barely able to look at everyone straight in their eyes. Her smiling face was nowhere to be found. All of Joe's brothers, their wives, and their children were there. Tommy explained that Pa's condition was critical. Uncle Jimmy took the news the hardest. He confessed to everyone that a few weeks earlier, Joe told him he wasn't feeling good and made him swear not to say a word to anyone. Tommy saw the pain in Jimmy's face when he admitted this.

"Uncle Jimmy, it wouldn't have mattered. The doctors said the tumors were there for a while. Pa was probably bleeding on the inside for months. We all know how proud he is, so there's no telling how long he's been feeling sick," Tommy explained, attempting to comfort Uncle Jimmy. "If you would've said something to us when he told you we'd still all be sitting here tonight.

Victor and his second and third-generation DaBone cousins stood listening to their Uncle Tommy in the kitchen hallway. In the past, when the kids gathered together at Joe and Mari's home for family gatherings, it was reckless abandon. They usually ran up and down the back stairs, in and out of the house, or played hide-n-seek in the backyard. But, on this visit, none of them ran, jumped, or effortlessly laughed. The youngest, like Celeste, Joe-Boy, Margaret Mary, and the twins, Mia and Santina, weren't old enough to totally understand what was happening. But, based on their parents, grandparents, aunts, uncles, and older cousins' demeanor, they knew it was something terrible about Grandpa Joe.

When Pa died, his wake was held for the usual two days and nights. Just about every person in Little Italy came to pay their respects. The empty parlor at Greemo's Funeral Home was transformed into a food and beverage station to accommodate the hundreds of attendees. Benito and Johnny Greemo were highly flexible with their funeral home's usual stringent rules and regulations regarding the solemnity and conduction of wakes. There were pastries, lunch meat trays, and pizza brought in by Fat Frankie, the Fontanelli Brothers, Snafuro's Bakery, La Joy Grocery Store, and Mitzie's Butcher. Besides relatives, friends, and neighbors in attendance, there was no shortage of Syndicate guys, police, and politicians. That was no surprise, considering how many contacts from all walks of life Tommy and Nicky made.

Of course, agents from the Chicago branch of the Organized Crime Task Force sat in their parked cars, wrote down license plate numbers, and took pictures of everyone walking in and out of the funeral home. Tommy was annoyed by that but didn't take it personally. He knew they were just doing their job. In the long run, it really didn't matter. It was all about people making time to pay their respects to a hardworking, family man who was a neighborhood fixture for the last 50 years.

On the second day of the wake, Victor sat with his cousin, Anthony Simonetti. Anthony's mother, Pauline, was one of Grace's sisters. He and Victor were always very close, not only just in age. Victor was two months to the day older. Anthony's father, Richard "Dicky" Simonetti, was doing a 10-year stint in Joliet State for money laundering. Added to his sentence were six individual counts of contempt which was a Cook County court record! When he was arrested, Dicky took his pinch like a man. He could've turned over on quite a few people knowing what he knew about dirty Mob money washed clean. But, instead of some high-end people getting jammed up, they remained free. Dicky kept the damaging information and incriminating evidence all to himself.

Victor and Anthony were huddled together on one of the uncomfortable funeral parlor couches.

"Grandpa Joe has big turnout, huh, Victor?"

"He sure does, Ant."

As the two cousins sat uncharacteristically quiet, a sudden hush came over the room. Clearing the path for Manny was Vinnie Champagne. Those waiting in line to offer their condolence gladly moved to the side. Vinnie supported Manny's underarm when he went to kneel down at the casket. Manny looked at Joe, got up, and made the sign of the cross. Then, he reached into the coffin, making sure not to disturb the authentic ivory rosary beads that were meticulously intertwined through Joe's fingers. Manny put his right hand on Joe's folded hands.

"Rilassati, mi amico mio. Spero di giocare presto a bocce con te. Dio ti benedica, Giuseppe." (Rest easy, my friend. I hope to play bocce ball with you soon. God bless you, Giuseppe.)

Manny slowly got up from the kneeler. He wondered if deliberately keeping his Bari friend at a distance for so many years was worthwhile. Manny knew the G would have bothered Joe for sure if they openly associated. Mari physically struggled as she tried to stand to greet him. He motioned for her to stay seated and instead sat next to her. Manny took Mari's hand, kissed it, and then put his arm around her while he kissed her cheek.

"Ora hai il tuo angelo in paradisio per vegliare su di te, Mari." (You have your angel in heaven to watch over you now, Mari.)

Mari nodded as she and Manny held hands. The entire family gathered around them and watched. Some sniffed, others wiped their tearful eyes. Vinnie helped him stand as all of Joe's brothers, wives, and children came up and kissed Manny on the cheek. Uncle Jimmy embraced him, weeping on his shoulder.

"Ti ha amato e rispettato, Manny," (He loved and respected you, Manny.)

"Avrei dovuto essere un amico migliore per lui. Giuseppe era un uomo da uomo, Jimmy." (I should have been a better friend to him. Giuseppe was a man's man, Jimmy.)

Nicky motioned to Victor to come over by them.

"Vic, you get to meet Mr. E.!" Anthony excitedly said.

When Victor walked to where his family stood, Nicky put his

arm around him.

"Say hello to Mr. Ingalleretta, Victor."

"I'm very sorry about your grandfather, Victor. He and I knew each other since we were young boys, probably even younger than you are now," Manny said.

Victor answered innocently and respectfully.

"Wow, that's a real long time ago."

Manny smiled.

Victor knew Manny was important. Based on his private Outfit puzzle, Ingalleretta was the largest piece.

"Yes, a very long time. What a handsome young man you are, Victor." Manny complimented.

"I take after Grandpa," Victor quickly answered.

Manny patted Victor on the cheek. Nicky nodded in approval and pointed back to the couch.

"You can go back by Anthony now."

Manny leaned in close to Nicky.

"When Tommy gets done talking with Father Geno, I want both of you to meet me in the washroom."

Vinnie walked with Manny to the restroom, and Nicky made his way to Father Geno and Tommy. After Nicky whispered into his ear, Tommy excused himself. He and Nicky walked to the rear of the parlor, where Vinnie stood guard in front of the men's room.

"He's waiting for you guys," Champagne instructed.

Tommy and Nicky opened the men's room door and found Manny sitting on the small chair near the sink. He was wiping his eyes with a handkerchief. Manny had been crying. He looked up at Tommy and Nicky after blowing his nose.

"Your father was a beautiful man, and I loved him. That's all I'm going to say about that."

Manny attempted to change his somber, regretful tone.

"Nicky, did Tommy tell you the story about how Joe used to follow me everywhere I went when we were children in Bari?"

"Yea, he did," Nicky answered.

"Joe used to call me, Mannuci. I always liked that," Manny shared.

Then, he reached inside his coat pocket, pulled out an envelope, and handed it to Tommy.

"This is for Mari. I didn't want to hand it to either of you where people could see. You never know who the fuck is watching. I saw those G cocksuckers outside taking pictures. I really don't give a shit anymore. I think Vinnie stood in front of me and pretty much blocked them from seeing me."

"Vinnie's big enough to block the sun, Manny," Nicky joked.

"Yea, he could," Manny responded. "I'm not gonna be around forever. I get tired really easily, and I'm starting to forget shit. Important shit, too. My body and mind don't agree with each other anymore. Anyway, listen. You two are good boys. Nicky, I always want you to listen to Tommy. Do you understand me?"

"Sure, I always do, Manny," Nicky agreed. "See, look?"

Nicky put his arm around Tommy and kissed him.

"Stop, ya fucking finocchio!" (Rhymes with Pinocchio. Homosexual slang)

Tommy laughed, pushing Nicky away.

"Maybe I should leave you two alone for a while," Manny said sarcastically as Tommy helped him up off the chair.

When Nicky opened the bathroom door, there was a line of four guys shuffling uncomfortably, patiently waiting to get inside the restroom. When Champagne gave them the nod to go in, the men rushed as if they were going to soil themselves.

"Remember, whatever Mari needs," Manny instructed Tommy and Nicky as he walked down the hallway.

"Thank you," they answered.

As they watched Manny and Vinnie walk out, Nicky nudged Tommy as tilted his head toward the parlor with all the food. There was Fat Roberta, hovering over the pastries, cakes, and pies, talking loudly and pointing to the vast assortment of sweets her and her 90-year-old grandfather, Jacco Snafuro, brought from their bakery. Roberta's mother, Vincenza, died a year earlier. It was apparent Roberta was picking up right where her mother left off as the keeper of the sweet table.

"I'm surprised Pa isn't getting up from the casket to kick her in her fat ass," Nicky commented to Tommy.

"I was just gonna say how proud I was of you. We're in day two of the wake, and you still hadn't said anything inappropriate," replied Tommy.

"Pa would've laughed at that, right? Nicky sadly asked.

Tommy put his arm around him.

"Yea, pal. He definitely would've."

"Guys, Michael Tunzi and Alderman Cosentino are in line, Cooches and JuJu just walked in, and Fazool told me he saw Mayor Daley's car pull up in front," Teresa said as she walked up to them.

"Nicky, you go talk to Cooches and JuJu, and I'll go by Tunzi and Cosentino," Tommy coordinated.

"What about the Mayor?" Teresa asked.

"Tree, you and Grace greet him. Then, maybe grab Victor and Anthony. They'll get a kick out of meeting him," Tommy suggested.

As they split up to go to their designated greeting assignments, Tommy took a minute to collect his thoughts.

"We have all our family, a top Chicago Mob boss and shot callers for two of the biggest gangs in the city. Standing a few feet away from them are decorated cops and detectives, an alderman, and the fucking mayor of Chicago! The Bishop and the Cardinal stopped by earlier. They even blessed some of the Outfit guys! Everyone from the neighborhood and beyond showed up to honor you, Pa."

On the day of Joe's funeral, there were five flower cars and over 300 vehicles in the funeral procession. Grandma Mari asked Nicky and Grace if it was okay for Victor to be a pallbearer since he was the only grandchild. They were honored and thought it was a great idea. When the time came to carry the casket, Victor joined his grandfather's four brothers and Fat Frankie. The slow ride from the funeral home to Our Lady of the Shroud Church for the mass, the drive past the DaBone's house, then to Queen of Heaven Mausoleum, took over two hours. The marble-faced indoor crypt already had a brass plate with Joe's full name, birth, and death dates inscribed on it. Victor thought that was a bit creepy.

The after-service brunch was held at The Flame Restaurant. The place was packed. Everyone dined on a steak-lobster combination and commented on how beautiful the wake arrangements and services were. For the next week, Teresa stayed overnight with Mari to help her transition to being without Joe. Fifty years married and five years before that was how long the two knew each other. Tommy even stayed a few nights as well. Family and friends came to the house every day. When Teresa left after the seven days passed, Mari walked into every room of her home and reminisced. What was especially difficult for her was looking at the indentations left on Pa's red leather recliner. Nicky, Grace, and Victor still lived upstairs, but when the love of your life for so many years dies, the loss is insurmountable. Every evening, Mari looked at all the pictures of Joe that hung in the house. She made the sign of the cross and said a prayer at each one. When done, she sat Joe's recliner, pulled out his red polka-dotted handkerchief, wept, and begged.

"Dear God, please give me the strength to get through this until I can be with my Giuseppe again."

1352 West Fillmore Street
1858-1970

The day Nicky, Grace, Victor, and Grandma Mari officially moved to west suburban Upper Cove should've been a happy occasion. It wasn't. The relocation to the suburbs was caped in more than one veil of sorrow. Mari cried on and off the entire day. Much of the DaBone's furniture was given away to relatives, neighbors, and friends, except a few pieces that were either newer or held sentimental value, like Pa's red leather recliner.

As the moving truck filled, Nicky gave longtime neighbor Bob Chinetti the keys, explaining that Micky Silvio would be by the next day to pick up the few remaining boxes in the basement. Victor was the last one to physically walk out of the house. He rode in Nicky's pickup truck with Willie from the Shop. As they headed to the Eisenhower Expressway north on Loomis Street, Victor saw some of his friends on the stoop in front of Phyllis's house. He asked Willie to stop for just a few minutes. Victor got out, walked over, and hugged and kissed them all.

"Oh, well, no Maria DiNapoli, I guess," he sadly thought.

As he climbed back into the truck, Willie saw the sadness in Victor's eyes.

"You gonna be alright, Baby Sweet," Willie said, attempting to console him.

Upper Cove was only 45 minutes away from the neighborhood. Victor felt it was more like the other side of the universe. It wasn't easy leaving his friends, especially the summer before his final year in grade school. The timing couldn't have been worse. For seven years, he waited to be an 8th grader at Our Lady of the

Shroud. Instead, he would be the new kid at Saint Vincent.

The phone call Nicky received from Bob Chinetti the day after the move was unpleasant. Bob explained scavengers had broken into the Fillmore Street house overnight and ripped out all copper and metal piping. Bob didn't recognize any of the pillagers but told Nicky they went through the entire house, poking holes in the walls. (It was common practice for old-timers to secure their valuables inside the walls of their homes.) Nicky left the Shop and met Chinetti in the alley. The first words out of his mouth were filled with disgust.

"Bob, you gotta be fucking kidding me!"

The scavengers had all but gutted the house. Four guys were struggling to carry the two bathtubs through the narrow gangway. The backyard wall to the basement was smashed, and most of the windows and their framing were extracted. The few remaining packed boxes temporarily stored inside the basement were long gone. Victor's comic book collection was in one of them.

"Nicky, I'm sorry. These fuckers came like thieves in the night," Chinetti explained.

"Fuck 'em, Bobby," Nicky answered. "It's all gonna get knocked down anyway."

When Nicky got back to the Shop, he called Grace, Teresa, and Tommy. When he explained what happened, Tommy was initially pissed, but he knew what was done was done. They all agreed it was best to say nothing to Mari. When Nicky got home that night, he broke the bad news to Victor.

"All my comic books and magazines, they're all gone?" Victor asked.

"I'm sorry, Victor," Nicky apologetically answered.

Victor couldn't believe the horrible news about his collection. All he could think about were the thousands of hours he and his friends spent reading, acting out, and dressing up, pretending to be the Super Hero characters of Superboy, Mon-El, Lightning Lad, Brainiac 5, and Ultra Boy. Those books played a ginormous part in his youth.

Nicky walked into Victor's new bedroom. It was twice the size of the one he had on Fillmore Street. He found his son blankly staring at the ceiling.

"Vic, can I buy you new books, or can we try and find copies of the older books? Tell me what you want me to do."

He answered his father but did not look at him.

"I don't want you to do anything, Dad. It was kid shit, anyway. They're gone, and that's that."

Later that night, Victor thought about his Taylor Street friends as he unpacked. When he came across his seventh-grade class photograph, he studied the individual squares, especially the girls, particularly Maria DiNapoli's. He wondered if any of them would think about him. Victor remembered the kids who moved away in third and fourth grade and how they were relegated as distant memories by him and his friends. He felt he was also headed in that forgotten direction. When he got to the last box, Victor saw the diary that Sister Christine insisted they keep. As he flipped through it, reading words from what felt like an eternity ago, he felt eased and amused. From that night forward, Victor wrote every single day.

Sometimes, only a few sentences, other times, a dozen pages and more. What he chose to write about ran the gamut.

It only took two days in his new home before the kids in Victor's subdivision came over to introduce themselves. In the days and weeks that followed, they included him in their bike rides, trips to the park, and get-togethers at The Tivoli Theater. But as accepting as they all were, they weren't neighborhood kids. Victor made sure to let his mother know that every chance he had. Grace knew the transition was tough on her son. So, in typical DaBone fashion, she encouraged him to be patient.

"Jesus Christ, Victor, you just met these kids! Give them a fucking chance, will ya? Who knows, maybe you'll all become great friends."

Victor doubted that. Instead, he spent most of his free time writing and listening to music. However, there was a girl who did catch his attention. One rainy night, he got together with Colleen Norton, the cute, red-head that lived a few houses away. They both snuck out and met under the secluded protection of neighbor John Majorowski's humungous weeping willow tree. Victor enjoyed that make-out session. It was also his very first-time french kissing. He secretly wished it was Loomis Street Maria DiNapoli instead of Janet Street Colleen Norton, but Maria was a million miles away in Victor's mind. He felt wrong about imagining his tongue darting in and out of her throat instead of Colleen's.

After all, Maria was Victor's first kiss. It lasted only a few seconds in seventh grade while playing Spin-the-Bottle at Fran Nolina's birthday party. However, the memory of Maria's tender lips, how they felt, and how they tasted were forever etched in his memory.

He felt a little better about himself and his fantasizing when he heard the recently released Stephen Stills lead single. It was a track from the artist's debut self-titled studio album, "Love The One You're With." Victor figured he wasn't the only one out there with someone, secretly wishing it was somebody else.

"And if you can't be, with the one you love, honey, love the one you're with! Love the one you're with!"

The day 1352 West Fillmore Street crumbled to the ground, there was a ferocious thunderstorm. Tommy, Nicky, Victor, and Uncle Jimmy sat in Tommy's Cadillac and watched the demolition equipment roll up to the front of their cherished home. Uncle Jimmy couldn't hold back.

"I'm glad Pa's not here to see this," he blurted out. "On top of it all, it had to be Polina Construction that's tearing down the fucking house?"

They watched the giant orange wrecking ball slam through the upstairs kitchen's outside wall. The attached enclosed porch, where Victor and Zeus sometimes took their afternoon nap, collapsed in a pile of roof shingles, bricks, and flooring. The front-loader moved in when the backyard filled with debris and scooped up the rubble. Tommy rolled his window down when Fat Frankie walked up to the car. The umbrella did little to protect his circumference from the rain.

"I'm so sorry, guys. This hurts me, too. I've spent as much time in that house as I have in my own," Frankie said, barely squeezing into the back seat.

He reached inside his coat pocket and pulled out some small glasses, along with his last bottle of Pa's wine. Frankie handed them off to Tommy and poured generous portions into each glass. Thirteen-year-old Victor also had a couple of sips.

"I was saving this bottle for a happy occasion, but I thought we could all use it today," Frankie sadly admitted.

As Nicky put the glass to his lips, Uncle Jimmy stopped him. The usually jovial Jimmy DaBone offered some heartfelt words in Italian about his brother.

"Con il miglior uomo che io abbia mai conosciuto, mi fratello Giuseppe. Grazie per aver spiananto la strada per l'America e darci tutte le belle vite. Dio ti benedica e veglia su di noi." (To the best man I will ever know, my brother, Giuseppe. Thank you for paving the way to America and giving us all beautiful lives. God bless you, and watch over us.)

"To Pa," they toasted.

For the next hour they all at in silence and watched 1352 West Fillmore Street disappear.

<u>Emmanuel Angelo Benito Ingalleretta</u>
Aka "Manny," "The Old Man," "Mr. E"
1893-1973

Manny died in his longtime Castle Street home bedroom two days shy of his 80th birthday. Vinnie Champagne told paramedics he found Manny unresponsive with his reading glasses cupped in his hands and a small picture of his deceased wife Lillian laying on the pillow next to him.

Every neighbor within a two-block radius gathered around Manny's house when the ambulance, squad cars, and fire truck arrived. They were crying, making the sign of the cross as Ingalleretta's lifeless body was hoisted into the ambulance. It didn't take long for the television and newspaper outlets to report Manny's passing. Some reporters attempted to get interviews with his Castle Street neighbors, but that proved unsuccessful. No one was willing to speak with them.

Primarily, the journalists focused their attention on his colorful association with the Chicago Syndicate. Their reports, columns, and comments were loaded with explosive verbs and overly-descriptive adjectives, documenting Manny's beginning as an Al Capone gopher throughout his reign as one of the Chicago Outfit's most prominent leaders.

Manny's death was big news. Channel 5's crime reporter, Sid Golden, used old news clips from the Racketeering Hearings. Tommy was pissed when the Ingalleretta footage they used was Manny saying how he owed his life to him. Golden ended his report with a commentary.

"There is lots of speculation in Mob circles about who will fill Ingalleretta's position. Will it be split between Primo Montalbano, Joey Balducci, and Jimmy Rio? Or, will the Mob turn over day-to-day Chicago

Near West Side operations to the banished ex-union chieftain and politically connected Taylor Street native Salvatore 'Sally Boy' Domenico? Mob insiders said they wouldn't be surprised if the Bosses gave a huge bump-up to alleged Outfit soldier and Ingalleretta-trusted neighborhood protégé, Tommy LaCosta. LaCosta is a banana company owner from SouthWater Market. As shown in the court testimony video we just aired, he supposedly saved Ingalleretta's life in what we found out later was a failed robbery attempt from years ago. More to come on who Chicago Mob Bosses will pick to fill the void left by Outfit legend Emmanuel 'Manny' Ingalleretta."

"THIS ROTTEN MUDDA FUCKER!" Tommy yelled as he and Nicky watched the noon replay of the news.

"That's lots of heat for you, pal," Nicky added. "What can I do to help?"

Tommy didn't immediately respond. Instead, he continued eating his prime rib eye sandwich from Mr. Lucky's. Nicky let him chew in peace. That lasted about a minute.

"What are you gonna do, Tee? Did you hear from Lenny or anyone yet?"

"Not yet. Nick, do me a favor. Get Mike Kampapas on the phone."

Less than five minutes into their conversation, Kampapas explained to Tommy there was nothing he could do in the way of filing a defamation of character charge about mentioning his name on television. Instead, Tommy learned a law lesson from his attorney-soon-to-be-judge friend. The word "alleged" carried a shit-ton of weight when used correctly. As a result, there was no legal recourse against Channel 5 or Sid Golden.

Manny's wake was a "Who's Who" of attendees. Vinnie and Lenny handled the arrangements. Manny's only living relative was a non-English speaking 90-year-old distant cousin from Rome whom he hadn't seen or spoken to in many years. The G got ballsy making their presence known. Agents openly walked the sidewalks and streets which surrounded the chapel instead of using the camouflage of their unmarked cars and vans. They strolled right up to mourners, taking videos and pictures of them, just as the news outlet cameras were doing. However, when a few of the guys from the Grand Avenue Crew walked into the funeral home, they told agents and press reporters they should go fuck themselves. That type of unwanted publicity and law enforcement attention were among the reasons Lenny and Vinnie decided to wake Manny for only one day.

It was almost 11:00 p.m. when the last group of people left Ingalleretta's viewing. Earlier in the evening, Lenny asked Tommy and Salvatore Domenico to join him at the end of the wake in the funeral home office of owner Benito Greemo. Lenny sat behind Greemo's desk and spoke quietly as he usually did. But, this time, there was no problem hearing him within the dead silence of a funeral home.

"This comes from "The Three," he began.

Domenico and Tommy knew Lenny meant Montalbano, Balducci, and Rio, the three remaining Bosses of the Chicago Outfit.

"Salvatore is Underboss, and Manny's territory is his. Sally Boy, that means everything, on top of all of the union business you've been doing since Jesus was a carpenter's apprentice. Tommy, they also said that you've been a great earner for years. It's always smooth sailing and big profits when you're involved. You'll be Salvatore's Top Lieutenant. All the envelopes that went to Manny will now go to Sally Boy. Also, Tommy, you handle SouthWater Market and the cartage companies. Salvatore handles Little Italy. Any new business, or problems with old business, gets filtered through Tommy. Sally, any territorial disputes between Crews or scores over 50K, those get sent up the ladder to you. Let's plan to l meet a few times in the next week for all the specifics. Needless to say, this would've been a unanimous decision, but I'm sure you know who complained."

Tommy and Sally Boy knew Lenny meant Primo Montalbano. Apparently, Montalbano's extreme jealousy of Manny didn't end because he was dead. Primo wanted every loose crumb Manny supplied to the Outfit's table swept onto his personal plate. Balducci and Rio adamantly disagreed and ruled otherwise.

"That's it, boys. Buona Fortuna," (Good fortune.) Lenny concluded as they hugged and kissed each other on the cheek.

Sally Boy needed to familiarize himself with Manny's responsibilities. There were more than a handful of things he needed to know about in a hurry. And who better to help him with that than his new Lieutenant and Little Italy friend Tommy.

"Tommy, I'll reach for you after the funeral. Does that work for you?" Domenico asked.

Tommy also wanted to hit the ground running.

"Sounds good, Salvatore. I'll talk to ya then."

Tommy looked forward to working with Domenico. He thought Salvatore had a lot of good traits, was intelligent, fair, and didn't have a giant ego to feed. Tommy also felt the two of them had similar work ethics. They both liked to get shit done quietly without fanfare or loose ends.

It didn't take long for the word to get out in the neighborhood about the change in Syndicate personnel. Nicky was as proud as could be about his brother-in-law's elevated Mob status, and he let him know about it.

"You just keep breaking records, don't ya, Tee?"

"What records?" Tommy asked.

"Are you too fucking important now to remember your first, as the youngest guy to work full-time at SouthWater, or your second, as a forklift driver? From what I've heard from a couple of the guys, you're now the youngest 'Outfit-official' Lieutenant the Mob ever had!" Tommy shrugged his shoulders.

"I should've left well-enough alone and stayed working at Lanzatorri, tossing loads of cabbage and driving the fucking forklift. Instead, this is gonna lead to lots of babysitting, jealous jagoffs starting shit, and me doing a ton of favors I wouldn't normally do.

Nicky opened his arms wide, hugged Tommy, and then proceeded to break his balls.

"Tommy, I have just one question. Do I have to kiss your ring?"

While they hugged, Nicky grabbed Tommy's ass. At first, Tommy struggled to break his grasp, but he quickly gave in, letting Nicky have his fun.

"You get a pass on the ass-grabbin' just this once. But, you still have to kiss my ring!"

When Nicky reached for Tommy's ring hand to oblige, the youngest Lieutenant in Chicago Mob history playfully slapped his adoring brother-in-law.

"Fuckin' around time is over, pal. There's work to do."

The dozen legal businesses Manny controlled were split up amongst the Bosses. The companies operated as they usually did, but now percentages were spelled out in black and white, so there wouldn't be any future confusion. Montalbano, Rio, and Balducci were insulated by go-betweens that acted as company owners and shareholders. This epic whirlwind of paperwork and addendums covering the asses of everyone took five lawyers to compose. The legality of Manny's last will and testament was simply spelled out. His $25,000 life insurance payout went to his estranged Italian cousin, $20,000 in his savings account was willed to Our Lady of the Shroud Church, and the ownership of his house in Oakbay went to Lenny. Manny's longtime Castle Street residence was left to Vinnie Champagne.

When Manny received his brain cancer diagnosis, he confided in Vinnie, giving him explicit instructions on what to do when the time came. Vinnie initially questioned Manny's immense generosity, but when Manny glared at him, Vinnie went silent. He knew Manny's stare, so he stopped talking and thanked him. There was also something else Manny instructed Vinnie to do for him. The last request involved Tommy and Lenny.

A week after Manny died, Vinnie asked both men to meet him at the Castle Street house. As they walked downstairs to the basement, Lenny commented on the beautiful custom black couch and matching chairs lined against the wall filled with old pictures. In the center was the portrait of Manny's wife, Lillian, on their wedding day. There was also an old Victrola next to the wall with a stack of albums neatly piled inside an ornate wooden case.

"Have a seat, guys," Vinnie instructed them.

Vinnie walked over to the bar. He reached behind it, pulled out three small wine glasses and a bottle of wine. Tommy recognized the bottle right away.

"That's Pa's wine."

"Tommy, all I know is that your father-in-law sent this over a while ago. Manny told me two things - where he was putting it and when he wanted it opened."

"That sounds exactly like our Manny," Lenny added.

Vinnie poured the wine into the three glasses and walked over to the Victrola. He grabbed an album from the stack and turned it on. It was Mario Lanza's "Nessun Dorma." (No Sleep.) Mario Lanza was Manny's favorite singer. In the early 1950's Lanza was gracious enough to appear at a private affair in the old Ambassador Hotel, which, at that time, was secretly owned by Manzie Marco, a longtime Florida Mob Boss. When the song was over, Vinnie got up, carefully put the album into its protective sleeve, and placed it back where he had gotten it from. Next, Vinnie walked to the wall where all the old, black, and white pictures hung. He removed Manny's wife Lillian's beautiful colorized wedding photo and placed

placed it on the table in front of where Tommy and Lenny were sitting. Vinnie also took down the remaining smaller pictures.

"Guys, don't be alarmed by what happens next," Vinnie explained as he laid a moving tarp against the wall and took a deep breath.

Then, Vinnie slammed his fist into the wall twice. Tommy and Lenny were startled. They looked at each other, shuffling uncomfortably in their chairs. Vinnie quickly put his hands up and motioned them to stay seated and remain calm.

"Va tutto bene, non preoccuparti," (Everything is okay, don't worry.) he reassured them.

Vinnie peeled away the remaining small chunks of drywall, reached inside, and pulled out an old metal box the size of a vacation suitcase.

"Come over here, guys," he instructed.

Tommy and Lenny walked over and stood with Vinnie as he opened it. There were three large manila envelopes with each man's name written on them. (It was definitely Manny's handwriting.) Vinnie spoke slowly but authoritatively.

"There's 100 G's in $50 bills in each envelope. Also, in your envelopes, there's a private note from Manny. When you're finished reading it, drop it in this ashtray. Remember what he wrote because he told me to burn them both after reading. The last thing he asked me to do is tell both of you that this $300K is his gift to us for our friendship, honesty, and loyalty to him. This money was never here, and the individual notes never existed. Do you both understand this?"

"Yes," Lenny and Tommy answered.

"Open your envelopes," Vinnie instructed.

Both men did as they were told. Lenny finished first. He shook his head as his eyes welled up with tears. His voice quivered, and he spoke even quieter than usual as he placed his note in the ashtray.

"This was a great man."

It took Tommy extra time to read and then reread Manny's message. Ingalleretta purposely used the Bari-style writing, knowing Tommy was only one of a few to understand its meaning. Tommy was in disbelief, realizing how vital the information was. As far as Vinnie and Lenny were concerned, he appeared poker-faced and emotionless.

Tommy's imagination ran wild.

"This is probably worth more than the entire $300K," he thought.

Tommy apologized for taking so long. When he finished his 2-page note, he placed it with Lenny's in the ashtray.

Vinnie took out his lighter and set the letters on fire. The three men watched the papers curl into small, dancing flames until all that remained were floating cinders.

"I don't know what Manny wrote to each of you, but I know that it meant the world to him that you had it," Vinnie explained as he filled the three wine glasses. "We bid a fond farewell to our Boss, our mentor, and our friend. Grazie di tutto, Manny." (Thank you for everything, Manny.)

As the three men ching-chinged their glasses, they knew they were forever joined at the hip. It's precisely what Manny wanted.

Marietta Francesca Teresa Spaccia DaBone
Aka "Mari" "Ma" "Grammy"
1903-1973

As peaceful as Ma DaBone's death was, it was difficult to watch her slip away. Surrounded by family, Mari closed her eyes, took a couple of labored breaths, and that was it. She was gone. The arrangements for her wake and funeral were first class.

When the services were completed, everyone gathered at Grace and Nicky's home. As they sat in the living room, surprisingly, Tommy openly wept first. Shortly afterward, there wasn't a dry eye in the house.

Teresa Marietta Giuseppina DaBone LaCosta
Aka "Tree," "Bella"
1923-1976

Out of all the deaths, sorrow, losses, and pain the DaBone and LaCosta families endured in the 1970s, Teresa's demise, by far, was the most unexpected, tragic, and devastating, especially for Tommy.

Teresa and Tommy's love for each other was not something you'd read about in some cheap dime store novel. Their bond was immediate and extraordinary from the first day Tommy came to live with the DaBones. The two of them spent many years not succumbing to their romantic desires. Their courtship was handled respectfully and delayed until they were adults. Disrespecting Ma and Pa DaBone was the last thing either of them wanted. Even then, they continued discreetly. Although there were many bumps in their relationship road, Teresa and Tommy maneuvered their path to be together with true love and dignity. There was no denying they were meant for each other.

Tommy never kept Teresa in the dark about his Outfit involvement. She never knew the particulars, just acknowledged how it came to be and accepted it. The details were guarded and elaborately coded for her protection when he shared. Teresa was smart enough to know that if she ever point-blank asked her husband if he ever murdered anybody, he would lie, denying it forever. Tommy knew in his heart that Teresa would never ask him that question. He was right. She never did.

When the call came over the police scanner about a "Level One" (Fatal Traffic Accident) on the Eisenhower Expressway, Detective Tunzi was parked in his unmarked squad. He just completed a 12-hour shift that ended with a successful overnight bust of a mid-sized counterfeiting operation just off of Western Avenue. Tunzi constantly monitored dozens of police calls while on duty, mostly ignoring them unless a need for immediate backup was requested. The police dispatcher on duty reported a semi-trailer carrying a load of steel beams had overturned near the on-ramp of the Eisenhower at Sacramento Avenue that caused another vehicle to flip over. What Tunzi heard next caused him to throw his coffee out the window, attach the red dome-light on the roof of his highly modified, souped-up black Chevy Caprice, turn on his siren, and speed to the accident scene. The police dispatcher reported that the fatality was the secondary driver, a 52-year-old Caucasian female named LaCosta, Teresa M., of Maple Creek. The last thing Tunzi heard was that emergency crews and an ambulance were en route. Tunzi immediately responded to the call.

"I'm 1107 in 5."

That was his badge number and accident arrival time. Tunzi spoke aloud to himself, throwing down his police walkie-talkie and grabbing his squad phone.

"Holy, Jesus Christ!"

Tunzi couldn't remember Tommy's phone number at Big Banana for the life of him. He maneuvered his vehicle onto sidewalks passing car after car until he arrived at the expressway. Then, he slammed his squad into the parked position and continued to go through his briefcase, looking for his personal phone book containing his coded contact list. Sirens blared as two ambulances, three tow trucks, and a front loader with a hoist made their way down the ramp onto the Eisenhower.

Captain Ned Devane arrived a few minutes before Tunzi. He just happened to be having breakfast a Sam Hatchell's Restaurant and heard the call. Devane walked up the ramp to Tunzi's car. Tunzi glanced up for a second as he continued shuffling through folders and papers.

"I can't find Tommy's phone number at Big Banana. Do you know it offhand, Ned?" Tunzi asked.

"Michael, don't call him yet," Devane warned.

"Don't call him? What do you mean, don't call him?"

"Michael, get out and walk down the ramp with me," Devane insisted.

Tunzi got out of his car and walked with him.

"Teresa's dead, right?" Tunzi asked.

"Yea, she is. But, there's more," answered Devane.

"More? Ned, what do you mean by more? What's more than dead?" Tunzi questioned.

As they walked past the crash debris to Teresa's overturned car and the semi-truck on its side, Tunzi noticed a distraught, very pale policeman being attended to by a couple of paramedics. The cop was white as a sheet and looked like he had just seen a ghost.

"What happened to that officer?" asked Tunzi.

"That's Officer Kane. He was the first one on the scene. Michael, I'm trying to tell you that Kane found Teresa's body hanging out of the driver's side door. She was decapitated. Kane found her head about 10 feet away from the car. First, he vomited, now he's incoherent. That's why he's being treated," Devane explained

Tunzi stopped walking. He squatted down, took a few deep breaths attempting to collect himself.

"Ned, we've got to get a hold of Tommy. Where is Teresa's head?"

"The paramedics wrapped it up in a severed limb medical bag and then put it inside a small cooler. They sealed the lid then put it on a stretcher with her body.

The paramedic told me her face was in 'Freeze Shock.'"

"Freeze Shock? What the fuck is that?" Tunzi asked.

"I asked the same question. It's when the deceased's facial expression remains frozen at the exact time of death. I heard Officer Kane telling the paramedics Teresa's two top front teeth were missing, and her mouth and eyes were wide-open, almost unnaturally. He said her eyes were bulging almost out of their sockets, and her face had an expression of intense fear. The ambulance driver told me they already reached out to some nerve doctor at Northwestern Hospital," Devane briefly explained.

"We've got to get a hold of Tommy before someone else does," Tunzi frantically suggested.

Tunzi's plan was to call Fazool Pirelli and meet at St. Luke's Hospital. Fazool was speechless when he heard what had happened to Teresa. Fortunately, he had Tommy's number at Big Banana. He gladly gave it to Tunzi, not wanting to make that call himself. But, as hardened, all-business, and professional as Tunzi was, Fazool was right. This was going to be one tough dial. Tunzi, Fazool, Tommy, and Teresa had been friends since they were teenagers. Anyone from Little Italy could tell you that if you grew up in the neighborhood with someone, it was almost as if you were related to them. So, Tunzi rolled up his car windows and dialed Tommy's number.

"Big Banana, this is Nicky."

"Nicky, it's Tunzi."

Before Tunzi had a chance to continue, Nicky began one of his usual comedy routines.

"What? You mean Special Detective Michael Tunzi, the most decorated police officer in the fine state of Illinois?"

Nicky held the phone to the side and yelled across the main staging area. "HEY, TOMMY, IT'S TUNZI FOR YOU!"

Nicky put the phone back to his mouth.

"How are you, Michael? I just stopped down here for a bit. Hey, if you're in the area, come over and have a cup of coffee with us. Maybe I can offer you a bribe in the form of steak and eggs."

"Nicky put me on hold, go to a private office, and shut the door. This is serious," Tunzi ordered.

Nicky's demeanor changed instantly. He looked at Tommy, put one finger in the air, and mouthed the words, "one minute" to him as he went into the main office. Nicky sat down and picked up the phone.

"Alright, I'm in Tommy's office by myself. Did someone get pinched?" Nicky asked.

"Nicky, I'm sorry to be the one to have to tell you this. But right now, for your brother's sake, you need to hold it together. Your sister Teresa was in a car accident. She's dead."

Nicky gulped as his breathing became erratic. He stared through the glass window at Tommy, who was laughing with a few customers.

"Michael, are you 1000% sure it's Teresa, and are you positive she's dead?" Nicky asked, barely able to get the words out of his mouth.

"Nicky, listen to me and do exactly as I tell you. Get Tommy and come to the emergency entrance at St. Luke's. Fazool and I will be waiting for you guys. Ned Devane is coordinating the ambulance's arrival. Stay with Tommy the entire fucking time, and do not let him out of your sight. Make sure he doesn't speak to anyone but me when you get there. I'm on my way now. Do you understand?"

"Yes, I understand," Nicky sadly answered.

Tommy looked at Nicky through the large window of the office. He immediately saw an all too familiar expression on his brother-in-law's face. It was the look of bad news, or worse. Nicky put his hands to his face, trying to make sense of the conversation that had just transpired with Tunzi. All he could think of was Teresa lying lifeless in a casket. He needed to pull himself together for Tommy's sake. Nicky could barely look at him when he walked into the office.

"Tee, we gotta go."

Tommy grabbed Nicky's arm.

"Nick, what is it?"

Nicky bolted out from the office with Tommy right on his tail. Then, he gave instructions to Marco Nicoletti, Tommy's most senior employee.

"Marco, Tommy, and I are leaving. Handle the phones and deliveries."

Tommy followed Nicky out to the dock. They both jumped off and got inside Nicky's car. Nicky fumbled to put his keys into the ignition. Tommy reached over and grabbed the car keys from his brother-in-law's trembling right hand.

"We ain't going anywhere until you tell me what the fuck is going on! Do you fucking understand me, Nick?" Tommy aggravatingly barked.

Nicky stopped fidgeting with the keys and just stared straight ahead. Tommy knew whatever the problem, it was something horrible. Nicky's lip was quivering and Tommy could see the tears rolling down his eyes.

"Nicky, goddamn it! What the fuck did Tunzi say?"

He turned to Tommy.

"Teresa was in a car accident. She's dead, Tommy."

Tommy's heartbeat tripled, and he struggled to breathe.

"Tunzi said to meet him and Fazool at the emergency entrance at St. Luke. I don't know anything else, except that it was definitely Teresa, and she's definitely gone."

Nicky was barely able to finish his sentence. Tommy slouched down in the passenger seat, mumbling in an almost unrecognizable voice.

"Let's go to her."

Tommy and Nicky used their matching red polka-dotted handkerchiefs to dry their tears and blow their noses as they drove to the hospital. Teresa had those gifts hand-made for them the previous Christmas as a reminder of the ones Pa carried with him for so many years. It was less than a ten-minute drive to St. Luke's. Still, Tommy recalled almost every moment he shared with Teresa in that short amount of time. He thought about the very first time he set eyes on her when he arrived from New York, all the way up to the romantic love-making session they shared five short hours earlier.

"Why? Why? Why?" Tommy cried out during the car ride.

Nicky just shook his head, struggling to concentrate on the road through unstoppable tears. When they pulled up to the emergency room parking lot, an ambulance with the back doors wide open was the first thing that caught Tommy's eye. Nicky quickly exited his car, remembering what Tunzi said about staying with Tommy and not speaking with anyone when they arrived. Tommy walked up to the ambulance and saw it was empty. Nicky put his arm around him.

"Let's find Michael first like he said we should. He's on top of this for us."

Tommy responded, barely nodding, unable to muster anything more. Nicky stood next to him as they walked through the large double glass doors leading to the emergency care area. Tommy saw Tunzi and Fazool standing with a doctor and nurse. They were huddled together in front of another door where a security guard stood. Within a flash, Tommy burst through the door like a bat outta hell. He was shouting at the top of his lungs.

"WHERE IS SHE? WHERE IS SHE?"

Tunzi and Fazool tried restraining Tommy. Nicky even jumped on top of him, holding on for dear life. The security guard also lunged in, trying to assist. Tommy dragged all four men about 20-feet before they finally got him down to the cold hospital floor. He shouted while squirming and shimmying on the slippery waxed floor tiles a foot at a time attempting to get free.

"DON'T KEEP ME FROM HER, YOU MOTHER FUCKERS! I WANT TO SEE MY WIFE! TERESA! TERESA! I'M HERE!"

Nicky hugged him tightly and repeatedly said the same words.

"Tommy, she's gone. She can't hear you. We can't do anything to help her."

For five straight minutes, Tommy battled desperately. He was physically exhausted. Although no punches were thrown, shirts and jackets were disheveled and torn from the ruckus. The security guard must've caught an inadvertent elbow or knee to the face because his cheek was bright red and swollen.

"Tommy, we're gonna stand you up. But, please, I don't want to cuff you. I just don't want anyone getting hurt. Do you understand me?" Tunzi asked breathlessly.

"No cuffs, Michael. Please, just let me see her. Guys, take me to her and let me hold her hand," Tommy begged as he gasped for air. "Alright, no more fighting. Now, get me up off this fuckin' floor."

After getting him upright, the men walked Tommy to a private waiting area. When a doctor attempted to walk in, Tunzi put his hand up and motioned for him to wait.

"Michael, just let him come in," Tommy said. "I want him to take me to Teresa."

"Give me one minute alone with him first, Tommy," Tunzi agreed, opening the door to privately speak with the doctor.

Before he walked out, Tunzi asked Fazool to make a few calls.

"Reach for Fat Frankie, Sally Boy, Micky, Lenny, and Vinnie Champagne, too."

Dr. Andrew Zinn was the head of the Emergency Department. He was noticeably shaken by the hospital hallway scuffle. Still nervous, he actually flinched when Fazool rushed past him to make the calls.

"Doc, before you go in to talk to Mr. LaCosta, I wanna find out if anyone's heard back from that Northwestern nerve specialist yet?" Tunzi asked.

"Yes, Detective, Dr. Cheni Indararash should be here within the hour," Zinn answered.

"He's gonna take care of the freeze shock thing, right?" Tunzi asked.

"Dr. Indararash's past procedures were on patients whose bodies were still whole. He asked us to keep Mrs. LaCosta in a cooler at exactly 33 degrees until he arrived. Time is of the essence. Her nerve endings have been severed from her skull and spinal cord base. We're hoping that they'll still be responsive to electrical shocks. That's what's needed to relax her facial muscles," Dr. Zinn explained. "I'm debating whether to give this information to Mr. LaCosta right now or wait until Dr. Indararash has had a chance to examine her."

"Doc, believe me, I'm not telling you how to do your job here, but with your permission and with you present in the room, I would like to be the one to explain this to Mr. LaCosta. I've known him since we were kids. As you witnessed, he is a physically strong man in an extremely agitated state. In my limited medical terms, his adrenaline is off the fuckin' charts. Hearing this news, there's no telling how he'll react. Don't you agree?" Tunzi asked.

"I do. I suggest you wait a few minutes and let me prepare a sedative for Mr. LaCosta, just in case."

Tunzi already knew what Tommy's response was going to be.

"Doc, he'll refuse it."

As Tunzi walked back into the room, he thought about how he should break the decapitation news to Tommy and Nicky. There wasn't an easy way to soften this type of blow, as if dying wasn't bad enough. Tunzi slid his chair across the slippery white tile floor next to Tommy as he sat down. Then, he directed Nicky to also sit. Doctor Zinn walked in and extended his hand to Tommy.

"Hello Mr. LaCosta, I'm Doctor Zinn. I'm so very sorry for your immeasurable loss."

Zinn turned to Nicky.

"I'm Nicky. Teresa's brother."

"My deepest sympathies on the loss of your sister," Zinn said, shaking Nicky's hand.

For almost a full unsettling minute after the introductions, everyone in the room sat in uncomfortable silence. The only noise was the humming electrical currents running through the overhead fluorescent light fixtures. Tunzi stared at Dr. Zinn, Dr. Zinn looked at Tommy, and Nicky and Tommy both looked at Dr. Zinn. Finally, Tommy took a huge breath.

"Doctor, in my mind right now, I'm bouncing from year to year, remembering all the wonderful times my beautiful Teresa and I shared. What I'm wondering right here and right now is, why haven't I been taken to see her? I understand she's dead. I've calmed down. Now, it's time for you to take me to my wife."

The question Tommy asked next was the most difficult one of his life.

"How badly is Teresa's body damaged from the accident?"

Tunzi looked at Dr. Zinn. Then, from behind his back, Zinn showed Tommy the syringe he had hidden in his hand.

"Mr. LaCosta, I prepared a sedative for you before we continue. I strongly suggest you agree to let me give this to you."

"They'll be no sedative for me. Somebody needs to start talking, or I'm gonna throw this entire fuckin' hospital up for grabs," Tommy warned.

"Mr. LaCosta, Detective Tunzi felt it was best for you if he was the one who explained what happened. Then, I will follow up with the medical facts. Is that acceptable?" Dr. Zinn asked.

"Yes," Tommy agreed.

Although Tunzi's explanation was short, it definitely wasn't sweet. There was no sugarcoating the sourest of news.

"Tommy, a semi-truck with stacks of metal sheets tipped over while merging eastbound onto the Eisenhower. One of the sheets sliced through the roof of Teresa's car. She was decapitated," Tunzi explained.

Nicky slid off of his chair and onto his knees. He clasped his hands together over his face and cried. Tommy closed his eyes, envisioning Teresa's headless body, twisted in metal, flesh, and blood. Then, he remembered the night he shot Sal the Barber and how Sal's head exploded against the wall. Tommy thought it was his time to pay to piper, the piper, being God.

"So, this must be my punishment for committing murder."

"Tommy, Nicky, I'm so fucking sorry. I'm just gonna let Dr. Zinn take it from here," Tunzi gulped, choking back tears.

Nicky got up off his knees and sat back in the chair. Once again, he wiped his eyes and nose with his red polka-dotted handkerchief.

"The rest of Mrs. LaCosta's body is intact. However, I noticed her two top front teeth were missing upon examining the head. Also, her facial muscles were overly-extended and accentuated due to the shock of the accident. Those muscles lock up because the blood flow traveling from the brain to the spinal column and back again abruptly stops. The medical term for this is AFPS, which means Acute Facial Paralysis Syndrome. I can't imagine how difficult this must be for you to hear. Should I continue?" Dr. Zinn asked.

Tommy's eyes were shut during the entire explanation. They remained closed as he answered.

"Yes, continue."

Although Tommy listened to Dr. Zinn's every word, he was also privately damning himself for his life choices, especially the Outfit deeds. He always knew he would have to answer for killing Sal.

"Mr. LaCosta, are you sure you're okay?" Please let me give you this sedative."

"Tommy refused once again, so Dr. Zinn continued.

"Here's what's happening right now. Dr. Cheni Indararash from Northwestern is on the way here. He is the foremost medical authority in the country on AFPS. He has a remarkable success rate performing electrolysis to nerve endings for deceased patients who suffered severe strokes, extreme facial lacerations, and Bell's palsy. But, those patients were whole, and their nerve endings, still responsive. Dr. Cheni feels Mrs. LaCosta's body should remain in a near-frozen environment until he arrives. He says it's the best chance to relax the muscles and get them to a pliable state as if she were asleep."

"Michael, where's the jagoff who was driving the truck that killed my sister? I wanna talk to him. Maybe the back alley would work best," Nicky fumed.

Tunzi knew where he was going with that.

"Nick, we're going by the book on this. Fazool has him in a room with the accident investigator from IDOT (Illinois Department of Transportation) and a State Trooper. The Trooper's one of my regular guys. He's VERY thorough, knows what questions to ask and what to look for. If the driver was at fault, if he was negligent, if we find even the slightest infraction, we'll do what legally needs to be done."

Nicky looked at Tommy.

"You alright with that, Tee?"

"My only concern is making Teresa right," Tommy answered.

A nurse knocked on the door. Dr. Zinn motioned for her to come in.

"Dr. Zinn, Dr. Indararash is here. He's waiting for you in Surgical Room 15B," she said.

"Gentlemen, use this room for however long you need to. Then, as soon as I have news, I'll come back to speak with all of you. The room across the hall has a private hospital phone in it. So, if there's anyone you'd like to contact, just dial the operator and ask for an outside line," Dr. Zinn offered before exiting.

"Nicky, you make the calls…."

Tommy struggled to finish his sentence.

"Just don't say anything about the decapitation. Not yet," Tommy instructed.

Nicky's phoned Grace first. She screamed so loudly it almost burst his eardrum. They both cried on and off for their entire 10-minute conversation. Thirty minutes later, Grace and Victor arrived at the hospital. Nicky took them into a private room and explained the brutal details of Teresa's accident. He also told them what was currently happening in Surgical Room 15B. They cried further eventually pulling themselves together for Tommy's sake.

Fat Frankie, Lenny, and Micky came to the hospital to show their support and see if anyone needed anything. As a result, the ordinarily strict rules regarding waiting room capacity were not enforced. Nicky ensured that by slipping $300 to the injured security guard who helped keep Tommy in check when they arrived. After three long hours, one of the nurses entered the private waiting room.

"Mr. LaCosta, Dr. Zinn, and Dr. Indararash will be in shortly to speak with you," she calmly informed.

"Is there anything you can tell me?" Tommy asked.

"It's probably best to wait for the doctors. I'm sorry," she answered.

Grace walked over and put her arm around Tommy. Victor did, too. Nicky paced around the room, his hands clenched in prayer. When the doctors entered the room, they asked everyone to sit. Dr. Indararash was the first to speak.

"Can I can speak openly about Mrs. LaCosta in front of everyone?" he cautiously asked.

"Yes, you can," Tommy replied, looking at Nicky, Grace, and Victor.

"Before I give details, let me first extend my sympathy to all of you. I'll start by saying that the procedure was successful. We relaxed the overly-extended facial muscles with electrolysis to the nerve endings. The reattachment of the cranium to the neck took the most time. The scaring is less than an eighth of an inch all the way around and should be easily hidden by the funeral home embalmer. But, there was one thing I couldn't do. I could not activate the nerve endings necessary to remove what appears as a slight smile, even with the highest voltage stimulation. Based on how well everything else went, I can only offer a spiritual explanation. Maybe it's a sign to us that she's comfortably resting at peace. In her present visual condition, an open casket would be at your comfort level and discretion. The only thing for you to consider is would you like to view her now, or would you rather wait until after the funeral home has prepared her?"

"I want to see her now," Tommy insisted.

He looked at Nicky, Grace, and Victor.

"If it's too much for you guys to see, please stay here. I can go by myself."

As Tommy got up, they all threw their arms around each other and followed the doctors to the elevator. The ride to the 15th floor took forever. There was no conversation. Everyone's eyes focused on the brightly lit numbers on the elevator panel. The incessant dinging noise that signaled every prior floor echoed, heavily accentuated, like something from an Alfred Hitchcock movie. Before entering the surgical room, Dr. Zinn felt it necessary to offer advice.

"Remember Teresa's body has been through quite a bit, so if you hold her hand, kiss her, or hug her in any way, please do so gently, so the extensive work that was done is not disturbed or compromised."

"Excellent point, Dr. Zinn," Indararash agreed.

The surgical room was cold. Teresa's body was laid on the table covered with a white sheet up to her chin. The lights that hovered over her were exceptionally bright. Tommy stood next to her. He immediately recognized the slight smile on her face. It was usually when Teresa unknowingly passed gas in her sleep. Tommy used to tease her about it like crazy.

"I don't fart in my sleep, you asshole," she would adamantly deny.

Tommy remembered how they both used to laugh about it. But then, that one night while they were on a short getaway in Lake Geneva, Teresa had one too many cocktails, and right before jumping in the pool with all her clothes on, she came clean and admitted she knew.

Dr. Indararash gathered the family around the metal table as he lowered the sheet revealing Teresa's neck. Although the stitches were tiny, the skin surrounding them was slightly bulged and swollen.

"Mr. LaCosta, the swelling will subside, and as I said earlier, the mortician will conceal the outer stitching with the cosmetic mixtures used during the embalming procedure."

Tommy looked at the stitches, but only for a few seconds. Then, he reached for Teresa's hand and held it.

"I'm sorry you're so cold, Bella. I know how much you hate that," he thought.

Nicky and Grace held her other hand while Victor chose her left arm.

"I love you, Auntie Tree," Victor said quietly.

They all took turns leaning over her body to ever so gently kiss Teresa's forehead. Their lips barely touched her skin.

"Thank you, doctors. Thank you both for doing what you did for her," Tommy quietly said, not taking his eyes off of Teresa.

"Mr. LaCosta, when you're ready, we'll go to my office. I have some forms to be signed so we can release her to the funeral parlor," Dr. Zinn concluded.

As they walked out, Tommy saw a stack of hospital blankets on a rack. He grabbed a couple of them, walked back to Teresa, and covered her just like he used to do with Ma DaBone's hand-knitted quilt while they watched television.

Grace held Nicky tightly and whispered to him.

"My heart is breaking for Tommy. This is just God-awful!"

Tommy made arrangements for a three-day wake. He wanted to make sure everyone had a chance to pay their respects. But, sadly, he knew there was no concealing the news of Teresa's decapitation. Everyone eventually found out, but not one person confronted him about it.

The dress Teresa wore was magnificent. The thick 24K Italian gold chain with an attached cross draped around her neck hid what little of the scar remained. Johnny Greemo did an excellent job preparing her body for viewing. Tommy knew deep down inside that everyone who knelt at Teresa's casket may have had their prayers directed towards heaven, but their eyes would be focused on her neckline. Oddly enough, what helped take the focus off of her scar was that oh-so-slight smile on her beautiful angelic face. It was a comforting sight for those who knew and loved her.

Hundreds of floral arrangements adorned Greemo & Son Funeral Home. Thousands of mourners came to pay their respects, even the Mob Bosses, including Primo Montalbano. Tommy was surprised at all of the Outfit guys who showed up. He knew they usually just sent floral pieces, sympathy cards, and envelopes due to G surveillance.

On the second day of the wake, Nicky went outside to get some air and a couple of cigar puffs. That's when he was approached by Tunzi.

"Nicky, I talked to my Chief. I explained that your family's been through enough over the past few years. I asked him to do me a personal favor and pull all surveillance for the rest of Teresa's wake and funeral. He gave me a pass."

"Thank you, Michael," Nicky gratefully acknowledged.

"Fuck them. The Task Force has enough license plate numbers and pictures. How's Tee holdin' up?" Tunzi asked.

"I guess he's doing okay. After that outburst in the hospital lobby, there's been nothing outta him except a few tears. He's been very calm. I went one-on-one with him a few times to see if he needed anything. I looked into his eyes, and they're fucking empty."

"Nicky, don't say anything, but the copper that found Teresa is still all fucked up. He's under heavy sedation in the psych ward at Elgin State."

"I've had a couple of nightmares about seeing her without a head. Johnny Greemo did a beautiful job. She really does looks like she's sleeping," Nicky answered.

"Speaking of Greemo, are we set up for later tonight?" Michael inquired.

"Yes. Is 10:00 good for you?"

"I'll be back at a quarter to," Tunzi agreed.

As the last few people exited the parlor later that evening, Tommy found himself standing next to Teresa's casket. After two full days and nights of nonstop mourners paying their respects and offering condolences, they were finally alone. Tommy knelt down and put his hand on hers. The rosary Ma made for her First Communion was wrapped neatly between her fingers.

"I'm sorry we never made it to Italy, Tree. We were supposed to grow old together. What am I supposed to do now? I feel like a fuckin' orphan again!" Tommy thought, gently squeezing Teresa's hands. *"I wanna crawl in there with you. I swear to Christ I do."*

Benito Greemo stood silently in the rear of the room. Tommy finished his private thoughts with Teresa and walked towards him. Greemo folded his hands, speaking softly and solemnly to Tommy.

"Once again, I'm so sorry for your loss. Teresa is with Ma and Pa now. I hope Johnny and I helped make her wake service everything you asked for."

"Yes. Thank you, Benito. Everything was exactly how she would have wanted it," Tommy appreciatively answered.

"My Johnny is a gifted boy, Tommy. He wanted to do his best for you and your beautiful Teresa," Benito proudly added.

"She looks perfect," Tommy sighed. "Do you have all the paperwork ready? I'd like to take care of everything now. What's easiest, check or credit card? I can do cash if you want, but you'll have to wait until tomorrow for that," Tommy offered.

"You can finish up with Johnny. He's waiting for you in the empty parlor in the back where we had all the food and drinks set up. It's Parlor D, Tommy, by the rear entrance," Benito explained. "They're waiting for you."

"They?" asked Tommy.

"The office was too small to accommodate everyone. Please, Tommy, Johnny is waiting for you," Greemo instructed, pointing to the end of the hallway.

Johnny Shovel stood outside Parlor D, his hands folded in front of him like his father's were. Unfortunately, Tommy was very familiar with the funeral home stance. He apprehensively continued to walk towards Johnny and spoke before he reached him.

"Johnny, I want to pay. Why aren't we going to your office?"

"They'll explain why Tommy," he answered.

Johnny stood sideways, extending an open hand to the doorway for Tommy to walk in first. Parlor chairs replaced the tables of food from earlier. Sitting on couches positioned in a half-circle were Nicky, Lenny, Silvio, Michael Gabriel Sr.,

Captain Ned Devane, Cooches, Sally Boy Domenico, and Detective Tunzi. JuJu, Fat Frankie, Donato and Rocco Fontanelli, Fazool Pirelli, and the Bolino Brothers stood behind them. Looming in the right corner of the room was Vinnie He dwarfed even the tallest of the elaborate flower displays. Greemo shut the door behind Tommy. Nicky stood, offering an explanation as to why everyone was gathered, his words apologetic, sheepishly delivered, and very un-Nickylike.

"Tommy, they all came to me and wanted to do something for you. I thanked them and said you didn't need anything. That's what you told me to say if anyone asked, and I did. But, they insisted. I mean, look at this group! How could I say no? That's why we're all here. We want you to know that we love you and paid for all the arrangements. It's all taken care of, including the luncheon tomorrow at The Flame. And before you say anything, I have to tell you it's not what we're PLANNING on doing. It's what's been done."

For a few seconds, Tommy blankly stared straight ahead. Then, he scanned the faces of every man in the room, one by one, in no particular order. There was little doubt he was exhausted, operating on little sleep and emotional fumes for the last 70 hours straight. Nicky was the first to approach him. The other men stood, followed, and shared a few private moments and words.

Tommy stoically handled the funeral and luncheon. But, unfortunately, the many months of grief that followed were rough. Torment and anguish unmercifully and methodically haunted him. It's what death's aftermath often does to the lost, broken-hearted souls left behind.

CHAPTER 15
MORE DEATHS, FRIENDS WITH CONNECTIONS, THE SPEEDY SICILIAN, AN EXCLUSIVE SCREENING

Victor grew out of his second black dress suit in less than two years. Most recently, the third of Grace's brothers passed away, preceded by her two oldest sisters, one of their husbands, and the youngest of the DaBone brothers, Dominic. Thus, throughout the 1970s, there was always a relative or family friend dying, which meant wake, funeral, grave/mausoleum site, and luncheon.

But, sprinkled in between the decade of death's sad, mournful, and challenging times, there were genuinely remarkable occasions involving some unbelievable people and incredible journeys, especially for Victor. Growing up in Little Italy was just a mere preview of what was in store for him. The move to the suburbs, which he initially dreaded, turned out to be a pleasant surprise, serving as inspiration when the time came for him to put pen to paper. That difficult relocation was the spark that ignited his writing career.

Besides the past make-out session with Colleen Norton, and more recently, Janie Genevicio, the hot, tiny blond from Orchard Brook, his usual routine was working with his father at the Shop or at the Big Banana with his uncle. Victor's leisure time consisted of writing, reading, jogging, and listening to music. He also secretly sized up his new classmates, comparing them to their counterparts on Taylor Street. He often thought about Grandpa Joe and Zeus, wishing they were still alive to enjoy the unlimited wide-open spaces, which Victor thought was the only redeeming quality about living in the suburbs.

The school year came and went, but Victor eventually made a handful of new friends with their own interesting ties. One of them was the son of a United States Treasury Department agent! A few others were children, grandchildren, nieces, nephews, and cousins of important Syndicate members. Victor learned he wasn't the only kid growing up privy to Mob activities and mindful of the men attached to the Chicago Outfit.

Dirk, Michael Jr., and Dino

Victor met Dirk Rigonest in September of 1970, a handful of months after Joe DaBone died. Their initial commonality was that they were the two new eighth-grade kids at St. Vincent Catholic Grade School. Dirk and his family moved to Upper Cove from Michigan when Dirk's father, Jerry, a longtime agent for the Treasury Department, was transferred to Chicago to oversee recruit training. Jerry Rigonest was also one of the government's hand-selected agents that protected United States presidents when they visited Detroit and Chicago. Very few had the proper clearance necessary for that unique detail. The G chose the right guy with Rigonest. He was admired and well known throughout all government agencies as a loyal, seasoned veteran. He had an illustrious 25-year career, a spotless work record, and distinguished service awards for his arrests during numerous undercover operations.

When Dirk's three older brothers attended their Michigan high school, they were successful athletes in three sports and excelled academically, achieving high honors. They wanted their little brother Dirk to follow their lead, especially as a new eighth-grade kid. The overly sports-minded Rigonest brothers were relentless. They frequently rode Dirk to practice hard, study harder, and develop consistency in everything he did. At the top of the brothers' list was to teach Dirk what they learned from their father and combine that with their own playing experiences. Dirk did everything according to the plan spearheaded by his dad and overseen by his brothers.

The last grammar school athletic challenge for Dirk and all of the eighth-grade boys in the area was the end of the school year's annual intramural flag football competition held at Doerhoefer Park. This game was a huge deal. A right-of-passage contest pitted Upper Cove's previous grammar school graduates, who were now freshmen, against the current outgoing eighth grade graduating classes. Most of these boys had played organized tackle football since they were in third grade and flag football for a year before that.

Jerry Rigonest couldn't attend the game, so he asked his sons to go in his place and report back to him with a scouting report of Dirk's performance. The Rigonest brothers were impressed with their little brother. Dirk played every down on both sides of the ball for the entire day. He held his ground and did quite well, even in their objective eyes. Finally, it was late in the game and time for Dirk to sit on the bench. The Rigonest brothers paced the sidelines, always standing roughly 15 yards away from the front of the line of scrimmage to get the angle-view. According to their father, it was the only way to successfully evaluate a player.

"Great job out there today, Dirk. Congratulations," Victor complimented as he sat next to his friend.

Victor admired Dirk's athleticism and technique. Although he didn't have great physical attributes, he more than made up for it with his game knowledge.

"Thanks, Vic. There's not much time left, and you're the only one who hasn't played yet. Are you going to get out there or sit here like, what do you call it, a chooch?" Dirk asked.

Victor was in for the opening kick-off but hadn't played a single down the entire game. He was a watcher, not a player. Victor knew how important this game was for his friends, so he spent his time cheering for them. A few plays earlier, the only other Italian eighth-grader at St. Vincent, Jimmy Polini, an acne-faced, five-foot, one-inch barely 90-pound feeble excuse of a kid, twisted his ankle and limped off the field.

"It's your time to shine, paisan," Dirk said, nudging Victor off of the bench and onto the field.

Victor was the only one of Dirk's friends the Rigonest brothers had never seen on a field or a court. So they laughed a little bit when they watched him jog out in his high-top red Converse gym shoes instead of spiked football cleats. Dirk's family always had nicknames they made up for each other's friends, classmates, and teammates. Victor's chosen name was "The Sicilian."

When Victor ran out on the field, he wasn't exactly sure where he was supposed to line up, so Dirk yelled and pointed. The only sports Victor played in the old neighborhood were unorganized pick-up games of 16-inch softball, a little basketball, and alley hockey with a rubber ball instead of a puck.

Victor ran a few routes as a decoy. On the next play, he miraculously snagged a non-spiraled pass thrown roughly three feet over his head. A few people applauded, but it was so late in the game that almost everyone was more concerned about socializing than watching, except the Rigonest brothers. They focused on Victor. They watched his reaction time, how quickly he ran downfield, how he blocked, and how he didn't shy away from the more than usual physical contact permitted during a typical flag football game. The funny thing was Victor was barely moving at half-speed!

"Jesus Christ, could he be quicker than Nat Jones was at that age?" Brian Rigonest asked his two brothers.

Nathanial "Nat" Jones was a Michigan all-state two-time MVP high school football wide receiver and former teammate of Brian, the oldest Rigonest brother. Jones drew national attention when he received a full football scholarship to Ohio State and wound up breaking two Rose Bowl records for pass receptions and kick-off return yardage.

Patrick and Tim didn't take long to answer their older brother. They both nodded yes.

"That's what I thought," Brian agreed.

"Maybe faster," added Tim. "And he's wearing fucking red Chuck Taylor high-top gym shoes!"

The brothers talked between themselves, wondering why Dirk never mentioned Victor's speed. That would be the question they couldn't wait to ask during post-game chalk talk at the kitchen table that evening. The Rigonests had a long-standing tradition. At the end of every sports competition, they broke down their games as a family.

Dirk wasn't paying much attention to his brothers, Victor, or the game. He was more concerned about flirting with Sue Ann Zimmer, one of the cheerleaders. She promised Dirk a hand-job at the party later evening if he played well. (Even at that age, the future attorney was pleading his case.)

With less than five minutes left, and the game winding down, Jimmy Slayton checked back in for the opposition. He wanted to get his fifth touchdown of the day, already tying the record earlier in the game. The only other player to score four touchdowns was Upper Cove's favorite son and claim to fame, Bobby Woodman. Woodman was a 1966 All-State high school football player for Upper Cove North and, more notably, the current starting running back for the Baltimore Colts.

When the ball changed hands, Victor played on defense as a cornerback. Four different guys had already played that position, and they all got lit up, burned by Jimmy Slayton. Slayton had quite the reputation. He was a freshman at Upper

Cove North High School. His stats on the day were impressive, even for a ceremonial flag football game. Besides his record-tying four touchdowns, he had three long runs and about five remarkable catches. He also had a diving, one-handed interception on defense. Slayton had been the talk of the town for a couple of years. Even the older players respected his game. Slayton's biggest drawback was being an arrogant, conceited ball hog who gave little to no credit to his teammates. What was even worse was the shit-talking premier athlete backed up his loud mouth with big-time plays. Slayton was only a freshman starting both ways on the varsity football team. He was also a sprinter, specializing in the 100 and 200-yard dashes and running the anchor leg in the relay races. Most of the local coaches referred to him as "The Franchise." The talk amongst local high school sports enthusiasts was how Upper Cove North could be a contender to win titles in both football and track because of Slayton. As critical as the Rigonest brothers were about young athletes, they agreed that Slayton was the real deal. Mr. Rigonest heard all the talk earlier in the year and had to see for himself, so he and Dirk attended a couple of Upper Cove North's Friday night home games during the season. After watching Slayton play, Mr. Rigonest agreed, saying he was one of the best all-around youth football players he had ever seen. That was quite an endorsement coming from a guy who had watched thousands of games and evaluated hundreds of athletes.

When Slayton lined up wide right and saw Victor defending him, he wasted no time taunting the opposing sideline.

"You have got to be kidding! So the slick-haired city kid who doesn't play football and wears high-tops is gonna try and cover me? Hey, sports fans, record-breaking touchdown number five is coming right up!"

Victor was more concerned about lining up correctly than Slayton's boastful prediction.

"DIRK, YO, DIRK!" Brian Rigonest yelled.

Dirk was on the bench talking to Sue Ann Zimmer while she cheered. He was working feverishly to ensure she was still on board to give him his evening rub and tug. He looked up and saw Brian pointing towards Victor and Slayton. Dirk stood, turned, and watched. Victor backed up a few steps as Slayton took off. Just as Victor turned to shadow him, Slayton made a head-fake move and then a cut to the sidelines. Victor slipped on the grass, and Slayton caught a beautifully placed pass for a first down.

Slayton tossed the ball to one of the referees and turned to Victor.

"Don't worry, Greaseball. This nightmare will be over for you very soon."

Victor ran up to Slayton and got in his face.

"What the fuck did you say?"

Slayton pushed him away as the referee stepped in between them.

"C'mon, guys. The game's almost over. So let's finish it classy," he reprimanded.

Slayton laughed on his way back to the huddle. Victor was fuming. He thought about Grandpa Joe lying in the casket a few months earlier. He remembered the stories about how he endured years of Italian slurs on the Polina Construction jobsites.

Brian Rigonest shouted to Dirk.

"GO TALK TO HIM!"

Dirk motioned for Victor to come close to the sidelines.

"C'mon, Vic, what the fuck's the matter with ya? Don't let that asshole get inside your head. Back up a few feet and don't slip. Nobody can hang with Slayton. Just try and do your best."

"Dirk, that jagoff called me a fucking Greaseball!"

Dirk remembered how pissed off Victor got when Bill Bohman, the huge seventh-grade bully, held back a year for bad grades, confronted Victor on the playground only two weeks after school started. Bohman made the mistake of calling Victor a Wop during a kickball game. The contest stopped, and the entire sixth, seventh, and eighth-grade classes surrounded them with chants of, "Fight! Fight! Fight!" Dirk especially remembered the look on Victor's face right before he hauled off and dropped Bohman with a quick right jab and the finishing blow, a solid left hook. (Victor told Dirk later those were boxing tips he learned from Taylor Street Champions Micky Silvio Luke Capezio.) Big Billy Bohman didn't even have time to get one punch off. He fell to the blacktop, bleeding from the mouth and nose, crying like a baby. The angered look on Victor's face now was the very same as it was that day.

"You're better than that, Victor. Fuck Slayton! Nobody likes him better than he likes himself," Dirk said, attempting to offer motivation.

Victor heard Dirk, but this went way deeper than being teased and made fun of for lack of football knowledge, slicked-back city hair, or floppy gym shoes. Victor's resolve was to somehow make an example of Jimmy Slayton in the most embarrassing of ways, on the football field and in front of everyone.

When Slayton lined up on the opposite end of the line, Victor ran over and switched sides with Eddie Fisk. Fisk didn't mind. Slayton already raced by him once in the first half for a touchdown.

"Thanks, Victor. Are you sure?" Fisk asked.

Eddie was a tremendous athlete in his own right but the game was almost over and Victor hadn't really played.

"I want him," Victor answered.

Slayton saw Victor was guarding him, so he leisurely strolled out wider and proceeded to talk shit.

"You just don't learn, do you, Slick. You're about to go down in history as the guy I scored my fifth touchdown on."

With less than fifty seconds left on the clock, Slayton ran what at first appeared to be another down and out pattern. This time, Victor was tightly on him, but Slayton quickly changed his route and added an up-field move at the end. Victor bit, slipped, fell, and rolled on the ground. Slayton caught the pass and took off. He had five yards on Victor just like that and was quickly on his way to an apparent record-breaking fifth touchdown. Slayton had some parting words for the slick-haired Italian city kid as he blazed down the field.

"BYE-BYE, GREASEBALL!"

As the crowd watched, they stood and cheered for what they thought would be Slayton's record-breaking score. That's not what they saw. Instead, Victor got up and took off. Thirty-five yards and only the blur of a pair of red high-top Converse gym shoes later, he not only made up the ground Slayton gained on him but for a brief moment, also toyed with him by running right alongside.

"That's all you got?" Victor asked, pulling Slayton's flag and knocking the clutched ball from his grip.

Slayton fell to the ground. Three ticks later the buzzer sounded, and just like that, the game was over. The park crowd was quiet, except for the Rigonest trio, who clapped and cheered in disbelief even though their brother's team lost by three touchdowns! Dirk couldn't believe it. His mouth was opened as wide as his eyes as he tried making his way through teammates to get a better view downfield.

Victor stood over Slayton, threw the touch flag into the shocked and embarrassed star athlete's face, and knelt as he issued a warning.

"If you ever call me a Greaseball again, I'll drag you down the middle of Ogden Avenue right in front of the Cock Robin and give you the beating of a lifetime. The only sport that you might be able to play after that would be wheelchair basketball."

Then, Victor delivered the most degrading line he could think of to someone like him.

"Oh, and for the record, when I was in fifth grade, I was faster than you are now, you little fucking cunt."

For the first time on a football field, Jimmy Slayton remained silent. Victor jogged off with no intention of returning to either his team or his friends. As he got closer to the end zone, he noticed two guys sitting on the hood of a car parked on the grass. The pair got off and walked towards him.

"That was WAY fucking cool, kid," the taller of the two said.

Victor looked at them but didn't stop or respond. Instead, he continued to make his way to the tennis courts, only to disappear through the back gate entrance to take the shortcut home.

"How do you like that, Dino? That disrespectful little shit didn't even say thank you," said the taller guy.

"Jesus Christ, Michael. I think I know him from somewhere," Dino responded. "He looks so goddamn familiar."

These teenagers were much more than just standout junior varsity football players from perennial powerhouse St. Benedict High School. Michael Gabriel Jr., the taller boy, was Michael "The Fixer" Gabriel's son. The other guy was Dino "Double D" Domenico. He was Sally Boy Domenico's boy. The Fixer was the Mob's political boss in Chicago's Tenth District. That's where all the top-level movers and shakers, the best attorneys, high-profile judges, important aldermen, and long-term council members had their offices. The politicos in Chicago were very well aware that Michael Gabriel was the Mob's man behind all their court cases. Gabriel had his hands in everything from the dismissal of unpaid parking tickets to the reducing murder charge sentences, especially for those with Mob connections. Michael Gabriel Sr. wielded a wicked web of power. When you're the

Syndicate's political point man, you've got both the legal contacts and the juice. So the Outfit created the 'Political Advisor' position specifically for Gabriel.

Sometime in the late 1940s, Manny suggested he legally change his name from Michaela Patricio Gabralina to Michael Gabriel to avoid law enforcement and political scrutiny of his prominent Italian name. For decades, The Fixer has been the most powerful, influential, behind-the-scenes Syndicate member in Chicago. If you were affiliated with the Outfit, got pinched, and needed legal advice or representation, there was no doubt someone high-up reached for Gabriel and his web of lawyer, judges, law firms, and court administrators.

Dino Domenico and Michael Gabriel Jr. were a few years older than Victor. Dino was raised in the suburbs but born on Carpenter Street while the Domenico's still lived in Little Italy. Dino finally remembered on the ride home from the football game with Michael Jr., where he had seen Victor. It was at one of Taylor Street Italian Festivals.

Later that afternoon, both Dino and Michael Jr. asked their fathers about Victor and his family. When it came time to compare notes, the cunning, always Outfit-minded, inquisitive friends were pleasantly surprised to discover that both of their fathers gave rave reviews. (That rarely happened.) Sally Boy and The Fixer had inside information about most of the connected guys in Chicago. In the past, when the boys questioned their fathers about someone they came in contact with suspected Mob-ties, Sally Boy and The Fixer's evaluations of those people were usually gospel truth, right on the money correct. Michael Jr. and Dino looked forward to the prospect of having Victor under their tutelage.

That evening at dinner, as the Rigonest brothers filled their father in on the game, they bombarded Dirk with questions about why Victor didn't join any eighth-grade sports teams. Dirk's only answer was that Victor never moved that quickly on the playground or gym class. It was the truth, he hadn't. The Rigonests strongly suggested to Dirk that he do everything possible to get Victor to join the freshman football team at St. Benedict.

After they finished supper, Jerry dropped Dirk off at Victor's house. That evening, the two soon-to-be grammar school graduates were headed to a huge bash at Mary Ann Collinsworth's parent's estate in Downers Grove. Mary Ann's mom and dad were out of town for the weekend and that meant one thing, her older brothers, Greg, Tim, and Ed were buying beer and supplying weed.

Nicky was in the driveway, waxing his pride and joy, a black, on black, on black convertible Cadillac.

"Hey, Jerry, how's my favorite government agent doing?"

"The Cadillac's looking good, Nicky!"

"Hi, Mr. DaBone, is Victor in his room?"

"Yea, Micky Spillane's up there bangin' on his fuckin' typewriter. Just follow the sound of the shitty music. And, Dirk, do me a favor, will ya? Tell him to lower it a little. Grandma's trying to take a nap."

Victor had just cranked the volume up a couple of notches. Dirk knew the song right away. It was "Layla" by Derek and The Dominos. They loved Eric Clapton.

"Jerry, do your other sons listen to that shit, too?" Nicky asked.

"All day and all night," he answered, shaking his head.

"In five years, nobody's gonna remember any of that crap," Nicky added. "They don't know what good music is. You can't even understand what the fuck they're sayin'!"

While Jerry and Nicky talked, Dino and Michael Jr. pulled up at the opposite end of the DaBone's semi-circular driveway in Michael's grey 1970 427 Corvette. Dino was able to get Victor's phone number with help from his father. He called a little earlier to say he and Michael would be stopping over. They got out of the car and walked up to Nicky, Jerry, and Dirk.

"Hi, is Victor home?" Dino asked.

"Hey, I know both of you, but I forget who's who," Nicky answered.

He knew exactly who they were. Nicky just wanted them to say their names in front of Jerry. He wanted to see how sharp the G-Man was.

"Oh, I'm sorry. I'm Dino Domenico, and this is Michael Gabriel," Dino said as they all shook hands.

"You guys are all grown up now! How's both of your family's doin'?" Nicky asked.

Jerry Rigonest smiled uncomfortably. He knew those last names.

"These kids are the sons of the Outfit!"

Nicky could tell by Jerry's expression that he knew the names.

"Hey, you're number 24 from the game today, right?" Dino asked Dirk. "You look like you know what you're doing out there. You're going to play with us at St. Benedict, right?"

"I am," answered Dirk, slightly intimidated by the upperclassmen.

"What about Victor? Is he going out for the team, too?" Michael Jr. asked.

"Victor? I doubt it. He writes, listens to music, jogs, and works at my place or SouthWater for his uncle and that's about it," Nicky interrupted.

Michael Jr. and Dino put their arms around Dirk.

"Let's see if the three of us could change his mind. Nice meeting you, Mr. DaBone, Mr. Rigonest," Dino said as he, Dirk, and Michael Jr. headed inside.

"Dirk, before you go, can you come here for a minute?" Jerry nervously asked as he walked to the other side of his car for a private conversation.

"What's up, Dad?" Dirk asked.

"You need to be careful. ALL these kids are related to mobsters, do you understand that? I've talked to you about Victor's uncle and father before, but these two kids' fathers? Jesus Christ!" Jerry warned.

"Dad, Mrs. DaBone is driving Victor and I to Mary Ann's house for her party, and when it's over, Mr. DaBone is picking us up and then driving me home. Do you want to give me your gun, just in case there's a problem?" Dirk sarcastically suggested.

"Don't be a smart ass, Dirk! I'm dead serious," Jerry angrily responded.

"It'll be fine, Dad. I'll see you later."

Dirk headed into the DaBone's house with Dino and Michael while Jerry walked back to Nicky.

"That's nice, the older guys taking an interest in our sons, right, Jerry?"

Nicky was busting his balls, knowing the Treasury Agent was sharp enough to know who those boys' fathers were.

"They seem like nice, respectful guys, Nicky. By the way, my older sons went to the football game today. I was working and couldn't make it. Did you go?"

"No, I was working, too. Grace wanted to go, but Victor said she didn't have to. He said it was mostly for the guys who played on the football team or some shit like that."

"Well, my sons went. They told me Victor didn't play until the very end, but when he got in, he was fascinating to watch, very fast. They also said he reminded them of a guy from Detroit they played with in high school. That kid wound up playing in college on a full scholarship," Jerry explained.

Nicky was half-listening and nodding respectfully to Jerry but more focused on the luster the Turtle Wax had on his Caddy.

"Jerry, Victor does what he wants to do. He's a very sharp kid but real low-key, so Grace and I don't push him in any direction, one way or another. A couple of the coaches on Taylor Street talked to me about getting him involved in the Park District teams. I think it was baseball, maybe basketball, and hockey, too. He told them all no. I do know he's fast. I've been watching him run his entire life, and there's only one time I knew for certain that he was trying his hardest. It was in the empty lot next to our house in the city. He was so pissed off when he lost that race!"

"Who beat him, one of the older guys?" Jerry asked.

"Naw, it was Zeus, our German Shepherd," Nicky answered with a straight face. "Jerry, the dog actually looked embarrassed! I mean, he did almost get beat by a 12-year-old kid. If anyone shoulda been embarrassed, it shoulda been me. After all, I spent $3000 on that fuckin' dog!"

Nicky winked at Jerry. Jerry smiled back, figuring Nicky was joking with him.

"Jerry, that's a true story. No bullshit. I swear to Christ, that kid came damn close to beating a fully grown, champion-bred German Shepherd police dog."

As the boys walked inside, Dirk said hello to Grace as she boiled pasta and washed dishes. Grandma Mari wasn't far away trying to take a late afternoon snooze in the cushiony, thick, clear-plastic covered chair. She'd been crocheting, as usual, and the knitting needles and yarn still sat in her lap. Dirk said hello then quickly took ok off upstairs to give Victor the heads-up, not knowing his friend already knew about the planned visit. Michael and Dino walked into the kitchen and introduced themselves to Grace. When she heard their last names, she knew the connection. Then the boys made their way to Grandma Mari. They knelt, hugged, and kissed her, telling her how sorry they were to hear about Pa DaBone's passing. These Mob sons were good, real good. Thanks to their fathers, they did their homework and knew the DaBone/LaCosta family dynamic. Their kind gesture of sympathy put a smile on that old lady's face.

Dirk ran into Victor's bedroom. He was lying in bed, looking up at the ceiling, listening to music, and daydreaming.

"Fucking Dino Domenico and Michael Gabriel are downstairs, and they're heading up here!"

"Yea, I knew they were coming over. Dino called me up a couple of hours ago. They were at the game today," Victor replied calmly. "I'm pretty sure I know why they're here."

After Dino and Victor reminisced about their Taylor Street experiences, Dino did his best to try and talk Victor into joining the freshman football team at St. Benedict. So did Michael Jr. and Dirk. For the next hour, they used every angle imaginable. Finally, Dirk jokingly told Victor that if he couldn't convince him to join the team, his older brothers threatened him with an ass-kicking, and his father said he would throw him out of the house. Michael Jr. and Dino got a hoot out of that. Victor politely listened to all three of them and then spoke.

"It's not for me, guys. Sorry."

"Okay, Victor, but let me ask one final thing. Were you ever timed in a 40 or 100-yard dash?" Dino asked. "You looked quicker than shit through a goose when you caught that prick, Slayton."

Victor quickly changed the subject, hoping to defer the attention onto someone else.

"No, I haven't. Oh, by the way, speaking of Slayton, he called me a Greaseball. I figured you guys would want to know that, you know, being Italian and all."

"WHAT? He called you a Greaseball?" Michael Jr. angrily asked looking at Dino.

"Slayton's a fucking punk. Victor showed him what's what. That's all that matters now," Dino said, attempting to calm his friend.

"Maybe, we should stop by Slayton's house next," Michael Jr. suggested.

"He's not worth it," Dino answered, changing the conversation. "Well, Victor, we tried to convince you to play, and you're not interested. But, we got to meet you and Dirk. For ALMOST freshmen, you guys seem pretty cool," Dino complimented as he and Michael Jr. headed out.

Those two guys became Victor's adopted big brothers. They took the young paisan under their wings and taught him how to enjoy the perks of suburban living related to bonafide members of the Chicago Outfit.

Victor got up and put another album on the turntable. It was Crosby Stills, Nash, and Young's "Déjà Vu" released a few months earlier.

"Every song on this album is unbelievable," Victor said. "We've talked about how good they are, right?"

Dirk walked to the bedroom door and closed it. Jimmy Rosselli's "Malafemmena" played on the old Victrola downstairs for Grandma Mari. It wasn't the first time there were different genres of music in the DaBone household. Frank Sinatra, Dean Martin, Jerry Vale, Tony Bennett, Jimmy Roselli, Bobby Darin, Tom Jones, and Sergio Franchi played downstairs. But, upstairs, Victor controlled the playlist. His choices were The Who, The Supremes, Three Dog Night, Eric Clapton, Steppenwolf, The Beatles, The Rolling Stones, Led Zeppelin, The Guess Who, and quite a few more.

Dirk was hurt and a little pissed. He didn't want to say anything while Michael Jr. and Dino were there, but he felt played. Rigonest didn't waste any time letting the speedy Sicilian know about it.

"What the fuck, Victor, I thought we were friends! You've been bullshitting everyone. Why would you do that? It's like you're ashamed because you're fast. All that half-assed finishing in the middle or near the end every time we had to run in gym class or play pick-up games! It's fucking stupid, man!"

"When I was little, I used to think it was my superpower, like in my comic books," Victor embarrassingly explained. "That fucker Slayton pissed me off this afternoon. I should've let it go and let him score his five fucking touchdowns, but I didn't. Look, I don't expect you to get what I'm saying. It's just best for me that I do my thing."

Victor opened his dresser drawer and revealed dozens of notebooks and stacks of typed and handwritten papers.

"I wrote these. They're short stories, and television show parodies. There's also some dirty poems like the ones I wrote on the inside cover of my religion book. We both love National Lampoon, MAD and Cracked, right?" Victor asked.

"For sure," Dirk agreed.

"I've been doing these for almost a year now, never showed them to anyone. I did send a few things to Cracked and MAD last month, but I never heard back. They probably tossed them. If you want to make fun of me, then go ahead, and make fun of me. My mom and dad know I've been writing, but they don't know about what."

Victor grabbed his most recent work and handed it to Dirk. Dirk flipped through it and found what looked like a script for the Andy Griffith Show. The eye-catching title on the page was "The REAL Mayberry."

"You read, I'm grabbing a 7UP. Do you want one?" Victor offered.

"No thanks. I'm just gonna peruse some pages."

Dirk was hooked by the second paragraph when he read how Andy yelled at Barney because Thelma Lou was giving him a blowjob on the bench outside Floyd's Barbershop. Dirk smiled, thinking it was something right out of National Lampoon. He laughed when he got to the part where Aunt Bee wanted to surprise Andy about Gomer teaching her how to drive. Victor wrote that Aunt Bee ran the squad car up on the front lawn of their house and hit Opie, breaking both his legs. The real kicker came on the next page when Victor introduced two Mount Pilot pimps that set up a brothel next to Clara Edwards's home. When Victor walked back into his room, Dirk put down the notebook.

"The first thing I gotta say is, you are one sick fuck. The second thing is, this is pretty funny. So, you made all this up? You didn't rewrite something somebody else already wrote?"

"Nope, all original, and all mine. Which one were you reading?"

"The Andy Griffith one," Dirk answered. "Thelma Lou blows Barney on a bench? Opie gets run over by Aunt Bee? A Whorehouse in the middle of Mayberry?" You're not right in the head."

Victor saw absolutely nothing wrong with those outrageous scenarios. Then, he shared his most recent abomination of another of America's most beloved sitcoms.

"I just finished a Dick Van Dyke episode last night. After a long day at the office, Rob comes home after writing some killer jokes for Alan Brady's opening monologue. He opens his front door, and there's Laura, Millie, and Jerry having a threesome on the ottoman he usually trips over. And to make matters worse, Jerry Helper's got a huge cock that Laura can't seem to get enough of, and all she keeps moaning is 'Ohhhh, Rob!'"

Dirk just shook his head. He wasn't quite sure what to think. (Later that night, while taking a shower, he pictured Jerry Helper pounding poor Laura Petrie into submission. He laughed like the fucking village idiot.)

"Okay, Victor, so you said you already sent stuff to Cracked and MAD Magazines?"

"Yea, I sent out a few things in the last couple of months."

"Vic, you're a 14-year old kid. Did you think they were going to print what you wrote and just send you a check?"

"That's what I was kinda hoping for," Victor naively answered.

Dirk delivered the bad news.

"I'm pretty sure it doesn't work like that."

Victor wasn't totally flabbergasted, it's what he figured, but he sent it anyway. The thought of his words being published was exciting.

"Dirk, let's keep this between us for now. And, one more favor, promise me that there won't be any more conversations about joining football, or any other team for that matter, okay?"

"You're missing out, but if that's what you want, you won't hear another fucking peep out of me. You know Coach Freud from St. Benedict was at the game today, and I'm pretty sure he saw you run Slayton down. So, you can count on him trying to talk you into playing football."

"Maybe he will, and maybe he won't. I'm taking a shower. Feel free to grab another notebook and read whatever you want."

Victor reached one of the newer albums from his growing collection and threw it on the Music Hall Classic Turntable he received as a Christmas gift from Fat Frankie the previous year. (Victor remembered laughing his ass off when Frankie told him to make sure and scratch the shipping label off!)

After his shower, Victor asked Dirk to help him with confusing submission guideline rules. After doing a little research in the months that followed, Dirk suggested to Victor that he make copies of everything, mail them back to himself, and then not open them. Dirk read in a copyright book that this simple method was a way to establish ownership and timeframe because of the postal date stamped on the envelope. Dirk's suggestion was legally not too shabby, especially considering he wasn't even 15-years old. Furthermore, it was the cheapest way for Victor to copyright his original work, even though he was only a minor.

As far as joining any sports team, Dirk never brought it up again. Instead, he watched Victor slide through four years of high school, bullshitting gym teachers, friends, coaches, and classmates, by finishing right in the middle of running drills and timed races.

Pio Birty, a fellow eighth-grader, summed up Victor and Dirk's entire family background early on when he shared his know-it-all father's nosey insight. Following closely in his daddy's drunken footsteps, Pio downed many mini bottles of Miller Beer in the Gilbert Woods Preserve during a sleepover at Lammy's house, only a couple of months after the school year started. Everyone was still referring to Dirk and Victor as new kids. Finally, after getting as liquored-up as an eighth-grader could get, Pio climbed up on a table, got everyone's attention, and loudly screamed.

"My father said Victor's family is 'Mobbed-Up' and Dirk's family is 'Lawed-Up.'

Victor and Dirk were the only two guys that laughed. Seconds later, Pio slipped, fell, and puked all over himself. The other boys smiled uncomfortably, quickly shuffled about, eventually laughing more from embarrassment than anything else. After learning more about the Rigonest and DaBone families as the months progressed, the other parents wound up agreeing with Mr. Birty.

Two years went by quickly, and as his sophomore year winded down, Victor got his driver's license the day after his 16th birthday. Unbeknownst to him, Grace and Nicky bought a black, low-mileage 1967 SS Camaro from Russo Chevrolet, owned by John "Little Johnny" Russo for his main gift. Victor's other present was purposely and teasingly kept very hush-hush. His parents felt he might appreciate that secondary gift even more than his car.

Little Johnny Russo and his family were Grand Avenue deep and had been for years. If you were Italian and wanted to buy a new or used Chevy, you purchased it from Russo. That's just the way it was. Little Johnny absolutely loved selling cars to the connected guys because they always paid with cash. The only downside to doing business with that type of clientele is that sometimes when they traded in or sold their vehicles, they either had no identification numbers, or the trunks were severely stained and reeked from spoiled meat. Little Johnny found out that the discoloring and stench in those trunks were from dried blood and small pieces of human flesh from God know who that hadn't been adequately cleaned or disposed of. So Russo adjusted his prices for the bleach-soaking and deep cleaning methods needed to hide the Outfit's trunk activities. Between that and forging titles and State of Illinois Vehicle paperwork documents with his dealership's name on them, hundreds of cars and trucks were illegally bought, sold, and sometimes even vanished from Russo's monster-sized Chevrolet lot. And Little Johnny? He made a fucking mint!

Guillermo Lupina was one of Nicky's Hispanic workers, and coincidently, Cooches Caballero's cousin. Nicky asked Guillermo to go over the Camaro with a fine-tooth comb to ensure it was mechanically safe because Guillermo knew his way around automobiles. He could take a vehicle apart all by himself and put it back together. In fact, that's what he did after hours at Cooches's many chop shops. Nicky trusted Little Johnny, but it was a used car. Once Guillermo gave it his seal of approval, Nicky drove it, parked it in the driveway, and excitedly waited for Victor. He and Grace stood and watched from the large bay window as he walked from the bus stop. When he got in the driveway, Victor circled the car a couple of times.

"Man, this is a sweet ride! I wonder whose it is."

Nicky couldn't stand it anymore. He grabbed Grace's hand, and they both walked outside while Grandma watched the excitement from the front door. As Victor walked towards them, he saw the look on their faces, especially Nicky. Victor knew that look. He'd seen it dozens of times over the years after his father made a good score. Nicky tossed him the keys, and wished him a happy birthday. Victor responded like he always did, saying the first thing that came to mind.

"NO FUCKING WAY!"

"USE IT IN THE BEST OF HEALTH, VICTOR!" Grandma wished, yelling from the front door as best she could. "E per favore, smettila di imprecare!" (And please, stop swearing!)

Later that following morning, Victor's second surprise slowly and mysteriously unfolded. On a rare day off both school and work, he stood in his driveway, waxing his Camaro and listening to the early release of America's "A Horse with No Name" as it played out of the speakers he placed in the open windows of his bedroom. He enjoyed the song but wondered why they never gave that poor horse a fucking name. When he saw Nicky pull up to the house in the Shop truck, he had a sinking feeling in his stomach. His father rarely came home during the middle of the day, and when he did, it usually meant he was bearing terrible news. Victor's first thought based on the last couple of years was kind of sad.

"Oh, Christ, I hope my black wake suit's back from the cleaners!"

"Dad, what are you doing home? Is everything okay?"

Nicky was smiling, so that was good.

"When you're done waxing your car, go grab a shower and put on some nice clothes. Maybe wear that handmade designer gray shirt and the black dress pants from Italy Auntie Tree bought for you. Then, pull the Cadillac out. You're driving."

Victor knew that wakes and funerals were usually the main reasons for Nicky's Cadillac made a roadworthy appearance.

"I'm driving the Cadillac? Where to, and who died?"

"Nobody died, and don't jinx us. It's been over a month, and we haven't had to smell embalming fluid or flowers. Get done and get dressed, we're picking up Uncle Tommy at his house first and then heading down to Japeto's to get Fat Frankie. God help my suspension with his fat ass in the back seat," Nicky dreaded.

"I'm not getting clipped, am I?" Victor joked.

"You're spending way too much time hanging around with Dino and Michael Jr. Now, hurry up and finish before I bury you under the fucking shed," Nicky sarcastically answered.

About an hour later, Victor walked into the foyer looking freshly dressed to the nines. Grace and Nicky stood in the front hallway.

"He's so handsome," Grace whispered.

"Alright, Mom, stop with the secrets and tell your only child what's going on."

"It's a wonderful surprise, Victor. You're gonna love it. That's all I'm allowed to say."

Nicky tossed him the car keys, and off they went to Tommy and Teresa's house. When Victor pulled up, they were already standing outside, looking as proud of Victor as Nicky and Grace were.

Teresa had her camera, and that meant pictures, whether you wanted to or not. She arranged her favorite men in a few different poses, but when she snapped one of them with their arms around each other, she couldn't contain herself.

"My God, this is going to be the best picture ever!"

"So, Auntie Tree, you know what's going on too, huh? Everyone's treating me like I'm a nu-nu. (Pronounced new-new. Means idiot) For Christ's sake, I feel like a Catutto!" Victor jokingly complained.

Victor was referring to longtime Little Italy residents, the Catutto family. If the Catuttos were light bulbs, there wouldn't have been one over 10-watts. The mother, father, and three kids were unintelligent. A simple common sense question asked of any of them, and they stared at you like deer caught in the headlights. In an arena filled with idiots, the nincompoop Catuttos would've stood out as the very stupidest of the stupid. All of them, even the parents, were held back a grade while in school. Mr. Catutto had to cut a deal with the principal in exchange for letting his youngest daughter, Ann Laura, graduate. Catutto offered to paint his home, the rectory, and the convent. The principal, the pastor, and Mother Superior Rita of St. Angelo's Catholic High School for girls agreed. They also wanted her out of school, the sooner, the better. Ann Laura was three months pregnant and starting to show.

"Victor honey, you're gonna love it!" Teresa promised.

"Mom said the same thing when I asked her what was going on. Did you guys practice your answers?"

Teresa laughed and kissed him.

"Auntie Tree will never tell, baby!" she teased.

"Let's go. I don't want to be late," Tommy urged.

Except for a large truck cutting Victor off at the Hillside Strangler portion of the Eisenhower Expressway, the maiden trip down to the city went flawlessly. Nicky and Tommy told Victor how impressed they were with his driving skills. He was way too embarrassed to admit that he practically crapped in his pants the whole way down just like Tony Shit Stains used to do when he drank.

As he turned on Loomis Street, Victor hoped he'd see Maria DiNapoli outside her house. But then, he remembered she was probably at school and that his day off from St. Benedict was due to a teacher's institute day. So instead, he glanced across the passenger side when he drove by and pictured her sitting on the front stoop waving at him.

"He's looking for the DiNapoli girl, Tee," Nicky said to Tommy, who was lounging like a king in the spacious back seat.

Victor shook his head and cracked a faint smile.

"Well, you got your driver's license and your own car now, so there's no reason you can't call her up and go on a date or something," Nicky suggested.

"It's not that simple, Dad."

Then, just as Nicky was about to tell Victor that he was his own worst enemy where Maria was concerned, Tommy leaned up from the back seat and put his hand on his nephew's shoulder.

"Do me a favor, Vic. Pull in the empty lot when we get to Japeto's. And as far as what your father just said, I agree. Call that cute girl up and ask her out."

Victor still felt nervous when he thought about her.

"Okay, maybe."

As they pulled into the empty lot, Nicky asked Victor to go inside Japeto's and let Fat Frankie know they were there. Tommy and Nicky got out of the car and stood in the exact spot of their home.

"It's been two years since Urban Renewal said the block was getting torn down. There's still fuckin' houses here! Then, they said it was because of the St. Luke's Hospital, and when that didn't happen, they said the reason we all had to leave was the University expansion. Still nothing, not a fuckin' thing built here!" Nicky disgustingly said.

Tommy gave his sad opinion.

"It really doesn't matter now. It was time anyway, Nick. You guys needed to get out, for you, Grace, Ma, and Victor's sake. It'll never sit right with me that Pa didn't get to come out and enjoy the suburbs with us. It's a fucking shame is what it is. Look around, pal. The block is dirty and rundown. It even feels different being here."

Nicky put his arm around Tommy who reciprocated. Victor slow-jogged back to the empty lot, noticing how much larger it was now that the old house was gone.

"Frankie's on his way out. He told me to tell you less than five minutes."

Victor could tell by the look on their faces that they were reminiscing, so he did the same. He walked a few feet away, standing where he thought his bedroom would be if the house was still there.

Victor wanted to break the sad, sentimental vibe that filled the air, so he made a humorous comment about something he wasn't supposed to know about in the first place. No big surprise there. He thought his father and uncle deserved a good laugh.

"This is weird to think the basement is still underneath us. Dad, I hope you and Uncle Tommy got all that cash you guys stashed out of Grandpa's empty wine barrels."

Before Nicky or Tommy got a chance to respond, Fat Frankie emerged from Japeto's. He was smiling, waving, and waddling across Fillmore Street, dressed in an obnoxiously colored matching plaid coat, pants, and tie. Tommy turned to Nicky.

"Nicky, please tell Frankie he looks sharp, and don't bust his balls."

"Aw, c'mon Tommy, this one's way too fucking easy! He looks like the flag of Czechoslovakia!"

Little did Tommy know, or maybe he did, that Nicky's mind was already racing a mile a minute for additional comments about Frankie's outlandish ensemble.

"Hey, how's everyone? I already said hi to Victor inside the restaurant," Frankie excitedly greeted.

"Frankie, I don't know if it's you or the suit, but this is the best I've seen you look in years. Nicky, what do you think?" Tommy asked, hoping Nicky heeded his warning.

Frankie proudly beamed as he looked at Nicky.

"I agree with Tommy. You're a diamond, Frankie. Salute!"

Frankie pulled up his pants to reveal matching plaid socks.

"Nobody has these!"

Nicky kept his response to himself.

"And there's a good fuckin' reason for that!"

Tommy could see Nicky was ready to explode.

"Alright, let's get going," he suggested, not wanting to see his brother-in-law's tongue bleed from biting it the way he must've been.

Victor was going to make a snide comment of his own, knowing Frankie wouldn't take offense. But he didn't want to come off as a wise-assed teenage punk. Instead, Victor admired his father's restraint. He also knew it had to be killing him not to say anything.

When Frankie squeezed into the back seat and plopped his sizable ass down, Nicky held his breath and said a silent prayer for the Cadillac's suspension. The luxurious made-in-Detroit vehicle bounced twice and settled. Victor waited to get in the car just so he could enjoy seeing the "Fat Frankie Two-Bounce" up close and personal.

"So, where are we headed, gentlemen?" Victor asked.

Tommy quickly interrupted, not wanting the surprise spoiled.

"Frankie, we didn't tell him yet."

"You didn't tell him yet? Vic, you're gonna go absolutely ape-shit!"

Victor couldn't take the suspense.

"C'mon, you guys! Frankie, are we going to a whore house? Please tell me that's it!"

"Nicky, let me give him directions. I know exactly we're supposed to park," Frankie proposed.

Nicky nodded but was still deep in thought, deciding what ball-busting comment to use.

"Alright, Vic, go like you would normally go to the Shop, but from that point, continue going east on Lake Street. When you get to State Street, turn right.

I'll tell you from there. But, wait a fucking minute, Victor's driving? HOLY SHIT! Victor, you're driving!" Frankie bubbled. "The children, they grow up so quickly, don't they?"

Victor rolled his eyes knowing Frankie was teasing him. He didn't mind one bit. He felt it was more like fitting in as an 'almost' adult. When they stopped at a red light, Victor looked at his father's face. Yep, Nicky was ready to unleash about Frankie and his plaid suit. Tommy knew it was coming too, and to some extent, so did Fat Frankie. As usual, Nicky didn't disappoint.

"Frankie, I gotta ask you. Out of curiosity's sake, how many polyesters did they have to slaughter to make that costume da pagliaccio?" (Clown costume)

Everyone started laughing, especially Frankie.

"Nicky, this is the longest you've ever waited to bust my culliones! (Balls) I'm so fucking proud of you!" he exclaimed.

As they drove by the Shop, Victor laid on the car horn loudly at Nicky's request. James and Willie were outside. They knew Victor since he was four years old. The guys hooted and hollered when they saw him behind the wheel of Nicky's Cadillac. Victor waved and turned right on Lake Street.

"Okay, a right on State Street, then what?"

"Stay in the right lane. When you get to The Chicago Theater, there's a small alley right after the marquis. Turn there, pull in the first lot, and don't worry about the 'No Parking' sign. Just find a spot," Frankie directed.

"The last time I went to the movies there, my friends and I took the bus from Taylor and Loomis to see "The Good, the Bad, and the Ugly," Victor announced. "So, we're seeing a movie today?"

No one responded. Victor pulled into the second spot next to a car he had seen before but couldn't immediately remember from where. When the four of them got out of Nicky's Caddy, Victor began walking to the main entrance on State Street, but Frankie redirected him.

"We're going the back way."

Victor did an about-face and rejoined everyone. When they reached a back door with 175 N. State Street stenciled on it, Frankie knocked two times, waited a couple of seconds, and then knocked two more times. Fazool opened the door. He was out-of-uniform but his Chicago Police badge was prominently displayed hanging on a strap around his neck. His arms and eyes opened as wide as his smile when he saw Frankie standing there.

"Come in, ya fuckin' mamaluke!" (Male who lacks masculinity)

Fazool's eyes quickly went to Victor. He didn't recognize him.

"Jesus Christ, I'm so sorry, I didn't see, uh…," he began apologizing.

"Hi, Sergeant Pirelli, it's Victor, Nicky's son. It's been a couple of years. How are you and your family doing?"

Fazool's facial expression changed from embarrassment to relief after remembering the not-so-young anymore Victor.

"Everyone's good, good. You sprouted up a couple of inches, huh? Alright, guys. Follow me and watch your step. Your eyes have to get adjusted to the darkness," Fazool warned.

Victor hoped to use that phrase the next time he wrote.

"Adjusted to the Darkness. I like that, lots of possibilities."

As Fazool led everyone up one of the side aisles, a Bugs Bunny cartoon started playing, brightening their way. Victor noticed small groups of seated guys but there were spaces in between the groups. Also, someone was standing in the middle of the aisle, way at the top waiving.

"There's Lenny," Victor heard Tommy tell his father. "They must be sitting up there."

After taking a few more steps, an arm reached out from one of the seats blocking their way.

"Hey, Tommy!"

Tommy smiled, shook hands, and exchanged a few brief words. Nicky joined the conversation while Frankie filled the aisle on his way up to Lenny. As Victor stopped and respectfully waited, he looked towards the middle aisle about halfway up. He saw the silhouette of two heads leaning forward in their seats. Since his eyes were still adjusting, he couldn't make out who it was. Tommy and Nicky continued with their conversation with the seated man.

"Tommy, Nicky, nice to see both of you guys again! Hey, Nicky, that ain't your kid from that day, is it?"

"It is," answered Nicky.

"Jesus Christ, he's almost a grown man! Where'd the fuckin' time go?" the seated man asked.

The man beside him adjusted in his oversized seat and extended his hand directly to Nicky.

"No hard feelings from back then, right?" he asked.

"Nick, you remember Big Charlie, don't you?" the first man reintroduced.

Nicky took Big Charlie's hand and shook it with both of his.

"Of course, how can I forget Big Charlie? All that matters is that everything worked out," Nicky quickly answered, deciding to leave well-enough alone where Carmine and Big Charlie were concerned.

Tommy excused himself and continued navigating his way to Lenny and Frankie. Nicky turned, grabbed Victor's arm, and lightly tugged, pulling him forward to their seats. Before following, Victor looked back to the middle aisle. The two heads were Michael Jr. and Dino! They were sitting next to their fathers and a couple of other guys he didn't recognize. His friends were smiling, nodding, and nudging each other simultaneously, appearing to enjoy his confused look. Victor took a quick second to collect his thoughts.

"What the fuck is going on? These two jadrools (Losers/Knuckleheads) *didn't say anything to me about being here today."*

Victor followed his father but glanced at Mr. Carmine and Big Charlie, who smiled and nodded. Victor returned their gesture. Two steps further are all it took for him to remember who they were.

"Those are the two guys from the Shop on that cold-ass Christmas Eve!"

When they reached the top of the stairs, Victor put his arm around his father.

"I remember those guys, Dad, Christmas Eve, 1965, in front of The Shop, right? The one guy pulled the fucking parking meter out of the cement!"

"All that turned out to be was a big misunderstanding. It's been resolved for a very long time, Victor. What's important now is that you go and shake hands with Lenny and Vinnie, and don't forget to kiss Mr. E."

Victor made his way down the aisle and shook hands with Lenny. Seated next to him was the man himself, Manny Ingalleretta.

"Hi, Mr. Ingalleretta, it's nice to see you again. It's Victor, Joe DaBone's grandson.

"Sure, I remember you! You look just like Giuseppe when he was a young man."

Manny turned and put his hand on what Victor thought was an armrest, but it wasn't. It was Vinnie Champagne's forearm. When he stood to shake Victor's hand, a few people started booing. Vinnie was so tall that his head blocked a portion of the movie projector's light. Vinnie ducked down quickly when he realized it. When those booing turned and saw it was Champagne that inadvertently shadowed the movie screen, the jeers ceased. Victor was shocked that the palm side of the ginormous man's fingers went almost halfway up his forearm when they shook! Victor felt like a newborn baby shaking hands with Wilt Chamberlin.

Frankie and Vinnie sat at opposite ends of the aisle where new double seats were recently installed for extra, extra-large moviegoers like both of them, and of course, Big Charlie.

Victor took the open seat next to his father. When the cartoon ended and the screen darkened, the conversations in the theater went silent. Tommy and Frankie leaned forward. They wanted to see the priceless look on Victor's face. The screen flashed brightly. The pyramidal mountain peak surrounded by tiny stars to create a circular dome used by Paramount Pictures to begin their movies appeared as it always did, only this time, it was accompanied by the sound of a single, melodically played trumpet.

The words "Paramount Pictures Presents" appeared and then faded to black. Then it happened, faded up from black to the movie title, all while punctuated with the ominous sound of that single blaring trumpet still echoing and continuously playing through. Victor's entire body exploded with goosebumps and chills when he read the words on the screen:

"Mario Puzo's The Godfather"

Oddly enough, the words struck Victor first. He thought they were printed exactly like the novel's cover, right down to the drawing of the hand holding the puppeteer cross with strings attached only to the 'father' portion of Godfather.

"Just like the book!"

Realizing this exclusive screening was the second part of his birthday present, he turned sideways and spoke quietly but excitedly to Nicky.

"NO FUCKING WAY! It's not scheduled to open in Chicago for another two weeks. It just premiered five days ago in New York, and people are still lined up around the block!"

Nicky smiled and nodded.

"This ain't New York, and the guys in this theater don't wait in lines, especially to see this movie."

Nicky pulled Victor in closely and whispered.

"Son, today we're here with The Chicago Outfit."

CHAPTER 16
EVERYONE'S GOT SOMETHING GOING ON

Besides the deaths, there were other significant changes in the mid to late 70s. Nicky sold his beloved company for a healthy profit and went to work at Big Banana with Tommy. The Shop was Nicky's pride and joy. It made him sick to his stomach to sell it, but the business move aspect was brilliant. It wasn't worth the cost of purchasing new punch-presses, lathes, or other equipment needed to remain competitive. Even worse was the thought of dumping thousands of dollars into that relic of a building that failed the last two city safety inspections. Besides that, technology was rapidly changing. More and more tool & die makers entering the job market had college degrees and rocket scientist mentalities. The new crop of toolers applied their computer knowledge to tridimensional (3D) programming, cutting, and plating. As sharp, mechanically inclined, and good with his hands as Nicky was, he was no rocket scientist. The majority of what he knew was self-taught, learning what he could from the older die makers he worked with along the way. This new digital age went way over his head. Also, the dozen or so government contracts, once a considerable chunk of the Shop's profits, didn't renew. Instead, the United States farmed out those jobs in trade agreements with Mexico, China, and other countries with cheap, penny-on-the-dollar labor. For months, the only projects that came through the doors were low-profit margin piecemeal drill tap orders. The only thing Nicky was happy about was that the older Shop workers were close to retirement and the younger guys quickly found other employment.

After an adjustment period, Nicky realized it was more or less a no-brainer to accept Tommy's overly generous offer to work with him at Big Banana. When he laid out the employment package, salary, and commission schedule, Nicky couldn't believe it.

"Jesus Christ, Tommy, I would've sold the Shop five fuckin' years ago if I knew you were gonna pay me this."

"Nicky, five years ago, I couldn't afford to offer you that. Now, I can."

Victor thought his father also working at Big Banana was the best thing in the world. So, in true DaBone fashion, he took a rare opportunity on his dad's first day as an official employee to turn the tables and tease him for a change.

"Hey, Uncle Tommy, who's the new old guy writing sales orders?" Victor asked loud enough so everyone at the main counter could hear.

The workers and a few customers knew the Nicky/Tommy/Victor relationship, so they laughed. Nicky pointed at Victor, smiled, and wagged his finger warning him to behave. Tommy was talking with one of the union guys, but that didn't stop him from quickly grabbing the microphone so everyone in the store could hear his response over the loudspeaker.

"That OLD guy is your NEW boss, Victor, so you better start working a lot harder."

Victor began throwing two and three boxes at a time on his pallet jack, rushing and sprinting down the aisle to Nicky's chair at the sales counter feigning to be out of breath.

"Is that fast enough for you, sir?"

"Move a little quicker next time, kid, like your ass is on fire!" Nicky suggested.

That type of shenanigans was the new norm at Big Banana. The employees turned the busiest, stressful work hours into fun, productive days that went by in a flash. Tommy loved having Nicky there to keep a watchful eye over things since he was spending some time traveling back and forth to Arizona at the request of the Outfit. The Bosses asked Tommy to help coordinate things at a cartage company in Scottsdale that they co-owned with Micky Silvio, who had moved there permanently the year before. Micky's company, Silvio Trucking, specialized in produce hauling, boasting the most current semi-truck refrigeration units available. What wasn't publicized was that there was more than lettuce, avocados, potatoes, and onions in those trucks when they got to Michigan, Detroit, Chicago, and Wisconsin. So Tommy drew up a plan for Silvio's trucks to use the least traveled, most inconspicuous routes. The goal was to keep Mob cargo away from weighing stations and state troopers looking to make a pinch.

Fat Frankie was doing his thing, making money for the Outfit hand-over-fist booking wagers. Japeto's restaurant business was also booming. Still, he made the time to start a side company featuring his famous hot giardiniera peppers and specialty sauces. The Japeto's label featured a cartoon version of Frankie. The caricature's belly had the jar's contents written on it. Nicky helped and built the equipment Frankie needed for his jarring assembly line, which was set up in the far corner storage area of Big Banana. So, for almost two full years before Teresa died, the three longtime neighborhood friends were all together under the same roof, joined by their favorite part-time employee/part-time College of DuPage student/part-time writer, Victor. They couldn't have been happier coexisting, busting each other's balls, and most importantly, making money.

Dirk was also keeping himself extremely busy. He graduated law school a full semester ahead of schedule, finished at the top of his class, passed the bar exam on his first attempt, and became one of the most sought-after new attorneys in the Midwest. Every large firm in the area was tossing offers of high yearly salaries and commissions, bonuses, incentive plans, country club memberships, and other employment perks at him. Dirk turned down every one of them. Instead, he opened his own office in Brookfield Terrace. Dirk was the only Rigonest son working in the private sector. The three oldest brothers eventually followed their father in the enforcement end of the law profession. Brian became a lead agent for the CIA. Patrick chose The Justice Department, and Tim Rigonest landed a lofty position in Kansas City as an Assistant Bureau Chief for the Drug Enforcement Agency.

Michael Jr. and Dino made good use of their father's influential connections to make some exciting moves of their own. First, Michael Jr. opened an advertising agency. He used his father's name often and wisely, especially when meeting prospective clients. Company owners wanted no problems with The Fixer feeling it served them best to stay, or get in his good graces. They knew the kind of political power Gabriel wielded, so they gladly signed up to do business with his son. Michael Jr. exceeded expectations with his ad agency. His next move was purchasing a small printing company so he could brand his own magazine. Chicago Style, Michael Jr.'s brain child publication, focused on the Windy City and its offerings. The magazine became so popular in the Chicago area, that there was a waiting list to advertise in it! Dino appeared in the magazine often, modeling the sharpest apparel and the most expensive suits from the very best shops. Michael Jr. teased Double D when he showed him the proof copies from his first photo shoot.

"Dino, is it me or do you look even more fuckable than usual?"

Victor even got in on the action. Before the second edition of Chicago Style went to press, Victor met with Michael Jr. at his plush East South Water Street office and pitched his idea over Chicken Parmigiano Marciano, an Angelo's Café specialty dish. He brought in dozens of public domain photographs and pictures of notable people from other magazines and newspapers and wrote humorous, obnoxious captions underneath them. Victor called his idea "CENSORED." He suggested to Michael Jr. that the actual word 'CENSORED' be lightly outlined, appearing as a red stamp over the reprints.

"The captioned photos give readers the impression they're seeing and reading something that wasn't authorized for publication Presenting it exactly that way makes it look you told the standards and practices legal douche bag to go fuck himself when he advised against printing it," Victor excitedly explained.

Michael Jr. twisted a popular quote from the popular "Kung Fu" television series to express his interest.

"That's very ballsy, Grasshopper."

Although the editorial staff was hesitant to share their boss's enthusiasm, fearing flack from conservative advertisers and readers, they reluctantly printed one of Victor's submissions. Michael Jr. was his biggest fan, pointing out that CENSORED was right in line with his own lay it all out there and take no prisoners vision and marketing attitude.

"We are fucking rebels! Edginess is our trademark!" he repeatedly told his staff. "If you're not on onboard with this, that's no problem. I heard "Christian Life" and "Better Homes and Gardens" are hiring. I'll write you a nice letter of recommendation."

Victor proved the thinner-skinned magazine staff wrong and carved out a nice little niche for himself in the process. Readers loved the photographs and the captions he wrote for them. Soon after seeing how cool and popular CENSORED was becoming, Michael Jr. asked Victor to write a full-page humorous piece for his December/January holiday edition. The title Victor chose was, "The Holidays are Over."

A few copies of Chicago Style made their way to the desk of Nation Lampoon Magazine creator Douglas Kenny. It was a stroke of luck that Kenny's good friend was Harold Ramis, a Lampoon original managing editor and a monthly contributor since the first edition hit newsstands. Ramis was a Chicago native who gained popularity as an actor, writer, and director at Second City Theater. He was involved in some of the most memorable skits ever performed on that stage.

Since Second City Theater was an advertiser in Gabriel's magazine, it was no surprise that Victor's sophomoric contributions would piqué someone's curiosity and interest from that venue. So when Chicago Style arrived in the mail at Second City, it made the rounds from directors to writers, to costume and set designers, to actors, down to stagehands. After it was feverishly passed around, it eventually wound up receiving the biggest compliment you could pay a magazine, cover to cover crinkled and shriveled, leaning against a bathroom toilet along with Playboy, National Lampoon, MAD, and High Times.

Another Chicago native and Second City alum enjoyed reading Michael Jr.'s magazine. This fan especially loved the bar/restaurant/nightclub review section with the full-page food and drink photos. When he spotted Victor's contributions, he wasted no time boasting to his New York and California peers and collaborators how Chicago-based comedy was the funniest. Since he was rapidly becoming a show business bad boy, nobody argued when he proudly touted and bragged about anything having to do with Chicago. This performer was amassing fans by the thousands. The public couldn't get enough of his intimidating brand of physical humor. Television critics, entertainment reporters, and famous actors and actresses agreed that watching him was hilariously addicting. His weekly on-screen appearances and character portrayals were almost as notable as his well-publicized off-screen antics. He started as a local favorite on the Chicago comedy scene but quickly became a national legend with stellar media attention. You could tell that he was someone destined to become very special in show business. His name was John Belushi.

Victor was unaware that the famous trio saw his CENSORED photo captions and Christmas piece. All Michael Jr. knew was that his magazine's circulation was rapidly climbing. Unfortunately, there was no way for him to determine who was reading it. He figured the rise was due to the hundreds of Chicago area medical and business offices that became new subscribers. Michael Jr. was excited at the prospect of getting at least a handful of them to purchase ad space for their companies in his magazine. Of course, his plan was to again use his intimidating last name, but with one addition, he suggested his own agency when it came time to design their advertising campaigns.

"This way, we're double bangin' 'em," he emphasized to his sales staff. "The agency gets a piece, the magazine gets a piece, we all get a piece."

Victor continued following freelance submission guidelines, sending out dozens of his articles to all types of publications. Most of them didn't make it to print, but some did. When complimented about something he wrote, Victor always downplayed it, quickly changing the subject. He was his own worst critic, constantly second-guessing himself, wondering if people actually understood what he wrote.

"Is it too inside? Will they see the irony? Am I the only one that thinks this? Will they get it without me actually writing it, or should I make sure and spell it out for them?"

Regardless of his apprehensions, Victor took on the most monumental writing task of all, a novel. It was a work in progress and already 60 pages deep. He kept its existence from everyone. The premise was simple, something the average reader could understand and relate to without the assistance of a dictionary.

"Build anticipation with the turn of every page. Use universal, recognizable words and phrases," he constantly reminded himself.

Victor was always looking for signs from above for everything he wrote. It's like he needed spiritual approval from beyond to justify every word. Then, a few months later, he entered a contest, as did tens of thousands of others. A popular, world-renowned satire magazine had challenged loyal readers to submit their own original stories.

In keeping with the magazine's no-holds-barred, tasteless, outrageous, groundbreaking humor, contest rules clearly stated in black and white that all submissions were required to be nasty, obscure, irreverent, or violent. Also gladly accepted were stories containing homophobic slurs, cannibalism, promiscuous activities between relatives, friends, and the clergy, blasphemy, bigotry, racism, or defilement of the recently deceased.

Since Victor was a big fan since the magazine's first edition appeared on newsstands in April of 1970, he jumped at the opportunity to enter. It wasn't about the $1,000 prize money. It was about having his work evaluated by the very people whose writing inspired him. After all, it was their outlandish words that thrilled him since he was old enough to sit cross-legged on the radiator on Fillmore Street. He recalled his 14-year old self, voraciously feeding that newfound insatiable appetite for adult, off-color, irreverent humor. Understanding the magazine's parodies, surrealist content, crass and bawdy jesting, nude cartoons, and an unusual mix of intelligent, cutting-edge wit made Victor feel as if he was actually part of some big inside joke. Only one publication on the planet had the balls big enough to hold a writing contest that encouraged its readers to stoop to such low levels. That was National Lampoon.

When Victor received the telegraph informing him he'd won, he threw up. Not once, but three times. His outlandish, satirical piece, "CELEBRITY FARTS," might have been his best work to date. Victor selected dozens of famous actors, actresses, athletes, and political figures. Then, he categorized their fart sounds and smells, comparing the noises and scents to musical instruments and various rotting meats, assorted cheeses, fish, and vegetables. The unflattering public domain pictures taken from various magazines sealed the deal for Victor in the eyes of contest judges - top celebrities photographed looking as if they were really farting or attempting to hold one in. Victor's raunchy, detailed descriptions of their gaseous releases were the icing on the cake. Besides an official release form authorizing National Lampoon to print his article, Victor received a handwritten note.

Your winning article was hilarious. I'm a fan of your Chicago Style Magazine stuff, too. So are Ramis and Belushi. You must be smoking some really great weed. (It's not as good as mine, though.)

Doug Kenny

Victor framed the telegram and proudly hung it on his bedroom wall in a prestigious spot, right between the picture of Zeus and him in the backyard on Fillmore Street and his most recent addition, an autographed picture arm in arm with Don Rickles backstage at the Mill Run Theater taken earlier that year. Winning the contest and receiving the personalized letter from Doug Kenny were the types of tangible signs Victor was looking for. But, his heavenly revelation arrived the following week in the form of a 19-word personalized letter.

How one handles success or failure is determined by their early childhood. Congratulations on winning the National Lampoon contest.

Harold Ramis

He read and reread it ten times. Ramis's words really blasted the shit out of him. Then, Victor noticed the scribbled, handwritten return address on the eleventh and final time before tucking the note back into the envelope.

Animal House New York, New York

Less than two years later, when National Lampoon began running television ads to promote their upcoming movie, "Animal House," Victor finally understood the meaning of the return address.

Things continued going well for Michael Jr. He received the "Entrepreneur of the Year" award from the Illinois Better Business Board and his magazine and ad agency were growing by leaps and bounds.

Dino wasn't sitting on the sidelines by any stretch of the imagination. Those who knew Dino "Double D" Domenico were divided into two camps. The first group thought he was unbelievably handsome. The second felt he was drop-dead gorgeous. Those that never saw him were definitely missing out on a visual treat. Dino was the type of guy you took a couple of quick glances at before you wound up just staring at him. People often thought they recognized him from somewhere. He generated the aura of someone famous, like an athlete, a movie star, or a celebrity of some kind. More times than not, women fantasized about performing at least a couple of sex acts with him. The guys were automatically jealous no matter how good they looked in their own right. There was something about Dino's physicality that made even the most secure men feel slightly uncomfortable and underdeveloped in their own skin. His thick, black, perfectly-coiffed, long, silky, wavy hair more than complimented his chiseled, smooth, and unblemished European-complexioned skin. His body was slender yet toned like a gymnast. He stood six-foot, one inch, and weighed 180 pounds. The clothing Dino wore clung to his frame as if he was a mannequin displayed at an exclusive boutique in Beverly Hills. Combine his universal handsomeness with the backing of Sam Baltic, head-honcho of the Illinois Film and Television Department, and Dino "Double D" Domenico's star was on an upward trajectory.

Baltic and Salvatore were friends since the late 1950s. So when Sam heard

Domenico's son was interested in appearing in magazines, television, and movies, he called Sally Boy to see if he could help. Salvatore actually planted that seed. He wanted to see if Baltic would reach out to him once he found out Dino's interest.

Sam and Sally Boy had more than a few mutual acquaintances. One of them was Ricardo "Eve" Everia. He was the burly, fully-bearded Sergeant at Arms for the powerful Electrical Engineers Union headed by Anthony "The Arm" LaPorte, who was Outfit Boss Jimmy Rio's brother-in-law. Everia delivered the seedling message to Baltic during casual conversation at a ribbon-cutting event. It wasn't uncommon for the men to run into each other on the job or at a dedication/groundbreaking ceremony. One of Everia's responsibilities as Chief Inspector for Illinois Electrical was ensuring that all of the electricians used on permitted film locations were union members in good standing. Ricardo was also in cahoots with the Outfit issuing illegal job permits at their various construction projects throughout Chicago and the suburbs. Everia was a perfect example of a connected guy in the Syndicate. He was honest, loyal, shrewd, intimidating, and most importantly, kept quiet about his Mob activity.

Sally Boy wondered if Sam would remember how he got his well-paying, cushy, city job with the Film Department. Baltic most certainly did. It was because Salvatore vouched for him with Manny. So when Ingalleretta got word to the mayor that Sam was one of his guys, it was only a matter of days before Baltic was hired as Director of the Illinois Film Department. If companies wanted to do any movie or television filming in Illinois, you needed approval, and Sam was the guy. The first official project authorized by Baltic's newly established Film Department was back in 1957. The production, filmed on the Streets of Chicago, was a black and white television crime drama starring Lee Marvin. The show was called "M Squad." Since then, more than a thousand projects came and went through Sam's office. He acquired a slew of contacts in the film, television and print industries in the 20 years that followed and learned how to operate between the lines. Sam knew exactly what he needed to do to help promote Dino. He casually let directors, casting agents, and extra coordinators know that he had a handsome, talented local guy for their productions. They all got the message. That was great news for Dino and the media companies that hired him. They all got their work permits minus the usual red tape.

Salvatore sat at the head chair on the morning of Dino's first assignment through Sam Baltic. He wore his trademark Dago-tee, admiring his most recent score, a newly installed marble floor for his kitchen, compliments of Joe Zito, a truck driver for Marble Roma of Lombard. Zito was only one of many that got their job because of Sally Boy. Domenico often called upon those he had secured employment for and asked them for help related to some kind of home improvement project. If Sally Domenico got you a job, you could bet your ass that soon after that, you were at his home. What you did there was show your gratitude for your bountiful employment by nailing, sawing, cooking, or delivering stolen construction materials and supplies. You helped Sally Boy with whatever he asked you to help with.

An ostentatious portion of the exclusive Ginger Pond residents where Sally

Boy lived wasted lots of energy overly concerned about their material possessions versus their Syndicate neighbors'. Their time would've been better well spent seeking professional treatment for the plethora of personal problems, substance addictions, and endless character flaws that plagued their own families. But, at the end of the day, it always came down to the makes, models, and quantity of vehicles owned, whose landscaping looked better, and what type of expensive motorized recreational toys you had. Like Salvatore, the few Ginger Pond families with organized crime ties couldn't care less about the 'Keeping up with the Joneses' mentality. Sally Boy let his Medigon (American) neighbors worry about that. As long as their privacy was respected, the only other thing of importance to Mob families was snow plowing. They were big on ensuring their Cadillacs, Lincolns, and Mercedes Benzes safely made it up to their winding 300-foot custom brick driveways, hidden on both sides by massive evergreens to their 4-car heated garages during the snowy winter months. One of the old-school connected Teamster guys even temporarily rigged a plow to his wife's Lincoln Continental Town Car!

    Anna Marie poured Salvatore a cup of imported espresso. Then, she got busy making him his favorite morning meal, sunny-side-up eggs, Greek toast, fried potatoes, and ever so slightly charred Canadian bacon. Before that was served, Sally Boy nibbled on fresh mozzarella and sliced ripe plum tomatoes that waited for him on a 150-year old antique Capodimonte plate handed down through the generations starting with his great grandmother.

    Dino was still sleeping from the night before. He was the recipient of a significant birthday shindig thrown by Michael Jr. in the private room of one of the most exclusive nightspots in Chicago, The 555 Club on Rush Street. On paper, the registered owner of 555 was well-known top Wheaton criminal attorney and late-night party veteran Raul McClendon. Raul was assuredly on the guest list any time a high-end soiree was thrown in the western suburbs. However, the real owners were the Stein family and Jimmy "Clams" Campione. Jimmy Clams owned a fresh seafood company on Fulton Street. He was protected by Joey Balducci and very friendly with top members of the Grand Avenue Crew, especially Underboss, Mr. Tony. Double D.'s birthday party lasted for almost 36 hours. Out of the 80 invited attendees, less than a dozen stayed for the duration. Those that made it to the very end were treated to breakfast by the birthday boy himself at Sam Hatchell's Restaurant at 6:00 a.m. Dino needed the entire day and night to recuperate, so he spent it napping, watching football, drinking a couple of gallons of water, eating fresh fruit, and taking aspirin.

    When Dino strutted into the kitchen that morning ready to take on the world, he looked like he had just stepped off the cover of a magazine. Not bad for a guy who spent 36 hours straight celebrating another trip around the planet.

    "Listen, Dino, before I forget, you need to do me a favor and keep track of how many jobs Baltic gets you and what you earn," Salvatore asked. "This is important to me."

    After an entire year, Salvatore still hadn't asked Dino about his earnings through Baltic. Sally Boy knew Dino was actively working, having spoken numerous times with him about the types of jobs he was being sent on, where filming was taking place, and what parts he had, but never about his earnings. Dino appeared in dozens of local magazine ads, commercials, and trade films. He also briefly appeared as a movie extra in a few television shows and two motion pictures. Over that stretch of time, the entire Domenico family sat and watched him when his commercials aired. Anna Marie cried the first time she saw her handsome boy on television. Dino's older sister, Connie, always told him he looked pale and skinny. Then, she'd give him the finger and silently mouth the words 'Fuck You' to her baby brother when her parents weren't looking.

Carol Kleinberg was a 50-year-old, bleached-blonde heavy, with or without her blusher, rouge, and mascara, Jewish fireplug of a woman. She was a well-known, top representative from the Chicago branch of The William Morris Agency for over 20 years, an eternity in that business. Carol represented about 100 clients, all actively working in their chosen fields. That was unheard of for an agent from Chicago. Carol and Dino met by chance one evening at a luxurious, north shore party hosted by Pierre St. Pabsy, an up-and-coming fashion designer. Carol's job was to supply the event with a dozen of the agency's top male and female models to wear St. Pabsy clothes, jewelry, and other apparel provided by Mob-controlled Ritz Designs. Attillio Pintozzi, a Syndicate Associate from Oak Brook, was a silent business partner with Genoa "Genny" Carlotti, a California-born/Chicago Heights-raised Street Boss. Kleinberg chose only the most physically attractive models to work that evening. They displayed four different ensembles, each in a 3-hour timeframe. In addition, they mingled socially with the crowd and promoted the new fall lines they wore. Carol indirectly heard more than just a few whispers about Dino earlier in the year. He was never referred to her by name but by similar descriptions to her by peers and modeling contacts. They called Dino things like "The Mobster's handsome son," "The too gorgeous guy," or 'The handsome one with the Outfit father."

Initially, Carol thought Dino looked like an Italian version of Elvis Presley, which was obviously a good thing. However, by the time it took for them to exchange pleasantries, Kleinberg's trained eyes and ears had seen and heard what was needed. She scanned the details of Dino's face, his hair, his teeth, his eyes, as well as his bodily motions during their brief conversation. Kleinberg used this evaluation technique with every person she ever considered representing. It was her proven method. As a result, she liked Dino's look, his deeper than his age voice, how intelligently he spoke, his eye contact, and how fluidly he carried himself.

One week after their brief meeting, Carol got Dino's phone number from Sam Baltic She called him and asked if he' like to meet at her agency office on Michigan Avenue for what may be a possible opportunity for both of them. Dino thought highly of his father's opinion, but he wanted to independently make moves and career decisions. So, he decided it best not to bother him with this just yet. So, instead, Dino called Sam Baltic to ask his opinion.

"Sam, do you think I need someone like her? I think I'm doing okay getting work on my own, right? You call me and tell me where to go, and who to see. I show up, they look me over, try me out, and it's been a done deal. I realize the only reason I'm getting my foot in the door is because of you, and I've thanked you every time, but, correct me if I'm wrong, if they didn't think I was right, they wouldn't use me, whether it's you referring me or not, isn't that right?"

Sam didn't want to offer advice to Dino without knowing what Sally Boy wanted, so he provided a generic suggestion.

"The feedback I've gotten about you is all positive, Dino. You show up for calls and auditions on time, you're always ready to work, you mind your own business, follow directions, and you do whatever is asked of you. Perfect. The photographers, the extras casting directors, the shoot managers, they love that kinda shit, it's fewer headaches for them. All I can tell you about Carol Kleinberg is that she's a serious broad. Everyone in the business knows her. So I say meet, listen to what she has to say, and see if it benefits you. No harm in that, right?"

Dino was intrigued, so he accepted Carol's offer to meet. He wore a dark sport coat, a white dress shirt (only one top button unbuttoned), a pair of black cotton dress pants, and a new pair of black dress shoes from Florsheim. When Dino walked into Deborah's office, the male receptionist looked at him, smiled, stood, and introduced himself.

"Hello, Mr. Domenico. My name is James. Ms. Kleinberg will be with you shortly."

While Dino sat in the waiting room, he looked at James.

"The guy that greets people and answers the phones is better looking, better built, and better dressed than me! What the fuck am I thinking? What am I doing here?"

James was, at best, above average looking. Dino couldn't see that. It was almost as if he was trying to talk himself out of being there. A few minutes later, Carol emerged wearing her usual array of heavy cosmetics. She also had a large pair of red horn-framed glasses that sat at the tip of her nose. She hugged Dino, air-kissed his cheek and the two of them retreated into her office. After five minutes of exchanged pleasantries, Carol was all business. She spoke, Dino listened. Kleinberg presented herself like she had a personal interest in his success. At least that's how Dino processed it. Carol didn't mince words, laying it all out as an official representation proposal.

"Let me mentor you, doll. Those good looks of yours will open a lot of doors. I know you already know that. But, if you truly want to be successful in this business and take your career to the next level, we'll need to fine-tune that earthy, Italian charm and magnetic personality of yours. That's going to take getting you enrolled in a special acting class with my friend, who happens to be one of the best instructors in the business. He's right here in Chicago, too. Once we get that going, I think we can write our own ticket."

Dino dug what Carol was saying up until her next sentence.

"You'll need to sign a contract with the agency, Dino. It's standard, clear cut, and used by every big firm in the business."

"I'm not thrilled about signing anything," he interrupted. "I like picking the jobs that I think are right for me."

Carol smiled. She took her glasses off and pulled up a chair right next to him so their knees were almost touching.

"Dino, it's an industry-standard document for one year of representation, by me, through the William Morris Agency. Do you realize the exposure you'll get? Have an attorney look it over. That's not a problem."

Carol changed gears. She went from selling herself and the agency to confidant and partner.

"Listen, I was born in Chicago. I worked in New York, Los Angeles, and even Paris for about ten years. I came back here because I love the city and the people. I know in my heart that this is where I belong. There are tons of opportunities for young talent here, but only if you know who's casting what projects. That's my specialty. Feel free to ask anyone in the business about me. Chicago is hot with a capital 'H.' It's what I always thought it could be; a stepping stone for national success in the entertainment industry."

Then, Carol addressed one of the things Dino wondered about, his father. She folded her hands on her lap, looked him straight in his eyes, and spoke a decibel or two lower than she previously had.

"Dino, I know who father is and I know he has lots of powerful, influential friends. I don't pull punches. I'm not here to fuck over you or anyone else I represent. Honey, I didn't ask for this meeting because of who you're related or connected to, you're here because I'd like the opportunity to represent you. That's the truth, plain and simple, babe. Do you understand where I'm coming from with this?"

Dino nodded.

"Go on all the auditions Sam Baltic lines up for you and continue to do what you've been doing. The only thing I'll ask is for you to include me in your job decisions. I may be able to offer you some insight and advice. For any jobs that I bring to the table, the agency receives a flat 15% commission. Thousands of models, actors, singers, and entertainers out there this very minute would kill to have this kind of representation deal. So, Mr. Dino Domenico, you need to give some thought to what I'm proposing. If you're not serious about this and not 100% on board, I'll wish you luck. Who knows, maybe we'll bump into each other at some function."

Since he was little, Dino dreamt about acting. His secret wish was to host his own show. Kleinberg slid her chair back to the spot in front of her desk and put her glasses back on.

"I'll be candid with you, Dino. As far as working freelance through Sam Baltic, you're on a nice roll. The local commercials, the movie-extra work, the print modeling, it all looks great on a resume, but when it comes down to it, there's bigger and better out there, but only if you're hungry. Chicago isn't California or New York. That's where the majority of the big action plays out. We've got to launch you from Chicago, like a rocket. We need to showcase that you're so much more than just a local pretty face. I mean no disrespect, but you need to step it up. Almost every successful actor and model working has an attitude. That's what makes or breaks you in this business. The major magazines offer unlimited exposure worldwide. There are also hundreds of products and services that would be a perfect match for you. If we do this right, you'll be able to pick and choose which of them you want to associate yourself with. Plan locally, but think nationally."

Carol promised Dino during their conversation that she'd also use her influence getting him enrolled in the prestigious Actor's Workshop on Clark Street. That famous location was where Chicago thespians, performance artists, singers, and musicians who were lucky enough to get an invitation to register for classes, wound up getting a steady flow of good-paying jobs. But, first, a decision needed to be made, and Dino needed some solid advice from his father. So, he thanked Carol for the opportunity, promising to get back to her. Then, that evening, Dino ran things by Salvatore. Sally Boy let him talk uninterrupted about his meeting - he already knew what was going on. (Sam Baltic called him earlier.) Salvatore waited until his son was finished enthusiastically laying everything out for him.

"So, what do you think, Dad?" Dino asked.

"First, that Jew-broad talent agent? Guess what, Dino? She's the real fucking deal. Look, I already talked to Sam Baltic. He told me not only is she the best, but she's righteous. Also, everyone in that business knows her. So, the advice she's giving you sounds legit to me. We'll get an attorney to look over any contract signing. And, for what it's worth, Baltic said she knows my friends and me, and I consider that a good thing because that means no jaggin' you around, capicse?"

Dino agreed.

"You know how much I love you, and I only want the very best. But, my business, all the union shit, the real estate, the things I've done in the past, the things I'm currently doing, and the things I will continue to do in the future, I don't want that for you. Believe me, I know how cool, exciting, and intriguing it all looks, but you see that from a position of safety and comfort. So, remember what I'm about to say. There's always some type of danger with my involvement."

Dino asked a question. He already knew the answer but wanted to hear his father speak the words.

"Dad, why don't you just stop with everything, you know what I'm talking about."

"Dino, now you're being naïve. My thing never stops. That's not how it works. Don't think that Senior (How Sally Boy referred to The Fixer) and I don't hear how much you and Michael Jr. know about street things. That's serious business that doesn't concern either of you. Keeping you guys away from all that shit is priority one for us. Take advantage of our connections and involvement without taking unnecessary risks yourself. You, Michael Jr., and a few others, all have a unique opportunity. Tell your buddies they need to be sharp enough to see that, too. God blessed you, Dino. Even though I've sinned like a mother fucker most of my adult life, He still blessed you."

Sally Boy and The Fixer were right. Their sons did love Chicago Syndicate gossip and trivia. The first time Victor heard them challenge each other, (They called their game "Who's Who in the Outfit") he was beyond impressed with their knowledge of the names, monikers, crew affiliations, Mob ranks, and specialties of almost everyone who had anything to do with The Chicago Syndicate. Victor thought it was way cool that they trusted him enough to play their very private game in front of him.

Dino slept on everything Sam, Carol, and his father said for a few days, taking all the valuable career advice he received into careful consideration. It was a no-brainer. Go with Carol Kleinberg and give it a year. So, two weeks later, after having an entertainment attorney from New York look at the contract, Dino signed. Next up, was the Actor's Workshop class. Dino came up with a plan to show his seriousness and enthusiasm. H needed to make his presence known and distinguish himself, just like Carol suggested.

On the very first day of class, Dino purposely showed up late. When he walked in, the professor was speaking. Dino didn't make eye contact with anyone, even though everyone's attention was focused on him and the 1920s-style iron-clad stage door that creaked when it slammed shut behind him.

"I apologize for being late. My name is Dino Domenico," he said quietly.

Dino slid into the first empty seat he could find, but that didn't stop the teacher from using his tardiness to explain why punctuality was necessary for not just his class but as an essential general rule in being a professional.

"This is perfect," he thought.

Double D.'s idea was to perform a scene explaining why he was late. If it worked, great, if it didn't, at least it showed initiative. He respectfully waited until the teacher finished stressing the importance of being on time. Then, he stood, looking at the instructor first. Next he made eye contact with as many classmates as he could in ten seconds, the amount of time he felt it would take to make his performance personal.

"A*CTION!*" he thought.

Dino wasted no time, diving right in, explaining he was late because of the funeral services for his parents and young brother.

"I don't know if any of you heard about that small plane crash on Tuesday, but that was my parents and little brother. They were on the way to Missouri to see my 81-year old grandmother who's on death's door," Dino explained, looking distraught, purposely struggling with words.

He continued with a fabricated back-story about his family, even adlibbing a few lines.

"My brother was only 11 years old. He was so excited about the plane ride. It was his first time. God, he didn't sleep a wink the night before. He had that little-kid anticipation, you know?" Dino continued, incorporating sniffles and a quivering lip into his performance.

The entire class, including Professor Tim White, was practically in tears. He expressed condolences, asked Dino to have a seat, and quickly changed the subject. White questioned the students, asking what specific entertainment areas interested them. One by one, everyone responded. When the last student finished, the entire class turned and looked at Dino. He was still in character, doing his very best to play the emotionally distraught, worn, visibly shaken son/bereaved older brother. Dino asked if they wanted to hear what his intended focus was. They all eagerly answered yes. Dino wiped away fake tears and blew his nose. Then, with that big, bright smile of his, he spoke loudly and firmly.

"DRAMATIC AND IMPROVISATIONAL ACTING!"

Dino quickly confessed that he didn't even have a little brother and that his parents were very much alive.

"I do have a married, older sister. Her name is Connie. She's five months pregnant and a pain in the ass. Actually, she's been a pain in the ass for the last 20 years."

The class collectively gasped. Professor White looked agitated, removing his spectacles and tossing them on his desk. Then, he stood and clapped. The students followed suit, rising to their feet applauding.

"A standing ovation!" Dino happily thought

Once everyone sat, Professor White laid it out for the Italian thespian.

"Mr. Dino Domenico, in my 30 plus years of teaching, I've never had a new student perform a scene as convincing as that on the very first day of class. That was very impressive. Thank you for sharing it with us. But, unfortunately for you, every session from here on in, you're going to have to prove to me and the rest of your acting peers that this scene you just performed isn't the work of a charlatan."

"CHARLATAN? Professor White, I'm Italian!"

Dino smiled. Luckily, he knew what charlatan meant. He hoped his sarcasm would be appreciated. It was, and the laughter and positive classroom response were tremendous. Professor White smiled and thought about his phone conversation with Carol Kleinberg.

"So, this is the Outfit kid. Well, he's got the looks, some acting chops, a quick wit, appears confident; not cocky. Maybe, we do have something here."

Anthony "Stones" Simonetti

Benny Stein gave Anthony Simonetti, the "Stones" nickname. The two knew each other very well from the hard-partying Rush Street scene where they were regular fixtures. Anthony loved weed and enjoyed alcohol, but his penchant was for pills. His tolerance was unbelievably high for Seconal, Darvon, Percodan, Valium, Tuinal, Percocet, and of course, his party biscuit of choice, the highly coveted Quaalude. He was a freak of nature, sometimes ingesting as many as four or five tablets in the course of an evening. Benny Stein said he never saw anyone swallow more stones (Pills) than him.

"Anthony, you're supposed to take only one, maybe two at the most!" Benny reminded him on more than a dozen occasions.

Anthony's answer was always the same.

"I just wanna make sure."

Stones purposely worked short stints at some of the top restaurants, clubs, and bars in Chicago since he was 16 years old, gathering information on how those establishments operated. Then, he moved on, with an end game to use all he learned to open his own place. Anthony's charm was his sense of humor and ability to supply people with whatever they wanted during their nightlife excursions. That made him valuable to club owners who wanted to keep customers coming through their doors. Anthony's choice of clothing, haircuts, jewelry, and on again, off again facial hair, constantly changed with all the new trends and styles. He was a fashion chameleon and the perfect choice as a front-end man in any restaurant or bar.

One night, while Stones was working as the main floor manager at Jillinotti's, an iconic, celebrity-laden restaurant/club, a group of Loyola University wrestlers came in for dinner to celebrate their conference championship. They arrived drunk, got drunker, and gave Anthony a hard time, making fun of his clothes, hairstyle, and outgoing personality as he enthusiastically welcomed guests, escorting them to their tables. All four grapplers were going bald. They had less than a full head of hair between them. Years of rolling around on sweaty, germ-infested gym mats not only damaged the few existing follicles they had, but scarred their faces with patches of deep acne. The manhandling and groping of their sport also played havoc on their ears, which were swelled, bulbous, and pocked.

Finally, Stones had enough of their unflattering, obnoxious remarks. He walked over to their table.

"Are you gentlemen having a good time? I see you guys valet-parked your hairlines. And those dress shirts are beautiful. You bought them at Robert Hall, right? Robert threw them out, and you hauled them in."

He wasn't done yet. Anthony put his hand up and motioned for Sherry, the shapely hostess, to come over to the table.

"Sweetheart, do me a favor. Bring these Neanderthals a jug of Clearasil, four straws, and a basket of breaded cauliflower ears. Put it on my tab."

The wrestlers got pissed. One of them got up but was stopped by the largest of the group, a wide-eyed, steroidal man child. Anthony sauntered back to his podium at the restaurant's front when he saw his two favorite couples walk in.

"Well, there they are! Mr. and Mrs. Senese and Mr. and Mrs. Potenzo! How wonderful to see you all! Mr. Potenzo, Mr. Senese called earlier. He said you were buying dinner tonight. So, I have four beautiful 2-pound lobster tails and a succulent bone-in prime rib roast ready to go along with two chilled bottles of Dom Perignon."

They all laughed. It was an ongoing joke for years between the couples. When they dined out, whoever was NOT paying for dinner, would make sure to pre-order only the most expensive menu items. Senese got Potenzo good this time. Everything he ordered was 'Market Price.' As Anthony escorted the couples to their reserved back corner table, he walked by the wrestlers, giving them one final verbal shot as they finished their fifth round of beers in less than an hour. Stones lowered his right hand, sliding it back and forth as if he was jacking off.

"Did you guys notice how extra special creamy and tangy your Italian salad dressing was?"

Stones learned an important lesson that night. Always have a contingency plan. So, at 2:30 a.m., after his shift ended, he walked out the alley door. Waiting for him were the four drunken behemoths he belittled earlier. They smacked Anthony around pretty good for about ten minutes. Besides some bruises and cuts, they also cracked one of his ribs and broke a finger. When they were done with him, Anthony stood half hunched over from pain, spit some blood out of his mouth, tucked his shirt inside of pants, threw back his hair with a flick of his head, and grinned.

"Are you bald-headed, pimple-faced douche-bags done? I've got places to go and people to see."

The wrestlers shoved him around a little more and left. They didn't want to run the risk of seriously injuring him. They got their point across, but Anthony clearly won the match. Standing five foot six inches (while wearing lifts in his dress shoes) and barely weighing 150 pounds soaking wet, Simonetti took a beating from four Division One wrestlers, and then basically told them to go fuck themselves. He was a sturdy little prick. Anthony watched them drunkenly maneuver down the alley, and when they were out of sight, he reached inside his pocket, took out a couple of stones, and swallowed them dry. After a minute, he downed another. This time, the additional tablet was more for the pain than the buzz.

"I just wanna make sure," he thought.

Finally, after years of saving and scrimping, Anthony opened his own place. The location he chose was spot-on. When asked to describe the vision of Full House, his new Little Italy Restaurant/Club, he was more than prepared.

"It's old-school cuisine with a new twist, not your average spaghetti, meatballs, and all-you-could-eat wilted salad and stale breadsticks joint. Did I mention a state-of-the-art surround sound system playing jazz, blues, rock, AND Frank, Dean, and Tony, too? Oh, and last but not least, I'll be running the show. Now, if that's not a fucking winning line-up, I don't know what is!"

Opening night came and went without a single glitch. The food, as promised, was incredible. Over a dozen local celebrities made it their business to show their support, and most importantly, their faces. As his chef, Anthony hired the talented up-and-comer, who many in the culinary end of the restaurant business called "The Kitchen Guru," Mateo Troostibella, from Calabria, Italy. The Guru's recipes included exotic mixtures of specialty herbs and spices, sauces, hand-rolled pasta, fresh seafood, and locally slaughtered meats. The results were orgasms on a platter. The perfect selection of music reverberated through the entire restaurant as promised, rivaling even the best concert venues. It was nothing short of stupendous. There was overwhelming support by neighborhood patrons, rave reviews from dining critics, and rabid word of mouth amongst avid foodies, nightlife searchers, and club-goers. Anthony achieved what he always wanted. He said he did it his way, sort of.

"Just like fucking Sinatra."

The Shady Lady and Ro-Ro

By the mid-70s, anyone who wanted to smoke pot usually had easy access through friends or friends of friends unless there was a dry spell. Then, unfortunately, the only weed available was stem-filed, seedy, weak warehouse stored Mexican or Indiana roadside ditch garf. They both smelled like manure. If you were lucky, you scored a pricy $40 lid of strong, eye-appealing 'Lumbo (Columbian) Gold' every once in a while. But, a handful of well-connected tokers had the premiere tea, a choice blend of flavorful, robust Hawaiian and sweet California sensimilla, as potent as it was aromatic. When a joint was torched, a distinctive fragrance filled the entire area. Michael Jr., Dino, Victor, Stones, and a few others were often surrounded by the smell of that great bud. Their marijuana came directly from Iggy Jr.'s sister, Heather Archibald.

    Heather's closest friends called her "The Shady Lady." She was in her mid 30s, but looked early 20s. After months of negotiating details and coordinating the particulars with the Outfit, Heather received their blessing and protection to move the expensive primo weed in the far western suburbs. She was one of the first women to have legitimate Mob juice. (Her brother Iggy Jr. set her up beautifully.) Heather washed the distribution profits through the web of legal businesses she personally set up with special 'Female Owned Business' bank loans. Everything on that end was on the up and up. Those limited corporations consisted of two beauty salons, a laundromat, three snack shops, an insurance agency, a custom car repair shop, and a popular, unpretentious Upper Cove bar called The DuPage Inn. Heather moved quite a bit of tasty grass through those businesses as well as thousands in Syndicate cash, passing herself off as a successful suburban female entrepreneur. She had no interest in the whole 'Queenpin' moniker. Heather's operation was on the down-low. She catered only to high-end clientele who were referred, which meant someone vouched for or pre-approved them. That was so the people in charge knew who to point the finger at if there was a bust. There was going to be no fucking around with her money laundering deal.

    Heather was thrilled when Michael Jr. and Dino introduced her to Victor. She gladly welcomed him into her tight circle. Victor smiled big when Heather told the story of when she was a little girl staring out of the oil-stained glass of the gas station customer waiting area, how his father and uncle would always stop in to fill up their tanks or get flat tires repaired.

    "Victor, honey, your daddy and uncle were always as kind, friendly, and funny as could be, especially your father. Nicky always made goofy faces that made me laugh! He and Tommy didn't treat my dad and brother like they were some kind of uneducated, low-life, step-and-fetch-it rednecks.

    Tommy and Nicky were also two of the few neighborhood people that attended The Hillbilly Godfather's wake. Many residents stayed clear of the gas station after the Tunzi airline container bust, but not Tommy and Nicky. Tommy suggested to Manny that it wouldn't hurt to have a set of eyes at the services to see who attended and what was being discussed. Manny wholeheartedly agreed.

    Heather was beautiful, street smart, and formally educated. Her monthly financials were always accurate to the penny. She operated quietly, professionally, and above reproach. When Dino and Michael Jr. played "Who's Who in the Mob, one of them always said that if Heather was a man, her hefty contributions would've easily made her an Associate, and quite possibly, a Soldier. When Heather socialized with her Italian boys, it was usually a smoke-filled extravaganza.

They would hang out and talk for hours on end. But, one thing was for sure. When they got together at a party and Heather walked in, all heads turned. She was pure rock star. Most girls and women were jealous, while other females were intrigued. Those women were the ones that heard the whispers about Heather and possible organized crime ties. Most made the intelligent decision to stay clear of her, which suited Heather fine. She always said she got along with guys much better. The few confrontations that did occur usually ended poorly, especially for the other women.

Proof of Heather's intolerance for drama-filled female interactions, was never more evident than the night Tina Johnson snorted a little too much coke at Maggie Galihad and Joey Adabeeci's wedding reception. The event was held at the posh Burnsides Lake Country Club. Tina was Derrick Johnson's daughter. He was the owner of the largest real estate agency in Illinois, DJ Investment Properties. For years, Tina conducted herself as if she were an entitled heiress. She and Heather had seen each other at a few different social functions and parties here and there, but never spoke. Tina was jealous and intimidated by The Shady Lady's fashion sense and attractiveness. She was also incredibly envious of how people treated, respected, and spoke about Heather, especially the men. Beside all of them wanting to get in her pants, the guys treated Heather as a successful business equal. The younger guys cared less about her corporate accomplishments; they just thought she was a hot, slightly older piece of ass. Heather knew Tina Johnson and intentionally ignored her on multiple occasions. The Shady Lady smelled the stench of entitlement right away with Tina and decided it was best not to associate with her, not even on the bottom level of being cordial.

Tina and her colossal ego were fed up with the "Heather this" and "Shady Lady that" gossip. In Tina's bought and daddy-paid for world, she alone was the one everyone should be talking about. Thanks to heavy cocaine consumption, Tina made the unfortunate decision to confront Heather in the washroom during the cocktail hour. Tina found refuge inside an unoccupied stall and consumed a couple of oversized rails of blow to accompany her double-shot of Chivas Regal on the rocks. Tina flung open the bathroom door, emerging energized, with the arrogance of an Egyptian Princess floating down the Nile. She stood next to Heather at the sink as they both re-applied their make-up in front of the large, custom vanity bathroom mirrors. White powder confidence filled Tina's nostrils. She adjusted her breasts, making sure they looked perky and plump in her low-cut designer gown. She inhaled, took a big sniff, and swallowed, allowing the numbing, chemical taste of the yolk to drip slowly down her throat. Her flippant age-degrading comment to Heather was cocaine-fueled and ill-advised.

"I've seen you around. Exactly whose mother are you?"

Heather was too smart for that shit. She knew a disguised insult when she heard one. So, the first thing Shady Lady did was make sure she and Tina were the only two in the bathroom. Then, Heather grabbed the wannabe socialite by the neck and swung her around awkwardly against the marble sink counter.

"Why, I'm YOUR mommy, Tina! Don't you recognize me? Mommy's tired of making excuses for her spoiled bitch of a daughter. Mommy's tired of watching her baby inhale mountains of cocaine. Mommy is also exhausted from watching you beg for attention from little boys with small dicks who only want to be with you only because daddy is filthy rich. Now, it's time for important mommy to go back to the reception. Be a good girl and remember this conversation never happened."

Heather released her grip on Tina's neck, gave her a shove, and continued.

"I'm so glad we had time for this mommy-daughter talk, aren't you, sweetheart? Now, get the fuck away from me before I kick you in your twat."

Heather reached inside her purse and pulled out a bottle of Chloe Eau de Parfum. Then, she hoisted her designer dress revealing her toned legs, partially covered by sheer, black garter straps. She pointed the expensive French perfume bottle at her silk, laced Victoria's Secret black panties, and gave the spray bottle two quick pumps.

Tina remained silent, stunned, and breathing heavily. Her dilated pupils struggled to focus. Heather exited the washroom and joined a few wedding attendees gathered near some couches and chairs in the lobby. They all watched Tina run out of the bathroom and leave the building just two minutes later.

"What the hell's going on with Tina? Did she forget her diamond-studded tiara?" one of the guys in the group sarcastically asked.

"Oh, that poor girl has diarrhea. She shit all over herself and the floor. It smells horrible in there like someone died," Heather coyly answered.

The guys all made disgusting facial expressions, and a couple of the girls chimed in.

"Ewww, that's gross!"

"It certainly was," Heather agreed. "It was quite explosive. Such a shame she ruined that expensive dress. She said something about period blood leaking out from her Kotex pad too."

While everyone gasped, trying not to vomit from the repulsive thought of Tina sprinting out to the parking lot with globs of wet shit and menstrual blood dripping from her, the side door of the lobby opened. In flounced Rose "Ro-Ro" Stafanti. Ro-Ro was a solid handful and then some. She strolled up to the group and kissed everyone. When she got to Heather, there was a pause. Ro-Ro leaned in to kiss her, but Heather put her hand up.

"Ro-Ro, you didn't just blow someone in the parking lot, did you?"

Ro-Ro didn't miss a beat.

"C'mon Heather, you know me better than that! No head before the appetizers!"

The two laughed, hugged, and kissed. Ro-Ro was only one of a few exceptions to Heather's rule about socializing with other females. The Shady Lady got a massive kick out of Stafanti's outlandish humor and the unpretentiousness in which she carried herself.

Ro-Ro was a huge-breasted, loud, red-blooded Italian girl whose cantaloupe sized tits always managed to make an impromptu, uncovered appearance regardless of the occasion. She loved alcohol, especially the pricy, top-shelf brands. If there was expensive liquor available, there was always at least one drink, if not the entire bottle, poured for her. Ro-Ro was also a very sexual person, almost to the point of whoredom. She was on a steady pace to blow-job her way across DuPage County, one cock at a time, all before her 25th birthday. No place was off-limits for Ro-Ro to give head, whether in a closet, kneeling in a tool shed, lying on a kitchen counter while preparing food, swimming pools, a bathroom stall at a bar mitzvah, or the back of a hearse parked right in front of a funeral home! Ro-Ro's fellatio escapades were famous among her group of friends with Michael Jr. being one of her early oral accomplishments. He retold the story more than a few times over the years.

"So, my parents were at their place in Lake Geneva for the weekend. Ro-Ro and I were maybe 18 years old. We were drunk. I mean, real drunk. She kept grabbing at me. I didn't know what to do. I had that whole 'taking advantage of her' thing in the back of my head with her grandfather and all that, so I didn't want to get in trouble. It got to the point where I had to climb up that big Oak tree in my backyard to get away from her. And what did Ro-Ro do? She gets bone-assed naked, wraps herself up in my mother's $7,000 mink stole, and climbs up after me! She scaled that fucking tree wearing that mink, like a north-woods black bear in heat. I mean, what could I do? So, I held onto one of the branches, swung back and forth like Tarzan, and let her blow me. We laughed our asses off when we sobered up. Then, we went to Omega Restaurant for a late-night breakfast. We ordered Grecian skirt steaks, eggs over easy, hash browns, buttered wheat toast, and chocolate shakes. We've been great friends ever since."

As funny as that tale was, Dino's question to Michael Jr. afterward was even more amusing.

"Michael, how disappointed was Ro-Ro when she found out you had more bush than dick?"

Ro-Ro was a loan officer and trustee of The First Italian American Bank of America. The branches were very popular with Italians. No big surprise there. One of the bank's largest depositors and best customers was Heather Archibald, whose last four business loans were all approved by Ro-Ro!

There was a whole back-story about Ro-Ro that even her outlandish sexual antics and creative loaning strategies couldn't top - the atrocities and brutalities committed by her infamous grandfather, Augustino "Augie the Animal" Stafanti. The Animal took over the juice loan business when Bartenzo died. Augie's torturous collection methods were legendary. He used Hokishari knives made from the sharpest metal on the planet to peel, slice, and carve the skin of the unfortunate souls who owed him money. Stafanti hacked, maimed, and dismembered his delinquent clientele using a 'pay or die' method. He'd sadistically laugh when bragging to his cohorts about being able to cut bone and flesh like a hot knife going through butter. Even though Augie was up there in age, the most ruthless, wild bunches of Mob enforcers around still kept their distance. Augie the Animal was a heartless, soulless, barely human being of a man. He was the ugly part of The Outfit. A few of the guys Ro-Ro blew openly admitted that they let her suck their dicks out of pure, unadulterated fear of her sociopathic grandfather.

LU-CHOW SHIN AND PETER KORINTHOS

Tadeo Shin and his two elderly uncles, whose first names were as close to unpronounceable in the English language as you could get, were the rulers of Chinatown. The best the Mob could do was to negotiate a piece of their lucrative gambling and drug operations. The Shins had deep roots in that three-square-mile patch. The Italians and the Chinese had the best working relationship between organized crime ethnicities in the city. The money was too big for it not to be. The old saying, "There's enough for everyone" was accurate.

The Shin family had many legal businesses, but their restaurant, Empire Noodle, was the most profitable by far. The Peking duck, the "She-She Twin Lobster Tails," the eggrolls, the spicy garlic crab, the cherry sauced spare ribs, the marinated prime tenderloin beef slices, and of course, their signature dish, hand-rolled noodles, were the best anywhere.

Tadeo's son, Lu-Chow, oversaw everything. He talked up the broken Chinese in front of his customers but spoke perfect English with his American friends. Lu-Chow rolled out the red carpet when Dino and Michael Jr. came for dinner. He knew who their fathers were, and so did his father, which was the reason that Mr. Shin always went out of the way to make a table-side appearance. The boys always let their guests know that when Lu-Chow's dad walked up, they needed to stand, bow, and shake his hand as a show of respect.

Initially, for Victor's 21st birthday, his friends planned an evening bash at a new club in Cicero called RAPTURE. It was earning quite the reputation as a place where debauchery was served nightly. Everyone was talking about how wild it was there and how the son of a ruthless Mob Underboss owned it. It was also receiving street recognition as a one-stop-shop designer drug store, where all types of illegal substances were available for purchase or consumption. Also, the wall-to-wall smokin' hot women and hungry young Mob Turks looking to make names for themselves added to the club's allure. When Michael Jr. told his father about their plans, The Fixer put the kibosh on it.

"Do NOT go there! There's a shitload of problems in Cicero right now, and if somebody who knows somebody recognizes who you guys are, they will intentionally fuck with you to see where it goes. Molto brutto. (Very bad.) Go someplace else, please."

The Fixer was correct. Cicero was rapidly becoming a Mob within itself boasting the most prominent, meanest, and profitable Crew. He made sure to let his son know about it.

"There's a bunch of guys walking around with bad reputations and chips on their shoulders. They all want to be known and don't give two shits about using violence. One beef, one fuck-up, one misunderstanding, it won't matter. Whether it's you and them or one of your friends and them, it'll result in a problem. And, God forbid one of their girlfriends looks at any of you guys for longer than five seconds? You know as well as I do that's a give-in if Dino's there. Backing down is not something they do in Cicero, even if your last name is Capone!"

When Dino talked to Michael Jr., he said his father more or less said the same thing. So, RAPTURE was out, and it was off to Empire Noodle.

As usual, Lu-Chow greeted them at the front door as if they were royalty. Then, he escorted the boys to their reserved table. It was a VIP area that you needed to walk over a small bridge to get to. The elaborate set-up was smack-dab in the middle of the main dining area and surrounded by a pond filled with Ryukin, the larger, fancier goldfish types. Even though the place was packed, Lu-Chow sat and shared the hysterical story of how he drove his father's brand new Cadillac, with less than 100 miles on the odometer, through a considerable swell at the bottom of a flooded-out street in their private subdivision.

"I thought I could make it through. It looked good at first, but ten seconds later, the Cadillac (he pronounced it 'Cad-Rack') was floating (he pronounced it 'froating') sideways next to a row of mailboxes! When they towed it back to the house, father opened the driver's door and dirty water poured out. He chased me around our driveway with a Tanaka Dynasty Sword. Father still moves surprisingly swiftly for a short Asian man," Lu-Chow laughed. "Father-San was screaming his ass off at me. You have no idea how hard it is to say, 'YOU FUCKING COCKSUCKER' in Chinese!"

As the guys sipped on specialty drinks like Blue China, Ming Martini, Jade Opium (Stones ordered that one), and Wong Warrior, Lu-Chow whispered to Michael Jr. and Dino.

"Peter's been downstairs gambling for a couple of hours. My cousin says he lost about $2,500 already."

"Unreal," Michael Jr. said, shaking his head.

After dinner and drinks, Lu-Chow led the guys through the kitchen and down a flight of stairs where a man in a dark suit who was the spitting image of Oddjob from the James Bond movie "Goldfinger" met them. When they got to the back cooler door, the stocky Oriental swung it open. Inside was a converted casino area, at least half the size of a football field. There were slot machines, individual card games, dice, roulette, blackjack, and of course, pai gow for the many Chinese gamblers. Michael Jr. and Dino spotted Peter at one of the dice tables. The other guys mulled around, marveling at how massive the gambling arena was. Dino walked up to the table first, waiting for Pete to throw the dice.

"Craps!" said the tuxedo-wearing box man.

"Shit!" Pete muttered.

Dino grabbed his arm, pulled him away from the table, and took him to Michael Jr.

"Pete, what the fuck are you doing?" Michael asked. "You're down $2,500 hundred already?"

"Fucking Lu-Chow! What did he do, run and tell you as soon as you walked in the joint?" Pete questioned.

Dirk won $500 playing slot machines by the end of the evening, and Victor got a blackjack for his 21st birthday on a one-time $100 play. Peter slowed his betting, but was down 4 G's by the end of the night. Victor and Stones tried to contain him, but when Pete Korinthos was at a table, he was incoherent to all non-wagering-related conversations. As tough as it was for them to admit, their good friend Peter had a serious gambling problem.

George the Greek was Pete's father. He was the owner of Fresh To You!, a popular grocery chain of smaller stores catering to shoppers in search of authentic Grecian specialties and delicacies. George recently opened up his eighth location off Halsted Street and the Eisenhower Expressway, right outside of Greektown. He gave that store to Pete. Within a year, Pete attached a substantial tented area and made it a garden/flower center. Right next to that, he installed a giant barbeque pit where he roasted whole lambs, chickens, pigs, and marinated sides of beef.

In less than a year, Peter Korinthos generated twice the revenue of any other of his father's stores, even out grossing the original location on the corner of Harlem and North avenues. Considering his significant problem, it was only a matter of time before Pete started siphoning funds from his store to feed his gambling appetite. It began slowly, but soon, he was in debt way over his head. The ass-chewing he received from his father at Vincenzo's Restaurant on Ogden Avenue in Downers Grove was a long time coming. George laid into him about his out-of-control wagering and threatened to beat the shit out of him. Pete respectfully listened and promised to stop. When The Greek finished his tirade, Pete left the restaurant, distraught, with his head down. Then, he drove directly to a high-stakes card game held in the honeymoon suite of the Naperville Hyatt Hotel. He lost $6,500 in three hours, got drunk, staggered out to his car parked next to a dumpster in the back of the hotel lot, put the convertible top down during a rainstorm, got in, got soaked, and fell asleep. There were many losing evenings in the months that followed.

About 9:15 a.m. one Sunday morning, Anthony and his family drove by the Halsted Street grocery store, as they usually did on their way to 10:00 a.m. mass at Our Lady of the Shroud. At first, Stones didn't think anything was wrong. He'd seen Pete's white Corvette parked there dozens of times on a Sunday.

Fresh to You! was the store's slogan for years, ever since Grandpa Stefano Korinthos sailed over from Athens, Greece. Billboard advertisements were plastered all over the city. But, on this particular Sunday, Pete's car wasn't parked in its usual spot. Instead, it was haphazardly left sideways on the curb, almost blocking the store's entrance. Anthony also noticed the passenger's side door was wide open.

"Angela, I gotta stop inside by Pete real quick."

"We're gonna be late for church, and I want to sit in the front by my parents," she complained.

"Just give me two minutes, Ange."

She looked at her gold Piaget watch.

"Anthony, I don't want to walk in late. The last thing I want is Fr, Hugh giving us stink-eye for the entire mass. He's such an asshole."

"You're right. Father Hugh is an asshole," Anthony agreed.

Sitting quietly in the back of the car was their three-year-old son, little

Carlo, dressed in blue, Calvin Klein kid jeans, and a white turtle neck.

"Asshole! Hahahaha," he giggled.

When Victor stopped by Angela and Stones's house to hang out or have a bite to eat, it was a huge treat when the little man Carlo repeated a swear word.

"He's good, but he ain't the champ!" Victor always reminded them.

Anthony crossed the street, circled Pete's Corvette, saw the inside door panel lightly splattered in blood, and jogged back across the street to his car.

"Angela, come and pick me up her after church."

"ABSOLUTELY NOT, you know we're sitting with my parents this morning. Daddy's treating all of us to brunch at Burnsides Country Club. They have the Eggs Benedict you love with the fresh crabmeat hollandaise sauce."

"Angela, I'll get a ride home. Then, I'll meet you back at the house."

"Okay, Anthony. What the fuck is going on?"

Angela knew Anthony better than he knew himself. She was well aware of his "Stones" nickname, partying escapades, and the group he surrounded himself with. But, she also knew when he was serious and concerned, so she slid behind the steering wheel while adjusting the seat and rearview mirror.

"Please be careful. Is Peter okay? Is it something with his gambling? Maybe you should call somebody. Anthony, you're not listening to me as usual, are you?"

She realized it was something urgent and stopped with the twenty questions routine.

"Alright, I'm going, just please be careful."

When she was visibly out of sight, Stones darted to the payphone on the corner instead of going to Pete's car. He dialed, hung up, and then redialed. Anthony was calling Victor, but remembered he was working at his Uncle Tommy's place doing inventory.

"Big Banana, this is Victor. Can I help you?"

"Victor, it's Stones," Anthony said nervously.

"What's up, my man? You haven't been up this early since Christmas morning of '66 when my father bought us those Remco Frogman plastic scuba divers," Victor joked. "Are you just getting in from an all-nighter?"

"I'm in front of Pete's store. Something's not right, Vic. His Vette's parked half on the curb with the passenger door open, and there's fucking blood on the inside panel. I didn't go inside the store yet."

"What do you mean, blood on the door panel?" Victor questioned.

"Vic, there's blood on the fucking door, like splashed on the inside. I'm just telling you what I see. I don't know."

"Don't go inside. Let me get someone to cover me here. I'll see you in about ten minutes," Victor cautioned.

Before leaving, Victor went to the bottom drawer of his father's desk. He opened the secret back panel and grabbed Nicky's 15-year old .38 caliber pistol. Anthony hung up and walked to Pete's car, purposely slamming the driver's side door shut with his hip.

"Nobody's gonna find my fucking fingerprints on this car," he thought.

Anthony's eyes immediately shot to the cement sidewalk. There were tiny droplets of blood leading to the store's front door. His mind was racing a million miles a minute, visualizing the different scenarios that might have unfolded. But, in the back of his head, the worst one kept replaying - Pete's substantial gambling debts. He owed lots of money. At last count, he was deep in the shitter for almost $80K. On more than a few occasions, Anthony and Victor both asked Fat Frankie for his advice on what Pete should do,

"He should stop gambling. That's what the fuck he should do! I know Peter is your friend, but he's way out of control," he explained.

Frankie tried to help Pete with a few hot wagering tips early on when it was all fun and games. Then, Frankie said he saw 'the signs,' when a gambler doesn't care how much is at stake if he loses. Frankie suggested to Victor and Anthony that at least for the time being, they stay away from Pete until he straightened himself out. That, coming from Fat Frankie, translated into something nasty being afoot. Dino and Michael Jr. had all but given up on him, having bailed his ass out numerous times and in more ways than just loaning him money. Every time Victor and Stones voiced their concerns, Pete told them he loved them, quickly offering reassurance that everything would turn out fine.

"I'll just double-down on the Lakers and the over!"

The sad truth was Pete often doubled down, lost, and then paid only the juice on what he owed. The following weekend, he'd bet heavily. As a result, he usually lost more than half of his bets. Pete's recent bad streak was going on for weeks.

Victor's car tires screeched around the corner eleven minutes from when he hung up the phone. Anthony joined him behind Pete's Vette.

"Vic, should we call someone? Who could we call?"

"Ant, who are we going to call? Uncle Tommy? He's in Arizona, and he's still way fucked up about Auntie Tree. Last month, he signed my birthday card, 'Love, Auntie Tree, and Uncle Tommy.' Auntie Tree's been dead going on almost two years now. Tell me there's not something wrong there. And, remember what Frankie told us? I'm not calling Dino or Michael Jr. because I think Pete still owes both of them cash. If I call my father, he'll tell us to back the fuck away and mind our own business. And you know goddamn well I'm not calling Pete's father until we see what's going on."

"So, what are we gonna do?" Anthony asked.

"We're gonna go inside. That's what we're gonna do."

"I don't think that's a good idea, Vic. This isn't one of your pretend stories here. You DO see the blood, right?"

"Maybe we start singing Kumbaya and call it a day," Victor angrily suggested.

"Hey, don't get pissy with me, Victor! I called you, remember? So I guess I should've driven right by and not done anything, right?"

"Of course not! I'm sorry, Ant. But, look, the only way we find out what's going on is to go inside."

They both cautiously walked to the store's entrance. As the automatic metal and glass doors swung open, Anthony pictured himself sitting with Angela's parents, trying to keep Carlo quiet while listening to elderly Father Hugh's drawn-out sermon. However, that quick daydream was rudely interrupted when he saw Victor un-tuck the hidden gun out of the corner of his eye. Victor wrapped his hand around the butt of Nicky's old, chrome-plated .38 caliber snub-nose revolver and pulled it to his side.

"What are you gonna do with that, Victor?"

"Don't make me nervous, Anthony, you jagoff!"

One step later, using the gun's muzzle, Victor lightly tapped a colorfully handmade cardboard advertisement poster hanging on the entrance corridor wall.

"Well, that's a sign of good news," he said, smiling at Stones.

"What? Anthony excitedly anticipated.

"Tomatoes are only twelve cents a pound."

"That's not even a little funny, Victor. What in the fuck is the matter with you?"

They crouched their way past the checkout lanes and produce section, maneuvering the aisles like elite members of a SWAT team. Victor raised his hand and motioned for Anthony to wait when he heard the sound of running water. He parted the long, ceiling to floor thick plastic strips that separated the shopping area from the refrigerated storage area. Peter was huddled over the deep-sink.

"Sorry, guys. The store doesn't open for another hour yet," he teased.

Victor tucked the revolver back into his pants.

"Pete, are you alright?" Victor asked.

"What the fuck, Pete!" Anthony added.

When they got closer, they saw the blood dripping from Pete's right hand into the sink.

"There was an open blade from a pair of wire cutters in my glove box. I sliced the shit out of my palm. Do you guys think I need stitches?"

He raised his bloodied hand for inspection.

Victor sighed in relief.

"Fucking wire-cutters? We thought something worse."

Pete saw the butt of the gun tucked inside Victor's pants.

"Vic, is that your dad's gun? The fucking piece is an antique now, isn't it?"

As the blood stopped dripping, he shut off the water and wrapped his hand with a white rag.

"What? Did you guys think Jenaro sent a couple of his balloon-head collectors over to give me a beating?" Pete asked them.

Jenaro Francis was a no-nonsense northside bookie who took Pete's action. If you won, Jenaro paid you. If you lost, you paid him. If you didn't, you worked out an arrangement. If you fucked and ducked him, he sent a couple of guys to remind you about it. The reminder was most unpleasant.

"Last night, my father and I sat down with Francis. My dad paid him everything I owed."

"Your father paid the whole nut off?" Victor surprisingly asked.

"Every fucking dime," Pete answered. "After we got done with Jenaro, he drove me to Dino and Michael Jr.'s houses. Those guys are paid in full, too."

"I thought your dad said you were on your own. What made him change his mind?" Anthony asked.

"You guys know us Greeks are a lot like you Italians when it comes to that father/son shit, so I had to be honest with how deep I was drowning. I broke down, told him I fucked up, gave him my number, and asked for help. When he heard $84,000 and change, he slapped me across the face and yelled his ass off at me. Then, right when it looked like he was gonna crack me again, he hugged me so tightly that I couldn't breathe," Pete confessed, his voice cracking.

He motioned Victor and Anthony to follow him to the office. Once inside, he sat down behind the desk while reaching inside the top drawer for some tissues. Victor and Anthony couldn't take their eyes off of him.

"I made my father cry. My father cried because he raised a fucking loser gambler of a son," Pete admitted.

He shook his head and looked up at his two friends.

"When my Grandpa Stefano died, my dad didn't weep a drop. He loved that old Greek bastard more than life itself. I mean, he was upset, but never cried. It was his fucking father, and he didn't shed one goddamn tear!"

Victor and Anthony never saw Pete's remorseful side in all the years they knew him.

"It was ME who made my father cry. That will never happen again," Pete promised.

"We've been telling you for at least a year, maybe more, that you're bleeding cash. I hope this fucking nightmare is over for you," Victor wished.

"Me, too," Anthony added.

"Your father loves you. You're lucky he's still in your corner," Victor continued. "It's about where you go from here."

Pete got up and walked to the couch where Anthony and Victor were seated. He opened his arms wide, and they all embraced.

"You thought I was in trouble, and you came to help me. I love you fucking guys."

Pete reached inside his grocery store apron and pulled out a joint.

"Gentlemen, this is a 'Julio Special.' It's got hash oil in it."

"HASH OIL? I'd eat the ass of some hash oil!" exclaimed Anthony.

"I gotta open the store in half an hour. So let's go inside the wet cooler and hit it. No weed-reek in there," Pete suggested.

"It sounds like you know that first-hand!" Victor laughed.

"I do, and speaking of hand."

Pete unraveled the rag from his sliced palm and closely examined it.

"It looks like the bleeding's stopped. Let's do this jay first, and then I'll get some gauze and bandages on it."

Right before the friends smoked up, Pete issued a warning.

"Julio said he, Zitters, and Reeco laced some Lumbo Gold with this hash oil and the taste and the buzz were fucking hellacious!"

"Those guys are the Heads, (Avid pot smokers) so they would know best," Victor confirmed.

Pete put the joint in his mouth and Anthony lit it with his father's 18K gold Zippo lighter.

"Thanks, Stones. Hey, you're going to have to give that lighter back to its rightful owner at the end of the year, right?"

"Yes, sir! Big Dicky finally gets out of jail in November, just in time for Thanksgiving."

Pete took a colossal hit and then passed the strong-smelling doobie to Victor. He grabbed it, took a quick toke, and passed it. Anthony's drag was deep. He held the smoke in longer than usual, wanting to get the full hash oil/weed combination effect.

"Anthony, do you know what the line is on the Celtics game tonight? I wanna throw a G-note on it," Pete jokingly asked.

Stones choked, spewing a hash oil infused cannabis cloud from his mouth and nose. Victor doubled over laughing. Pete grabbed the spliff, took another hit, and gave it final approval.

"The Heads were right. Smells great, tastes, great, and is good for you!"

Moving forward, the small-money monthly card games at Victor's house was the only gambling Peter did. He usually lost.

CHAPTER 17
RUN FOR YOUR LIFE

When Tommy rescued Ingalleretta from being shanked in the alley by those bums, his future changed forever. What unfolded for him was a Mob mentorship and wealth beyond his wildest dreams. Although Victor and Tommy's defining experiences were decades apart and entirely different scenarios, they both happened one morning at SouthWater Market.

Almost three weeks had passed since Tommy had his blowout with Nicky and Victor. His initial thrill with the exciting news regarding Victor's pending book release lasted for about 20 seconds. Since Teresa died, it was the first time Tommy showed a positive, emotional response to anything. The famous LaCosta smile faded as quickly as it appeared when Victor explained the book's summary in quick, semi-nervous detail. When he shared the title with his uncle, it did absolutely nothing to soften the blow.

"You wrote about WHAT and then called it WHAT? My Grandfathers Are Bosses? So that's the name of your book? Are you out of your fucking mind? What were you thinking? What planet have you been living on for the last 20-something years? Of all the things you could write about, you pick Outfit shit? I don't give two fucks that you made everything up! I don't care if it's funny. I thought you were a sharp guy, Victor! You're going to trick-bag all of us with this, do you realize that?"

Tommy was as pissed as Victor had ever seen him, which is why he asked Nicky to come with him for moral support. Who was better than his father to act as a buffer? Unfortunately for Nicky, Tommy wasted little time getting in his face too.

"Nicky, how long have you known about this? You're sitting there awfully fucking quiet for a guy that always has something to say. What's the matter, no funny remark or comment? Hello? Hello? All of a sudden, you're deaf and dumb like the guy that used to limp sideways down Taylor Street selling those fuckin' pencils!"

Victor wasn't about to sit by and witness his dad get lambasted.

"Uncle Tommy, Dad didn't know what my book was about until last month. When I got back from St. Jude's Press in New York, I told him. That's where the publishing house is. I stayed at my friend Mary Ann Collinsworth's home for three days. She and her husband Bill have that huge spread in Mamaroneck. Don't get mad at my father. He was just as pissed as when I told him about it, well, almost as pissed as you are now," Victor explained, trying to take his father out of the line of fire. "This is all on me."

Tommy was long overdue to explode. It had been standing room only for the demons that tormented him since Teresa's tragic death.

"All on you, are you fucking kidding me? Don't you realize I'm going to get calls about this? Did you even think about that? What am I supposed to say? How's this? Don't worry about it, guys. No big deal. He didn't even mention your names. But, hey, I have an even better idea, Victor. YOU go and talk to them when they call, and they WILL call, you can bet your mudda fuckin' typewriter on that!"

"If you say I have to go talk to somebody, I will, Uncle Tee. No problem."

"No problem?" Tommy condescendingly chuckled.

He turned his attention back to Nicky while cupping his hands as if in prayer, shaking them in an up and down motion.

"Nicky, did I hear your son say no problem? No fucking problem?"

Tommy turned back to Victor.

"What have I always said? Always be low-key about that shit! Low key! What you're doing is **NOT FUCKING LOW KEY!**"

Tommy continued to rage. For someone emphasizing low-key, he got louder as he said it. Victor felt it best to lay everything on the table.

"Uncle Tommy, I have a radio interview on WLUP tomorrow. You know, THE LOOP. It's with Anthony Simonetti's friend, Big Irish Tony Fitz. He's the guy on the billboards with all the tattoos. He hosts their evening talk show, the one where the listeners call in. Well, Steve Dahl, the disc jockey that blew up all those disco records at Comisky Park, his show is on right before Tony's. Big Irish told me that he'd put Dahl and his partner, Garry Meier, in a headlock and make them stick around on the air during my interview. All those guys are red hot, and that kind of publicity could be huge for me. And, it won't cost a penny. It's all for free. Isn't that great?" Victor explained.

Tommy didn't answer. He just shook his head, mumbled, and thought while throwing clothes together for another trip out west.

"What the fuck is this kid thinking? Why hasn't Nicky said anything? Should I reach out and see if this is gonna be a problem, or just let it go? I don't need this unnecessary shit on my fucking plate right now!"

"Tee, this is a good thing for Victor. Be happy for him. Neither one of us could spell worth a shit, and this kid's....," Nicky abruptly stopped talking, realizing what said.

He turned to Victor, back-tracking his previous words.

"Victor, I'm not calling you a kid. You're MY kid, of course, but I don't mean, 'kid.'"

Victor understood. Nicky turned back to Tommy, attempting to stand up for his son.

"Tommy, Victor's getting an actual, honest to goodness fucking book published! I think that's fantastic."

In the last few weeks since that heated exchange, before Tommy angrily left for Arizona, Victor replayed parts of their conversation repeatedly in his head. Especially concerning was Tommy's parting response to Victor's last words.

"Uncle Tommy, you were younger than me when you saved Mr. E. You did what you did then, and you do what you do now. You've made all our lives better, and you did it with hard work, commitment, and dedication to our family. You're the most selfless person I've ever known. Did you know that any time there's ever been something good that happens in our family, who my father says to thank? It's not God or Jesus. My father says to make sure and thank Uncle Tommy. And we have, all of us, time and time again, year after year. Look, I love and respect you, I value your opinion, and I always want you on my side. But, I write what I write. It's my thing. I'm going full steam ahead here with this because it's what I was born to do. I'm going to make my own way here, just like you, Dad, and Grandpa did."

Victor's speech was well thought out and delivered, but Tommy was only half-listening while packing his bags. He couldn't wait to get the hell out of Dodge. Victor could still see his uncle standing at the front door with his valigia (Suitcase) in hand.

Before Tommy exited, he did what he had done every time he left his house since Teresa's death. He kissed his hand and touched the painted, full-length wedding picture of her that hung in his foyer. Tommy's last words are what Victor remembered best from that day.

"Victor, I wanna wish you, Buona Fortuna! (Good Fortune) Who knows, maybe they'll dig a hole deep enough to bury all three of us in."

Tommy ended the conversation, closed his front door, and headed to O'Hare Airport. Nicky hung his head with no follow up wise comment. That's when Victor knew there might be a problem. The first words out of his mouth were filled with apprehension.

"Dad, bury the three of us together? NO FUCKING WAY! I mean, Uncle Tommy's overacting, right?"

That morning, Nicky's response was the only comfort Victor had during the long wait to continue the conversation with his uncle.

"Yes, Uncle Tommy's exaggerating. Nobody's getting buried. But, I'm not going gonna bullshit you, Victor. He may have to explain what you're doing to somebody, somebody. Uncle Tee's upset right now. Give him a little time to soak it all in. It took me a couple of days to understand everything, right? I came around. He'll come around, too. The whole Teresa thing, you see what's going there, right? Everything your uncle has ever done has been for our family, Grandma, Grandpa, the great aunts, uncles, their families, Auntie Tree, me, you, Mom, and her family. He's been doing that forever. Do I even need to mention all the other people that he's helped, too? You just said all those things to him yourself, but the most important thing you need to remember is that he was younger than you now when he got involved with some serious people. He made a huge decision there. I know it always looks like everything he touches turns to gold, but that's not the case. Believe me when I tell you this. The personal shit you think you know about Uncle Tommy? You haven't even scratched the surface. Think about what it must've been like being in his shoes back then. Starting at that age, not knowing what was around the corner, involved and doing shit for Manny and a bunch of other dangerous guys. And guess what? He's still here doing it, with more responsibilities and pressures, and I'm not even talking about running a successful business like Big Banana. He's gotta do ALL that and more while pretty fucked up in the head."

"I guess you're right," Victor agreed.

"You keep doing what you're doing. When Uncle Tee's ready to talk to you about everything, he will," Nicky finished.

It was day seventeen, and Victor was still counting and waiting. When he arrived at work that morning, Nicky was already there. The docks and street were packed, which was usual for a Friday, but since Monday was a national holiday and SouthWater was closed, it was exceptionally crowded and crazy.

"Morning, Dad. Did you talk to Uncle Tommy last night?"

"I did. Nothing about your thing, just work stuff. Listen, we're busier than shit. Grab a few pallets of ripe bananas for the Finer Foods, Pedi Brothers, and Testa Produce orders. Bring them down to Tony at Cee Bee Cartage when you get done. Start on Fresh To You!, Gino's Warehouse and Big Apple for the afternoon run when you get back. We're splitting a semi-trailer with Mandolini, Auster, and City Wide for those orders," Nicky answered without looking up from the delivery board.

"Dad, we're getting close to three fucking weeks and nothing. I don't ever think I went that long without talking to him," Victor panicked.

"Uncle Tommy said he'll be back from Arizona next Wednesday or Thursday. So just wait until then, Vic, okay?" Nicky answered.

For the next few hours that morning at work, Victor went through the motions. But, unfortunately, this whole thing was taking a toll on him. He always played things cool on the outside, but this time, he was a nervous wreck, outside, inside, and even in between. While deep in thought about the whole fiasco, Victor heard a familiar voice.

"What's up, brotha? Are you still my EYE-TALIAN?"

He knew it was Reece Walker. Reece worked on and off at SouthWater for a couple of summers during breaks in football training camp at The University of Notre Dame. Reece was a great guy. He was intelligent, respectful, and blessed with abundant physical talent. In his senior year, he graduated with high honors, was a consensus First Team All-American wide receiver, and was also an alternate sprinter on the USA Olympic Team in the 100 and 200-yard dashes. Anytime local Fighting Irish sportscasters and newspaper columnists in South Bend, Indiana referred to him, it was always as Reece "Fast as Lightning" Walker. His newest accomplishment was as a recent pick in the second round of the NFL draft. Reece was headed to California to be an Oakland Raider.

The summer before his senior year at Notre Dame, Reece played in a few televised Saturday afternoon games. One of those was against powerhouse Ohio State. Walker had 8 catches for over 100 yards and two touchdowns, including the winning score with a one-handed grab in the end zone at the buzzer. (Fat Frankie and the Outfit made a bundle with the 5-point spread.) When Brent Mussburger interviewed Reece after that game, the talented athlete was humble. He thanked God, his family, teammates, coaches, and the Fighting Irish fans. Mussburger called him a class act. From the day of that interview on, Reece officially overtook Kelvin Duckworth, the lanky 6-foot 10-inch center on Purdue's Big 10 Championship Basketball Team who worked as seasonal help at Ira Fisher, as the most famous athlete on the Market.

Reece and Victor worked together, breaking down truckloads of produce more than a few times over the two previous summers. They got along great, and even better, was how they made the time fly by sharing their love and knowledge of movies, television, music, and comedy. They constantly challenged each other, pitting their favorite bands, singers, actors, and comedians against each other. Reece always chose the blacks. Victor always chose the whites. Regardless of who won, the loser always wound up calling the winner a fucking racist. Of course, they'd laugh their asses off, especially when the winner picked someone of the opposite color.

"You can't use George Carlin or Lenny Bruce," Victor often complained. "And Don Rickles is definitely off-limits."

"You can keep fucking Rickles, with his 'Colored guy in the back,' 'The Mexican broads over there,' or 'The Chinese guy from the war in the corner.' His shit's getting real old. Just keep your skinny, cracker ass away from Dick Gregory, Richard Pryor, and Redd Foxx. They're mine!" Reece would shoot back, using his best, exaggerated black street thug voice. "You wanna use someone black? I'll give you Bill Cosby. I can't put my finger on it, but something ain't right about that mutha fucker. You can have him, and I'll throw in Flip Wilson and his ugly bitch, Geraldine."

They always argued over Motown, Blues, and Jazz picks. Victor always knew his choices would get a rise out of Reece.

"I gotta take Muddy Waters, B.B. King, Buddy Guy, and Robert Johnson for starters. Then, maybe, Howlin' Wolf and John Lee Hooker, too," Victor claimed. "We can share Ray Charles and Stevie Wonder. They won't know the fucking difference."

"Making fun of my blind soul brothers? Man, that's some cold, funny-ass shit, DaBone! So you think you know about Negro music? You're fucking EYE-TALIAN! That music is MY people's music! It's all about our struggle, the pain we've suffered, the poverty, the oppression. The only struggle y'all know about is when you run out of ways to cheat the black man, or in your case when someone eats the last cannoli!"

Reece and Victor's banter was brutally honest, socially unacceptable, and culturally biased. They shit all over the color barrier. The very best of times was when Reece brought his Panasonic Dynamite 8-track plastic tape player and hung it off the back door of trucks they were unloading. More than a handful of hustlers stopped between delivering their orders so they could enjoy a couple of tunes. As Victor and Reece unloaded full pallets or stacked floor loads, the jams echoed in the trailer as it became emptier. Everyone thought that sounded very cool.

Every so often, during break periods or lunch, Reece spun a longer than usual yarn about a gridiron or track story with Victor and other co-workers. It was during those extended tales that Victor's mind wandered. It wasn't Reece's fault. His stories were fun to hear. During this particular daydream episode, Victor pictured himself shoulder to shoulder next to Reece in the "On your mark, get set, go!" position. The first time he imagined that scenario, Victor actually typed up a few paragraphs about it. A few weeks later, when rereading it, he thought before tearing it up.

"Something like that would never happen."

Reece and Victor caught up and congratulated each other. Victor told Reece how cool it was that he was drafted. Reece said he couldn't believe it either. Then he teased Victor about his book saying he didn't know EYE-TALIANS could read, much less write. Victor got a huge kick out of that. The chat with Reece was just what he needed to get his mind off things. But, the good-time feelings didn't last long. Less than an hour later, the two were side-by-side at one end of the street, ready to race, while everyone else on SouthWater lined the front docks. The starting line was in front of The Watermelon House, and the finish line ended at The Market Café.

    At first, everyone thought the contest was a big joke, like when Tim Hoverstein from Hovie and Son Lettuce paid High-Ass Charlie and Tiny $100 each to race each other down the alley, knowing full well they were piss-ass drunk. That 50-yard debacle was about as far away from a dash as anyone could imagine. Between tripping, falling, and leaning against garbage cans to puke or catch their breath, that race turned into a literal 15-minute shit-show. It ended when 300-pound Tiny crawled across the finish line. He had chards of broken whiskey bottle glass from the alley protruding from his bloodied hands and knees. His beige pants were half-off and filled with a freshly laid load of dark brown diarrhea. As ridiculous as that was, every swinging dick on the Market bet on it. Victor was confident what he and Reece were about to run was being viewed as the same, just-a fun diversion after a tough work week and prelude to a three-day weekend. After all, he was just an Italian guy from the neighborhood who never played an organized sport in his life, racing against a black, soon-to-be professional football player known for his speed. Everything about this race was surreal and it all came about because of Walt Kramer, and surprisingly enough, Tommy LaCosta.

    Walt was president and chief financial officer of the Homer Grocery chain in Wisconsin. His stores doubled in size for the last three years, which gave Kramer prominence as a significant player on the Market. The store owners kissed his ass, and the workers that loaded his trucks received $50 tips. Even though most of Homer Grocery's produce was delivered directly to their central warehouse in Delevan, Wisconsin, Walt usually purchased at least three or four full semi-trailers a week from SouthWater filled to the brim with whatever he could buy the cheapest. It gave store owners the chance to purge their inventories of items that weren't moving or the opportunity to get rid of stock that had been sitting too long and needed to get blown out before spoilage started. Walt knew it and offered only a dime or two on the dollar. Other times, if there was a shortage or a high-demand item, he gladly paid up to double the asking price to get what he wanted. If that wasn't enough of an incentive to want to sell to him, it was Walt's chosen payment method - cash in full, on the day of purchase. Since cash was always king at SouthWater, Hebrew Walt Kramer was like King David on the street.

    Years earlier, Walt and his drivers had labor problems. Salvatore Domenico was still union president, and he wanted Kramer's guys to join up, just like everyone else on SouthWater. There were threats, delivery delays, issues with final counts, and the usual punctured truck tires and radiators. Sally Boy was shocked when Ingalleretta instructed him to back off Walt and the drivers. Salvatore had a real hard-on for Walt and wanted a signed union contract. Manny told Domenico the reasons why, and that was that. No more strong-arm tactics, no more intimidation and no more truck vandalism. Almost overnight, the union business agents went from pushing and shoving to turning a blind eye to Walt. Bottom line, Walt was tight with a powerful, wealthy group of Jewish and Italian mobsters from Wisconsin. The Bosses in both states had to get involved when it became a union territorial problem. They even had an official sit-down over the whole thing, which in itself was a huge deal. Once the powers reached a resolve, South Water viewed Walt in an entirely different light. He already had reputations as a shrewd businessman and an intelligent gambler with a big bankroll, but when you added 'connected guy' to that mix, there was weight. Walt's winning ways were pretty well-known, having cleaned out some of the heaviest Greek, Italian, and Polish gamblers on more than a few poker-playing occasions. Even Fat Frankie made a few hefty payouts to him on football and basketball wagers.

Reece was only a freshman at Notre Dame when Walt first approached him about making side cash. Since Reece was a Wisconsin guy, Walt convinced him to sign autographs, take pictures, and do fan meet-and-greets at the Homer grocery stores. Walt saw the potential in him from day one, and since Reece had four immediate family members working at Homer Groceries, he trusted Walt and let him handle things. Reece's share of cash was always under-the-table. Walt was sharp enough to know about the strict NCAA (National Collegiate Athletic Association) rules and regulations regarding student-athletes, especially when it came to gift acceptance. Reece explained to Walt that he was good, just as long as he didn't have to throw football games or lose track meets. Even better than the promotional store appearances was Walt's most recent scheme, running races under the guise of charity, which was acceptable under college guidelines.

A month earlier, Walt promoted a race between Reece and a very speedy Green Bay Packer kick returner named Steve Odom. The 100-yd event was heavily advertised and designed to raise donations for Wisconsin food pantries. (It was no coincidence the race was in a recently manicured grassy area behind the newest Homer Grocery parking lot during that store's grand opening.) But, again, Walt knew every angle, and the event was a monster success. Throngs of Wisconsinites showed up with food pantry contributions and watched a member of their beloved Packers race one of their talented homegrown kids. What spectators didn't know was that thousands were being bet under the table. Interested bookies said the smart money was on Odom. Walt knew better. He bet heavily on Reece. When Steve Odom crossed the finish line, Reece Walker was already there, two whole steps ahead of him. He glanced back at Odom just before breaking the tape and smiled.

Walt tried putting together one more score before Reece left for rookie training camp, but word quickly spread when he beat Odom. The competition, even for the sake of charity, dried up quickly. Reece was on his way to the west coast to start his NFL career, and SouthWater was the pair's last opportunity to take advantage of their sure thing.

Walt walked up and down the street that entire day, buying produce and looking for race action. He approached every store owner, every loan shark, and even the big-shot gamblers. Finally, he had coffee with Cristofano Milano, a heavily connected guy who worked a part-time salesman job at Anthony's

Tomatoes. Milano needed that part-time job for proof of employment to keep the G off his ass. Cristofano practically choked on his espresso when Walt suggested the bet.

"What am I, some kind of an asshole? If I'm gonna throw money out the window, you sure as shit ain't gonna be the one to catch it!" he told Walt. "There's no one on SouthWater who's gonna beat that fuckin' black kid from Notre Dame."

Kramer even broke down and talked to a couple of the union guys hoping to pique their interest. Joe Boyson, longtime Gino's Warehouse employee and newly elected Secretary-Treasurer of the local, was one of those guys. Boyson was Salvatore Domenico's eyes and ears relaying day-to-day labor business ever since Domenico's removal from his union position. But, of course, he also filled Salvatore in about anything out of the ordinary that was happening.

Since Tommy was spending so much time in Arizona over the last six months, Boyson was the guy coordinating Mob and union business in his absence. Given Salvatore and Walt's history, Boyson made a phone call to Domenico.

"That Jew cocksucker's got a set of fucking matzah balls on him, I'll give him that! Joey, I'm with my son Dino having breakfast. We'll stop down real nonchalant, like we don't know what's going on with this whole fucking thing. Meet ya in an hour at Big Banana," Sally Boy said.

It was almost 11:00 in the morning, and Walt still had no takers. He was coming to the sad realization that his sure-thing money-maker was over. Of course, the best move was to walk away with the thick bundle of cash already made. But, as logical as that reasoning was, he still had to talk himself into it.

"Time to count all the scratch I made off this. No one's gonna beat Reece no matter what odds I give. Maybe, I'll have a little fun with the whole thing."

Walt heard earlier from one of his Market gophers that LaCosta was still out of town, so when he walked inside Big Banana looking for bettors, he took advantage of Tommy's absence by being extra loud and overly obnoxious. Walt knew Tommy didn't care for him much. The feeling was mutual. The two men did little produce business with each other, and when Nicky came aboard, he followed right along with Tommy. At best, they were all cordial, but nothing more than that. The few times they did try to conduct a transaction, posturing and personal feelings always got in the way. They knew what side of the fence each of them stood on. After all, Big Banana was one of the few SouthWater houses that refused to sell to Walt during that whole union beef.

Manny spoke privately to Tommy shortly after Sally Boy was told to back his union guys off Walt and his drivers. After that conversation, Tommy better understood why things went the way they did. Walt's silent business partners were also his very personal friends. Manny explained to Tommy that Walt's friends mattered because they were the guys that sat at the very top of the Milwaukee Mob.

Walt boldly walked behind the main counter of the Big Banana showroom and stood on Tommy's oversized, hand-carved wooden chair so everyone could see and hear him.

"This is the last chance for any of you chosen Jews, lowly Gentiles, or Shvartsas (Jewish slang for blacks.) to win big! A single bet of $5,000 gets you 5-1 odds against future Oakland Raider Reece Walker. How about it? One hundred yards right down the middle of legendary SouthWater Market for a chance to win 25 fucking grand, and all it costs you is five lousy G's! C'mon, ya cheap bastards, I got the hard part here. I have to find someone who's stupid AND rich enough to take that bet!"

    Walt was really enjoying himself.

    Victor shook Reece's hand as he tilted his head towards Kramer.

    "Good luck with whatever that whole fucking thing is about. What's Walt trying to do, find some asshole to race you?"

    "No takers yet," Reece answered. "This is our final chance to make some green."

    Victor threw the final box of ripened bananas on his pallet jack.

    "Alright, man, I gotta go. Have a good camp. You guys are playing at Soldier Field this year, so I'll be there - cheering my white ass off for the Bears."

    "FUCK YOU!" Reece laughed. "I gotta go, man. My partner just gave me my cue."

    Reece pretended to sprint, but it was slow motion. He continued with his theatrics all the way up to the main counter where Walt was standing. When he joined Walt, he posed as if starting a race. Nicky was in one of the coolers working a deal with the Bastounes brothers, Dean and Tom from Capital Produce. When he heard the commotion Walt was causing, he headed to the front of the store.

    "Who wants a shot at the 'Fast as Lightning' champ?" Reece asked, shuffling his feet, jabbing, and throwing shadow punches and combinations like Muhammad Ali.

    After a few seconds of boisterous laughter from the growing crowd, the piped-in music playing over the Big Banana's loudspeakers abruptly scratched to a silent stop.

    "Make it $25,000 straight up. No odds. Take it or leave it, Walleshishka."

    Walleshishka was Walt's official Hebrew name. Up until that point, no one on SouthWater knew that. Everyone's attention turned towards the large bay window of the raised office that overlooked the entire main floor. Standing there, holding two bricks of cash in his hands and waving them, was Tommy, back from Arizona a lot earlier than anyone anticipated. He put the money stacks down on his table and grabbed the microphone. The speakers loudly crackled when he turned the volume up full blast.

    "And Walleshishka, get the FUCK, off my FUCKING chair!"

    Walt couldn't leap down fast enough. Reece stopped flashing and posing. Nicky, who had just wrapped his hand around the police baton he hid under his desk, set it back down in its place. His initial intention was to thump the metal counter with the club to intimidate Walt to get down from Tommy's chair. When Victor heard his uncle's voice over the intercom, he slammed his pallet jack to a halt so fast that the whole top layer of bananas boxes slid off the top stack.

    "Walt, I'll be down in fifteen minutes. Nicky and Victor come to my office," Tommy finished.

    The thump of Tommy's microphone hitting his desk echoed inside the building. He turned the speaker volume back to where it had been, reached into his desk, and pulled out an 8-track. It was "The Best of Frank Sinatra." He threw in inside the player. The song "My Way" played throughout the store.

"NO FUCKING WAY! WHAT THE FUCKING FUCK!" Victor thought.

On the way upstairs to his uncle's office, Victor looked down and saw Walt and Reece huddled together. Some of the crowd shuffled out, no doubt spreading the word up and down the Market that a race was about to go down. Other customers and Big Banana employees appeared to be carrying on with their morning. When Nicky and Victor got to Tommy's office door, they looked at each other before walking inside.

"Victor, I swear to Christ, he told me he wasn't coming back until next week."

"Come in, close the door, and sit down," Tommy authoritatively said.

Tommy didn't face them when he spoke. Instead, his back remained turned as he stared at the blown-up black and white overhead photograph of SouthWater Market from the late 1940s that hung on the wall behind his desk. It was the most famous of all the reprints.

"You know, I'm probably in the crowd somewhere. But, Jesus Christ, that was a long time ago. Every time I look at this fucking picture, I think about how some things have changed, and some are still the same. Do you follow me?"

Tommy turned, faced Nicky and Victor, and smiled a rare smile. They respectfully returned a nod and an uncomfortable grin.

"There's a reason I'm back early, but first things first. Victor, you're going to race Reece," Tommy decided. "You have your running shoes in your locker, right? I mean, you jog back and forth to the neighborhood three or four days a week, so I know you're in good shape, correct?" Tommy asked.

Victor was shocked.

"Good shape? Uncle Tommy, you have got to be fucking kidding me! Shape has nothing to do with it! ME race REECE? That's, that's insane!"

Victor thought his uncle was playing a sick joke on him.

"I get it. You're fucking with me because you're still pissed about the whole book thing. Okay, Uncle Tommy, you made your point. I'm sorry I didn't tell you about things sooner."

"Nope, I'm not pissed, and I'm also not fucking around. I'm betting $25,000 on you," Tommy answered. "Life is all about signs. You're a big sign guy, right, Victor?"

"I am," Victor agreed.

"I've spent the last few weeks doing a lot of thinking and soul searching. First, I felt miserable about how I acted and what I said to both of you before I left. I'm ashamed of myself, and I apologize. But then, Victor, I thought about how Auntie Tree and how she would've been so proud of you no matter what you wrote. Maybe almost as proud as she was when you read that Dr. Seuss book to her. That was always special for her because that was the first book she read to you when you were still a baby."

"It was "The Cat in the Hat." I was 5-years-old the first time I read it back to her on my own. Auntie Tree cried."

Physically, Tommy looked great with his tan, fresh shave, and recent haircut. It was also the most he had spoken at one time about anything other than business for months. Yet, as he continued, his voice took on an ever-so-slight tremble.

"So, I'm sitting outside on the deck one night in Arizona, like usual, by myself, looking up at the stars, missing Teresa. I walked into the bedroom and put a gun inside my mouth. I would've pulled that fucking trigger, too, if that dresser didn't have a mirror attached to it. Staring back at me was a weak, sorrowful, regretful man that let grief get the best of him. I looked like my birth father! That's not how I want to be remembered. I cried and yelled harder than I ever had before. The fucking security guys from the guardhouse came to the front door because the neighbors called them and said they heard screams."

Nicky and Victor sat stunned.

"I'm not gonna lie, it was a bad night," Tommy admitted. "The good that came from it was that I decided it was time for me to live again. I wanted to come back home, be with my family, and dive headfirst into the next adventure."

"You're okay, now? I mean, you sound great, you look fantastic, but betting 25 G's on Victor racing Reece? Come on, Tee, that's just fucking nuts!"

All Victor could do was nod. He was in total agreement with his father but more in a state of shock, trying to put everything into perspective.

"This is straight outta the fucking Twilight Zone," he thought.

"Victor, this is more about you than it is me. I wanted to do something to show you that I'm 100% behind you in whatever you do. We're a family, that's how it's been, and that's how it's always going to be," Tommy explained.

"That means the world to me, Uncle Tommy, but I have one question. What in the fuck does any of this have to do with me racing Reece? I'm sorry, it's just plain stupid! And, you're going to bet 25K? I have a better idea, Give ME the $25,000, we'll have a nice hug, and I'll thank you for your confidence in me

Tommy laughed.

"Sure, Victor, I could easily hand you all that cash and tell you to use it in the best of health just like Grandma used to wish, but I was looking for something else, something deeper. I kept thinking, what can I do for Victor personally that will always remind him of my support? What can I do for him to make sure he always remembers WHO he is and WHERE he came from?"

Victor turned to Nicky.

"Dad, tell Uncle Tommy that I already know who I am and where I came from. I think there's something wrong with him. I'm serious."

Tommy smiled as big as possible and laughed a billowing laugh. Then, he walked up to Victor, grabbed both sides of his cheeks in his hands, and planted a loud kiss on his forehead.

"MUAH! You're really somethin'! Nicky, this kid…. I'm sorry, this MAN of yours? He's a fucking beauty!" Tommy exclaimed, proudly admiring Victor.

Still seated in a state of borderline bewilderment, Victor turned his attention away from Tommy and looked at his father.

"Dad, feel free to dive right in."

Nicky raised his hand, stopping Victor from continuing.

"Let your uncle finish what he was saying, Vic."

Tommy walked to the front of his desk and plopped his ass down backward, half-seated over the edge.

"So, where was I? Oh, yeah, I'm walking up the steps by the back dock, feeling fresh as a fucking daisy, excited to see you guys, Fat Frankie, Grace, you know, everyone. I want to start living again. But then, I heard that big mouth, arrogant prick, Walt. At first, I didn't pay much attention to what he was saying. Now I'm halfway up the stairs to my office, and I stop and listen for a minute. I already heard from somebody, somebody about his fucking charity races. Charity my balleens! (Testicles) He had a sure win with his underground betting bullshit. I'll give him that."

Tommy looked at just Victor.

"I like Reece. He's a grown-ass man with a great future ahead of him. And I'll be honest; if I were him in his position, I'd be doing the same fucking thing. It's a smart, safe gig. Good, God bless. But, Walt? He thinks everyone on SouthWater is a strunzo (Worthless piece of shit) and that he's a genius. Fuck Walt! Then, I looked down at you and Reece talking by the west exit, and BOOM! It hit me! VICTOR IS THE SIGN! He is the last guy in the world, well, at least on the Market, Walt would expect to race against Reece! And the beauty of it all is that this move serves two purposes. First, it fucks with Walt's head because he thinks there's an angle he missed. Second, and most importantly, is the bigger picture."

"BIGGER? No Uncle Tommy, BIGGEST. As in, I get to go down as the BIGGEST ASSHOLE in the history of SouthWater Market!"

"Stop thinking so much and just listen for a change," Nicky sternly advised.

The whole time Tommy spoke, dozens of people ran in and out of Big Banana. The commotion was loud even with Tommy's heavy metal office door closed. Then, as he was ready to continue, his private phone rang.

"Let me get this call, guys."

"Hello. Okay. Tell Walt I'm opening my sliding glass window."

"Victor, come here and stand by me."

Victor got up and stood with his uncle. Tommy opened the sliding window so the entire main floor could see and hear him. Walt was still standing next to Reece at the front counter. Reece nudged him when he saw Tommy's window open.

"Tommy, unless you're hiding Jesse Owens Jr. in your office, I'm a lock here," Walt confidently stated.

"My nephew is gonna race Reece," Tommy answered.

Although there wasn't an all-out burst of hysterical laughter from everyone on the main floor, a struggling comic would've been more than satisfied with the ha ha's and snickers when Tommy announced Victor was the one who would be racing Reece.

I cannot fucking believe this!" Victor thought. *"Now, if I don't run, I'm gonna look like a chicken-shit cunt!"*

There was a common look of disbelief on every main floor face, especially Reece's. He opened both of his arms palm sides up, looked directly at Victor, and widely mouthed the words, "WHAT THE FUCK?"

"Tommy, come on, the kid standing right there, for 25 large straight up? What's the catch?" Walt asked

"There's no catch, and he's not a kid," Tommy answered, locking eyes with his nephew.

Walt quickly responded.

"Of course, he's not a kid! I didn't mean anything by that. But, hey, they're both kids to us, right, Tommy? So listen, one hundred yards, down the middle of the Market. You and I are the judges. Sound good?"

"We'll start in a half-hour. Nicky will be down to help coordinate," Tommy answered as he closed the window.

"Coordinate what? What am I coordinating?" Nicky asked.

"First, let me finish with what I was saying," Tommy answered as he turned his attention back to his nephew. "Victor, what was the name of that show? Wait, it was "This Is Your Life!" Do you remember that?"

"Barely," Victor answered.

"Well, THIS IS YOUR LIFE, VICTOR DABONE!" Tommy enthusiastically exclaimed. "My little nephew, what you need to do inside that head of yours, is envision something much bigger here. The main character in this story is you, and you're about to have a huge moment. Isn't that what you writers do? You call it character development, right? So let's see how developed your character is."

"I'm trying hard to understand where you're coming from with all this, Uncle Tommy. None of it makes sense," Victor answered.

As Tommy was about to continue, Reece knocked on the door. Tommy motioned for him to come in.

"Hi Mr. LaCosta, hey, Mr. DaBone, I'm sorry to interrupt you guys," Reece respectfully apologized.

"Reece, I heard about you on the news! Congratulations on being drafted! You deserve it!" Tommy congratulated.

"Nice job. A professional football player! Wow, holy shit! That's fucking fantastic!" Nicky added.

"Thank you, both. I appreciate it. But, please tell me, what the hell is going on with me racing Victor? I mean, we're friends," Reece questioned. "Mr. LaCosta, no disrespect, but if this is something personal between you and Walt, I don't want to be a part of it."

"Reece, this is just a fun race. Yea, there's an expensive wager attached to it, but nothing more than that where you're concerned. You said that you and Victor are friends. Great! And, you'll be friends after the race, too." Tommy explained.

"I don't understand," Reece added as he looked at Victor.

"Join the club. I just said the same fucking thing," Victor agreed.

For a good thirty seconds or so, there was dead silence in the office as the four of them exchanged glances, waiting to see who was going to speak next. It was

Reece.

"If you guys are all okay with this, then let's do it and get it over. Racing is a money thing for me. That's all it's ever been."

"Good. So it's settled," Tommy concluded.

What Reece said next was directed at Victor. Tommy could've talked all afternoon about his intentions with what he was thinking, and it wouldn't have gotten his point across better or accomplished more than what Reece said next.

"I'll try not to embarrass you too badly out there, Victor," Reece confidently stated.

It was evident that Reece was genuine. His offer was heartfelt and not meant to be disrespectful or intimidating. In his mind, he was offering Victor friendship mercy.

"I hate to see you lose all that money, Mr. LaCosta. But, I mean, I'll try not to shame any of you," Reece added as he made eye contact with Tommy and Nicky.

"This is beautiful! I couldn't have set this up any better on my best day," Tommy thought.

Nicky was doing some thinking of his own.

"Now I see where Tommy's going with this whole thing! That sly mudda fucker!"

Tommy and Nicky beamed. Tommy was barely able to contain himself.

"Victor, that's real decent of Reece not wanting to embarrass any of us, don't you think?"

Victor's response didn't disappoint.

"Yes, that's nice of Reece. I was about to extend the same courtesy to him and Walt."

Tommy would've bet 25 million he was going to say something like that.

"Right on fucking schedule!"

Reece smiled and imagined.

"You can't be serious, Victor! Wait, I get it. You're just trying to save face in front of your father and uncle."

"Okay, Victor, okay. Great, then they'll be no hard feelings, either way, right?" he asked, semi-chuckling.

"We'll always be friends, Reece. We're good," Victor assured him as their standard handshake went from conventional, to soul-brother style.

Thirty minutes later, thanks to Nicky's coordinating, Reece and Victor slowly jogged down the center of the freshly cleaned pavement of SouthWater to the starting line at the Watermelon House. The odds against Victor, depending on how much you were betting and who you were betting with, varied. He was going off as a 5-1 underdog, but there was a catch. To get those high odds, you had to come up with a $500 minimum bet. Mostly, there were individual $20-$100 wagers at 2-1, and that was if you could find someone willing to pick Victor. There was quite a bit of white against black betting going on too, but in a non-threatening way, which is precisely how different ethnicities interacted on the Market. Reece looked confident, just like he had at every sporting competition he was involved with since grade school. Victor's appearance was more like a condemned man approaching the gallows. Almost every produce business was empty as workers, owners, truck drivers, and buyers lined the front docks. Words of encouragement for Victor were few and far between.

"Hey, DaBone, you got a better chance at winning a typing contest, and Reece would probably beat your ass in that, too!" someone teased.

"GO WRITE A POEM AND GET THE FUCK BACK IN THE BANANA COOLER!" shouted Al, the driver for Quam Brothers Cartage.

"You ain't Rocky Balboa, lay!" laughed Berle from Ira Fisher.

Victor didn't take the shitty comments personally. He was seasoned enough to know that SouthWater had almost as many ball-busting jagoffs working there as it did decent guys. He also knew that a 50-yard dash would've personally suited him much better, but 100 yards it was.

"There's a helluva lot of cheering for Reece. Fuck it! So what! No half-assed shit today. Everything like it means everything. My time! My time!" he repeatedly thought while the song "Run Run Run" by Jo Jo Gunn played in his head.

As they both stretched out, Victor side-eyeballed Reece, watching him go through his pre-race ritual.

"Reece's warm-up routine is right out of the fucking text book. Shit!"

"VICTOR! HEY, VICTOR! WE GOT ALL OURS ON YOU!" a voice close by yelled.

It was Pete Korinthos who was screaming.

"MY PARTNER AND I GOT TWO GRAND AT 5-1 ON YOU! LOOK AT WHO MY PARTNER IS!"

Pete's father, George the Greek, popped his head out behind Peter and pointed at Victor.

"Malaka, (Greek slang. Means either friend or masturbator.) you win, and I buy you a nice dinner, you lose, and I'm gonna shoot Peter in his fucking head."

Victor knew George was kidding, and normally, he would've thought that was hilarious, especially in The Greek's heavy Athenian accent. But there was nothing normal, or remotely funny, about what was happening. He was about to run a race against the devastatingly fast Reece Walker in front of everyone on SouthWater. Fazool just happened to be at LaMancha Produce picking up some fruits and vegetables for a weekend party at his son Vito's house in Oak Brook. He walked with Nicky down the middle of the street. Everyone on the Market knew Fazool was a cop from Taylor Street. When he was a young patrol officer, he did a 5-year stint on SouthWater. (The Chief of Police assigned him there at Manny Ingalleretta's request.) Nicky jogged away from Fazool, clutching the top pocket of his shirt so the five pens and two DiNobili cigars he had tucked in there wouldn't spill out. He joined George the Greek and Peter in the crowd. Fazool strolled up to Victor at the starting line.

"I don't talk to you for a few years at a time, and when I do, it's always under interesting circumstances, isn't it, Victor?"

He knew what Fazool meant. Besides a few wakes and a couple of weddings, one of the last times they spoke was almost seven years earlier at "The

"Godfather" premiere.

"And speaking of interesting, your father just told me an interesting story about you from back on Taylor Street. He asked me to remind you about it."

Fazool didn't need to be a 35-year veteran police officer to recognize the nervous look on Victor's face. He interrogated more than his fair share of suspects and interviewed thousands of witnesses in his time, both on and off, the job. In the meantime, Reece was busy chattering with a group of black workers who gathered on the starting line's other side. They were shouting different versions of encouragement - everything from "Kick that white boy's ass" to "Light up dat mudda fucker!" Fazool thought it best to relay Nicky's message as quickly as possible because poor Victor appeared ready to pass out.

"Your father said I should remind you about that race you had with your German Shepherd about ten years ago. What was your dog's name? Oh yea. It was Zeus."

Fazool turned and walked out about five yards away from the front of the starting line. He took the gun from his holster, raised it in the air, and shouted.

"RUNNERS, TAKE YOUR MARKS! GEEEEET SET…"

The blast was as loud as the crowd. Victor would've won by about a half-step if the race was only 15 yards long. It was the fastest he ever started. Fifteen yards was also the distance it took for Reece to wipe that over-confident, shit-eating grin off his face.

"Well, I'll be goddamned! My EYE-TALIAN'S got some wheels!"

For the next 30 yards or so, it was back and forth. First, it was Victor. Then, it was Reece. At the halfway point, they were neck and neck, until Reece started striding out with those long, muscular, athletic legs of his. He was beginning to pull away slightly.

In the next split second, out of the corner of his eye, Victor saw the Lanzatorri Produce sign precariously dangling from the front entrance of the building as it had done for the last 50 years. It was the unofficial halfway point of the first section of SouthWater. That aged, weather-beaten, hand-painted wooden plaque, jarred flashes of past stories in his head. They were the tales about the struggles his uncle faced as a kid, the winter cold he endured walking miles to and from the Market, the hard work trying to keep up with full-grown adult men, and of course, that morning on the back dock with Ingalleretta. Victor also remembered his father working on his hands and knees in the garage on Fillmore Street to fix pallet jacks and other equipment. He also recalled his first day there and what a nervous wreck he was trying to blend in and not embarrass either of them. At that moment, the Lanzatorri Produce sign brought all three of their stories to life. Two questions ran quickly through his mind.

"Is this race my turn to add to my family's SouthWater legacy? Is this what Uncle Tommy was getting at?"

The only thing for sure was that Victor was in the process of losing the race. At about 70 yards, he was roughly a full body length behind Reece. It was now or never, so the speedy Sicilian shifted into that extra gear. Reece smelled another victory.

"Nice try, Victor, but I got you now, boy," he thought. *"Your ass is....OH, FUCK!"*

Reece couldn't finish his thought process. He was a seasoned sprinter, and natural speedsters can always sense when an opponent closes in on them. He felt Victor coming on quickly, so he buried his head in anticipation of breaking the tape with his signature finish, a long, leaping final stride.

The race was so close that you wouldn't have known who won if you weren't standing parallel to the finish line. Those lucky enough to have positioned themselves there ahead of time, like Walt, Tommy, Sister Vanna Rose, the food buyer from Brother Lucien's Food Pantry, Sally Boy and Dino Domenico, Joe Boyson, and also, at the last minute, Fat Frankie, Michael Jr., JuJu, and about fifty Market guys, - they all knew immediately.

For as quickly as it started, for how tightly it ended, and for as many times as the lead changed hands, there was a definite winner, and if you blinked when they crossed the finish line, you would've missed it. Finally, about 15-20 yards after the finish, Reece and Victor came to a stop. They both bent over, trying to catch their breath. A few people tried to make their way to them, but truck drivers from Finer Foods and Cee Bee Cartage waved them away shouting.

"GIVE THEM SOME ROOM! GIVE THEM SOME ROOM!"

Reece was the first to stand. His hands were raised, attempting to fill his lungs with air. He used this particular technique to catch his breath quicker. It must have worked because he looked like he was ready to run again. On the other hand, Victor was struggling. He was bent over, panting and breathing as deeply as possible between coughs. He felt like puking, thinking he was dying right then and there.

"Oh, this fucking hurts! My heart's gonna burst out of my chest just like that thing in Alien!"

"Stand up, Victor." Reece encouraged. "Breathe slowly. Take short puffs a little at a time. You're full of surprises, my man! That was a good fucking race! I'm not used to running on the blacktop. I like a cinder or rubber track, or even better, the grass on a football field. You wanna run it one more time to make sure who won?"

Reece wasn't even out of breath. He babbled as if he had just taken a brisk stroll through Peanut Park. Victor, on the other hand, looked like death warmed over.

He choked out a response, hacking through the entire three words.

"Fuck you, Reece!"

Reece laughed and patted Victor's back.

"Maybe we'll do a rematch one of these days. But, seriously, you should have done something with that kind of speed. The biggest shame here is that it's wasted on an EYE-TALIAN boy!"

Walt and Tommy disappear into the crowd, which dispersed as quickly as it formed.

"I think I'm gonna call you 'Clark' from now on, like Clark Kent. That mutha fucker's a writer, too! You were hiding that faster than a speeding bullet shit, just like Superman! GET THE FUCK OUTTA HERE!" Reece laughed.

A handful of guys finally made their way through to offer both men congratulations on a great race. Unfortunately, others felt it necessary to voice their critical comments. After all, it was SouthWater. But, as pissed and disappointed as some people were about the race outcome, no one doubted both runners went balls-out. The guys who won money gloated, and the guys who lost money complained. They knew they had no reason to. They just picked the wrong horse. Through all the grumbling, moaning, and whining, not one person on the entire Market cried 'Bullshit." The winner won, and the loser lost. Neither Walt nor Tommy could contest the outcome. They were right there and saw it for themselves.

Sally Boy and Dino were talking to Nicky on the Market Café steps. Fat Frankie was busy scarfing two folded slices of sausage pizza fresh out of the Pompeii Bakery truck while talking to Michael Jr., who, of all things, showed up out of the fucking blue five minutes before the race started!

When Victor was finally able to stand, he looked at his friends. They waved and pointed, but he barely acknowledged them, only offering a head-tilt.

"Dirk is gonna shit when he hears about this!" Dino gloated.

"I want a twenty-five hundred-word short story about the race for the magazine next month," Michael Jr. added.

Victor, barely able to take more than three breaths in a row without coughing, responded to Dino.

"Yea, I know!"

Then Victor pointed at Michael Jr.

"Nothing here for me to write about. Sorry."

Reece got sidetracked as he headed off the Market when a few guys asked him to sign autographs. That led to also shaking hands, receiving encouraging pats on the back, and receiving well-wishes for his rookie season with the Oakland Raiders.

When Victor walked up to his guys, they surrounded him with a group hug. Fat Frankie joined in, squeezing tightly. Victor winced from ribcage pain and coughed from the added pressure of Frankie's girth and the repulsive smell of anchovy pizza still lingering on his breath. Dino was the first to congratulate him.

"That was unfucking real, Victor! By the way, did you happen to see who won? Oh, and did Frankie tell ya, Peter bet $50,000 of his dad's money on Reece!"

Victor smiled and rolled his eyes.

"Hey, let's call up Coach Freud and tell him that Victor's finally ready to play!" Michael Jr. added.

An hour later, still feeling the physical side effects of the race, Victor puked. Not once, but three times. As he slowly walked out of the shower stall at Big Banana, he took solace in the profound peace of the basement. It was precisely the silence he needed. The only sounds were remaining drops of water draining into the sewer. It was the most exhilaratingly satisfying shower he ever remembered taking. Standing in front of the sink mirror, his waist wrapped in a Quality Inn bath towel, Victor took a deep breath, held it, and exhaled, still feeling a slight bit of pain.

"Almost normal, but not yet."

He reached into his gym bag, took out a comb, and just like Nicky had taught him, slicked his hair back, duplicating the perfect swirl of a curl. As he continued staring at himself, he thought.

"So that's what the adult version of 100% feels like! I am never going to put my body through that again, EVER! How can Reece run that fast and hard week in and week out? I can't wait to get home and lie in bed with headphones. Shit! Why are my back teeth hurting?"

He pulled out a new pair of blue jeans that he bought a week earlier at Chess King in Yorktown Mall. Gina Guzzaldi, the unbelievably beautiful long black-haired Italian girl from Woodridge who worked there, confessed that she snuck a peek when he walked out of the fitting room and stood in front of the three full-length mirrors.

"Victor, your ass looks great in those pants," she whispered right before he left.

Gina and Victor knew each other from crossover high school parties and flirted back and forth for years. Victor told her he overheard her say the exact same thing to the guy in front of him right before he checked out. Gina laughed. But, what Victor really thought about was the punch line from the joke about the guy with the five dicks.

"His pants fit like a glove!"

As he trudged up the back staircase to the main floor, JuJu walked down from Tommy's office.

"There he is, the man of the fucking hour!" JuJu excitedly greeted. "Walt and Reece just left Tommy's office. Speaking of your uncle, he's waiting for you, your dad and Frankie, too. Look at these pictures. Before Reece left, he autographed a bunch of them for me to give to the young brothers at Black Power Gym."

"Reece is a good guy," Victor affirmed, looking at the glossy football photographs.

He handed them back to JuJu who intentionally stopped on the last step blocking the way. Victor over-exaggeratedly looked him over from head to toe.

"I'm way too tired to try and climb over you, JuJu."

As he stepped aside, JuJu asked Victor the question that was undoubtedly on the minds of everyone who saw the race.

"How in the fuck did you beat Reece?"

Victor answered confidently, assuredly, and analytically.

"I ran faster than he did."

CHAPTER 18
THE HOLY TRINITY

In Christian doctrine, the Holy Trinity holds that God is one God and exists in the form of three coeternal and consubstantial persons; the Father, the Son, and the Holy Spirit. The three are distinct yet are one substance, essence, or nature. The Chicago Mob had their version of The Holy Trinity - Joey Balducci, Primo Montalbano, and Jimmy Rio. Thanks to Tommy, Victor was going to meet them.

"You told me that if you had to talk to someone about your book, that you'd have no problem doing that. So tonight, you're going to get that opportunity," Tommy casually explained to Victor. "I'm sitting with them on something entirely different, but I asked for a few minutes of their time afterward, so you could explain to them in person what you're doing. Trust me on this. Being honest and upfront is the best play here."

As he sprawled on the oversized brown leather couch, Victor remembered telling his uncle a few weeks earlier that he would talk to whoever he had to talk to, if necessary.

"I can't believe Uncle Tommy took me seriously!"

Nicky and Fat Frankie agreed wholeheartedly with Tommy, voicing their opinions. Victor heard only a few of their words here and there. Instead, it all blended, like muffled conversations of others when first waking from a deep nap or sleep.

"Tommy, they're expecting you about 6:00, and then Victor and Nicky at around 7:00," Frankie explained.

"Tommy, it's okay that I go, right?" Nicky asked.

"It's what I asked for, pal. I wouldn't want this to go down any other way," Tommy confirmed. "Now, Victor, do you have any questions? And, before you answer, hear me out for one second. All you have to do is be respectful, speak respectfully, and show respect. You get the common denominator, right?"

"Yes, I do," Victor agreed. "I need to say something here, and this is for my sanity, more than anything else. I think I must be unconscious because I cannot believe what just happened with that whole fucking race thing, which, by the way, I'm not even 100% certain was real. And now, you're telling me that I have to explain to the three most serious and powerful men in Chicago why I wrote a book about a topic they don't like? Please, for the love of God, someone shake me awake!"

"Go home and get some sleep. All of this is nothing more than explaining what your book is about exactly the way you told me, capicse?" Tommy said encouragingly.

That was the Tommy LaCosta of old talking. The guy who planned, maneuvered, saw all the angles, and accomplished just about anything he set out to do.

"Nicky, I'll meet you and Victor at Japeto's about 6:45. Then, we'll walk across the empty lot to my apartment. Tommy will already be there. When we walk in, you make nice and say hello, and then I'll make the introductions with Victor," Frankie explained.

"Your apartment in Charlie Landa's old building?" Victor asked.

"Yes, that's where they're meeting this…," Frankie said, stopping himself mid-sentence.

He looked at Tommy before continuing, realizing he was about to say something containing semi-privileged Mob information. Even though he knew Victor would remain close-lipped, he wasn't about to go any further without Tommy's approval.

"Go ahead, finish," Tommy instructed.

"When The Holy Trinity meets, they do it at about half a dozen safe locations. My apartment is one of them," Frankie shared.

"Victor, I'm going on record, right here, right now. I do NOT want to read anything about 'safe locations' in your next book," Tommy laughingly warned his nephew.

"What about burying all of us together in one hole? Can I write about that? And, is Frankie included?" Victor sarcastically responded.

Frankie looked puzzled, but Tommy and Nicky immediately knew what he meant.

"WHO'S GETTING BURRIED IN WHAT HOLE?" Frankie nervously asked.

Tommy took a minute to explain to Frankie what he had previously said to Victor in the heat of that moment

"That would never happen over something like this, Vic," Frankie reassured him.

"Yea, if they threw Frankie in with us, they'd have to dig it a helluva a lot deeper AND wider!" Nicky piped up.

Everyone laughed, except Victor. He was too exhausted.

"Can I please leave now?" he tiredly asked.

Nicky was the first to notice the concerned look on his son's face. Tommy and Frankie also saw it, so they attempted to ease Victor's trepidation by feigning nonchalance over the meeting.

"Vic, you got this, no problem. Just greet them and speak to them like you did the few times you were around Manny," Frankie suggested.

"Frankie, I was just gonna tell him the very same fucking thing!" Nicky agreed.

Victor stood up from the couch and grabbed his gym bag.

"Wait a minute," Tommy interrupted.

He took the gym bag out of Victor's hands, reached inside, and took out his Asics running shoes, tossing them to Nicky.

"I want you to put these in a glass frame, just like you did with Frankie's broken steering wheel. Then, get a nice plaque. I want it all in gold, etched real nice and classy with Roman-style writing. Go see Mr. Marco, the jeweler from St. Charles, he's the only one I trust to do it the right way. Here's what I want written on it," Tommy instructed.

VICTOR DABONE
THE FASTEST MAN ON SOUTHWATER MARKET

"Put today's date on there too, Nick. I'm hanging it up behind my desk next to the 1940s Market picture."

Before Tommy handed Victor his gym bag back, he slid in a large manila envelope that was sitting on his desk. Then, he zipped up the bag.

"That's half of what I won from Walt, Victor. If you've been following YOUR story, and I know you have, that's 12.5K," Tommy explained. "That's an awful lot of cash for a young man. I have other plans for you with the remaining 12.5. But, for now, you deserve this. We're all proud of you. That was one helluva race. Buy a new pair of shoes with it, and maybe a house, too."

Victor took the bag and set it back on the desk. He also began unzipping it.

"I can't accept that."

Tommy put his hand on the bag's zipper.

"You CAN accept it, and you WILL," he matter-of-factly stated. "Not only is this because you won, but not once during this whole thing did I ever hear you say that you were going to lose. Not once. You fucking stood up and owned it, pal. That's probably the most important thing that happened here today, well, that, and Walt and me coming to an understanding. We're going to start working together on produce deals instead of always butting heads. Domenico and Joe Boyson talked to him, too, while you were showering. Walt agreed to sign his five Chicago truck drivers up with the local. That's how things should've gone down ten years ago, instead of all of us acting like a bunch of fucking teenage hard-ons. Everyone's going to benefit from what happened here today. I will say I took some personal pleasure when I heard the puckering sound of Walt's asshole when he handed over the scarole (Cash)."

Victor hoped his father would intervene and be the voice of reason.

"Dad, please tell Uncle Tommy I can't take that money," Victor pleaded.

Instead, Nicky did what he did best. He reached for the envelope with the overtly greedy intention of making Victor's hefty payday his own.

"All right, I guess I gotta step in, here. Let me hold on to it for safekeeping," Nicky said, selfishly making a move to confiscate the gym bag.

Both Fat Frankie and Tommy smelled that coming from a mile away and burst out laughing.

"Nicky, you touch that bag, and I'll snap your fuckin' fingers off," Tommy threateningly joked. "Seriously, Victor, I knew in my heart that race was going to be close, but you shocked the shit out of the whole fucking Market. You made your history here today, and tonight? Well, tonight, your journey continues."

Too tired to argue and too fatigued to express the proper jubilation, he hugged and kissed his uncle for such a significant gift. But, as worn out as he was, there was one thing he wondered.

"Frankie, did you bet on the race?"

"No, I was in the back jarring some fresh Fra Diavolo (Brother Devil) sauce and by the time I came out, it was too late. I did see the finish, though. It was un-fucking believable!" Frankie answered.

"Tell me the gospel truth, Frankie. If you would've bet, who would you have picked?"

"I don't have to tell you the smart money was on Reece, but I would've picked you, odds or no odds, just like your uncle did, and that's the fucking truth," Frankie answered. "It's not always about betting smart. Sometimes, it's a feeling. Other times, it's about having inside information, knowing the things that no one else knows," he continued explaining.

"What inside information?" Victor questioned.

"A long time ago, I was outside the restaurant grilling sausage on the pit your father made me. I watched you as a kid race Zeus in the empty lot. Honestly, I could not fucking believe that you almost beat him. That was maybe what, 40 or-50 yards? It was from your fence to the side of Tony and Lena's house. You were like 12-years old?"

Nicky stood up like his ass was on fire.

"I thought I was the only one who saw that! I told Fazool that same fucking story right before the race! I asked him to remind Victor about it. I can't fucking believe this! The only other time I remember saying anything about that was to Jerry Rigonest. Yeah, it was Jerry the G-Man! I was in our driveway waxing the Caddy, and Jerry dropped Dirk off. That was the first time Dino and Michael Jr. stopped by the house, too. They all tried talking Victor into playing football," Nicky remembered. "It was right at the end of eighth grade. Frankie, I can't believe you never said anything to me!"

"My mother was standing there with me, too. Do you know what she said?" Frankie asked, hoping someone would request his famous Graziella Pope impression.

"Your mother was watching, too? What did she say?" Nicky asked, encouraging and intentionally baiting Frankie.

"Madre di Maria, Frangee, proprio ieri il piccolo Victorio stave cagando nel suo pannolino quando l'ho tenuto in braccio, ora corre come una gazzella!" (Mother of Mary, Frankie, just yesterday, little Victor was shitting in his diaper when I held him in my arms, now he runs like a gazelle!) Frankie proclaimed in his mother's high-pitched voice.

Frankie was proud of his updated interpretation, even adding exaggerated hand gestures and stances since his last performance. He translated his mother's earthy Italian version to English. Victor secretly thought the Italian version sounded much better. Nevertheless, Frankie had Mama Pope's voice down pat. It was as if she was standing right there with them. The only difference was that Graziella wasn't a 490-pound man. (She was every bit of 225, though.)

"So, here's my answer to your question, Victor," Frankie continued. "Besides almost beating an adult German Shepherd police dog in a race and witnessing you fly around the bases all those years playing softball, I had an even bigger reason to bet on you. The family NEVER bets against the family."

Victor hugged and kissed him.

"Thank you, Frankie. Speaking of dogs, I'm dog-ass tired. I'll see everyone later."

Victor's 35-minute ride home to Upper Cove was as if a dreamscape had unfolded. He blinked when he merged onto the Eisenhower Expressway, and by the next flutter of an eyelash, he was exiting onto Highland Avenue. He didn't even remember seeing the usual, familiar landmarks, like the large red Magikist lips sign, Loretto Hospital, the Ferrara Candy Company smokestack, The Hillside Theater, or the Oakbrook Mall.

In the few hours before his meeting, he relaxed and listened to his "Dreamy Tea Drifters" mix. Victor transferred dozens of individual tracks from albums onto a reel-to-reel tape. It was the very best falling to sleep song collection ever. There was music by Pink Floyd, Traffic, The Allman Brothers, Robin Trower, Crosby, Stills, Nash & Young, The Steve Miller Band, Cream, Bob Seger, The Doobie Brothers, UFO, The Doors, The Beatles, The Rolling Stones, Jethro Tull, Bad Company, Chicago, Boston, Tangerine Dream, Grand Funk Railroad, Aerosmith, Marvin Gaye, and many others. As tempted as he was to grab a couple of tokes before Traffic's "The Low Spark of High Heeled Boys" began playing, Victor was too tired to move from the comfort of his king-sized water bed. Plus, he wanted to keep his head clear for the evening meeting; the one he still couldn't believe was going down.

Victor was overly cautious when he wrote "My Grandfathers are Bosses." His priority was ensuring the character names he used were not the same, or even similar, to actual Outfit members and associates. When he was halfway through the book's final rewrite, he received a valuable gift, thanks to Dirk's oldest brother Brian and his connections within the law enforcement community. It was a yet-to-be-released copy of the Chicago Organized Crime Task Force Mob Chart. The updated Outfit member information on that list was immensely beneficial as Victor neared his book's completion

"This chart is for your eyes only. It doesn't get officially released to the press until the end of next month," Brian warned at the time.

Over 200 guys appeared on the list, and at least 60 were new. Victor recognized some names, others he heard mentioned here and there over the years. He was mildly disappointed at his cluelessness regarding who the majority of them were.

"Dino and Michael Jr. are going to have a field day with this chart when the time comes to share it with them. I can't wait to watch them play 'Who's Who in the Outfit.'"

When he recalled reading the new list for the first time, Victor's favorite memory was when he compared it to the old chart from five years earlier. Tommy's upgrade was accurate as Near West Side Lieutenant instead of a Taylor Street Soldier. Fat Frankie got bumped up from Bookie to Top Bookmaker. Michael Gabriel Sr. remained in a category all his own as Head Political Fixer. Salvatore Domenico maintained his position as Little Italy Captain, and the biggest surprise for Victor came when he read his father's name added as an Associate. He wondered what took the G so long. There were tons of guys that knew Nicky was Tommy LaCosta's protected brother-in-law. And, if that wasn't enough, there was his 20 plus year involvement handling stolen merchandise, taking down scores, and participating in Mob-sanctioned schemes and heists.

Because of that updated chart, it took almost a month to revise the manuscript with character name changes. The biggest challenges were the nicknames. The similarities to real ones were WAY too obvious. Some of the actual Outfit guys had two, three, and even four monikers! After more than a few attempts, Victor finally fabricated new sobriquets for his imaginary gangsters. When completed, the changes to their nom de plumes were even better than the originals. Brian Rigonest did a solid getting that updated chart. So, to ensure the list's secrecy, Victor hid it in the most secure spot he could think of, with his weed, under the kitchen floorboard of the side apartment attached to his parents' house. Since moving there after his grandmother died, it was his premiere hiding spot. Just about every time he retrieved his herbage, he thought about Grandma Mari.

"She's probably doing summersaults in that mausoleum wall watching me smoke this shit!"

Although he jerked himself awake every 30-40 minutes, those short bursts of rest in between allowed him to catch a pretty decent snooze in the five hours that preceded his Holy Trinity meeting. Besides experiencing more than a few rational thoughts, which Victor felt was due to lucid bouts of hypnagogia and hypnopompia, he finally convinced himself how well he covered his bases.

"I did my fucking homework. There's not one similarity in my book to anyone living or deceased."

For the entire ride down to Japeto's, Nicky reassured him about the meeting being informal and casual. They did not discuss the elephant in the room - that the men involved were Syndicate Bosses. Nevertheless, Victor was awful glad Nicky was doing the driving. It gave him more time to concentrate.

"Victor, they have more pressing shit going on. So this is what it is - a clear, stand-up show of respect. The last thing you want is them feeling blindsided hearing something about you or your book from someone else," Nicky reminded.

"Dad, what if they say I should've asked for their permission first?" Victor asked.

Nicky didn't respond. Instead, he made the sign of the cross. When Victor realized where they were, he did the same. Since Teresa's death, anytime any of their family drove inbounds on the Eisenhower, they made the sign of the cross and offered blessings to her at Sacramento Avenue. They did it out of love and respect. It was the exact location of the car crash that claimed her life.

"I miss her," Nicky solemnly stated.

"Me, too," Victor added. "It's coming up on three years."

"As far as them asking you about getting their permission first, I honestly don't know what you should say. Just remember what we're all telling you, and I know you're already tired of hearing it, but I'm going to repeat it, be respectful. And, maybe, say a little prayer to Auntie Teresa. Ask her for some guidance. I mean, it's pretty fucking weird that this is what we're talking about at that spot on the expressway. But, if they do ask you that question, I'm certain you'll have a great answer for them," Nicky encouragingly added.

Within minutes, Victor noticed the red neon Japeto's sign. It was then he realized it was the first time ever passing Maria's house without looking for her. He briefly thought about how on a Friday night during the summer, ten or fifteen years ago, Loomis Street would've been packed with kids, teenagers, and parents. Now, there were barely a handful of people scattered between Flournoy and Fillmore Streets. As he walked in the empty dirt lot where his old house once stood, he repeated the same words over and over in his head.

"Be respectful and act and speak respectfully."

When they walked inside the apartment, Tommy was sitting in the corner on a couch that Frankie brought over from his Marina Towers place. (At last count, Frankie had five different known residences. There were at least two more that only a select few knew about.)

"Uncle Tommy's smiling and looks happy. I guess his meeting went well," Victor thought.

Nicky confidently sauntered around the dining room table. It wasn't his first rodeo greeting Outfit Bosses. He shook their hands, said a few words, and kissed them on their cheeks. The return responses to Nicky were genuine, friendly, and cordial. As for Victor, his stomach was spinning upside down as he watched his father.

"Shit! What am I supposed to do? Should I shake their hands? Should I kiss them on the cheek? Should I do both? Mother fucker, why didn't I ask someone that before I walked in here? That's going to set the tone. Okay, calm down, calm down, and for the love of God, don't start sweating. Fuck it, handshakes and kisses on the cheek it is!"

"And this is Nicky's son, Victor," Fat Frankie introduced.

The Holy Trinity looked at Victor but said nothing. It was like they were waiting to see his reaction.

"Here we go!" thought Victor. *"Don't be nervous like Luca Brasi was when he thanked Don Corleone for the invitation to his daughter's wedding."*

Victor followed his father's lead. Where Nicky sauntered to greet them, Victor's approach was more reverent, like a Catholic schoolboy approaching the altar for first communion or confirmation. After all, they were the Holy Trinity! The three Bosses all had full plates of food in front of them. The pasta was definitely from Japeto's. The steaks looked and smelled like they came from Gino and Georgie's.

Jimmy Rio was first. Victor leaned in, kissed him on his left cheek, and grasped his hand with both of his. Then, in a voice not much above a whisper, Victor spoke, trying not to concentrate on Rio's diminutive height which was evident even though he remained seated. Rio's feet barely touched the floor!

"It's an honor to meet you, sir," Victor said, slightly bowing.

"The bow may have been a little much, and I should've called him Mr. Rio! Son of a bitch!" Victor thought.

Jimmy shuffled in his chair and turned it outward. Then, Victor noticed a small leaf of lettuce dangling from Crap Game's lip.

"Nice to meet you, young man," he warmly said.

Victor watched the lettuce slide off Rio's mouth and onto the red cloth napkin tucked neatly inside the neckline of his sheer silk shirt. The white dago tee he wore underneath it was visible from up close. When Rio smiled, he revealed a second, much larger large piece of lettuce lodged in the noticeable gap of his front upper teeth. Being from SouthWater Market, Victor accurately identified the suspect greenery.

"That's romaine. Jesus Christ, I bet he could fit a whole fucking head of it in that tooth gap!"

Next was the man himself, Joseph "Joey Good Times" Balducci. Three powerful men sat at that table, but there was no doubt which one of them cast the immense shadow. Victor almost shit himself right then and there when Balducci pushed the chair he was seated at away from the table and began standing. Instead, Victor politely placed his hand on Balducci's shoulder stopping him less than halfway.

"Please, Mr. Balducci, don't get up from your meal," apologized Victor while bending over to give a respectfully light hug and brush-kiss of Joey's right cheek.

"That's alright. We knew you were coming, Victor," Balducci said, positioning himself back in his original position at the table.

Sitting on his plate appeared to be Linguini di Mare. (Linguini of the Sea) There were overly generous portions of calamari, squid, clams, shrimp, and lobster pieces sprinkled throughout the entire dish.

"Wait! Did he just call me Victor? I mean, I know he knew I was coming. They all fucking knew I was coming but did I hear Joey fucking Balducci call me by my first name? He called me Victor. He said my name! Of course, I realize that's my fucking name, but what the fuck!" Victor thought as he gulped loudly.
"Composure, mother fucker, keep your fucking composure! The next guy is going to be the toughest to win over."

Victor knew Primo the Hitter was probably the most all-around treacherous of the three. Some of the stories that floated around about him over the years were terrifying. Although Primo appeared inattentive, Victor was 100% certain that he had watched and listened to everything happening.

"Mr. Montalbano, I'm so sorry to interrupt you during your dinner. Please, forgive my timing," Victor said in the most genuine, respectful voice he ever mustered.

Montalbano put his fork down and accepted Victor's handshake and cheek kiss. Although Primo didn't look him in the eyes, Victor could tell he chose the right words by observing his face. As Victor walked around the table's end, Montalbano spoke aloud first.

"I gotta ask you one thing, kid," Primo said, pointing his fork at Victor while swallowing a large chunk of what looked like Chicken Vesuvio.

Victor's heart skipped three full beats, and all normal breathing ceased. He braced himself waiting for Montalbano to continue with what he feared was the dreaded question asking why he didn't come to them first.

"*He's gonna drill me a new asshole,*" Victor thought, clenching his butt cheeks in preparation for a verbal anal intrusion.

"How in the fuck did you beat that moulinyan?" Montalbano asked.

Jimmy Rio and Balducci laughed while taking bites of their food. Tommy, Nicky, and Frankie joined them with some light chuckling.

"I'm fucking serious! You guys had to have had a side deal. That shine intentionally threw the race, and you split the winnings, am I right? And I bet that Jew cocksucker Walt was in on it from the start. He's a cunning Heeb, that mudda fucker. I'm just saying that there's no way something like that happens for real. The black kid's a professional athlete, for Christ's sake! Tommy says it was legit. What do you gotta say?" Primo aggressively questioned.

Victor stared at the floor momentarily before responding. He knew how important it was for his answer to be short, humble, and precise. That's when he noticed the antique Persian rug beneath his feet. He briefly thought about the extraordinary story attached to that pricy piece of fabric.

"*That's the rug that Frankie accepted instead of cash when Gordon Terminelli from Bridgeport couldn't pay on a $2,000 lost bet. Frankie went nuts when he had it professionally appraised and found out it was worth over $15K!*"

Victor felt his intentionally planned pause lasted long enough. With his hands folded in front of him, he looked at Montalbano.

"I beat Reece Walker fair and square, sir. There was no side bet. That race was as real and honest as me standing in front of you now," he reassured.

"*Oooh, that's a great answer!*" Victor thought, congratulating himself.

"May I continue speaking to explain why I'm here tonight?" Victor respectfully asked.

"*Yet another winning line! Me asking for permission to speak! I'm on a roll, now!*"

"Your uncle tells us that you wrote a book that's getting published. Congratulations. He also said you wanted to explain what it's about, so there's no misunderstanding when it gets released. That's very respectful, Victor. So tell me, tell us, about your book," Balducci inquired.

Without hesitation, as if he were a high-powered Hollywood agent pitching a movie idea to studio heads, Victor spoke from his heart. He explained to the Bosses how it was light-hearted and more of a comedic family story. He openly admitted a touch of organized crime references but explained the use was sparingly for entertainment purposes. Victor spoke slowly and concisely. He pointed out the focus of his book being more about the competition between the two grandfathers and their adventures as they vied for their only grandson's affection. Victor used actual examples of them purchasing expensive toys, hosting lavish birthday parties, acquiring the very best seats at sporting events and concerts, and treating the grandson and his friends to all-expenses-paid vacations to places like Disneyland and Hawaii.

Victor stopped speaking and looked at the couch where Nicky and Tommy were sitting. They were smiling and seemed pleased with his performance. Frankie walked in from the kitchen with a tray of homemade tiramisu. As he cut a few slices, he nodded in agreement with Victor's every word. The Holy Trinity sat in silence as Frankie poured them small cups of espresso. Victor was feeling more than confident. So, he thought it best to wrap things up. How he went about doing that was so last minute, so unscripted, and so unplanned that even he couldn't believe what he was going to say next.

"Gentlemen, I've already taken up too much of your time tonight. The only thing I have left to say is that my book is make-believe. It's fiction. It's not real. If I wrote about a Teamster president surviving a point-blank, ambush-style, 12 gauge sawed-off shotgun blast in the face, or about his son, the secretary-treasurer of that very same union, who walked away after the car he was backing up blew to smithereens, smack dab in the heart of Little Italy, those are the types of stories that cause concern because they're real. Guys like John Drummond, Art Petaque, and John O'Brien? Those are the ones who write about stuff like that. And then, there's me, a neighborhood guy with an overactive imagination trying to make his dream come true as a writer."

Balducci and Montalbano shifted in their seats. The look of disbelief on Tommy's face was the same as he had when Victor first told him about his book only this time in addition, he needed to read the reactions of The Trinity. Tommy nervously attempted to disguise what he was sure was a shocked, slightly embarrassed expression.

"Minchia (Fuck) Victor, why would you bring something like that up?"

As accurate as his nephew's analogy was between the book being fictional and the recent Father/Son union assassination attempts being real, Tommy knew Victor should not have brought it up, especially in THAT room, in front of THOSE guys. It didn't matter that it made headlines in every newspaper, was reported on every Chicago television channel, and was the current hot topic of conversation in and around Mob circles. Tommy's mind was already in damage control mode. He hoped the Bosses realized that Victor didn't know any better and would take his off-the-cuff comment at face value as nothing more than a mere snafu in an otherwise well-thought-out and respectful presentation. Fortunately, Tommy was on top of it. He already had a few defensive replies lined up inside his head on Victor's behalf.

"Victor innocently repeated information already available to the general public. Victor spoke with no maliciousness whatsoever. In no way, shape, or form would Victor ever be intentionally disrespectful!"

The shooting and the car bombing were a current sore spot within the Outfit hierarchy. No one owned up to it. The official investigation, spearheaded by no less than three branches of law enforcement, all came up empty-handed. Even the handful of lower echelon Outfit guys, the ones who talked openly more than they should, weren't saying shit. The only thing for sure was the abundance of gossipy rumors swirling on both sides of the law about why someone would target the pair. Still, no one was able to agree on a definitive motive. Some thought it might have been a well-planned attempt by a rival union to remove the family from their elected offices - on a more permanent basis.

But, for now, the widespread consensus was that unknown renegade organized crime members who may, or may not, have union ties and affiliations with at least one or more Street Crews botched the assassination attempts. Most confusing was that both men were well-known charted Syndicate members. They were amongst the few union officials with Mob-ties that successfully avoided government prosecution and removal from office during The Labor Judgment days. Both were deeply connected, liked, and respected across the board. Someone very high up in the Outfit knew more than they were admitting. Shootings and bombings don't happen without the approval of someone in authority. The closest of the closest felt the failed hits were more personal-vendetta related than they were about territorial or business disputes. That entire Father/Son assassination debacle, cloaked in a dark shroud of secrecy, was a pinched nerve unknowingly tweaked by Victor. Those assassination attempts were a sign that there was serious internal strife between fractions of The Chicago Mob.

Thankfully, Jimmy Rio didn't react to Victor's comparison example. Instead, he ignored it, choosing to concentrate on devouring his tiramisu. Tommy, Nicky, and Victor exchanged quick panicked looks in the interim. Frankie thought it was best to pretend he didn't hear anything, not wanting to add to the confusion. Instead, he kept himself occupied by eyeballing the uneaten portion of bone-in rib eye still sitting on Balducci's plate. Joey Good Times stood and cleared his throat.

"Well, Victor, aside from that last part, which doesn't concern you, me, or anyone in this room, I don't see any problems with your book. On the contrary, it was very considerate of you to let us know what was going on," he concluded, looking at Montalbano and Rio to make sure they agreed with his decision.

"That's the best fucking news ever!" Tommy thought.

Nicky was also thankful.

"Victor dodged a bullet there. Sometimes my kid's too fuckin' sharp for his own good."

Fat Frankie also had a thought.

"I wonder if Joey's gonna eat that prime rib eye. If not, I'm gonna have it when they leave."

Victor hoped and prayed.

"Thank you, sweet baby Jesus. Thank you, God. Thank you, Auntie Tree! Dear Lord in heaven, please strike me temporarily speechless, and get me the fuck out of here safe and sound!"

"Frankie, wrap a few slices of the tiramisu up for me. I promised my wife I'd bring home some dessert," Montalbano said, totally ignoring Victor's faux pas as he stood. "Antoinette loves her sweets. That's why she married me!"

Everyone nervously laughed, except for Victor. He was still in disbelief and beating himself up internally for what he said.

"Why, in the fuck, did I just say that? I'm a fucking idiot! I should jump out the window right now and save them the time and effort of whacking me."

"So, that's it for tonight, right, Joey?" Primo inquired.

"I guess it is," Balducci confirmed, turning to Rio. "Jimmy, do you have anything else?"

"No, I don't. All I gotta say is, Frankie, everything was fucking delicious. Please pack up my leftovers," Rio complimented, un-tucking and placing his napkin on the table. "Good luck with your book, kid. I don't read much, unless you count newspaper betting lines, so all I can say is, God bless. You know, I was pretty fast in my time. Do you think you coulda beat me in a race?"

Victor remained unresponsive. He was still calculating how many steps it would take for him to leap out of the third-story window. He wondered if the fall to Taylor Street would be enough to kill him instantly.

"Fuck it, you don't have to answer that," Rio laughed. "I probably woulda beat ya!"

The best Victor could do was offering Rio an awkward smile. Then, Montalbano walked around the table. He stopped in front of Victor, looking at him from head to toe.

"Oh, Christ, I hope he's not sizing me up for an Indiana cornfield burial," Victor nervously thought.

Montalbano raised his hand. Victor didn't flinch. Not one centimeter. Instead, Primo pinched his cheek, just like an overenthusiastic great uncle would do to a little boy as an expression of tough-love affection.

"You do look like you're in good shape. Maybe you did beat that tutsoon," Montalbano admitted. "You showed a lot of respect here tonight. Most guys your age act like a bunch of fucking mamalukes. I wish you lots-a-luck with your book. Maybe next time, choose another subject. Also, stay away from stories about shootings and car bombings. Nobody wants to read that kind of shit. It's much too violent and depressing."

Victor chose the safest reply, expertly skirting a response to Primo's suggestion.

"Thank you for your time this evening, Mr. Montalbano. I'll certainly do my best to avoid those topics in the future."

Montalbano turned his attention to Tommy, pointing at him.

"Congratulations on your thing. Just remember what I said about those fucking Bolino brothers. You keep a close eye on them, Tommy," Primo reminded.

Montalbano put his index finger up to his eye as he spoke. It was a symbolic Italian gesture. Tommy needed to WATCH the Bolinos CLOSELY. Nicky, Frankie, and even Victor all thought the same thing simultaneously.

"Why did Montalbano congratulate Tommy, and what the fuck is going on with Johnny and Michael Bolino?"

Tommy motioned for Nicky to get up. Frankie walked out with Rio and Montalbano, cradling their take-home goodie packages in his arms, deeply inhaling the combination of aromas like a dying man taking his last breath.

"Thank you for everything, Mr. Balducci," Victor graciously said as he made his way to the hallway door."

Joey had more to say.

"Wait one minute, Victor," he interrupted.

Nicky turned his head when he heard Balducci ask Victor to remain.

"You come back in, too, Nicky," Joey instructed. "And close the door."

Balducci stood and grabbed his box of Pall Mall cigarettes off the table. He slid one out, lit it, inhaled deeply, and spoke after exhaling.

"If, and I'm thinking out loud here. If Victor's approached by the O.C. (Organized Crime) pricks because they got nothing better to do than to try and shake our tree, I want to make sure we all understand each other about how I want it handled" he said, taking another deep drag. "Maybe somebody's jealous, maybe somebody's trying to score some points with these jagoffs, or maybe it's them trying to jam us up."

Balducci stopped speaking, putting his train of thought together before continuing. Tommy, Victor, and Nicky patiently waited for what was next.

"Victor, if they stop you in the street or while you're working, if they come to your house or pull you over in your car, whatever, and maybe this doesn't happen, but if it does, you need to act like you don't have a fucking care in the world. The reason for that is because I say you don't, that's why. Understand? No acting cocky. Just play it very cool and calm. Respectfully ask to see their badges and memorize their names and faces if you can. The most important things are WHAT and WHO they ask about. My guess is they already know Tommy's your uncle, so they'll probably ask you about him."

Tommy nodded in agreement.

"You see where I'm going with this, right?" Balducci asked Tommy.

Tommy presumed Joey was referring to the private meeting before Victor and Nicky showed up.

"You think it's because of our conversation earlier. The G uses Victor's book as a pretense to stop and rattle him, maybe for leverage to see if he says something. That's a real good possibility, Joey," Tommy agreed.

"I knew you'd follow me. I'm thinking the timing and shit. It's perfect for them," Balducci said, winking.

Nicky and Victor were in total darkness on Balducci and Tommy's confusing conversation and eye wink. But, of course, it didn't stop either of them from trying to piece things together on their own.

"Joey, how does this sound?" Tommy asked Balducci, turning to Victor.

"Do just like Mr. Balducci said, Victor. If you get approached by law enforcement, politely ask to see their credentials and remember everything precisely as it happens. More than likely, they'll be two of them. Other than giving them your name and address, respectfully decline to answer any questions or say anything. Maybe they'll play nice, or perhaps they'll be jagoffs. Either way, that's how you should handle it. If they ask about your book, don't say anything, even if it sounds innocent. Just know one thing. Your book may be the hook they use to stop you in the first place. I really and truly don't think any of this will happen, just my opinion. The G's doing what they always do. They look for information. If they keep asking you questions, just ask for permission to make a phone call. Under no circumstance do you get an attitude and be smart with them. And please don't start talking about your legal rights. More than likely, they'll leave you alone, maybe even hand you one of their business cards. If they do, take it, then call me," Tommy specifically explained.

"Beautiful, Tommy, if it happens, that's how I want it to go down," Balducci concurred as he walked up to Victor. "Do everything exactly like that, okay, Victor? I'd consider it a personal favor."

"Did I just hear Joey Balducci ask me to do him a personal favor?" Victor thought. *"Now would be the time to make up for my earlier stupidity."*

"I'll handle it exactly the way you and Uncle Tommy want me to."

Balducci extended his hand. Victor shook it and kissed Joey's cheek. Joey turned to Nicky.

"You raised a good son. That's something to be very proud of. So go and enjoy your evening. Tommy, you stick around for a couple of minutes."

Victor moved almost as quickly out of the room as he did when he started the race against Reece. Nicky walked to Balducci and hugged him.

"Thank you for everything, Joey," he whispered.

Balducci walked back around the table, lit another cigarette, and sat down. Nicky closed the door behind him and joined Victor.

"Manny was right, Tommy. You have a wonderful family. No one's ever in trouble, everyone is respectful, never any problems," he complimented. "Your nephew handled himself very well."

"I could tell he was nervous," Tommy laughed.

"Are you gonna say anything to them tonight about us making you Captain of the western suburbs?" Balducci asked.

"We're going to Japeto's to have dinner. Maybe I'll bring it up in conversation. I think the first thing I should do is buy my nephew a drink. I think that poor kid could use a stiff belt or two," Tommy chuckled.

"Okay, that sounds good. Please tell Frankie I'd like my stuff wrapped up," Balducci said. "And Tommy, also tell him to keep his hands off of my rib eye! All fucking night he's been staring at that hunk of aged beef like it owes him money!"

"Joey, he's always hungry. What can I say?" Tommy laughingly answered. "Thank you again for the bump up. I won't disappoint any of you."

"Tommy, you've done real well for lots of years, even Primo knows it, and you know how fucking critical he is. But, I'll be honest. When your wife died, well, we didn't know what to expect from you. It looks like you pulled through from that horrible experience, thank God. You'll never get over it. I know that. As I told you at Teresa's wake, concentrate on your family, take care of business, and carry on in her memory. One last thing, I do want you to be very careful. There's a lot of jealousy out there about a lot of different things. Some of the moves we're making? Well, they're a little risky. Keep an eye out for everyone. And what Primo said about the Bolinos? I don't think you need to be concerned about them," Balducci advised.

Victor and Nicky waited in the alley behind Frankie's apartment. Nicky hugged and kissed Victor telling him how great he did. When Tommy walked out, the three of them waited for Frankie. After some idle chit-chat, Fat Frankie waddled sideways down the back outside wooden stairs. The timber creaked and crackled loudly with every footstep he took. As they walked across the empty lot to Japeto's, Tommy held Victor back a few paces, put his arm around his nephew, and showered him with praise.

"You did a great job tonight, Vic. Really great!" Tommy beamed proudly. "Next time, if there is a next time, don't bring up things that don't concern you."

"I know I shouldn't have said anything about Dom and his son. I'm sorry Uncle Tommy, I was nervous and I…."

Tommy interrupted him.

"Victor, what happened to Dominic and his kid? Guys that deep don't get shot and blown up without a real good reason, and most importantly, without at least ONE of the Holy Trinity giving it the green light. That's all I'm going to say about that. As far as everything else, you finished strong, just like you did in the race today," Tommy confided. "You came across as intelligent and respectful. I'm proud of you! Listen, I think Frankie roasted a small pig for us. I even brought one of my last bottles of Grandpa's wine. I've been saving it for a special occasion. When the time comes to pay the dinner tab later, I told Frankie to give your father the check. I can't wait for that!"

Victor was excited, but there was something else going on with him.

"That all sounds outstanding, Uncle Tommy."

As he stood in Japeto's doorway, Tommy noticed his nephew's sickly appearance,

"Are you okay? You look a little pale."

"Yea, I'm fine. I just need some fresh air. Give me a few minutes, Uncle Tee."

As soon as Tommy walked inside Japeto's, Victor hastily retreated to the backside of the restaurant towards the Grenshaw Street alley. He knew goddamn well what was coming next. The exhaustion and excitement of the race compounded by the nervousness and stress of his Holy Trinity meeting finally caught up with him.

He bent over and threw up. Not once, but three times.

CHAPTER 19
ONCE UPON A TIME, THERE WAS A ROBBERY YOU NEVER HEARD ABOUT

In 1852, Henry Wells, William George Fargo, and other investors, established The Wells Fargo Corporation in New York to handle the banking and express business prompted by the California gold rush. In June of 1952, after 100 years in business, an elaborate party was held at one of the oldest operating hotels in America, the luxurious Palmer House of Chicago.

Everyone was included on the nationwide company guest list - from top executives, board members, stockholders, in-house lawyers, and accountants, right down to office managers, clerical staff, drivers, guards, and maintenance workers. More than 1,500 employees from coast to coast attended the lavish celebration held under massive, garnet-draped chandeliers and surrounded by Louis Comfort Tiffany masterpieces.

While partygoers dressed in their Sunday best, ate, drank, and danced the night away, an unauthorized evening withdrawal was taking place at the main Wells Fargo depot on Mannheim Road just south of O'Hare Airport. The following morning, longtime driver, Stash Krinicky, arrived to work at the usual time, just as he did for the last 33 years. The senior employee slowly sipped his coffee as he read his driving assignments for the day. When he came to the route page, he couldn't believe what was first on his schedule - a delivery to their Wacker Drive Bank vault! That meant the truck he was about to get in was already stocked with the previous night's collection and left overnight, parked inside one of the maintenance bays.

Stash nervously concentrated on checking and double-checking the company truck numbers, license plate, and paperwork he received.

"This has to be a misprint. It can't be right," he thought.

Finally, after walking around the fully armored vehicle, Stash stuck the keys into the rear safety latch no less than three times number checking.

"Well, that's good. At least it's locked," he softly spoke, swinging the heavy metal doors open.

According to the tally sheet, Stash expected to find 15 bags of currency totaling more than 3.5 million dollars. Instead, he found an empty cargo bay. Krinicky didn't panic. He closed the doors, locked them, and quickly made his way to speak privately with the plant supervisor.

An eight-month-long secretive internal investigation ensued, which turned up something quite unbelievable. Erroneously diverted, the fully-loaded money truck came in for routine maintenance AFTER daily pickups but BEFORE a bank vault drop-off. Under normal circumstances, this would've come to someone's attention. But security staff didn't follow standard safety procedures due to the excitement of the company's centennial festivities and the mass arrival of hundreds of out-of-state employees who were visiting the central hub. Also, the newly implemented video surveillance system invented only five years earlier shorted out, melting the tape. As a result, the Wells Fargo investigative team had a shitload of missing money, no physical evidence, and absolutely zero leads. They were back to square one.

Solving this major federal crime could NOT be blamed on law enforcement ineptness. No one ever notified them. Wells Fargo knew they fucked up and were on the hook for the massive amount of money. That meant fronting funds into the accounts of their depositors. Anyone with knowledge of the internal investigation, even the out-of-state company primary executives, like the president, vice-president, and treasurer, legally covered their asses by signing official NDA's. (Non-disclosure agreements) They could never discuss missing money, the apparent robbery, or the investigation. Corporate big-wigs knew how damaging it could be for them if news of the theft ever went public. Legal FDIC (Federal Deposit Insurance Corporation) ramifications, fines, and probable lawsuits for Wells Fargo AND company executives charged as individuals were also distinct possibilities.

Driver Krinicky, the plant supervisor, Harobed Windsor, and security chief Squibby Unklchester, were three of five men at the depot with direct knowledge of money left in the truck. The fourth man, the early-on prime suspect who parked the loaded vehicle in the warehouse in the first place, was Chata Seenta-Peenta, a Nairobian-born rookie driver who had only been on the job for a month. Surprisingly, Chata was the first to be ruled out. Seenta-Peenta's whereabouts before and after the money went missing were solid. His money-bag count for the day was punch-stamped and signed at each stop. His route sheet, which errantly directed him to return to the main depot instead of the bank vault after the last pickup, was due to a typographical error made by elderly office secretary, Philomena Welty. Seenta-Peenta's actions were flawless. He did as he instructed. When questioned about the unwritten rule regarding NOT parking trucks filled with cash in the warehouse, Security Chief Unklchester was clearly on a fishing expedition, secretly hoping to get the black immigrant to feel pressure, slip up, and confess to the robbery. Instead, Seenta-Peenta, who spoke and understood Nairobian better than he did English, apologized, explaining no one ever told him not to do that. He was right. No one did.

"If I no told, how I know?" Chata innocently asked in his heavy Kenyan accent.

Wells Fargo implemented a stringent hiring and training process for all newly hired drivers and guards from that day forward. They also retrained their existing crew nationwide. The robbery was the biggest cover-up by a national financial institution ever. The fifth man, who saw the bags of cash, was a lowly janitor who just happened to catch a glimpse of the cargo as he was sweeping the garage floor behind Seenta-Peenta when the Nairobian locked the rear armored cargo doors before leaving for the day. By the time this employee's name was alphabetically brought up as someone in the building when the truck arrived, investigators were already at their wits' end, running around in circles with nothing to go on. Finally, they unanimously agreed, it would be a waste of costly time looking into the guy who emptied the garbage, cleaned the toilets, and made coffee for the mechanics. In the company's eyes, this employee was above reproach with an unblemished attendance record, never missing a single workday in his 24 years on the job.

What Wells Fargo investigators never knew about the janitor, and how would they, was that he had a long-running $200 monthly debt owed to a low-level Outfit loan shark. He needed that advance to pay for his sick daughter's mounting medical bills. He eventually got buried deep in vig, and the meter was still running. The lowly worker felt that a tip about the bags of cash to the right person might help resolve his debt. He chose wisely. That ten-cent phone call he made was the reason 3.5 million dollars vanished into thin air.

Victor was confident he completed his puking bout in the parking lot. When he opened Japeto's front door, Frankie flagged him down. He was with Tommy and Nicky in the private, elevated corner booth reserved explicitly for Spaccones. (Means wise guys/braggarts/show-offs) As they popped the cork and cautiously sipped Grandpa Joe's wine, which was famous for sneaking up and packing a wallop, Tommy asked everyone to lean in closely over the table. All their faces were inches from each other.

"They made me Captain of the western suburbs," he whispered, smiling coyly.

Nicky was barely able to contain himself. So much so that Tommy had to shush him twice. Fat Frankie said he knew it was only a matter of time before that happened. Victor offered congratulations, kissed his uncle, and quickly remembered what Joey Good Times had said about an hour or so earlier.

"So that's what Balducci was referring to earlier when he said the G might try and squeeze me for information about Uncle Tommy. It's because they put him in charge of the western suburbs," Victor thought.

Feeling as if they were on top of the world, the men confidently nestled back into the roominess and comfort of the Spaccone Booth. They made many toasts honoring Tommy's news and Victor's successful race, meeting, and pending book release. A long list of other toast recipients followed. There was one each for Ma and Pa DaBone, Teresa, Frankie's father Japeto, and Manny Ingalleretta. Even Zeus had a glass raised in his honor.

Frankie went all-out with the food spread. He put on a 3-hour cooking clinic consisting of stuffed pig, pasta dishes, grilled seafood, thinly sliced, lightly breaded pink veal, and just about everything in between. Victor's favorites were crabmeat and lobster stuffed mushrooms, fried zucchini flowers, and rolled eggplant. At the same time, Tommy couldn't get enough of the manicotti with crumbled hot sausage and Pecorino Romano cheese sprinkled on top. Nicky ate a little of everything and kept everyone entertained and in stitches the entire time with his endless stories and impressions. Victor couldn't remember his dad ever being on such a comedic run. He figured two full glasses of Grandpa Joe's wine were playing a massive part in his father's creative overzealousness.

"It's like watching a combination of Rickles, Buddy Hacket, Shecky Greene and Dangerfield on Johnny Carson," Victor thought.

Tommy laughed so hard he cried. Fat Frankie roared and howled between massive forkfuls of Linguini Gamberi e Broccolini. (Linguini, Shrimp, and Broccolini) Even though Victor felt he somewhat arrived as a trusted adult peer in the eyes of the men that meant the most to him, in the back of his mind, he was still in disbelief about the events of the day. He never thought something as big as winning the race against Reece in front of the entire Market would take a backseat to anything, except maybe, a successful first book. But, in actuality, it was the replay of his Holy Trinity meeting that eclipsed both of those things by a country mile. The most unbelievable fact was when Joey Balducci asked him for a favor. That, to Victor, was inconceivable! It's something he couldn't imagine ever happening, even on his most successful writing days.

"Joey Balducci! Shit, even Primo Montalbano sorta liked me! I'm so fucking happy right now I might even consider letting Jimmy Rio beat me in a race! I can't wait to tell the guys."

Victor wasn't the only one with a wandering mind seated at the table. Tommy was also preoccupied. As much he enjoyed the outcome of the day's exciting events and being made Captain, there was something serious that needed to be discussed. Since his Holy Trinity meeting went well and there were no problems with Victor's book presentation, Tommy felt it was time to share.

Danny Peanut Butter was the last Japeto's employee to leave for the night. As he came out of the kitchen to jokingly stutter good night wishes, Frankie followed him, carrying a freshly made Disaronno Amaretto Originale cake with homemade whipped cream frosting infused with pulverized vanilla beans. Tommy walked Peanut Butter to the front door and tucked a C-Note in his pocket. Danny attempted to refuse the generosity, but, after all, it was Big Banana LaCosta who insisted he take it, so he respectfully accepted.

Tommy locked the front door and walked to the classic Seeburg Jukebox in the bar area. He smiled when he remembered how he and Silvio swiped three of them in the Lanzatorri Produce truck on one of the coldest days of the 1960s, thanks to a tip from Grace's brother "Handsome Joey" who worked on the Seeburg loading dock. Tommy reminisced as he loaded the jukebox with quarters. He studied the songs and picked Dean, Frank, and various Motown artists. The first tune he played was Frank Sinatra's "My Kind of Town." (Chicago Is) When Tommy slid back into the booth, Fat Frankie, who was already three pieces deep in Amaretto cake, hung his massive arm around him.

"This fucking guy!" he proudly stated, with a half-cheek full of smeared whipped cream.

Everyone nodded and smiled. Nicky motioned to Frankie to wipe his face, which he did, but only after intentionally dunking his napkin deep into Nicky's water glass. They all laughed.

"Frank, is the back door locked?" Tommy asked. "Yea, if you locked the front door, everything's sealed up nice and tight," Frankie answered. "Why, Tee?"

Frankie and Nicky recognized the 'Tommy-Look' right away and knew something was up. Not oblivious to his uncle's sudden intense demeanor, Victor wondered what was next.

"Put a pot of coffee on, Frankie," Tommy suggested.

As they enjoyed the jukebox music, the boys had a few big gulps each of the imported Bolivian coffee Frankie bought from "Rozzie the Gypsy" on Carpenter Street. Then, Tommy began to lay the groundwork.

"What I'm about to tell you guys must never leave this table, capicse?" Tommy began. "I made a promise that I've decided to break tonight. Right, wrong, or indifferent, it's what I feel is best for all of us. Victor, I want absolutely no written variations of this story. No sharing it with any of your friends in any way, shape, or form. Every part is off-limits, and you cannot use any aspect of it, period. And Nicky, no fucking around or joking about it at anytime whatsoever. Frankie, all I could say is that you're gonna explode when you hear this."

The boys all sat up and attentively listened to the man they looked up to, loved, and respected.

"There's a shit-load of information I'm going to put out here tonight. I spent two full days at the Chicago Public Library researching and going through old newspaper articles on their slide machine, not to mention all the undercover work I did sorting everything out. To tell this the right way, I have to start at the end and work my way to the beginning. Victor, feel free to use that technique on your next writing project!" Tommy half-jokingly encouraged.

"That's not such a bad idea, Uncle Tee," Victor agreed.

Tommy wasted no time throwing it out there with scorching opening sentence.

"Twenty-seven years ago, Manny, Joey, and Primo stole 3.5 million dollars and never told anyone about it."

Nicky, Frankie, and Victor were awestruck.

"Joey and Primo don't know that I know, correction; that WE know about this. If things didn't go well tonight, for Victor or me, I planned to say two words to them without Jimmy Rio in the room because I'm pretty sure he doesn't know anything about this. Those two words would've given me a pass on whatever problem there was." Tommy confessed.

"What two words?" Nicky excitedly asked.

"Wells Fargo," Tommy answered.

As he began the story, Victor couldn't help think how intriguing his uncle's tale would be in book form, but he received a warning, and that was that. However, it didn't stop him from doing what he had done his entire life, putting himself in the plot as if he were an invisible third party.

In detail, Tommy explained how Manny, Joey, and Primo swore an oath to each other, agreeing that upon their death, whoever came to the remaining two and said the words 'Wells Fargo' would be a good friend, worthy of favors and considerations. But, most importantly, it would be someone who could keep secrets. Those guys knew anything could happen at any given time because of the life they chose, and this was their way to make sure that their family or assigned designees would be able to enjoy the massive spoils of their secret caper in the future.

"Since Manny was the oldest, I think that had a little something to do with the hard-on Primo's had for him. It's my opinion that Montalbano always felt Manny would wind up dying first, and he didn't want to be stuck doing favors for a friend of Manny's. Primo was very mellow with us tonight, but I know goddamn well that if I would've played that Wells Fargo card, things would have gone down much differently. At least that's how I see it."

Tommy continued backward storytelling, detailing his experience with Vinnie and Lenny in Manny's basement the week after Ingalleretta died. When he explained how Vinnie punched holes in the wall to retrieve the chest, Nicky admitted he probably would have shit in his pants right then and there. Tommy also told them about him, Lenny, and Vinnie receiving 100K each. Lastly and most importantly, Tommy shared the contents of Manny's two-page note written in Barese (Bari).

"You guys try and translate something THAT important in just a few fucking minutes! And to top it off, Manny wrote it all out in multiple one-line sentences! I knew Vinnie and Lenny were curious because my letter was so long. Lenny's short note took him less than a minute to read, and it looked like Manny wrote it on a piece of scrap paper," Tommy explained. "Come to think of it; it wasn't paper. Jesus Christ, it's all coming back to me right now! Manny wrote Lenny's note on a Gino and Georgie's cocktail napkin! I was so focused on what I was reading that night that it slipped my mind until this very fucking minute. Wow! Anyway, whatever Manny wrote to Lenny made him cry. Other than a couple of wakes, including Teresa's, I never saw Lenny break down. And believe you me, that fucking guy has had a lot to cry about in his time. Frankie? Nicky? Am I right, or am I right about that?"

"You're right," they agreed.

"Vinnie didn't tell Lenny or me whether Manny left him a note, and I wasn't going to be the one to ask. The way I look at it, why press it? After all, Manny trusted him enough to make sure he carried out his last wish. Vinnie could've fucked Lenny and me over and made off with the entire 300K, read our notes, and no one would've been the wiser. That speaks volumes about who Vinnie Champagne is. I want you guys always to remember that, okay?"

Tommy paused and took a sip of coffee.

"Tommy, THE NOTE! What was in the fucking note?" Nicky eagerly asked.

Tommy put down his coffee, smiled, and lit up a cigarette.

"Now, things get immensely interesting."

Frankie cut himself another peninsula-sized portion of cake, Nicky torched a crooked DiNobili cigar, and Victor poured his third cup of coffee.

"With this much caffeine in me, I'm gonna have to smoke at least three one-hitters of Heather's weed just to fall asleep tonight," Victor imagined, looking forward to his self-imposed challenge.

"For me to try and explain what Manny wrote word for word would be too confusing, so I'm just gonna tell you guys everything I pieced together based on the translation AND what I pieced together on my own."

Tommy spelled out how Manny, Joey, and Primo were fed up with the chain of command back then. The Bosses weren't kicking back the proper zort (Money) to the guys doing all the heavy lifting – which was the three of them. Tommy also shared one of Ingalleretta's confidential Castle Street front porch tales about starting out in the Syndicate.

"Manny said he was clipping guys left and right and taking down scores like crazy. So were Montalbano and Balducci. The Old Man was fucking disgusted. He said all they got in return from the cheap fuck Bosses was ugatz." (Shit)

Tommy took another sip of coffee. He put out his cigarette in the personalized crystal Stardust Hotel ashtray Frankie got as a gift from Mr. Tony, the Grand Avenue Underboss. Mr. Tony was the Outfit's go-to guy in Las Vegas.

"Alright, before I go any further, I gotta go to the washroom. The fuckin' coffee from Rozzie the Gypsy is running through me like Grant took Richmond," Tommy announced.

"Like Grant took Richmond? I don't think I ever heard that one before! That's fucking hysterical! I gotta go too," Victor laughingly piped up.

"Me too, and maybe a nice cacca," (Shit) added Frankie.

"Well, I guess I'm the only one that's good for now. But listen, Frankie, I hope you don't mind. I took a leak on your floor about a half-hour ago!" Nicky teased.

"The mop is in the basement, you ball-bustin' cocksucker, you!" Frankie shot back while Victor and Tommy laughed.

Victor patiently waited for his turn in the bathroom. Tommy grabbed the men's toilet, and Frankie stuffed himself into the more petite lady's room. He glanced back at his father.

"Dad's getting older, but he still has that thick hair of his. I hope I look as good as him when I'm his age. And, I wouldn't mind having his energy, either. Shit, he was down at SouthWater at 3 a.m. yesterday. He's been going for almost 24 hours, and he still looks fresh as fuck!"

Nicky raised his hand in the air, jokingly gave Victor the middle finger, and shouted over the music, smiling from ear to ear.

"Good luck getting Fat Frankie outta the pisciatore." (Pronounced: pee-sha-tore-aye. Means pisser.)

Not two seconds later, Frankie performed his famous sideways slide to make it out of the lady's bathroom.

"I heard what your father just said," Frankie confirmed, barely making it through the doorway.

Barely was an understatement. The front of Frankie's stomach and back of his ass brushed heavily against the wood trim framing even though he was exiting sideways!

"Vic, I'd stay out of there for at least an hour. Fucking amaretto cake is delicious but it ran right through me."

"Duly noted, thanks for the heads-up," Victor appreciatively answered.

Tommy walked out of the men's room as Frankie stopped behind the bar.

"Vic, sorry it took me so long, I was playing with it for a few minutes, and then, you know, by the time I reel it back in," Tommy joked, referring to the size of his dick.

Victor laughed, breezing by his uncle for a quick bathroom entry. While he peed, he thought.

"*No wonder I turned out the way I did, surrounded by these fucking guys for guys for the last 20 something years!*"

As they settled back in the booth anticipating the second half of Tommy's story, Nick spoke first.

"Tee, before you go any further, I gotta ask. Did Manny ever pop anyone big, maybe someone we knew, or someone we heard of?" he hesitantly asked.

"I'm in the middle of telling you the most important story on the fucking planet, and you ask me that? You're unfucking believable!" Tommy sternly answered.

There was silence for about ten seconds. Then, finally, Tommy couldn't pretend to be upset any longer.

"I got ya, Nick, ya fuckin' inquisitive mudda fucker, you!" Tommy laughed.

Victor and Frankie joined in the laugher, and then all breathed a collective sigh of relief, especially Nicky.

"Okay, fine. You got me. You successfully stuck it in my ass and broke it off. Now, are you gonna answer my question or not?" Nicky asked.

"Can I please finish this story? We're going to be here all fucking night as it is!" Tommy answered, skirting the question.

Frankie and Victor were equally curious if Manny clipped anyone notable, and Tommy knew it. So, he decided to throw them a bone.

"Nicky, the answer is yes, he did. That's all I'm gonna say about that. Can I please continue? I'm getting to another interesting part," he half answered.

Temporarily satisfied with that response, they let Tommy continue.

"Enter Michael Tunzi's father, Sabino, into the story. He was upside down with some semi-connected loan shark for about $200 a month. Mr. Tunzi needed that extra cash to pay Frieda's medical expenses. She died right about the time Victor was born, maybe a few years before that.

"Who's Frieda?" Victor asked.

"Frieda was Detective Tunzi's crippled sister," Tommy answered. "She was five or six years older than Teresa, Michael, and me. Anyway, Mr. Tunzi was buried in VIG alone, month after month for years, because of Frieda's doctor and medicine expenses. Remember, we're talking about a $200 monthly loan, rolling over every month since that poor girl was a kid!"

"Jesus Christ, that's tens of thousands," Frankie quickly calculated.

"Exactly," Tommy responded. "Manny was in the process of helping old man Tunzi square the whole thing away, but the loan shark was less than cooperative. So, Nicky or Tommy, do either of you remember where Sabino Tunzi worked?"

Nicky and Tommy looked at each other, shrugging their shoulders.

"Wells Fargo?" Victor guessed.

"That's right! Victor, how the fuck did you know that?" Fat Frankie asked, slamming his fist down on the table.

"Yea, how DID you know that?" Nicky also inquired, blindsided by his son's correct response.

"I'm just paying attention to the story," Victor replied.

"Tommy, Manny wrote all of this to you in his note?" Nicky interrupted.

"No, no, no. Remember what I said. A lot of this I had to put together on my own. But, it's good as gold," Tommy explained.

"Jesus Christ, do you think Michael knows about any of this?" Frankie asked.

"I don't know. But, let me finish, then I'll tell you what I think," Tommy answered.

For the next 15 minutes, Tommy explained how Sabino Tunzi saw the open doors of the fully-loaded truck right before the Wells Fargo hub closes for the evening.

"Keep in mind, Sabino was only a janitor, but even HE knew the trucks were supposed to be empty before they came back to the yard. So what does he do? Sabino calls Manny and tells him everything, from the easiest way to get into the building unnoticed, right down to the truck number and key location. Manny used exclamation marks when he wrote the sentence about Sabino not doing anything other than making the phone call. I think it was old man Tunzi's way to thank Ingalleretta for helping him with the juice guy," Tommy surmised.

"That makes sense. Let me guess what's next, Tee. Manny reaches out to Joey and Primo. He tells them he's got something, and they suit up. Then, they see how fucking much it is, sit on it and wait to see who knows what and how much heat there is?" Frankie intuitively guessed. "That's definitely the right fucking play on a heist that huge."

"Nice job, Frankie! So, low and behold, time passes, and no one says nothin' about nothin'. Those three lucky bastards! They kept all that cash and whacked it up just between themselves, NO BOSSES. That's 3.5 million twenty-six years ago!" Tommy exclaimed.

"A fucking dream score," Nicky added.

"You ain't shittin'!" Frankie concurred.

Victor was amazed.

"Wow. Just, wow! "So Mr. E. and the other two guys did what with all that cash, Uncle Tommy?"

"After they agreed to the whole secret 'Wells Fargo' code thing, you know, in case one of them died, naturally or otherwise, they had to come up with a plan for what to do with all that fucking cash, and the worst part, they had to do it inconspicuously. So, for starters, they decided to kick up more than usual to the Bosses with every score they made to keep them happy. It was a small price to pay to stay under everyone's radar, and most importantly, it made them look like they were doing the right thing. The three of them were shining fucking stars, earning with both hands as far the Bosses knew. Now I'm not saying Manny, Joey, and Primo didn't pay their dues to get bumped up as quickly as they did, but, what Manny wrote next, explained it all. It's pure, unadulterated genius to the tenth fucking degree, and it was so simple, it blew me the fuck away," Tommy teased.

After Frankie and Victor both guessed incorrectly, it was Nicky's turn.

"Nick, ya got anything?" Tommy asked.

"I do. Manny, Joey, and Primo used the money they stole, spread it out over all of their scores, and inconspicuously paid themselves with it. They wanted everyone to think they were hitting home runs. So they sweetened the pots with what they had already stolen from Wells Fargo. They disguised all that fucking cash as profits from new heists, hijackings, robberies, scams, and whatever."

"Give that man a cigar!" Tommy declared.

Nicky relit his crooked DiNobili, stood, bowed, and slowly waved, just like the Pope in his motorcade when greeting throngs of followers from foreign countries.

"Thank you. Thank you very much," Nicky appreciatively said, impersonating Elvis.

As Tommy took a break from speaking, the guys sat in amazement, shaking their heads at such an unbelievable revelation. Finally, Nicky, still feeling strong from his previous correct answer, asked Tommy the question on all of their minds.

"That's a major fucking briscala card in your back pocket, Tee. So, how ya gonna play it? What's next?"

"What's fucking next? I really don't know, Nick. I honestly don't know. But, here are some of my thoughts."

Tommy lit his last cigarette of the long evening.

"Right now, there are at least six of us who know about this - Joey, Primo, and us four. I'm saying six of us because I don't know who told who what. You follow me?" Tommy asked.

"Yea, I mean Michael Tunzi could know, maybe even Vinnie or Lenny. Shit, Joey and Primo could've already said something to somebody on their end, too. Or, they could've written a letter like Manny did, and then it's whoever winds up getting that when the time comes. Or maybe they write a letter, and it somehow makes its way into the wrong hands by mistake. Fuck, I hate to be the one to say it, but as we sit, the odds are in favor that there are more than six of us who know. Those odds get worse the longer you wait to use it, not even counting the minute Joey or Primo die," Frankie pointed out.

"They do," Tommy agreed. "Best case scenario for right now is that just the four of us know. Manny's been dead for what, five, six years? Maybe Primo and Joey figure they're in the clear with that much time passing without anybody saying anything," Tommy guessed.

"Or, somebody could've already gone to them. Maybe Uncle Tommy wasn't the only one Manny wrote to, or for that matter, said something to," Victor brought up.

Tommy pointed at his nephew.

"I thought about that too, Victor. But, knowing the Old Man the way I did, I gotta lean towards me being the only one he let know about it," Tommy figured. "At least I'm hoping for that."

"Maybe Primo and Joey figured Manny was so fucked-up from his brain cancer that he forgot about doing it, or mentally couldn't do it, because his mind was going," Frankie added.

Everyone looked at each other and agreed that it was another distinct possibility.

"So, like Dad said, what's next, Uncle Tee?" Victor questioned.

Jet lag, compliments of an early morning flight from Arizona was setting in. Tommy was yawning loudly and the coffee wasn't helping keep him awake any longer. Plus, he needed to go to the bathroom again. Fat Frankie's ass was noticeably dragging too, even more than it usually did due to the earth's gravitational pull. Victor was also winding down. Instead of 'Miller Time,' he was looking forward to 'Bong-O-Rama' hits when he got home.

"After all, it's only a weed that turns to a flower in your mind," he thought. *"God, I love that saying!"*

Tommy wrapped up his story with a suggestion, a summary, and an important direction of how he wanted things to proceed.

"I think we should all go home, get some sleep, and get together early next week. Check your schedules to see what days work best. Things are all going our way right now. If we use 'Wells Fargo,' maybe shit changes somehow. Holding on to that gem for an emergency may not be the worst idea in the world either. Whatever we decide, I'll go to Joey and Primo alone. It's safer that way. Remember, we get one shot here, and we're dealing with a dozen unknowns, including an expiration date on the whole fucking deal if they somehow both die. Speaking of dying, I have to say this, just in case. If I croak out of the fucking blue, God forbid, you three decide what to do. If you play the card, Frankie's the one that goes to them. We have an opportunity to do something huge with this, boys, capicse?"

Instead of verbally agreeing with Tommy's plan, they used various physical approval forms. For Nicky, it was the sign of the cross. Victor chose the thumbs-up. Fat Frankie signaled positively with a nod and a wink, right after shoveling the final two slices of amaretto cake into his mouth.

CHAPTER 20
THAT'S UP TO YOU

"Victor, do you need anything ironed for tonight?"

"No thanks, Ma, I'm good. Well, wait, maybe my black shirt. What do you think?"

Victor held up the shirt for Grace to examine.

"That's up to you," she replied.

Victor would hear the phrase 'That's up to you" multiple times from various people before the day was over.

"I talked to your father before he left for work this morning. He told me you did very well at your meeting last night. Were you nervous?"

"I puked three times."

Grace looked flabbergasted.

"It was my usual, three times in five minutes, right before I walked inside Japeto's. I was in the back of the parking lot. Nobody saw me." Victor admitted. "Please, don't say anything to Dad or Uncle Tommy about that."

"Jesus, Mary, and Joseph, Victor! Wait a minute. You heaved your guts out, ate like a gavone, PLUS drank Grandpa's wine?"

"Yes, mother, I did. And I'm feeling every bit of it this morning."

"Well, you have another big night ahead of you. So try and get some rest. I think it's very nice of your friends to throw a dinner party in your honor. Dad and I are so proud of you, your writing, your book release, and the man you've become."

Victor hugged and kissed her.

"Thanks, Mom. I owe it all to you and Dad for my horrible upbringing and lack of parental guidance when I needed it most."

As Victor braced for his mother's response, Grace removed one of her slippers to throw at him.

"Oooh, Victor, you little shit!"

"I'm sorry, I'm sorry. Please don't hit me! You make it way too easy sometimes," he laughed.

Grace got serious for a second.

"Victor, I wanna ask you something, and I want you to be honest. You don't mind that Dad and I are stopping by tonight too, do you? I mean I know it's your night with all your friends. We don't wanna make you feel stupid by showing up."

"Mom, you're seriously asking me that? It's more than okay! Everyone thinks Dad's hysterical, and I know for a fact that you're my friends' favorite mom ever since the day you served them beer when they were barely 18 years old."

Grace thought about it for a few seconds.

"Did I?"

Victor wasted no time helping her recall the exact day.

"Oh, indeed you did! It was my junior year. We were going to Billy Kay's house for a huge Halloween party. When I got home from work, I walked downstairs and found ten of my St. Benedict friends all liquored-up waiting for me.

Craig, Dirk, Gerbs, Frank, Mike, Benj, Nick, Donny, Niner, and Lammy were all sitting around the bar area drinking beer out of frosted glasses!"

Grace remembered.

"Ohhhh, that's right! Well, in my defense, I was trying to be hospitable."

"Hospitable? Ma, between that and the meatball sandwiches you fed them, I'm surprised they ever left! For the next few months, all they talked about was Grace DaBone, the hostess with the mostest!"

"They went through three cases AND about twenty-five meatball sandwiches. Niner ate three of them himself! When your father saw all the empty beer bottles in the garbage the next day, he asked me how much money I made turning tricks for Fifth Platoon! A volte, e un tale stronzo!" (Sometimes, he is such an asshole!)

"The Fifth Platoon? Christ, where does Dad come up with that shit?"

"Are any of the St. Benedict guys going to be at Full House tonight? I haven't seen some of them in a few years, especially Frank," Grace wondered.

"I'm pretty sure most of them are, but I'm not positive about Frank. Anthony told me that Michael Jr., Dirk, and Dino were taking care of the guest list. I only asked that they don't go crazy inviting people - the fewer, the better. They told me to go fuck myself."

"Try and relax, Victor. Between yesterday and today, you've been going non-stop. The only thing I wish is that I could've seen you race Reece," Grace confessed. "I bet you don't remember this, but when you were about 5-years old, you were so fast that Dad and I had to clamp Zeus's leesh to the belt buckles of your pants because if you took off, we sure as shit wouldn't have been able to catch you! Anyway, your friends are wonderful. They love you, and you love them. What more can you ask? See, moving to the suburbs worked out for you after all. Mama knows best, sweetheart. You always need to remember that!"

"Yes, you do know best, Grace Rose! Oh, Mom, I forgot to tell you that St. Jude's Press told me there's an outside chance I may have to do an official book signing. The publicist said it's rare for an unknown author, but it occasionally happens. And that reminds me, I have to tell Dad and Uncle Tommy not to run out and buy 500 copies each. They'll think they're helping me, but the book stores monitor the sales and report to the printer. I also don't want to pull in the garage and see ten boxes filled with my books getting cobwebs on them. Did I mention that I'm already working on a second novel?"

"Really, what's it about?" Grace excitedly asked.

"It's the story of a beautiful, almost Christ-like little Italian boy that grows up with no supervision because his mother and father are too busy dealing drugs and guns to street gangs. The title is called "Victor DaBone's Parents Suck.""

He ducked and ran for cover when he saw Grace reach for her slipper again.

"You're worse than your father! You're really gonna get smacked this time. You know I'm deadly with slippers!"

That afternoon passed slowly, like all afternoons do when there's something of significance planned for the evening. Luckily, Victor's 5-hour nap was interrupted only twice, once by Michael Jr. and once by Dirk. First, Michael Jr.

suggested to Victor that he consider packing an overnight bag.

"Dino's father told him we could crash at the Aberdeen Street rehabbed loft if we needed to, but just to sleep, no parties, and positively no drinking or smoking," Michael explained. "I'm staying for sure. So are Dino, Pete, Craig, and Nick."

"Should I stay, too?" Victor asked.

"That's up to you," Michael responded.

Victor picked up on the "That's up to you" right away.

"That's twice now."

Dirk's call was to find out what the dress code was for the evening, and to bust Victor's balls about beating Reece. The two hadn't spoken about it yet.

"Now you decide to run fast? You're 23 fucking years old! Ten years ago, Victor! TEN FUCKING YEARS AGO, we talked about this! I did a conference call with my brothers and father about you beating Reece. Do you know what they said? Nothing. Not a fucking thing. As a matter of fact, they all hung up on me!"

"Dirk Rigonest, I find you guilty of harassment by telephone. That's a federal charge, correct counsellor?" Victor joked. "Okay, you had your little rant. Now, hopefully, it's all out of your system. But, seriously, did you wake me up from a great dream to find out what the fucking dress code is? I was just about to get a blowjob from Farah Fawcett."

Dirk was never going to let it go.

"All I can say is 'Get used to it' because you're going to hear me shit-talk at least once a week…FOREVER! Now, what should I wear? Is this a sport coat deal, jeans, bulletproof vest, or what?"

"Wear what you want. I'm wearing jeans and a black dress shirt. You know how great my ass looks when I wear jeans. By the way, what color panties do you have on right now?" Victor asked in a deep, seductive voice.

"I'm not wearing any, you sick fuck. I'll see you tonight, Mr. Sand-Baggin' Bitch!" Dirk finished.

"Back to Farah," Victor pleasingly thought.

After a close shave and a relaxing hot shower, Victor checked himself out one final time, admiring his reflection in the full-length sliding closet mirror doors in front of his waterbed.

"Not too awful shabby. I'm no Dino Domenico, but then again, who is?"

When he walked out to the driveway, Victor noticed the garage door was open, and Nicky's brand new convertible Cadillac was gone. He remembered something about his parents catching a matinee before heading down to Full House.

"I wonder if they went to see that new movie about H.G. Wells traveling through time to catch Jack the Ripper. What was the name of it? O, yea, "Time After Time." That would've been my choice."

He climbed inside his black Monte Carlo SS. Thirty-five minutes later, after making the sign of the cross at Sacrament Avenue, driving by Maria DiNapoli's house, and passing by the empty lot on Fillmore Street, he pulled into the back parking lot of Full House. When he walked to the front door, he saw his father's Cadillac parked right on Taylor Street in front of the restaurant's entrance.

"I bet Dad called Anthony and told him to keep that spot open."

After making the rounds, Victor was overwhelmed. Almost 40 of his friends filled the dining area, the bar, and the small party room. One minute, he was shaking hands, hugging, and kissing. The next minute, his arm was around someone getting a picture taken. As great as it was that Heather and Lu-Chow made the time to stop by and congratulate him, there was a surprise attendee. Victor saw Stones's wife, Angela, sitting at a table with Heather, Tia, Ro-Ro, Carla, Gina, Jo Ann, Phyllis, and Leah. Angela was the only girl he hadn't seen yet, or so he thought.

"Hello, handsome! Congratulations! What, you're too busy getting your picture taken to come and see your biggest fan?" Angela teasingly asked.

After standing to give Victor a full-frontal embrace, she turned sideways.

"Listen, I want you to meet a friend of mine. Victor, this is Veronica, Veronica, this is Victor."

Angela was already slurring her words after a couple of tall, slow gin fizzes.

"Nice to meet you, Veron…," Victor said, stopping short, his heart skipping a beat.

It was Maria DiNapoli. Victor couldn't believe it! Her back was purposely (per Angela's instructions) towards him the entire time. Maria's hair was the longest he ever remembered seeing it.

"Hi, call me Veronica."

Marie was playing right along with Angela's ruse. She casually shook Victor's hand as a person does when meeting someone for the very first time. She caved in quickly and hugged him.

"Congratulations, Sweetheart."

"God, she smells heavenly," Victor excitedly thought.

"Thank you. Maria. You look amazing. Your hair is so long. I love it like that."

"I wish the two of you would just bang each other and get it the fuck over with," Angela suggested, as her third drink in less than an hour arrived at the table.

"Okay, then," Victor responded. "That settles that. Veronica, what do you think?"

"Veronica is a slut, so I'm sure it's alright with her," Maria jokingly agreed.

As he made small talk with the girls, Victor noticed four men at the end of the bar. They were slightly loud and semi-obnoxious. He didn't recognize them as neighborhood guys, but did notice one of them was a huge man with long hair.

Nicky stood and waved from the back corner of the restaurant.

"Victor, Victor. Come over here!"

He walked to his parents' table. They were sitting with two attractive couples.

"Victor, this is Mr. and Mrs. Potenzo and Mr. and Mrs. Senese," Nicky proudly introduced.

Victor shook hands with the husbands and kissed the wives. Grace and Nicky had no idea they were going to be there. Victor had only met them a few times when he was younger but had most definitely heard their names fondly mentioned during dozens of stories. Just then, Anthony walked back to make sure his favorite customers and favorite aunt and uncle were enjoying themselves.

"How's everything, Unc?" Anthony asked, putting his arm around Nicky.

"Fantastic, Ant," Nicky quickly answered. "The drinks are weak, and the fish was raw, but other than that, beautiful, pal."

Everyone laughed, knowing Nicky's ball-busting antics.

"Nick, stop," Grace spoke up. "Anthony, everything is perfect! The lobster ravioli and filet are delicious. Your Uncle Nicky ate his order and half of mine!"

"Anthony, this meal is so good it's going to be a shame to take a shit later," Nicky uniquely complimented.

"If there are any complaints about the music tonight, talk to this guy," Anthony instructed, pointing to Victor.

"Don't worry. I made sure the special tape I made for tonight has Frank, Dean, Jerry Vale, Jimmy Roselli, Vic Damone, Perry Como, and Tony Bennett."

Mr. Potenzo was a music aficionado. When he talked about the concerts he and his wife saw between November and December of 1968, Victor and Anthony were shocked.

"We saw four groups, front row center, at The Coliseum and The Auditorium in less than 30 days. The Doors, Paul Revere and The Raiders, The Vanilla Fudge, and a guy you might have heard of by the name of Jimi Hendrix," Potenzo said. "Over ten years later, and my fucking ears are still ringing!"

Before Anthony could ask about the other concerts they had attended, he shared his backstage International Amphitheater experience at the Eric Clapton concert on his 18th birthday.

"I'm sitting there wearing my VIP pass around my neck, minding my own business, and someone tells Clapton it's my birthday. He walks up, hugs me, wishes me happy birthday, and then gives me his guitar pick from that night! His encore was 'Layla.' I couldn't believe it! The pick was still hot!"

Nicky tugged on Victor's arm and whispered.

"Uncle Tommy told me to tell you that he's sorry for not stopping by tonight. He had a couple of meetings in Oak Brook with the 'Way-Ups.' Also, before you go back by your friends, make sure you stop by the corner table and say hello. You see who's sitting there, right?"

Victor looked in the corner.

"I'm gonna go over there right now, Dad."

Victor excused himself, but a voice from the bar area called out before he and Anthony separated.

"Hey, Stones! Stones! Come over here!"

"Oh, Christ," Anthony muttered, putting his finger up that he'd be there in a minute.

"Who's that?" Victor asked.

"That's Billy Cirillo and a few of his Cicero boys. I better go take care of this."

The rugged, dark figure dressed in all black with thick, silver chains draped around his neck was Billy "Wild Child" Cirillo. Typically, it's a good thing when a person is told their reputation precedes them. However, it was doubtful that Wild

Child ever heard those words when introduced to someone. Billy was bad news, from the front page to the sports section. He was a tough-guy thug driven by drugs, alcohol, and power, whose father just happened to be the ruthless and well-respected Underboss of the largest Crew in the Chicago Outfit, Frank "Saint Francis" Cirillo of Cicero.

For the last few years, Billy was honing a sordid reputation as the leader of wayward, hard-partying, 30-something no-gooders that looked to him as if he was some street messiah sent by Mob Gods. Held on a pedestal by his peers, the older Syndicate-connected guys, at best, tolerated his shenanigans, and that was because they respected and feared his old man. Billy Cirillo was barely 35 years old, but it was a rough 35. Heavy cocaine usage, Jack Daniels, and sleep deprivation have a way of doing that. His classmates voted him "Most Likely to Commit Recidivism" when he was in high school. Billy had gotten suspended a total of three times. Then, right before graduation, two police detectives came onto school property and arrested him for some shenanigans he was involved in from the previous weekend. It was ironic they slapped the cuffs on him while he was taking a nap during religion class.

Wild Child was also a talented middle linebacker who many thought could've been an all-state selection. But, his senior year stint on the football team was short-lived. He was uncoachable, uncontrollable, and eventually got kicked off for, of all things, excessive violence. The fifth game of the season was the last he ever played. It was his school's homecoming. At the start of the third quarter, after brutally sacking the quarterback for the third time, Billy kicked him in the helmet as he lay on the turf. Then, for his finishing move, he stepped on the Q.B.'s chest and spit on him. Every official threw their yellow flags in the air, briefly huddled together, and tossed Billy out of the game. By the time authorities and school faculty wrestled him off the field, Billy had already punched the head referee and an opposing coach. He also kicked his own team's mascot. Wild Child's fond farewell to his football career was an over-the-topper. Before being forcefully escorted into the field house, he pushed an elderly nun from a local convent into a patch of thorn bushes. She broke her hip.

Out of high school for seventeen years and almost ten spent in jail. Billy was one of the new scary faces looking to make a name for himself in The Chicago Outfit in the late 1970s.

On his feet for almost two hours straight mingling with family and friends, Victor finally sat down. But, right before he did, he casually walked by Maria as she and the girls were laughing at one of Leah's stories. He lightly brushed Maria's shoulder with his hand. When she looked up and saw it was Victor, she responded by squeezing it with hers. Their eyes locked for a brief second.

Dino, Michael, Peter, and Lu-Chow stood at the dining room entrance. Victor had no doubt they were discussing Wild Child and his cronies.

"There's a lot of posturing going on. I hope everybody plays nice tonight and nobody starts any shit," Victor hoped.

Instead of having a typical sit-down dinner, Anthony decided it was best to let everyone order whenever they were hungry. When he joined Victor at the table, he saw that Niner was already on his second order of Tuscan Wild Boar Ragu with Pappardelle pasta.

"Jesus Christ, Niner! Are you going to the fucking electric chair tomorrow? Do me a favor. If you need to shit later, please go crap in the alley and spare my bathroom," Anthony requested.

"Ahhhhh, this is phenomenal!" Niner complimented between swallows. "I could eat a whole loaf of the Italian bread with it."

"Well, there's at least a pound of crumbs on your lap and the floor, so maybe finish those and go from there," Craig sarcastically pointed out.

Victor thought about what his mother said when he the banter and saw the seats at the table filling with his great friends.

"She's right. We love each other."

On that note, he decided to stand and formally thank everyone for attending.

"I appreciate all of you from the bottom of my heart. Thanks for your encouragement, your friendship, and for being here this evening. Oh, and by the way, who do I thank for this?" he joked, insinuating he wasn't picking up the tab.

Angela shouted, clanging her glass with a spoon while sipping her fourth slow gin fizz.

"AND YOU BETTER THANK ME FOR GETTING MARIA TO BE HERE!"

Anthony knew Angela was drunk. It was months since she'd been out with the girls for an evening. In addition, little Carlo was overnight at her parents' house and she wasn't driving.

"Attention! All bartenders! Please do not serve that woman any more alcohol," Anthony instructed them.

"No, Ant, she's right. Thank you for that, Angela," Victor acknowledged as he sat.

"You're goddamn right, I'm right!" Angela agreed.

As she attempted to sit, Angela almost missed the chair. The girls were laughing uncontrollably. While waitresses were busy taking food and drink orders, Victor whispered in Anthony's ear.

"Why did Cirillo want to talk to you?"

Anthony shook his head.

"Fucking guy wanted to use my office so he and his buddies could do some blow. I told him absolutely not. He was a little pissed, but fuck him! That whole crew is already tuned-up to the max."

As Victor finished his small plate of Frutti di Mare alla Griglia (Grilled Seafood), a few baked clams, and a 12-ounce flame-broiled filet mignon, Nicky and Grace stuck their heads into the party room. When Anthony saw them, he stood and asked for everyone's attention.

"My Auntie Grace and Uncle Nicky have a presentation," he announced.

Anthony reached under the table and handed them a gift-wrapped package with a giant red bow. They gave it to Victor.

"Well, well, well. What do we have here? Did Dad dig up all my comic books?"

Victor tore the wrapping paper. When he saw what it was, he smiled as big as he ever did. His breath was taken away. A few guys at the end of the table couldn't make out what it was.

"Hold it up!"

"What is it?"

"We can't see it!"

Victor proudly displayed his gift. There were lots of ooohs and ahhhs. Grace and Nicky commissioned their talented artist friend, Luella Rangus, to draw a sketch of Victor's book cover. The masterfully printed bold, shaded lettering and illustration was a 'from behind' shot of two slightly hunched-over grandfatherly types wearing fedoras holding hands with a young boy positioned between them. The sidewalk and the house the grandfathers and grandson strolled past was 1352 West Fillmore Street. Victor remembered searching for that picture taken years earlier by his Aunt Teresa. That specific cover was the one thing he insisted on during book negotiations. Luella's rendition was perfect, from the side view of the house, right down to the steep front staircase and waist-level cement block fence where Pa and Uncle Jimmy always used to sit. The cappellino (Little hat) worn by the grandson was an exact duplicate of the one Victor wore in kindergarten. As everyone clapped with approval and raised their glasses, Victor hugged his parents.

"Thanks so much for everything," he whispered. "I love you both."

Grace began to tear up. So did Nicky, but, he fought through it, instead choosing one of his old adages.

"Have fun tonight and remember..."

Nicky looked at Victor's friend Donny, hoping he'd get the hint to finish the sentence. Before Victor and Donny left the DaBone house for weekend parties during high school, the last two words of fatherly advice out of Nicky's mouth between voracious gulps of dinner were always the same.

"**BE careful!**" Donny remembered, firmly accentuating the word 'be' just like Nicky used to.

There was nothing but great music and unbelievable food and drinks for the next hour. So many conversations erupting in fits of laughter were taking place at the same time. Anthony was up and down quite a bit tending to the restaurant business, doing his best to accommodate other diners. Dino and Michael Jr. were still busy side-eyeballing Wild Child and his guys. They had met Billy a few times over the years and were well aware of his bad reputation and arrogance. They also heard multiple stories from their fathers and other Outfit guys. There was always some problem involving Wild Child. Tonight wouldn't be any different.

The large guy with the long hair, who didn't leave Billy's side for the entire time, was the first to walk into the party room. Everyone continued with their conversations, but all eyes focused on this massive individual. Wild Child strutted in behind him. The other two guys followed.

"What's this, a Handsome Contest?" Billy roared, looking at the table and pointing. "We got Italians, Greeks, Chinese, and what, Irish and Polish? It looks like The League of fucking Nations in here!"

Mike leaned in and whispered to Nick.

"The big guy is Ivan Binkowski. He played defensive end at the University of Iowa. Had a try-out with the Bears, but got pinched for vehicular homicide, drunken driving, and possession."

Billy, as usual, was happy to be the center of attention. He strutted to the section of the large party table where Dirk and Nick sat.

"I'm not sure what country you two guys are representing, but based on those sport coats, you're either lawyers or morticians! Hey, same fuckin' thing right?"

Wild Child looked back at his guys to make sure they were laughing at what he just said. And, right on cue, they were.

"But, we know who the MOST handsome guy here is, right, Dino "Double D." Domenico?"

Dino shifted uncomfortably in his chair but maintained coolness and composure.

"What's up, Dino? You still pullin' Fredos out there?" Billy asked.

"Fredos?" Dino questioned.

"Yea, bangin' broads two at a time," Billy explained, assuming Dino would get the Moe Greene/Fredo Corleone/cocktail waitresses reference from "The Godfather."

Dino put it together quickly, and rebounded with a great reply.

"Okay, Sonny," he responded, throwing Billy a "Godfather" character reference of his own.

"SONNY? I fucking love that! The only difference is I'm better looking and not one bullet hole in me," Billy reassuringly smiled.

He opened up his black leather jacket to display his non-bullet-riddled body, also revealing the butt of a .45 caliber pistol tucked inside his pants.

"Peter the Gambling Greek God Korinthos, and Chinatown's Number One Son, Lu-Chow Shin! Wow! What a table this is!" Billy continued. "And there's Michael Gabriel Jr., the Business Man of the Year lookin' like a million fucking bucks as usual!"

Michael Jr. half-smilingly nodded. Victor noticed the room's atmosphere becoming slightly uncomfortable, so he felt the need to say something. It was uncharacteristically NOT well thought out and just plain stupid.

"Sonny and Fredo both die at the end."

"Jesus Christ! How fucking lame was that?" he thought.

Billy approached him.

"Well, well, well, this must be young Mario Puzo, the guest of honor," Billy sarcastically assumed.

Victor stood and extended his hand.

"I'm Victor DaBone, Billy. It's nice to meet you."

Wild Child's eyes opened wide.

"WOW, finally, someone with a little fucking class! Standing, handshake, all formal with the proper etiquette and shit," Billy responded. "The rest of youse could learn a thing or two."

Billy grasped his hand tightly with an overly aggressive squeeze, but Victor was prepared, returning an equally firm-gripped response. Billy was surprised, but not impressed. Likewise, nothing impressed Wild Child, except Wild Child.

"A couple of my guys told me they heard you on Big Irish's radio show a few weeks ago, something about you writing a fairy tale about Mob grandfathers. It's all make-believe shit, right?" Billy asked, half attempting to get a rise out of Victor or anyone else in the room.

"It's fiction," Victor responded.

"Oh, fiction, right, I heard of that. Well, maybe you should come and hang out with me for a few days. I'll show you some for real shit," Billy suggested. "That's if you think you could handle it."

As Billy waited for a response from Victor, Anthony interrupted with a prompt hoping to encourage Billy and his guys to leave.

"All right, then. Thanks for stopping by, Billy. I hope you and your guys had a good meal."

Wild Child wasn't finished.

"Everything was good, Stones, but that fucking waitress slapping down plates of food on my table? I felt like I was back at Joliet State," Billy criticized.

It was a poor attempt at being subtle. He wanted everyone in listening distance to know that he did time in the joint.

"Billy, her name is Danica. She told you that three times. But even after that, she said you kept calling her 'Tits Plus,'" Anthony awkwardly explained.

Billy's guys laughed, waiting to hear what their leader would say next.

"It was a fucking compliment, Stones! Who remembers a name like Danica! But TITS PLUS? Now that's a name you don't forget!" he proclaimed.

Before another verbal exchange between Wild Child and whoever was next in the line of fire could take place, the party room entrance got a lot more crowded. A large arm draped around Billy's neck. Cirillo swung around, agitated that someone touched him. He was preparing an aggressive response until he saw who it was.

"BILLY! What a surprise to see you here!" How ya doin'? You guys all havin' a good time tonight?"

It was Fat Frankie. JuJu stood next to him. Their combined width blocked every fire exit in the restaurant. Ivan took a short step towards Billy to show his support. He stopped abruptly when a hand engulfed his shoulder. It belonged to the only guy in the territory he didn't hover over, Vinnie Champagne. Ivan turned his head and saw something he wasn't used to, a man who was a head taller than he was. Vinnie whispered into the Russian's ear.

"Let's keep things nice and friendly here, little guy."

When Billy saw Fat Frankie, JuJu, and Champagne, his demeanor changed, and the coke buzz he was riding disappeared. He looked like he had a mouthful of shit.

"What's up, Frankie?"

"Billy, can I talk to you for a minute privately?" Frankie insisted.

"Hi JuJu, hi Mr. Champagne," Victor greeted, smiling confidently.

Ivan moved to follow Billy. That wasn't going to happen. Instead, the sizable Russian was held firmly in place. Ivan's second attempt to advance was also unsuccessful. Vinnie's grip tightened and he offered some not so friendly advice.

"If you try and move again, I'm gonna dislocate your shoulder."

Binkowski looked at Wild Child for guidance. Billy motioned for him to stay put. It was undoubtedly the best news Ivan heard the entire evening. The other two guys with Billy attempted to make themselves relevant with some movement but decided to remain still, especially when they saw who walked in next.

"Victor, meet Johnny and Michael Bolino," Frankie introduced.

Talk about preceding reputations! Wild Child turned a whiter shade of pale, as did his little Crew of trouble makers. They knew who the Bolino brothers were. They also realized the most dangerous thing about Johnny and Michael. There were two of them. The feared brothers gave Billy a disgusted look when they ignorantly and purposely brushed him off to shake hands with Victor. A few guys in the know couldn't believe it was the Bolinos, especially Anthony, Peter, and Lu-Chow. On the other hand, Michael Jr. and Dino were smiling ear to ear, hoping to meet them.

"Look at this! We've got OLD friends and NEW friends!" Frankie jubilantly stated, guiding Billy out of the room for a little one-on-one conversation.

Fat Frankie stood face to face with Wild Child next to the coatroom.

"Billy, there's a bunch of good guys in there. You and your friends do what you do, and that's your thing. But they're here tonight celebrating. None of them are playing the part, do you follow me? But that's not why I wanna talk to you. Listen, a little birdie, actually it was more like a big stool pigeon, told me you and a few of your Cicero buddies are taking heavy betting action at RAPTURE, something about college football. That's your joint, right, or is it your father's?"

Frankie knew his information was on the money, correct.

"MOTHER FUCKER! Who in the fuck beefed? I'm gonna crack somebody's skull wide fucking open!" Billy angrily thought.

"Yea, just a few friendly wagers, Frankie," Billy smartly admitted.

"Is your father good with that? I mean, him, me, and a couple of the 'Way Ups' agreed a few years ago that ALL the big coins roll to me. So if that's changed, well, we gotta talk about that."

Billy knew his father would be furious about secretly taking wagers, especially at RAPTURE.

"Frankie, we were just trying to generate some extra cash and run it clean through the club. That's all. Can I cut you a healthy slice?" Billy offered as a bribe.

Frankie shook his head no.

"Billy, how about we do this. You stop taking big action. A couple of G's here and there, that's fine. But $10,000 plus every week, week in and week out like you guys have been doing? That has to stop. You're not just fucking around with my bottom line, but a lot of other people's too. So, keep what you've made so far. That's all on the hush. It's my gift to you. Or, your father and I can talk to who we have to talk to, and we'll see what they think. Either way, they're probably gonna tax you with a penalty, juice, or God-forbid, maybe something else. That's not even counting how your dad's gonna react."

Billy didn't want any part of his father's no mercy approach to anyone who didn't follow a street agreement.

"You know how St. Francis could be," Frankie reminded, sinisterly chuckling, purposely using Billy's dad's well-known street name. "I ain't gotta tell you that, though. I mean, he's a very serious fucking guy when it comes to that kinda shit."

While Frankie read Billy the riot act, Wild Child's guys weren't fairing much better on their end. Ivan was making sure not to move implicitly following Vinnie's instructions. The other two guys attempted to make small talk with the Bolinos. One of them made the mistake of mentioning his cousin's name to Johnny hoping to find some common Mob ground.

"My cousin is "Sammy Checkers" from Elmwood Park. Do you know him?"

Johnny did know him, but instead of continuing the conversation further, he chose a different route. Unfortunately, the response was less than friendly.

"I don't know anybody, kid. And you don't either."

Dino and Michael Jr. whispered back and forth to each other, dying to go up and introduce themselves. Finally, Michael Jr. grabbed Dino's arm and whispered.

"Fuck it, let's go."

So, the two sons of very important Outfit guys walked up to the Bolinos.

"We wanted to introduce ourselves. I'm Michael Gabriel Jr. and this is Dino Domenico."

Both Bolinos knew who their fathers were. They shook hands and even cracked smiles. As the four exchanged small talk, Billy did some side eyeballing of his own. When he saw how friendly the Bolinos, Dino, and Michael Jr. were getting he made a decision.

"Time to get the fuck outta here," he wisely thought.

"Billy, think about what I said, and let me know what's what. The other thing I wanna point out is that it's always good to have friends. That's the theme for tonight, 'FRIENDS.' They're all over the place. So I want you to take a quick peek behind you," Frankie advised.

Billy turned his head. The man and woman sitting at the back table Victor visited earlier were Frankie's sister Gina and her boyfriend, Special Detective Michael Tunzi. Billy made eye contact with Tunzi. The two never met but heard of each other. Tunzi knew the only reason Billy wasn't dead or in jail was because of who his father was. That didn't sit well with him. So, Tunzi acknowledged Billy by looking at him, furrowing his eyebrows, and scrunching his lips as if to say, 'Who in the fuck are you supposed to be?' At the same time he gave Billy the disrespectful facial expression, he purposely opened his sport coat, revealing his platinum badge and pearl-handled Magnum .357 cannon.

"Billy, now I want you to look at the bar where you and your boys were sitting earlier," Frankie advised.

Taking those seats were Street Captain Anthony Carosha's three sons. They recently bought Mitzie's Butcher Shop. They spent a ton of renovation money and turned it into an old-school Italian specialties deli called La Bella Vita. (The Good Life) Nico Carosha, the oldest brother was called "Right Hand" because when he hit you with his sledgehammer punch; it was the last thing you remembered before blacking the fuck out. It was also the first thing you remembered when you eventually woke up. All those pummeled by Nico agreed. His strike hurt twice.

The Carosha's Sheridan Park cousins, Anthony "Tony Knockout" Jacalui and Paul "Wreck It Paulie" Timmerino, weren't far behind. They were responsible for issuing dozens of well-deserved impromptu beatings over the years between the five of them. Their specialty was disposing of drunken tough-guy college frat boys that strutted around Little Italy flexing their beer muscles. Other times, it was to straighten out rich suburban goofs or the chooches from other neighborhoods that treated local bar and restaurant staff like they were indentured servants. If you were flagrantly disrespectful when visiting the Near West Side joints, these guys were right there to teach you the proper etiquette. Taylor Street area residents knew them, loved them, and affectionately referred to the five as "La Vigilanza di Quartiere." (The Neighborhood Watch.)

From across the bar, Nico Carosha loudly overstated a greeting to Fat Frankie. He also waved so Billy would notice him.

"Frankie! Franganucci! How ya doin' pal, are you alright over there?"

As the Neighborhood Watch guys settled comfortably into their seats, they focused on Wild Child, not taking their eyes off him. If the group look they were going for was intimidation, they oozed it. Billy picked up on that vibe right away. Frankie knew he would.

"Billy, here's my suggestion. Go back in the party room, wish Victor good luck with his book, tell the other guys to have fun, and then you and your boys continue on your merry way enjoying the rest of your Saturday night. I'll wait for you to call me on that thing. How's that sound?"

Billy shook Frankie's hand, knowing full well that starting any kind of beef there tonight would create nothing but huge problems for him, his guys, or worse, his father.

"Okay, Frankie. You're right. No need for me to call you on that thing. No more bets. Anyone that wants action, we'll refer them all to you."

"That's even better," Frankie concurred.

"I got lots of stops to make tonight," Billy said, attempting to exude an air of importance.

What was really on his mind was snorting a couple of giant rails of coke.

"Hey Frankie, maybe tell those hoodlums at the bar to behave," Billy facetiously said, pointing to La Vigilanza di Quartiere. "They look like a pack of fucking hungry wolves."

Billy strutted back into the party room.

"Time to go, Cicero boys," he announced.

The look of relief on their faces was evident, especially Ivan's, whose shoulder was going numb. Frankie followed right behind him. But, as usual, he was hungry.

"I'm starving. Vinnie, JuJu, Bolinos? Are we dining tonight, or are we dining tonight?"

They agreed to dine.

"Mr. Simonetti, can we have the back table?" Frankie politely asked Anthony.

"Mr. Frankie Pope, you guys can eat wherever the fuck you want!"

Anthony was confident that there would've been an all-out melee inside Full House if it wasn't for Fat Frankie and his guys. Billy walked up to the main table and spoke loudly enough for everyone to hear.

"I want you ALL to have a wonderful evening. Victor, good luck with your book, and if you and all your buddies here wanna stop at RAPTURE one night, let me know. Seriously, dinner, drinks, snatch, and party favors, my treat."

Billy tweaked his nose with his fingers when he said 'party favors.'

"Thanks, Billy. We'll let you know when we're ready to step up to that level," Victor joked.

"That's up to you," Billy answered.

Victor couldn't believe it was Wild Child who said that!

"Again with that shit?" Victor imagined. *"This has gotta be a sign, but what? There's something I'm not seeing with this whole fucking thing!"*

"It's all aboard the crazy train if you guys do come out. And do you know why? It's because we're ALL friends here, ain't that right, Frankie?" Billy asked, turning to Frankie.

Frankie nodded. He and Niner were busy dipping slices of Focaccia bread into an imported olive oil and Pecorino Romano cheese mixture.

Billy and his guys exited quickly. Everyone else milled around, stretching their legs.

"Maybe tomorrow you'll tell me what that was that whole fucking thing was about," Dirk whispered to Victor.

"Not sure," Victor answered. "Maybe I'll ask Fat Frankie. Maybe I won't. I'm thinking I won't."

"Whatever the fuck it was, it sure mellowed Wild Child's ass the fuck out," Stones added. "You gotta put what happened here in your next book, Cugine." (Pronounced Koo-Gene. Means cousin)

"There's no way I could put it into words. It was too ethereal," Victor explained.

"ETHEREAL! What the fuck does that mean?" Stones asked, slyly sliding a Quaalude into his mouth.

"It means spiritual, something too perfect for this world," Victor answered.

"I thought it had something to do with ether because I'd eat the ass out some ether!" Anthony boasted. "They use that shit for freebasing coke!"

Victor decided it was best not to tell his cousin that 'ethereal' also meant, of or containing or dissolved in ether. He was confident if he did, Stones would've made a phone call to Benny Stein and had a tank delivered to Full House within the hour!

As the trajectory of the evening's mood took a noticeable upswing, waitresses served after-dinner drinks, coffee, espresso, cappuccino, as well as freshly baked cakes, pies, and Italian cookies.

A tipsy Angela sauntered into the party room with a bit of help from the girls.

"Anthony, we're stopping over at Tufano's real quick. I'm driving."

"THE FUCK YOU ARE!" Ro-Ro interrupted. "You don't even have a car here, Angela! You're such a drunken hooker!"

Heather put her arm around Angela and looked at Anthony.

"I got this, Stones. The Shady Lady is driving her girls."

Victor walked up to Maria.

"You're coming back, right? We didn't even have a chance to talk."

"Victor, honey, I'm so sorry. I'm exhausted. I worked all day, and I'm just beat. I'm staying at my dad's tonight. The girls are going to drop me off. I'm just so happy for you, babe. I'm glad Angela asked me to be here tonight."

"Let me walk you to your father's house instead, okay?" he asked innocently with the crush of a schoolboy.

"You can't leave, Victor, all of your friends are here!"

"Your dad's house is a block and a half away. Five, ten minutes! They won't even know I'm gone. It'll be fine unless you'd rather me not."

Victor over dramatically batted his eyes, hoping to get approval.

"Okay, fine. That would be nice. Just please don't do that with your eyes. You look like the blind guy that used to sit in the last pew at church."

Victor laughed. He knew exactly who she meant.

"Alright, girls, let's go," Angela announced. "Anthony, babe, we'll be back in a few minutes."

Anthony was busy talking to a couple of the guys. So he didn't immediately respond.

"Anthony, I said we'll be back!" Angela said a little louder.

Still, there was no response from Stones. Instead, he continued telling a story to Donny, Benj, and Lu-Chow. Niner was also listening while feverishly working his way through the large tray of cannolis, eclairs, and cookies. Victor and Maria watched, listening to Angela become more and more frustrated with futile attempts to get her husband's attention. Finally, Angela screamed at the top of her lungs.

"ANTHONY!"

The entire room went silent.

"Angela, Jesus Christ, I heard you the first time!" he irritatingly responded.

"Good. I love you, baby," she playfully cooed.

"I love you, too," Anthony condescendingly answered.

Angela was about to deliver the line of the evening.

"We'll be right back, sweetheart, and remember, while I'm gone, DON'T BLOW ANYBODY!"

Everyone was hysterical. Angela smiled, knowing she had just bested Anthony for ignoring her. She walked out with the girls like the Queen of Sheba.

"My father and grandfather have been telling me not to blow anyone for years!" Ro-Ro admitted. "I haven't listened to them once!"

"Now, THAT was awesome!" Victor said to Maria.

"Angela is SOOO blasted," Maria added.

Anthony looked around. Everyone was still laughing. He needed to set the record straight. He stood on a chair and made a very important announcement.

"I SWEAR TO GOD, I NEVER SUCKED A DICK IN MY LIFE!"

"She nailed you good, Stones," Dino teased.

"She sure the fuck did," Pete agreed.

"Sometimes, I look at Angela and can't believe how blessed I am. She puts up with me, she's a great mother, and cooks like a chef. Broad still looks phenomenal, too. Then she opens that fucking mouth of hers, and I wish I were a widower," Anthony admitted.

"Yea, you're lucky she didn't hear you say that," Danica teased as she cleared dishes from the table. "And if anyone ever calls me 'Tits Plus' again, I'm gonna cut 'em. I don't give two fucks who they are or who their fathers are."

"Okay, sweetheart, just don't use my good steak knives," Anthony warned. "Alright, I've waited long enough. I'm ducking out to smoke a jay. Who's in?"

Stones proudly displayed a Cheech and Chong-sized doobie.

"Me," Peter answered.

"I'll hit it a little," Dino added.

I'll take a whack or two," Michael Jr. also responded.

As the boys made their way through the kitchen and into the alley to enjoy their herbage, Victor and Maria took advantage of the opportunity to blend in with the crowd and exit through the front door.

In boyfriend and girlfriend history, there have never been two people that weren't together but should've been together, more than Victor and Maria. Wishing, hoping, and dreaming was the closest the two of them ever came, not counting the extended, one-time closed-mouth kiss they shared playing Spin the Bottle in sixth grade. They simultaneously reached to hold hands when they walked out of Full House. Victor thought it was more instinct than coincidence. It gave him the self-confidence he needed for what was about to happen next.

Right before they arrived at the corner of Taylor and Loomis streets, he couldn't control himself any longer. When they got to Chinetti's building, he lightly but assertively swung Maria inside the gangway. Victor leaned her up against the east building wall. Street lights partially shadowed one side; the other was darkened by night. You could see Taylor Street, but Taylor Street couldn't see you. Maria gasped for a split second, and then exhaled a romantic moan. She panted when Victor's hands lovingly cupped her face. Maria grabbed his hips, pulling him against her. The very second their lips touched, their mouths simultaneously opened wide as both of their wet tongues intertwined, glided, and rolled. Even though it was uncharted territory, it felt natural and familiar. Victor always wondered what it would feel like to deeply kiss Maria. It was even more exciting than he imagined it would be.

"This is what's missing! Fuck everything else! I'm right here, right now, with Maria, finally!"

Their bodies lined up perfectly, penis to pussy, and pussy to penis, sliding back and forth, and then, slowly, up and down. It was a dry-humping bodily symphony conducted by years of yearning. Victor was as hard as a rock, and Maria was feverishly hot, becoming damper by the second.

"I've wanted you forever. Why did it take so fucking long for this to happen?" Maria thought, letting her mind wander.

In that moment of time, everything in the world felt perfect, until their loving, passionate entanglement was interrupted by approaching music. They stopped kissing but remained in each other's arms. Their heads turned towards Taylor Street. Victor recognized the song. It was Nazareth's "Hair of the Dog." It was blaring from a car radio, the car, driven by Wild Child. Victor and Maria watched the vehicle stop short of the intersection traffic light. Billy ducked his head down and brought his thumb/forefinger area up to his nose. It was pretty obvious what he was doing. The other guys in the car were obnoxiously singing along with the music. Billy and his boys were continuing their cocaine consumption right where they had left off, six minutes and four thick lines each ago in the parking lot of Full House. As Nazareth's song ended, Ted Nugent's opening guitar riff of "Just What the Doctor Ordered" began. Maria looked up at Victor.

"Isn't that the guy you were talking to at the restaurant? Him and those dirtbags he's with look like trouble. I'm sorry. I shouldn't say that if they're friends of yours. They look mean."

Wild Child looked around, checked his rearview mirror, and took another massive sniff of ale. Then, he threw his head back, and in perfect synchronicity with the song, shouted out:

"THIS IS JUST WHAT THE DOCTOR ORDERED!"

The childhood sweethearts were in disbelief. When the stoplight changed from red to green, Wild Child floored his black Coupe de Ville, smoking, spinning, and screeching the tires as he turned right down Loomis Street. The deep, pulsating rock sounds bounced off and reverberated against the brick two and three-story buildings. Seconds later, all that remained were faint, distant echoes in the alleys they passed. Victor wondered where they were off to and who they would terrorize next. It wasn't going to be the gang at Full House, that's for sure.

"What the fuck was that?" Maria shockingly asked.

"As Sister Christine would say, those are the bad boys," Victor answered.

Maria lightly gripped the bulge still protruding from Victor's jeans.

"Speaking of bad boys, who's this for?"

"For you, it's always been for you," he answered.

"Why did you have to move, Victor? I mean, I know that you had to. It's just that…,"

"What?" Victor asked.

"There's a lot that's happened in 10 years. Between tons of bullshit dates, a bunch of one-night stands, and my fucked up 5-month engagement to that cheating asshole, I'm not some pure as the driven snow chick," she confessed, tears welling in the corners of her big, beautiful, dark brown eyes. "You deserve better."

She embarrassingly buried her face in Victor's chest. He held her tightly then gently pulled her head up to look at him.

"Can either of us do anything about what's already happened? I know I can't, for you or me. I must've picked up the phone to call you a million times, probably more, but I never even dialed your number, not once. When I got my driver's license, you were the first one I thought about asking for a date. Did that ever happen? When I'd bump into someone, and they'd mention your name or say that they'd seen you, do you know what I did? I changed the subject. I couldn't stand myself for not making a fucking attempt to be with you. As happy as I was seeing you the few times we did over the years, it always bothered me afterward," he admitted. "The absolute fucking worst was when I heard you got engaged. I stood in front of the mirror and called myself a jagoff."

Maria wiped her tears with her sleeve and sniffed.

"This doesn't sound like a terrific love story to me, does it, Victor?"

"No. No, it doesn't. But, I'm a writer. So maybe I could add an extra chapter, starting right now."

"That's up to you," Maria answered, gazing into Victor's eyes.

"And there it is. My sign," Victor happily thought.

"It's up to us, Maria. If we try something here, you have to help me out. Look, I'm almost 24 years old, and I haven't had more than five dates in my entire life. There was always a problem. None of them were you."

"Wow. That might be the most beautiful thing anyone has ever said to me. Thank you, Victor," Maria whispered. "I'm heading back to my condo tomorrow. If I give you my number, will you complete the call?"

"Yes, I will," he responded immediately.

As they walked out from the gangway shadow, a sizeable white limousine headed east down Taylor Street.

"Jesus Christ, that's a big one," Victor pointed out.

The brake lights of the luxury stretch lit up when it pulled in front of Full House. It parked exactly where Nicky's Caddy was earlier. As they stood on the sidewalk holding hands, Maria and Victor watched the limo driver get out and open the back door. Four guys piled out. They were all laughing and guffawing as they walked inside Full House.

"Do you want to go back and see who they are?" Victor excitedly suggested.

"No. You go back with your friends. Can you walk me to my steps? Geez, that's something I've wanted to ask you since third grade!" Maria confessed.

When they finished passionately kissing for the final time that evening, Maria wrote down her phone number and handed it to Victor.

"I'll be home after eleven or twelve tomorrow. I'm going to be doing laundry and cleaning my house. I might be having an overnight guest next weekend."

"Wow. Good for you. Anyone I know?" Victor asked.

Maria shyly answered.

"Someone special from my past that I'm hoping will be even more special in my future."

As he walked away, Maria called out to him.

"Victor?"

He turned to see Maria standing on her tippy toes, looking over her shoulder, and playfully lifting the back of her skirt. Her perfectly curved ass was half-covered by a pair of bright pink bikini undies. Victor's jaw dropped so low it almost hit the sidewalk. She smiled, blew him a kiss, and then disappeared through the side door.

During his walk back to Full House, Victor said a prayer. He knew how fortunate he was.

"Thank you for my marvelous family, my loyal friends, my blessed and interesting life, for the burst of speed I needed to beat Reece, for getting me out of the Holy Trinity meeting in one piece, for a wonderful party with no Wild Child problems, and most of all, for giving Maria and me a chance."

He felt overwhelming comfort when he glanced up and looked at the street sign.

"There it is! Taylor and Loomis! Well, 1980 is just around the corner. I hope it'll be as good to me as this corner's been."

As he strolled past Snafuro's Bakery, the Allman Brother's song "Midnight Rider" blared from Full House's sound system. Victor looked at his silver Rado Diastar watch. Sure enough, it was 12:00 sharp. That meant only one thing. Stones was time-coordinating the jams.

When he walked back inside, Victor saw his friends gathered around four men seated at the main party table. His first thought was correct.

"They're probably the guys that got out of the limo."

As he got closer, his heart skipped a couple of beats when he realized who the foursome was. And just like he'd done since he was a youngster, the Taylor Street Swearing Machine blurted out the first thing that came to mind.

"NO FUCKING WAY!"

Made in the USA
Coppell, TX
28 December 2022